CW01020520

UNDER A CHANGING MOON

ALSO BY MARGOT BENARY-ISBERT

The Ark
Rowan Farm
The Shooting Star
The Wicked Enchantment
Castle on the Border
Blue Mystery
The Long Way Home
Dangerous Spring
A Time to Love

Under A Changing Moon

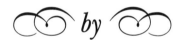 *by*

Margot Benary-Isbert

Translated from the German by
Rosaleen Ockenden
and the author

BETHLEHEM BOOKS • IGNATIUS PRESS
WARSAW, N.D.   SAN FRANCISCO

ISBN 1-883937-33-7
Library of Congress Catalog Number: 97-77063

Bethlehem Books • Ignatius Press
15605 County Road 15, Minto, ND 58261

*For Margaret
with love and gratitude*

Contents

Winter I

T HE JUDGE, in top hat and black greatcoat, had been walking up and down in front of the posting station for a good half hour. It was a cold afternoon toward the end of December in the year 1865. He had tried warming his cold feet in the inn opposite, but the coffee had tasted of chicory, and the room smelled of tobacco and stale beer. So he soon decided that the fresh clean winter air outside was preferable.

"They're late, Herr Amtmann," said the postmaster, using the Judge's title. He had come out into the street to look toward the Frankfurt Gate for the mail coach. Fresh horses had already been sent back to the stable twice. "All this snow makes hard going for the beasts," Postmaster Gellert said. "Even the railway train got stuck yesterday." He chuckled maliciously. "Folks must be crazy who think that our good, dependable coach will soon be outdone by this newfangled thing on rails. Unhealthy, that's what the doctor called it the other day. The human body won't be able to stand this mad speed. Never was meant to. Would Your Honor care to come into our warm room? My wife would feel honored to serve a cup of hot coffee to the Herr Amtmann."

1

"Thanks, Gellert. It won't be too long now. I'll wait outside so as to be on the spot."

"Fräulein Paula is coming home today, isn't she? How has she traveled if I may ask?"

"By mail coach all the way. We—and the nuns in Nancy—thought that the safest way for a young girl to travel. One of the nuns took her as far as Strasbourg, where she slept in a daughter house of the convent. The second night she spent with friends in Frankfurt. Quite a journey, but it'll soon be over now."

"She'll be a big girl now, the Fräulein. I remember Your Honor taking her to France in the autumn of '63, and the five lads—her brothers—standing there and waving good-by and then running behind the coach as it left."

"Here it comes!" said the Amtmann.

Four steaming horses trotted around the corner, the heavy coach jolting behind them. Today the coachman did not blow his horn as usual. He reined in the horses and jumped down from the box, touching his shiny hat with the jaunty cockade. "Your servant, Herr Amtmann. After-noon, Gellert." His cheeks glowed like two red apples; the skin was tight over the high cheekbones. "No weather for horn-blowing today. The young lady had a good journey, plenty of room in my coach, too. Only two gentlemen from Cologne and young Herr Overberg from Bad Ems besides her. People stay at home if they needn't travel in weather like this."

He stamped his feet, clapped his hands, and rubbed his cheeks. The stableboy from the posting station came out to change the horses and unload the luggage. There wasn't much today: just one large pigskin case with the letters K.O. engraved on it and Paula's small traveling hamper.

The coach door was opened, the steps let down. The judge reached out his hand to his daughter, and she jumped down the two steps right into his open arms. "Here I am, Papa."

"At last, dear child. Are you frozen stiff? They're all waiting for you at home. Holwein will fetch the hamper in the handcart, Gellert."

"Allow me to say good afternoon, Your Honor," said a voice behind them. The Amtmann turned and shook hands with a young man in a cinnamon-colored traveling coat with a marten-fur collar.

"Back from France, Overberg? Have you discovered all the secrets of making champagne in Epernay? And will you stay home for a while now?"

"I wouldn't take my oath on that, sir. In our field of business, there remains always much to learn. Lately they have been praising the Crimean wines to the skies. Another reason to pack the old trunk again. My father's traveling days are over."

"Herr Overberg from Bad Ems," the Amtmann said in introduction. "This is my daughter Paula, just returned from the convent school in Nancy."

The young man bowed, and Paula curtsied. During the journey he had laid half of his warm fur rug over her knees, and she had not been certain how to behave in such a situation. Dear Mère Monique had forgotten to mention such an eventuality in her etiquette classes.

"I guessed so, sir," said Overberg. "The family likeness is unmistakable. Unfortunately, I had no chance of talking to the young lady."

Paula raised her eyebrows. Talking to her, indeed! On this point, at least, there could be no doubt: Mère Monique's little black book on *The Correct Behavior in All Circumstances for Young Gentlewomen* would never have approved conversation with a strange gentleman in a mail coach. Besides, she had been much too preoccupied with her own thoughts to feel inclined for conversation with anyone. Half of her was still in the convent with her friends and the nuns; the other half, already at home. The convent was close and familiar; home had become almost strange. For more than two years, she had not been back. She had even asked her parents to let her spend one more Christmas at the convent, although her time at Nancy had really been ended last fall. Her first term in the convent she had been miserable with homesickness, and now, she felt, she would be just as homesick for the convent. Under her black short coat with its three collars, she was still wearing the convent girl's gray Sunday dress, along with the matching felt bonnet, under which two braids of dark hair were framing her cold little face.

The Amtmann took his daughter's arm, and, accompanied by young Overberg, they went along the snow-covered cobbles of Grabenstrasse to the Dom Hotel, where Konrad Overberg was to await the carriage his father was sending for him from Bad Ems. No doubt it had also been delayed by the snow. The two men talked animatedly about wines and the best vineyards and vintages, an inexhaustible topic in this part of Germany blessed with the best wines of the country; then about books, which also were a common interest. At the door of the Dom Hotel, Overberg took his leave. Father and daughter walked on along Grabenstrasse, and now Paula started to talk. "How is everything at home?" she asked eagerly, evidently pleased to be rid of the strange gentleman.

"Good and lively as always," her father replied. "Mama is looking after all of us and a host of others as well; I'll never understand how she manages. Babett watches the kitchen from her armchair the same as ever. Aunt Stina is still busy writing and sending her novels to various ladies' journals, and the ladies' journals are sending them back to her. Aunt Rikchen still paints her dainty watercolors and gives piano lessons to the boys whenever she can get hold of them—with the patience of a saint, I must say. Uncle Emmerich lives with his books, which he never seems very anxious to sell. Once in a while he has a customer, but he treats each of them as if he were asking a favor. It's in the boys you'll find the greatest change. August was fifteen last summer . . ."

"Do you think he is going to study law as you used to hope?"

"Don't you remember that Mama had other plans for him? However, as far as his future profession is concerned, I believe it will be neither the Roman Church nor the Roman law. His greatest interest is history, from old Egypt to present-day Prussia which he thinks is the nation of the future."

"And Adolf?"

"It's hard to predict yet how he will turn out. In school, he is not as brilliant as August, nor as unconcerned and lazy as Georg. He isn't a problem like Ferdinand, nor as ambitious a student as little Karl. At home, he is handy with everything that has to do with animals. With my new horse that Holwein considers unreliable, he gets along without any difficulty. Incidentally, he writes surprisingly good compositions for a boy of his age. He and you were always rather close to each other, weren't you?"

"Yes. Perhaps because we were both a little lonely."

"Lonely, when there were six of you? What do you mean?"

"Well, I was the only girl, you know, and Adolf the middle one of five brothers. It was rather hard for him. Georg has always been as inseparable from August as his shadow, since they're only one year apart. And yet Adolf adores August, who is the hero and model of all his younger brothers. Ferdinand and Karl are much too young for Adolf."

"Well, I never would have guessed that it was this way. Besides, one would think that August had more in common with Adolf than with harum-scarum Georg. I imagine August has no idea that Adolf would like to be more friendly with him. He *is* a rather reserved young fellow, though."

"Not toward me. He wrote me the nicest and longest letters—mostly about his dog, Aquarius. I suppose he called him that because he pulled him out of the water?"

"Right! That was a typical Adolf incident. Ask him to tell you how it happened sometime."

They had reached Erbach Square now, where the courthouse was—that is, the back side of the courthouse with the main entrance; the front faced the river. Three sandstone steps led up to the carved oak door over which still stood the coat of arms of the Abbot of Eberbach, who in 1777 had built the stately baroque structure as a branch of his rich monastery on the Rhine. The crowned dolphin on a blue background stared down haughtily on all who passed through the door; above him, the black boar of Eberbach held back the heraldic curtain.

"Welcome home, Paulinchen!" said the Amtmann,

squeezing his daughter's arm affectionately. She smiled up at him, rubbing her cold cheek against his sleeve, as she had done when a child. It was good to be with him again.

"What a beautiful house it is!" she said in surprise, anxious to show that she had learned something. "Funny that I never noticed before. But Mère Marie-Ignace was a real scholar in art history."

She looked up and scrutinized the house as though she was seeing it for the first time. How well proportioned it was, how unpretentious and noble! The window embrasures of red sandstone, the pale yellow of the walls, and, above it, the blue slate roof and the five dormer windows of the attic with their pointed gables—all this was of a convincing harmony. "Generally we studied religious art, of course, but in architecture we did secular buildings as well," she said importantly.

A single-storied wing had been built out into the garden that ran along the river down to the tall gray cliffs on which, with its seven towers, one of the oldest cathedrals of Germany stands. In this wing was the big kitchen, next to it old Babett's room, and then the rooms in which Uncle Emmerich and the two great-aunts lived, called simply aunts by the children in everyday life.

The wide stone-paved hall smelled the same as it had always done, of yellowing files, ink and wood smoke, and the unaired clothes of country folk, working people, and peddlers who waited here, when the court was in session, for Wittich the beadle to call them into the courtroom.

Upstairs, they had been heard. "Here they are!" shrilled the little-boy voice of Karl, and with earsplitting noise the five brothers rushed down the staircase with its elegantly curved banisters. Mama, Paula remembered, used to say that these shining banisters never needed any dusting: her sons took care of that with the seats of their pants. Four of them were shouting and talking at the same time, almost knocking each other over in their eagerness to greet their big sister. Only August came down a little more slowly, the eldest one, the chief of the clan whose dignity did not need any proving. Above the heads of the other four, he shook hands with Paula, raising hers to his lips, the perfect young cavalier. "Welcome home, Paula! Glad you're back."

Almost at the same moment, Georg grabbed her hand and pumped it extravagantly—Georg, even handsomer than two years ago, with his shining auburn hair and challenging eyes. "Hope you haven't become a goody-goody in the convent," he shouted.

A red-and-white cat sat on the banisters grooming himself absent-mindedly, indicating that he had nothing to do with this rather vulgar upheaval.

"Nicki, Uncle Emmo's cat, remember?" small Karl asked.

A big shaggy dog joined in the tumult with joyous barks.

The Amtmann retreated into his office, while the two youngest brothers fought over Paula's embroidered traveling-bag, grabbed her hands, tugged at her shoulders, all the time telling her some lengthy story of which she did not understand much. She would have to get accustomed again to the Nassau dialect in which all the last letters were dropped.

"Careful or you'll pull her to pieces!" August admonished them. "I'm sure she hasn't been used to such high-wayman manners in the convent." He was taller than she, with the narrow hips of an expert young swordsman, the thoughtful eyes, the humorous mouth, and the oval face of his father. All the children had the dark hair and eyes of their father's family, but in the four younger boys the rounder face, the full curved mouth, and the small nose of their mother's clan, the Thours, prevailed. Ten-year-old Ferdinand was the darkest of them all with the almond-shaped eyes and impudent smile of a Murillo street-urchin. *Gamin!* Paula thought, remembering some of the escapades of the wildest of her wild brothers. Karl, the youngest, just eight years old, had still the grace of childhood, enchanting the hearts of all the women of the household. Nobody would ever have believed that he sometimes joined delightedly in Ferdinand's adventurous tricks.

And there was Adolf, his hand on the collar of the dog. He took Paula's hand and put it on the dog's head. "Here he is—Aquarius!" he said proudly. "He has killed more rats than that lazy Nicki."

"And stolen more eggs," said Georg.

"You be quiet. No one has ever caught him doing it."

"No, but a muzzle smeared with egg yolk is circumstantial evidence. You just ask Papa."

"He's a grand dog, Paula," Adolf said, ignoring Georg and exchanging a glance with his sister, confirming their old companionship. Paula smiled fondly. Her favorite brother's hair was as shaggy as that of the dog—all cowlicks. He would never be able to get his part as smooth and straight as the two older boys.

Father came back from his office, where he had been signing some documents. And now Mother's voice was heard above.

"Why don't you come up, children? The coffee is getting cold. Paula will be dead tired after the long journey, and you mustn't keep her standing down there."

She was waiting on the top step in her blue house dress with the small white collar; her light brown hair was coiled over her ears and gathered in a little crown on top. Her lively blue eyes welcomed her daughter happily, home at last after more than two years away. Paula remembered well how those eyes sometimes darkened like a stormy sky when Mama was annoyed, and there was often some reason for annoyance in this tumultuous house—about the boys; about the two hired girls; about stubborn old Holwein, groom, odd jobman, and gardener in one person, who had served two of the Amtmann's predecessors already; and about old Babett. Most of all about her. But luckily, the straw fire of her anger usually died away as quickly as it had flared up.

"Good day, Mama," said Paula, curtsying and kissing her hand. Her mother embraced her and kissed her on both cheeks. Heavens, she had a grown-up daughter suddenly! Taking Paula by the hand, she led her, with her entourage of brothers, cat and dog, into the drawing room, where the other members of the family were waiting. There were the two great-aunts in the same gray alpaca dresses and black lace caps they had been wearing for years. There was Uncle Emmerich, one of father's older brothers, standing in one of the three deep bay windows, wearing his long coat, embroidered waistcoat, and pleated jabot and raising his lorgnette in a welcoming gesture.

"Welcome, welcome, *chère enfant,*" twittered Aunt Christine and Aunt Ulrike. Again curtsies and hand kissings from Paula, kisses and embraces from the aunts. Uncle Emmo, too, could not resist pressing his young niece against his fine waistcoat, one of those waistcoats in petit-point with which the aunts supplied him every Christmas.

"How she has grown!" Aunt Rikchen remarked fondly, contemplating the slim, shy girl.

"But so thin and pale!" lamented Aunt Stina. "Didn't you *ever* get fresh air at your convent, child? Nothing but studying and praying and probably fasting. You wait and see. A spoonful of cod-liver oil a day and your mother's good kitchen will do wonders."

"But believe me, we weren't starved," Paula protested. "Some of the girls put on pounds and pounds. It wasn't the fault of our kitchen sister that I didn't, just lack of talent for putting on weight on my part. And we could stroll in the beautiful garden between lessons and were taken out for a walk every day, too."

"On a leash?" Georg asked.

"Nonsense! Two by two like the Pallottine girls here, one nun in front and one in the rear," Ferdinand said.

"Dreadful!" Karl said, raising his eyes to the ceiling.

Paula shrugged. How could the boys know how beautiful it all had been!

"Konrad Overberg has asked to be remembered to the ladies," said the Amtmann. "He traveled from Frankfurt in the same coach with Paula."

They all sat down at the long table with an enormous pound cake in the middle of the white damask tablecloth.

"Ah!" said Aunt Rikchen. "So he is back again."

The aunts exchanged a quick glance.

"Well, some mothers' hearts will be jumping like spring lambs, I bet. He is, after all, the most eligible bachelor in Nassau, if only he weren't such a Don Juan." That was Aunt Rikchen again. She had a hard time keeping her tongue in check, even though gossip was strictly barred from the family table.

"Rikchen!" Aunt Stina admonished her mildly, but it was Uncle Emmo who suavely saved the situation. "A young gentleman with perfect manners, I'd call him. Well-read, widely traveled. You've only got to see him handling rare books to know that they are more important to him than the prettiest girl. I wonder what he has brought for his father's library this time. Maybe even a *Livre d'Heures* for me! I've been looking for one for years." He smacked his lips like a gourmet anticipating a delicacy.

Meanwhile, the boys had been devoting their attention to the coming-home cake. It needed a special occasion for such a cake to be baked in the middle of the week. But this family knew how to celebrate whenever an opportunity turned up, and there were opportunities enough in a house with so many birthdays and name days, besides all the feast days of the year.

"May we be excused?" Georg asked when only a few crumbs of the cake were left. "On the ice, men! Only five more days and they'll put our noses to the grindstone again."

"Your grinding never seems to start before Christmas, my boy," Uncle Emmo remarked. "May I recommend my well-known services as a coach in Latin and Greek? I presume you want to pass at Easter, anyway."

"Thank you, sir," Georg answered without enthusiasm. It was true that he never started to work before Christmas, and against all the laws of fairness, he had so far managed to pass each year.

"Out with you," Mama said. "Fresh air is good for you."

In an instant, the boys had left the room, clattering down
the stairs with shouts and laughter, the dog joining in with
his barking. Nicki just blinked behind them unconcern-
edly from Uncle Emmo's shoulder.

"I'll take you up to your room now, Paula," Mama said.
"You'll want to wash up and comb your hair. There is a
clean dress for you hanging in the cupboard on the landing. You mustn't forget to see Babett before supper or
she'll grumble for days."

"Dear old Babett! Papa said she was just the same as
ever," Paula said as she went up to the top floor with her
mother, where her old room was between the maids' room
and that of the boys.

"The same indeed," Mama confirmed with a little sigh.
"She still helps with the darning and patching and knitting. In addition, she advises me how to handle my husband, bring up the boys, and run the house. Through her
ever-open door, she rules the maids in the kitchen, who
consider her a holy terror but mind her or else! Poor thing,
she'll be ninety this fall, and she has become rather stiff
with rheumatism lately. She scarcely leaves her room now,
and I often send one of the boys down to read a little to
her or to listen to her stories about the glorious reign of
King Jerome of Kassel."

"Oh, I remember . . ." Paula said. Like all the children
in the house, she had grown up with these stories about
court life in Kassel. Babett was a relic of the Amtmann's
first marriage to the beautiful Françoise Dudon d'Enval,
to whose mother Babett had been chambermaid. With the
two ladies—the *belle-mère*, as the Amtmann called his
mother-in-law, and the young bride—Babett had come,

and she had stayed on when after only one year of marriage Françoise had died in childbirth and her heartbroken mother had followed her soon. It was then that the Amtmann's two aunts, Christine and Ulrike, had come to comfort their widowed nephew and, for ten years, with Babett's help, had taken care of his ménage and brought up little Franziska. At this time, Jacob Eisenberth had been a young judge, transferred almost every two years to another part of the small duchy of Nassau. Eight years ago he had become Amtmann—both judge and administrator—in Limburg, the cathedral town on the river, where he hoped to spend the rest of his active days.

When he married again, ten years after the death of his first wife, his bride, young Margarete Thour, took over the reins of the household, but nobody thought of parting with the three old women who had taken care of him and little Franziska when he was in need of help. They were part of the ménage and were taken along the same as bed and chest, table and chair, from one place to the next. Four years ago, Emmerich, Jacob's unmarried brother, an antiquarian and bibliophile, had joined the household; in fact, he had come to spend a few weeks with his relatives and had stayed on. There was ample room in the garden wing of the courthouse, and families were a close-knit unit.

Franziska, Jacob Eisenberth's daughter by his first marriage, lived with her husband—also a judge—and family in a small town in the Taunus Mountains, near enough for her much younger half brothers and Paula to visit her in the holidays. Her eldest son was almost the same age as Karl.

Paula was thinking of all this as she stood in the room that was now to be hers again in the early dusk of the

December day. The walls had been newly whitewashed; there were starched muslin curtains around the bed and the windows. A small cherry-wood desk from her mother's girlhood had been brought down from the attic and an old armchair covered with gay chintz. Behind a screen, which evidently her brothers had made and painted, the iron washstand was hidden, and opposite the bed was her little shrine with the Madonna; even the small basin with holy water at the door was still the same. Mama had dipped her fingers in it and made the sign of the cross on her daughter's forehead. "God bless your return, child," she had said, and gone downstairs again.

The room was cold. Bedrooms in the courthouse were not heated, whatever the temperature outside. Mama did not believe in coddling her brood; she trusted in cod-liver oil, fresh air, and what she called her "blood-cleansing tea" during Lent. To this and other beneficial herb teas, she credited the fact that, apart from mumps and measles, her children had scarcely ever been ill.

Paula walked over to the window and looked down at the river and the familiar landscape of rolling countryside beyond the thousand-year-old bridge—the fields now covered with snow, the hedged orchards, the dark patches of forest. The river was a sheet of sparkling ice, interrupted only by an island with wintry-looking trees. It was still called the *leper island* because, long ago, the lepers had been brought out there and, according to an old chronicle, a monk, sick himself, had nursed them and cheered them with sweet songs in praise of the Queen of Heaven. Now the ice was tinged with pink by the setting sun and dotted with schoolboys chasing to and fro. The three arches of the bridge stretched across to the farther bank and to the grim tower that had once been the town gate and was now the prison. On the parapet of the central arch, where the gray stonework thrust out over the river, stood a statue of St. Nepomuk in episcopal attire, cross in hand. For five years, Paula had walked past him, in rain and shine, summer and winter, on her way to the girls' school run by the Pallottine nuns. How long ago it all seemed! It was like another life, and she did not yet know how to pick up the threads.

She heard her brothers' voices from the ice below, where they were playing with their friends, moving as easily as though they had been born with skates on their feet. Right now they were in a contest, jumping over a barrel at full speed, the barrel presumably being on loan from the courthouse cellar. Adolf's dog was competing as eagerly as the boys; with four legs and no skates, it was easier for him than for them. There was shouting and laughter, scorn for those who landed on their stomachs or on their seats, and clapping and shouts of admiration for the successful jumpers. Paula had never had the chance to become so good a skater or swimmer as her brothers. Her long skirts and starched petticoats had always been a handicap to her in the boys' games, and Mama was cross when she came home with her braids undone, a tear in her dress, or a cut knee. Things like that were not proper for a girl. From the age of eight, she had had to look after her youngest brothers, to knit and darn stockings, and to perform all kinds of duties in the house and garden. The boys, also, had to do some chores, but not nearly so many as she.

How different life in the convent had been! Of course,

there were duties there, too, and strict rules, but everything had been shared by forty companions of the same age, enlivened by ardent friendships, little jealousies, deep secrets; by discussions about the few carefully selected books that, apart from their textbooks, they were allowed to read; by the daily excitement of seeing which girl an adored nun would choose to walk by her side in the promenade or which would be chosen to wear the blue ribbon of the *Enfants de Marie* on the next feast of our Lady. They studied languages, geography, history, and art, as well as music, all within the limits of what was regarded as suitable for the education of a young lady. They did fine embroidery, and there was some instruction in cooking and running a household, just enough to enable them to rule their servants one day. Nobody had asked them to knit ghastly, long black-wool boys' stockings, a task Paula had had to learn as a very little girl with clumsy, sticky, hot fingers. And every day at the convent school had begun and ended with prayers in the lovely chapel; all the hours had passed peacefully against the golden background of a sweet and untroubled piety, as yet unshadowed by doubt. When the girls left to go back into the *world*, the good nuns warned them gravely of the dangers they would encounter "out there." As to the precise nature of these dangers, they had only the vaguest ideas.

I wonder . . . Paula thought, sniffing with her straight little nose, as though she could catch a whiff of the fire-and-brimstone smell arising from the abyss of this dangerous world.

She took off her school dress, washed her face and hands in the ice-cold water from the big jug, combed her long hair and put it up again, donned the checkered wool dress Mama had hung in the big cupboard on the landing for her, cast a rather uninterested look at her reflection in the little mirror, and prepared to go downstairs, where the new duties of daughter-of-the-house awaited her.

From the cathedral and the other churches of the town came the ringing of the Angelus bells, and all the village bells from the countryside answered. St. Lubentius in Dietkirchen, equal in age and dignity to the Limburg Cathedral, also joined in the evening song.

In Nancy, Paula thought, they would now be going in procession two by two, followed by Mère Celeste, to the chapel for the Angelus and rosary—and a wave of home-sickness flowed over her as she prayed. But then, Mère Celeste's beloved voice, along with the voices of the bells, was with her in her cold room. "Patience!" it said as it had done so often, and just as often Paula had shaken her head half-embarrassed, half-smiling: "Patience is not the most notable characteristic of my family, *ma mère.*" Only Papa was patient—how could he have been a judge otherwise?

". . . but you will have to prove now what you learned while you were with us, *ma petite Paulette!*" the voice said with the gentle firmness that was never contradicted.

"*Oui, ma Mère,*" she replied, ready to begin her new life.

Winter II

ON JANUARY seventh, the day after the Epiphany and the first school day after the Christmas holidays, Adolf went alone for the first time to the cathedral to ring the Angelus bell and serve Mass. The vacation was over; the austerity of school life would start once again. They had celebrated New Year's Eve in the courthouse, as they did every year, with a crowd of friends and relatives. The women had been hard at work in the kitchen for two days beforehand preparing everything, since on the evening itself there was only a cold buffet so that the maids— Gretel and Kettchen—could have the time off to go dancing. The enormous traditional salad had to be made the day before in any case so that it had time to marinate properly. Paula had helped her aunts with the unending task of cutting up and shredding. The three of them sat at the bright, scrubbed kitchen table and diced the roast veal, the apples and celery, hard-boiled eggs and pickled herrings, beetroots and cucumbers, and the long kidney potatoes, which were grown specially every year in the garden. Nuts were cracked and chopped to put in, as well. The black coal stove glowed. Eclairs, cheese straws, and white bread were baked. The Amtmann and Uncle Emmerich discussed the choice of wines. On the day itself, Mother filled big dishes with what was left of the Christmas baking—cinnamon stars and almond cakes, honey cake, shortbread, gingernuts, and hazelnut macaroons. The brothers were given their share in advance, each a plateful, for who could say whether or not the guests would leave any!

The big drawing room next to the living room was opened up, and the dust covers taken off the furniture. In the prisms of the chandelier, the multicolored light from forty candles was reflected. The festivities continued long past midnight, and on New Year's Day, all the friends met once again at Mass in the cathedral.

Yesterday the Three Wise Men had made their journey through the town, the well-known figures that appeared every year on the sixth of January. They went from house to house, piously singing the endless verses of their song and collecting a few coins for their efforts, for they had to recover from the cold and the strain of holiness at every inn on the way. Alas, they were by nature neither holy nor wise, and no one for a moment supposed they were, least of all they themselves. Nonetheless, on this one day of the year, under a cloak of shabby velvet, a burnoose made from a patched bed sheet, and a piece of threadbare brocade, some of the splendor of the old legends was about them. There were some tongues in town wagging about the old reprobates, to be sure, yet everyone would have missed them had they not gone through the streets on the evening of the Epiphany. They were a part of the Church's changing seasons; a venerable custom, even though in themselves far from venerable; a part of the established devout ritual that gave life its rhythm and meaning.

Adolf was already awake when the clock from the

Cathedral of St. George sang out a single resounding stroke over the sleeping town—a quarter past five. It had not really been necessary for Mother to knock from the floor below on the ceiling with the handle of the broom she kept ready.

"Are you coming to early Mass, too?" Adolf had asked his sister the evening before. But this was the bread-baking day, and Paula was to prepare the dough herself for the first time.

In the boys' room, there were two beds against each of the long walls. August and Georg slept along the opposite wall. Ferdinand and Karl shared a bed on Adolf's side. They were lucky, particularly in winter: two get warm more quickly than one. In compensation, Adolf had his dog as a foot warmer, although this was kept a secret from the adults in the family. There was an old carpet beside his bed for Aquarius, but every evening as soon as Mother had said evening prayers with her sons, wished them good night, and put out the candle, the dog jumped up, snuggled his head into Adolf's armpit, and they went off to sleep peacefully together.

"You can't come with me today," said Adolf as he felt for his clothes in the dark. "You're not allowed in the church, and it's too cold outside." The dog understood him, as he understood everything his master said. Wherever he came from, it was in his blood to obey every word or signal.

The boys wore the shirts, which Mama put out clean for them on Saturday evenings, day and night—a charitable custom, since it saved them from having to slip into a cold shirt in the mornings and let them take some of the comforting warmth of bed into the cold outside world with them. Adolf pulled on his long underwear and black hand-knitted stockings, then his thick winter suit, and he was ready. In winter, thorough washing was done in the evening in the washhouse, which was warmed a little by the embers in the kitchen stove next door. On Saturdays, water was heated in the big copper wash kettle, and all the members of the family bathed in a large wooden tub. Again and again Holwein would have to fetch more wood from the shed; again and again he would take turns with the maids and the boys to go to the pump and carry in pailfuls of water. Saturday was a black day for Holwein.

Adolf ran the washcloth once quickly over his face (it was frozen and crackled nastily) and the comb through his hair. He didn't light the candle, as that would have disturbed his brothers, who need not get up yet. By common consent, a boy old enough to go and ring the bells in the morning dressed in the dark. Previously, it had been only August and Georg. But now Adolf was going to take turns with the older brothers every third week.

He wound the knitted scarf around his neck and crept downstairs in his stocking feet. In the hall on the ground floor were two benches, one in front of his father's office, the other next to the courtroom. Beyond was the chancery, where the young clerks wrote with their quills in thick pigskin tomes or on paper stamped with the arms of the Duke and where the filing shelves reached up to the ceiling. Beside the front door, Holwein had his room, but nothing was stirring there yet.

Adolf sat down on one of the benches and laced up his high boots. From the box room under the stairs came the heavy breathing of someone sleeping there. Sometimes a suspect would be locked up there overnight, if Wittich the beadle or the nightwatchman had picked him up late in the evening, ready for the Amtmann to question early the next morning.

Outside, the dark January morning lay bitterly cold over river, valley, and town. Adolf hunched up his shoulders, dug his chin deeper into the folds of the woolen scarf, and stuck his hands in his pockets. Schoolboys neither wore nor indeed possessed overcoats. Even the rich Trombetta boys put theirs on only on Sunday to go to church.

Adolf walked quickly up the steep narrow alley that led from the courthouse to the cathedral. In a few of the workmen's houses, candles were already flickering. There was no question of lighting lamps in the mornings; oil was expensive and had to be saved for the long winter evenings.

On top of the hill, the street became wider, and the vast sky stretched moonless and milky. The sharp early-morning wind coming down the valley buffeted him as though it had been lying in wait for him, stung his cheeks, and made his eyes water. The broad street led straight to the portal of the cathedral, along the wall of the graveyard. "Anyone who runs past the graveyard wall is a coward," Georg had said when Adolf had gone with him once in the Christmas holidays. And "I won't run," he said to himself under his breath now, but involuntarily, he quickened his pace, looking straight ahead. How could you know what you might see if you looked to the left, where at this hour the crosses loomed up as darker blurs in the misty darkness and morning haze and night shadows held their ghostly dance between the graves? Babett had often enough told stories of terrifying meetings that people had had when

should know better than old Babett, who talked to the
spirits of the dead as though they were still alive. The Poor
Souls who still languished in Purgatory would often wake
the old woman out of her light sleep and not give her
peace until she had prayed an Our Father for them. Not a
night passed but they made their presence known by
knocking on the bedstead and making rustling sounds in
the beams. "I've so many friends among them," said Babett. "If I help them now, they'll help me later."

Adolf had now reached the narrow door behind which
the ropes of the early bell hung. The key was in a niche in
the wall, hidden in the folds of a stone saint's coat. Adolf
quickly unlocked the door, felt for the tinder and candle,
and as the wick took light and the flame flickered upward,
all the terrors he had felt outside were left behind. Once
on consecrated ground, he was safe. It was good to feel the
rough hemp of the bell rope in his hands, hear the bell
answer to his pull; clear and beautiful its note resounded
from the tower. Above him the crows and, in the town
below, the people awoke at the sound. Adolf knew how to
do it. He had more than once rung the bell under the
supervision of his older brothers, but today he was doing
it by himself for the first time. The watchman Michel
Anderwand, who lived high up in the tower, with only the
crows and the sky for company, would listen to judge if it
were properly done. He was old and plagued by rheumatism, so after his wife's death two years before, the dignitaries of the cathedral chapter had allowed him to find a
substitute for the morning ringing. Michel knew the Amtmann and his five sons well. Occasionally, the Amtmann
would climb the many stairs up to his room to have a

bird's-eye view of the world. "It helps to get things in perspective," he said to Michel, who knew every roof in the town and every human soul beneath it. He rang the bells for christenings, weddings, and funerals. For close on forty years, he had kept watch over the town from his eyrie. His choice for a boy to ring the morning bell had fallen on the quiet and reliable August. Georg, who never rested until he could do everything his brother did, took turns with him the second year. And now Adolf was allowed to share the honor and the early rising with his older brothers. He had been surprised when they finally gave in to his pleas. Since making his lonely way today past the graveyard in the dark and cold, he was much less surprised.

Three times three double strokes of the bell with a brief pause between them, as though the world were holding its breath at the angelic greeting—then the bell's jubilant morning song. The ringing gave Adolf a happy feeling, but as he walked over to the sacristy, he felt somewhat ill at ease. Father Müller was a strict, relentless man who chalked up every black mark against you. Adolf had had him for three years as a religious instructor and as a confessor. A holy terror the boys called him. You needed to miss only one single question from the catechism and you had to stay in. In addition, there were three raps with the ruler on your fingertips and sometimes a thrashing with the hazel rod, which always stood by the desk. Adolf sighed. Georg had told him that, after Christmas, Father Müller would be saying the early Mass in the cathedral.

But when Adolf came into the sacristy, a strange young curate was kneeling there at the *prie-dieu*, reading his breviary. His hands and the tip of his nose were blue with cold. Adolf felt an enormous sense of relief and crept around on tiptoe so as not to disturb the young priest at his prayers. He took out the Mass vestments and laid them ready; the amice, alb, and cincture, and the white chasuble. Then he slipped into his own red cassock and white surplice and went into the cathedral to light the candles on one of the side altars. A few women were already kneeling in the front benches; the fringes of their long shawls hung down right to the stone floor, where the light from the sanctuary lamp made a red pool. As they whispered their rosary, their breath rose like curls of white smoke into the cold air.

The curate was waiting already vested when Adolf came back into the sacristy. "Good morning, Father," he said. "I'm Adolf from the courthouse."

"Good morning, Adolf," replied the young priest, as warmly as if he were greeting an old friend. "You must be called after the Duke?"

"Yes, the Duke is my godfather, but I like my other godfather, Uncle Adolf Waterloo of Montabaur, much better."

"Well, even godfathers are a matter of taste. I am Kaplan Knodt, the new curate. Give your parents my regards and say that I shall be visiting them shortly. The Eisenberths and the Knodts are related. You are twelve, I should guess, right?"

"I'll be thirteen in August."

"In the seventh grade?"

"Yes, Father."

"Then I'll be your teacher for religion from now on, and probably I'll be taking your class in Latin, too."

"Good for us! But what about Father Müller?"

"Father Müller has gone to Wiesbaden. Now, Adolf, let us give our attention to holy Mass."

The boy picked up the missal and carried it to the altar in front of the priest. It was big and heavy for a twelve-year-old; and he could hardly see over the top of it. He had to be careful not to trip over the altar steps, as he had once done when serving Mass at the Pallottine convent, but he had only been ten then. Some of the schoolgirls had giggled and told their brothers about it afterwards, and Adolf had never heard the end of it until he gave the two biggest bullies, Emil Müller and Sebastian Meckel, a good licking. He felt a contented glow at the memory of his sweet revenge. But then he remembered what the curate had said and made a real effort to think of the sacred ceremony.

"Dear God, I thank you for giving us a new religion teacher," he prayed. He liked the curate. He moved with such measured solemnity that it was really beautiful to watch, and he spoke so clearly that you could understand all the Latin words and make the right responses. This is what his brother August would be like celebrating Mass, thought Adolf, if he did become a priest. But probably he had no such intention: his head was full of secular history. Under his leadership, the brothers and their friends had run through the Egyptians, Greeks, Persians, and Romans and almost every period of history in their summer games. They all agreed that this was far more fun than the everlasting games of cops and robbers that had been the fashion for years among the schoolboys. Even famous robbers like Schinderhannes could become boring after a while. But when August was by turns Alexander, Theseus, Hannibal, or Caesar, a victorious general leading the entire gang of neighborhood boys to India or Crete, over the Alps or into Gaul—man alive, there was nothing boring about that! The cliffs running down from the cathedral heights into the garden of the courthouse could substitute for any mountain range in the world and the River Lahn for each one of the seven seas. Adolf's favorite period was the medieval age of chivalry. He often dreamed of being Walther von der Vogelweide or Tannhäuser, riding from castle to castle with his harp and his sword, singing songs and telling ancient tales; jousting at tournaments in the cause of the innocent; overcoming dragons that demanded maidens as their prey; winding his way through endless forests with a falcon on his wrist. How lucky people were to have lived then! Now everything was so awfully modern that it was enough to drive any boy with a spark of adventure to despair. Oh dear, his thoughts had run away with him again! Thank goodness, he at least hadn't made any mistakes in the Mass.

"You did very well, Adolf," the young curate said approvingly when they parted afterwards, and Adolf blushed with pleasure. But now he was in a hurry to get home to his breakfast. Dawn was gray over the valley, with the first hint of daylight. Something was scurrying along at the foot of the graveyard wall, and in spite of his hurry Adolf stopped, bent down, and felt for it with his hands. It wasn't something scurrying but something flapping. A bird? A bat? Yes, it was a bird, injured or half frozen and unable to fly away. Adolf pulled off his mittens and reached for the animal. Carefully but firmly, he put his hands around the bird. One of its wings was hanging limp. A sharp beak snapped at his thumb; a pair of talons clawed his hand. Adolf felt suddenly warm in spite of the cold. A bird of prey! Could it be a falcon? Oh, Lord, let it be a falcon!

"Don't make such a fuss." He soothed the wild thing as he licked the blood off his hand. "Silly! If I leave you lying there, the cat will get you and the crows will pick your eyes out."

He pushed the bird under his jacket and held it firmly with one hand, so that it wouldn't do itself further harm by its furious efforts at resistance. Then he went bounding down the steep narrow alley as fast as he could. In one of the empty stalls in the stable was the old cage that had belonged to Aunt Stina's parrot. He put the bird into it. It snapped once more, malevolently, at his hand and then sank down onto the floor of the cage to lie there exhausted.

When Adolf went into the house, a man was already sitting on the bench outside his father's office, a dark, thin fellow who didn't look up when the boy said good morning. He must have been the one spending the night on the makeshift bed under the stairs. Holwein was lighting the stove that heated all the official rooms from the hall; at the same time, he kept a watchful eye on the sinister stranger.

Aquarius came down the stairs to greet his master; however short their separations, there was always the same wild joy when they were reunited, as though the dog could never be quite sure that Adolf had not disappeared from his life for good.

The family was already sitting in the living room, which also served as the dining room. Only the aunts were absent; in winter they had breakfast in bed, so that they didn't need to come out of their room before the house had warmed up. Adolf quickly sat down at his place, and the dog slipped under his chair. He had learned long ago that he was only allowed in the living room on condition that he kept absolutely quiet.

"How did you get on?" asked Mama. "Did you do everything right?"

"Perfect," said Adolf. "And what do you know, the new curate is called Knodt and says he is related to us and will soon pay you a visit. We're going to have him as our teacher for religion and perhaps for Latin, too. Say, aren't we lucky to be rid of old Müller?"

"Of whom?" asked Father.

"Reverend Father Müller. He's gone to Wiesbaden."

The brothers wanted to know more about the new curate, but Adolf could only say that he was nice and tall and lean.

Papa sat there at the head of the table, clean-shaven, in his high stand-up collar and wide black stock. Other fathers wore cinnamon or plum-colored tail coats, but the children had never seen their father except in black. Only when he went to court did he put on the dark blue, gold-embroidered coat of the ducal councilors, with the stars of two orders on his breast, the small tricorn hat under his arm, and the short sword at his side. There was yet no trace of white in his thick dark hair, although he was nearly sixty.

Their mother sat at the other end of the long table. In front of her, she had a pile of sturdy bread slices, which she buttered one after the other, spreading the butter fairly right to the edges but skillfully gliding over the holes in the home-baked bread so that the expensive butter did not stick in them. The children could have either butter or plum jam on their bread at breakfast—to have both was a treat reserved for Sundays and feast days.

Adolf thought of nothing but his bird as he ate his bread and drank his hot milk. Would he be able to mend its broken wing?

"Eat up and don't dream, Adolf," said Mama when he had been staring into space for quite a while. "What have you done to your hand? It's bleeding, isn't it?"

"Oh, nothing much," said Adolf, and luckily Mama's attention was distracted.

"Paula, Karlchen has finished his milk," she admonished her daughter.

Paula hurried to fill the beaker that Karl held out to her. She kept on forgetting that she had to look after the two little boys at table and thought, anyway, that Karl could have asked for more himself: he could speak up well enough at other times.

"Could you send Paula to me for an hour later on to do some writing?" asked Papa. He suffered from writer's cramp, and she was the only one of his children who wrote a clear hand. The brothers all had a terrible scrawl. Paula liked nothing better than being able to escape from the turmoil of the household for a while into the quiet of her father's room.

"As soon as she has finished the bread, Jacob," said Mama. "It must rise now, then go into the oven. While it is baking, she can make the beds and dust her aunts' room."

The Amtmann nodded. "I'll send the man to you in the kitchen after I've had a word with him." Evidently, this was the continuation of a conversation they had had earlier in the morning.

"Did Wittich really have to wake you up in the middle of the night because of that tramp?" asked Mama.

"Indeed he did. Wittich couldn't take the responsibility of locking up a sick man in the tower. If he hadn't come across him in the hayrick behind the mill, the fellow would have frozen to death in the night. It was ten degrees below freezing last night. He coughs a lot and seems to be injured. He needed a drop of brandy badly. Give him a decent breakfast and a glass of hot milk with honey."

"And then what?"

"We'll see. In any case, I have no intention of sending him to the workhouse in his present condition, and I don't want to shove him over the border either."

"Yet those are surely the two courses prescribed by law in the case of tramps, unless I'm mistaken."

"You're not mistaken," said the Amtmann good-humoredly. Nothing amused him more than his wife's occasional remarks on legal matters. "But the law was made for man, not man for the law. The fellow must have a roof over his head for the winter. He's a mere boy, nineteen at the most, a gypsy I should think. Probably he's been cut off from his clan for some reason or other."

The boys pricked up their ears. Their mother remained silent.

"You're always complaining that Holwein never has time to help with everything that needs doing in the house and in the yard. Well, the stableboy's room at the back of the stables is empty, and once he's got his strength back, the gypsy will almost certainly be willing to make himself useful. As long as he has a roof over his head for the winter and enough to eat, he won't need to steal, and that's a lot to be thankful for. It does more harm than good to put such a young lad in prison. I know I can rely on you, Margarete."

Mother stood up and smoothed down the folds of her full skirt. There was suddenly a twinkle in her eyes, which was reflected in Father's as though in a looking glass.

"Your time's up, boys," she said, "unless you want to be late on the first day back at school. Paula, they have a roll and apple each for their break at ten o'clock. Make sure the two little ones have clean handkerchiefs and then put your bread in the oven. First, hold a piece of paper in the oven. If it turns light brown, it's the right heat."

"Yes, Mama." Paula looked tired. Adolf stroked her smooth hair quickly as he went past. "I've something to tell you," he whispered in her ear. He would have loved to have another look at the bird before he went. As yet, he had said nothing to his brothers about it. He was always unwilling to broach anything of importance in the presence of Georg, who had a way of chiding him that drove him mad. Would the bird perhaps have been able to fly away if he had not caught it, he thought desperately? No, the cat would have gotten it, he answered the accusing voice of his conscience. So what? replied the voice. Perhaps a swift death would have been more merciful for a bird of prey than imprisonment.

Aquarius ran to school with the brothers. Every morning it upset the dog when Karl and Ferdinand separated from their big brothers at the first corner. They went to the primary school, the older ones to the high school. Aquarius would look at his master inquiringly to see whether or not he should follow his sheep dog's instinct and keep

the flock together. It was so easy; he just needed to nip the
legs of the deserters a little and they would know they had
to stay with the others. But Adolf shook his head. "Come
on, Aqua; leave those two."

It was nearly a year now since Adolf had rescued the
dog from the river when it was in flood. He had seen him
being carried past the garden of the courthouse clinging to
the remains of his kennel and whining piteously in the
muddy waters of the River Lahn. It had been a cold,
windy March day, and all the tributaries of the Lahn had
been swollen by the snow melting in the mountains and
by heavy rains. Without a moment's thought, Adolf, fully
clothed, had waded into the raging water, which had
swept over the path by the river, swum as he got out of his
depth, and finally brought the dog to land. The brothers
supported the escapade from the bank with encouraging
shouts and good advice: "Watch out or you'll get caught
by that beam. More over to the right. Yes—now you can
get him. Slip his collar off. Easy, boy! That's it!" Long
poles and helping hands were outstretched as he struggled
up the slippery bank, dragging along the spluttering animal. Since then, the dog would have gone through fire for
him—though not through water. For that, he had an
invincible distaste ever since his adventure. For Adolf, it
meant accepting a thorough beating, chiefly for ruining his
clothes but also for endangering his life so foolishly. But
what risk had there been for a boy who had grown up by
the water and could swim like an otter? And you would
have to be a miserable coward to let a poor dog drown
before your very eyes!

"And now just you dare get pneumonia!" said Mama.

"And don't think for one moment I'll put up with a dog in the house."

So Aquarius was first put in the stables, but even Mama had to admit that this was far from being an ideal solution, for it merely meant that to all intents and purposes Adolf lived in the stables, too. By and by, Aquarius was tacitly adopted into the family when inquiries about his rightful owner had come to nothing. The Amtmann had insisted that a notice be put in the Limburg paper, and Adolf had spent a couple of sleepless nights, that someone would reply to it. No one did, however, and Aqua became Adolf's dog, although in the beginning he would often run around as if looking for someone and sometimes would sigh deeply in his sleep.

"A gypsy, Papa said. Did you hear?" said August as they made their way to school.

"I must have a word with him about the gypsy language and the signs they leave at the doors of people's houses," said Georg.

"What sort of signs?" Adolf asked.

Georg threw his brother a pitying look. "They must have dropped you on your head as a child. Haven't you ever heard of gypsies' signs? They make them at the gate of the yard with chalk or coal to warn or guide the others coming after them. Here you get something; here the hausfrau will take pity on a poor devil; or here they set the dog on you."

"Mean, setting a dog on them!" Adolf was always ready to take the side of the underdog.

But August was of the opinion that you had to protect yourself against gypsies. "Didn't you hear what Mama said recently: they wring a hen's neck before it can so much as squawk. And the gypsies don't stop at hens; they're just as likely to take a horse or calf if it comes their way. They crop the horse's tail and mane and disguise it till its own mother wouldn't know it and then take it to market. With that lot, stealing's an art. They teach the children when they're little."

"Boy, they sure know all the tricks in the book!" Georg said appreciatively.

"Do you remember how they pinched the bay horse from the Wiesenhof farm last year?" August chuckled.

"But they were caught three days later," Adolf put in. "Little good it did them giving the horse two white feet and covering up his white markings with shoe polish."

"And Papa sent them off to work for three weeks on Wiesenhof's farm instead of putting them in jail," August recalled, full of admiration for his father's highly individual way of administering justice.

"They had to pump out the cesspool and then manure the fields!" Georg tittered.

"The farmer liked that better than if they'd just had to serve time, I should think."

In the meantime, the boys had nearly reached the high school, and their schoolfellows were joining them from all sides.

"So long, Aqua," said Adolf. "We won't set you on gypsies; that's for sure."

Winter III

ONCE the brothers were out of the house, silence reigned like the calm after a storm. Paula stood for a moment listening and discovered that, in spite of their noise, she had a weak spot in her heart for them. Smiling, she went into the kitchen to put her bread in the oven. "Has it risen enough, Kettchen?" she asked anxiously. "Shouldn't it be much higher? What shall I do if it goes flat?"

The kitchen maid couldn't help laughing at the ignorance of the daughter of the house. She had long ago forgotten how inexperienced she herself had been when she came to the house four years ago and how many tears there had been over her mistakes. "No need to worry, Fräulein Paula," she said comfortingly. "That dough won't go flat. I couldn't do it better myself."

Paula put a piece of paper in the oven, inspected it after a few moments, and said, "That's right now—in with the bread!" It was just like Schiller's poem about *The Bell:* "To the dark womb of the sacred earth we entrust the toil of our hands."

"God watch over it!" said Kettchen, making the sign of the cross on the oven door.

But now there came the sound of Babett's stick tapping an angry staccato on the floor. "My camomile tea! Is no one going to bring me my camomile tea this morning?"

Paula quickly picked up the blue earthenware jug and its matching cup from the back of the range where they were keeping warm and carried them in to the old woman. She was sitting at the window wrapped up in rugs and a shawl, her feet on a heated stone. Every morning Gretel helped her to get up and dress. "You've not even come to say good morning to me yet, child," she said to Paula.

"Good morning, Babett. You were still fast asleep when I was preparing the dough early this morning and later on when I was kneading it."

"Asleep! Why, I haven't shut an eye all night. I'd be far better off in the almshouse, I'm thinking. At least you have someone to talk to there, and when you look out of the window, you can see the people going past and the mail coach setting out. Here there's nothing to see but water and trees. But I couldn't do it to the Amtmann; I couldn't leave him when he depends on me so."

The Amtmann looked in on Babett every day; he knew what was good for an old heart. Nonetheless, Paula doubted that he would be inconsolable if Babett accepted the place in the old women's home run by the church that the parish priest had already offered her twice. But naturally one couldn't suggest that she move, although she had gradually become quite a burden. Nothing happened in the house but she would have her say in it; she was an obstinate, cantankerous, domineering old tyrant, but when all was said and done, she belonged to the family, and they couldn't help loving her.

Now there was the bedmaking to do. Up in the parents'

room, Gretel, armed with broom, tin of polish, and the heavy buffer for the parquet floors, was getting on with the cleaning. She was a big-boned country girl with red cheeks, her blond hair combed back severely and twisted into a tight bun right in the middle of her head. For going to church on Sundays and holidays, the bun was covered up by a tiny black silk cap with long ribbons. Her full hand-woven skirt with the many stiff petticoats under it swung merrily to and fro with her nimble movements, showing the white stockings beneath. Beside the delicate Paula, with her ivory skin and big, dark eyes, Gretel was like a solid, useful Westerwalder earthenware jug next to a piece of transparent Dresden china. She had been in service in the courthouse for three years, and next autumn she was going back to her parents' farm near Dietkirchen to marry the son of a neighbor whose fields bordered conveniently on theirs. When a girl went into service in the town, she earned something toward her dowry, and every year at Christmas she received presents of household linen. The farmers' wives round about were happy to have their daughters in service with Frau Eisenberth. True, they had to work hard, but they learned something from such a skilled housewife, and they were well looked after.

"How do you manage to have such pretty rosy cheeks, Gretel?" asked Paula as they made the beds together. Gretel laughed. She laughed or sang all day long as she did her work. "Why, nothing at all, that's what I do. You know what, Fräulein Paula? Being pale is much more refined. Every country girl's got red cheeks."

That was no comfort to Paula. The aunts were forever lamenting her pallor and thinness, and she herself was conscious of the fact that she didn't look like the other

young girls, for instance those who had come to the New
Year's Eve party with their parents. And how free and easy
they had been! How they had laughed with the young
men and teased one another during the round games, and
they had been so cheerful and fresh and charming. How
she envied them!

Her bread turned out successfully. It was the very first
she had made from beginning to end entirely on her own.
As soon as it was cool, she had to take a loaf to old Frau
Feiler, who had helped on washdays in the courthouse for
six years. Now she was too old and ill to do any more
washing. In between, there was just time for a quick hour
with Papa in his quiet office, which looked out over the
river. His first wife's portrait hung above his writing desk,
a sketch in pastels of a very young girl with three ringlets
on either side of a delicate face. How beautiful she was,
thought Paula every time she sat here and copied for her
father. How much he must have loved her to wait ten
years before deciding to marry a second time!

Today Paula was given a report that had to be handed
on to the Duke. "Take your time," said Papa, and it was
lovely not to rush for once. She filled up the beautiful
smooth paper with her clear script at a comfortable pace.

"Good!" said Papa when she handed him the finished
letter. "Not one of the clerks has nearly such a fine hand
as you, nor have any of your brothers. Thank you, Paula."
It was pleasant to be praised for something for a change.

Shortly after twelve o'clock, the brothers came in for
their dinner; at two they had to be back in school again.
At the table the conversation was again about the gypsy,

who had in the meantime moved into the stableboy's quarters.

"A real live gypsy!" said Georg. "Has he been stealing things?"

"Yes, a real gypsy," replied the Amtmann. "Or Romany, as he calls himself."

"Is he going to stay with us?" asked Karl.

"For the time being. Mind you, leave him in peace. The man has a chronic cold and a knife wound in his side. How bad it is, I don't know—he wouldn't let me see—but he limps a little when he walks and holds his hand to the spot. He's probably had to leave his clan because of a fight with knives. His name is Janosch."

"How romantic!" Aunt Stina, in whose unpublished novels gypsies played a part from time to time, sighed.

"Would you be good enough to put a couple of clean rags in the stable for him, Margarete," requested the Amtmann. "And leave a bottle of tincture of arnica, too. He would only clear out if we sent for a doctor."

"How unreasonable!" said Aunt Rikchen. "I hope Wittich had a good look to see that he no longer had a knife on him. He could easily get through our window on the ground floor and cut all our throats."

"He would come to me first, without a doubt," said Uncle Emmerich. "Then Nicki would jump in his face, and I would have time to seize my old rapier from the wall and defend myself. I guarantee that he'd have lost all desire to attack you by the time I'd finished with him."

"Don't joke about it, Emmo. Someone was murdered in the Rhineland less than two years ago."

"If I thought the man looked like a cutthroat, I wouldn't

have brought him into the house, nor even into the stable, Aunt Rikchen. Besides, you have the bell pull up to our room right beside your bed."

"Let's say grace," said Mama, as she noticed that the boys were sitting impatiently in front of their empty plates. They were desperate to fit in another hour on the ice before school began again.

As soon as Karl had said grace, they shouted, "*Gesegnete Mahlzeit!*" and rushed down the stairs like a thunderstorm. At the side entrance, they strapped on their skates and hobbled over the hard-frozen garden paths, through the lower door in the garden wall, and out onto the river, where a few friends were already waiting for them. Only Adolf, normally the most enthusiastic of skaters, lagged behind: today he had more important things to do. Followed by Aqua, he went over to the stable.

The stranger was standing in the stall of the gray gelding that the boys had named Silver. Aqua growled softly but was silent immediately as Adolf gave him a warning tap on the head. "It's all right, Aqua," he whispered. The dog hesitated a moment, sniffed, and then followed his master over to the two goats who had their stall farther away. The young horse whinnied behind Adolf, moved its ears uneasily, and sniffed the stranger's scent. Then, as the man ran his hand over its neck, a shiver rippled over the smooth skin.

"He's all right when you get to know him," said Adolf. "His name is Silver. I'm going to look at my bird."

The man did not respond. He stood beside the horse and touched it now and then gently. Adolf could not help remembering what his brothers had been saying on the way to school about horse thieves. You've got to watch out, he thought, and then felt ashamed of himself.

In the empty stall next to the gelding's, the bird was sitting on the lowest pole in its cage, its feathers fluffed, its yellow eyes staring straight ahead. It took as little notice of Adolf as the gypsy had done.

The boy filled the drinking bowl with fresh water. He had smuggled a piece of meat from the table in his trouser pocket, and he pushed it between the bars. The bird did not move.

"Don't die, please don't die," whispered Adolf. "This evening I'll bring you a mouse if I find one in the trap."

He stood there motionless, looking at the bird, his hand on his dog's head. It was a peregrine falcon that he had caught, a fine, strong one with a yellow speckled breast and the sharp beak of a bird of prey. But its right wing was hanging limp. Adolf willed with all his might that the bird would one day be well again and not hate him so much any more. He wanted to tame him as the knights had tamed their falcons. Uncle Emmerich had two books on falconry that he would study down to the last detail.

"Its wing is broken," he said to the gypsy over the half wall that separated the stalls. The bird's proud suffering would have broken his heart if he had not had someone to talk to about it. The man laid down the comb with which he had started to clean the horse and came over to him. Aqua sniffed the hand that he calmly held out to him, made a polite little movement with the tip of his tail, and placed himself between the stranger and his master.

"Suspicious," said the man scornfully, nodding at the

dog. "Suspicious like you." Adolf felt himself go red and stood, scarcely able to breathe, while the man inspected the bird with a frown.

"Janosch," he said beseechingly, "my name is Adolf." But what did that mean to the stranger? The glance that fell on the boy was as wild as that of the falcon.

"Yes," he said. "Wing broken." He pressed his hand to his hip, as though his wound and the bird's were one and the same. Then he waved his hand toward the door in a gesture of dismissal. "Go!" Silver whinnied again as though to remind Adolf that he hadn't yet had his apple. Adolf went. The dog followed him, his tail between his legs.

The Amtmann and his wife had stayed behind in the living room after the meal as they did every day at this time. The Amtmann was smoking a pipe; Mama had taken out some sewing. "I hadn't thought it would be like this at all, having a grown-up daughter in the house," she said. "Her thoughts don't seem to be on what she's doing. She forgets everything and makes more mistakes than a new maid. Am I asking too much of her?"

"If you really want my opinion, then I must say yes," answered the Amtmann. "Give her time. After all, everything here is strange for her."

"You, too," she said. "As if it weren't enough having the aunts looking at me reproachfully and Babett, the old grumbler, telling me to my face that I'm too strict with the poor child."

"She's not a poor child, and if I know her, there's nothing she wants less than to be pitied. But don't forget that she's come from another world. In the convent she didn't have five brothers filling the house to bursting point with their noise, and now she's suddenly responsible for them and has to darn their stockings and mend their pants and supervise their homework, at least that of the two little ones. Nor were there three old women who had to be attended to and entertained. We shouldn't be surprised if at first it seems to her as if pandemonium has been let loose."

"Sometimes it *is* like pandemonium here," replied Margarete, her blue eyes shining with suppressed tears. "No one stops to think whether I too don't need a bit of peace and quiet at times."

"*I* think about it, dearest. And does it really seem to you that you never have any peace and quiet? Aren't our evenings together peaceful when the children are asleep and we play chess or simply sit quietly together? But with the children, too, it's peaceful when we all have a singsong or play games or one of us tells stories before the lamp is lit in the evenings. Think of our long walks in the summer or the evenings on the terrace beside the river when we're having a glass of wine with friends. Would you really wish our life to be different? Easier children to manage perhaps, for I admit our brood is far from easy. Or perhaps not quite so many. Or a different husband who wouldn't have brought you three old women as a dowry and who, for good measure, arrests a vagabond from time to time for you to feed. Hm?"

"A different husband!" said Margarete, and now there were dangerous sparks in her eyes. "That's one thing you must never say, never even think!"

He had laid his hands on her shoulders and looked at her. "Margarete!"

"What else do you want?"

"The lad, the gypsy, he *did* steal something. He was hungry. Please don't let the boys know."

The next morning, when Adolf went to the stable for a moment before school to take the falcon a plump mouse from the trap in the larder, its wing had been fixed to a wooden splint. This time Adolf had not forgotten Silver and had brought an apple for him, his own precious apple for the ten o'clock break, for apples in winter were a rarity in those days. The horse crunched the fruit and looked in Adolf's pocket for more. Adolf was wondering whether he ought to thank the gypsy for having taken care of the falcon when Georg came into the stable and poured out a stream of questions at Janosch, idiotic questions about gypsy signs and such-like rubbish. Adolf was furious. "Shut up, can't you?" he snorted at his brother. "Didn't you hear Papa say we were to leave him in peace?"

"Except for you, eh? And what's this miserable creature you've picked up somewhere? It looks as though it's going to die any minute."

"It's a falcon. You couldn't tell a falcon from a crow. And I bet it's not going to die."

Janosch was in the rear part of the stable, filling the goats' water trough. He acted as if Georg simply didn't exist, which gave Adolf great satisfaction. On the other hand, he showed no sign of noticing Adolf either.

This morning Adolf was given a black mark in catechism by the nice Father Knodt for not paying attention. It was one of those days when everything seemed to go wrong. When he went back to the stable in the afternoon to take the falcon a piece of meat (the mouse he had brought in the morning had disappeared—a sign that at least the bird wasn't refusing to eat), Aunt Stina was standing there, with notebook and pencil, addressing Janosch, who was feeding the horse. Adolf drew a deep breath.

"Good evening, Janosch," he heard her say in her delicate ladylike voice. "Would you perhaps have the goodness to answer a few questions for me about gypsy life?"

Heavens above! Adolf signaled to her to be quiet, to beat it, to sink into the earth—but she didn't understand. And now Janosch came out of the horse box, shut the door with a bang, threw Aunt Stina one of his black looks, turned his back on her and Adolf (on me, too, thought Adolf unhappily), and disappeared into the rear of the stable, not to the goats this time but to the pig, as though this would emphasize his distaste for such importunities.

Winter IV

FEBRUARY had come around already. One evening Paula was sitting in her room writing a letter to Mère Celeste with numb fingers. Why couldn't she write her letter in the comfort and warmth of the living room, Mama had asked when she had gone upstairs earlier than usual today. But you had to have Mama's iron nerves to write letters with this overpowering family all around you, Paula thought rebelliously. Not to mention the continual interruptions—"Paula, a button is loose on my jacket!" "Give me a hand with this French translation, will you? What did we send you to France for?" That was Georg. Or Mama: "Be a dear and fetch some hot water for Father's nightcap, would you; and while you're there, take a cup of fennel tea in to Aunt Stina. At suppertime she looked as though she were starting one of her colds again."

Sometimes Papa would read aloud to them or Uncle Emmerich would bring a volume of pictures in for them to look at. But Paula would have preferred to read by herself; there was so much of literature that she hadn't read yet. Practically everything, she thought, every time she dusted the books in Uncle Emmo's room. Suddenly, she was seized by a desire to read everything at once. Mama often read in the evening, but she could knit at the same time. Couldn't Paula knit while she was reading? No, that was another thing they hadn't taught her in the convent. In the evenings it was recreation time and no work was done; no knitting, and anyway not horrible thick black boys' stockings.

"*Ma chère Mère,*" wrote Paula. "I have discovered that it is impossible to be good and holy in the *world.* At least I can't do it. Every day I lose my temper dozens of times— with my brothers, with my aunts, with old Babett who always wants something or other, with Mama who is so strict and expects so much of me. In the evening when I examine my conscience, I feel ashamed that I have had such wicked, angry thoughts. The days are so full of noise and bustle and duties that there is never time for quiet prayer; from morning till night I am busy with worldly concerns. I can't even get to holy Mass every day. Do you know, a dress is being made for my first ball and, oh, *ma Mère,* if you were to see how low it is cut! It's true that old Babett, who can remember King Jerome's court, says it's hardly décolleté at all and that I should have seen the ladies at the balls in the palace at Kassel. But that's more than half a century ago, and I haven't the slightest desire to be a great lady, let alone one of 1811. My aunts, however, speak very effusively of the Empress Eugénie whom they call the most beautiful woman of the century. And why is she so beautiful? Because she washes her face every day in rain water or buttermilk. Where would I find the time to do that even if I wanted to? The Empress Eugénie wears dresses with absolutely bare shoulders to balls. Bare shoulders, *ma Mère!* What a false picture we girls had about life in the world! How lucky the postulants in the convent are! I hope that one day I too may be one of them . . ."

She was so deep in her letter that only now did she become conscious of the row going on in the boys' room next door. Of course, it was full moon! In January also the brothers had gone completely wild when there was a bright moon at night. Any minute now there would be a knock on the ceiling below and Mama's voice would call up, "Paula, can't you hear that there's blue murder being done in the boys' room?" It was probably a harmless pillow fight or a dramatic acting-out of part of a Schiller play.

But suddenly there was a frightening dull thud, like something heavy striking the floor. Paula heard footsteps running to and fro, the patter of bare feet across the corridor to the broom cupboard, muffled shouts—and then, as she had feared, her mother's knocking from below. Paula rushed out. As she opened the door of the boys' room, she found herself in the midst of a battlefield. One of the big water jugs had been knocked over, a pillow was swimming in the water, and the moon outside the window was smiling serenely at its reflection in the flood. August was sitting on his bed, his legs crossed like a pasha, directing his forces. Georg and Adolf were trying to mop up the flood with cloths from the broom cupboard. "Come on, men, under the beds, too!" ordered August calmly. Ferdinand was holding on to Karl, who threshed about with his arms and legs, struggling desperately in his short shirt, his cheeks glowing with fighting spirit, trying to attack Georg with whom he seemed to have something to settle. "The boy Karl is beginning to irritate me," said August. "March him off to be shot!" At this threat, Karl took a deep breath in order to have enough air to yell, but

Georg slapped him around the ears with the wet floor cloth and Adolf threw himself into the fray by putting a hand over his mouth. If Mama heard screams from her youngest, she would come up herself, and then there'd be trouble.

"Quiet!" hissed Paula. "Into bed with you, Karl. No, first I must dry your feet. Are you all out of your minds? Let him go, Ferdinand."

"Go back to your convent, you old nun," shouted Ferdinand. "This room is for men. We don't want girls here."

"Men!" said Paula angrily. "As if men threw pillows around at night." She seized the struggling Karl, dragged him to a chair, and began to rub his bare ice-cold feet dry. "August!" she implored. "For heaven's sake, tell them to stop!"

"All over now!" came the order from the sultan's bed. "Back to bed, men. Otherwise, Paula will get it in the neck in the morning from Mama, and we won't be allowed on the ice."

They obeyed instantly; as suddenly as if there had never been a fight, there was peace. Paula wiped up the rest of the water from the floor. It was icy, and her hands, cold already, felt as though they had lost all feeling when she got back to her room. There was no question of going on with her letter. She stood for a few minutes at the window and looked down on the river where the moonlight lay like a patch of molten silver on the sheet of ice. The fool's moon, she thought. In four days it would be Carnival Sunday, and she would go with her parents to her first big ball in the Casino. Actually, it was quite touching the way all the women in the house had joined in with advice and assistance to show her off to the best advantage.

Her dress was of white *broderie anglaise*, which old Isidor, the peddler who came to Limburg three times a year, had brought especially from Frankfurt for the first ball dress of the young courthouse lady. The sewing had been a terrible lot of work; three rows of flounces on the five-yard-round skirt set over a crinoline stiff with horsehair.

"Millions of stitches!" Aunt Stina said. "How it will swing when you dance!"

There were three rows of narrower flounces on the bodice. "That makes her look a little fuller," remarked Aunt Rikchen.

Paula's waist, naturally narrow enough, would be kept in further by stays, so that it looked like a flower's delicate stem, which a puff of wind could break off. It was a ravishing dress, Paula had to admit, even if she still thought the décolleté too daring. But what if all this work had been wasted? Did she really look forward to the ball? She felt a shy anticipation, a curiosity rather, mixed with anxiety. Perhaps she would be a wallflower, and how terribly embarrassing that would be for her and for her family! The alternative was that each of those strange young men could ask her to dance and lead her away, his arm around her—when up till now she had at most offered the tips of her fingers to strange young men! How gay and uncomplicated the Shrovetide celebrations in the convent had been, with plays put on by the pupils and fancy dresses and dancing in the evening on Sunday, Monday, and Tuesday from eight till ten, whereas normally they had to be in bed by nine. And all this gaiety without the trace of a man around, and even the plainest girl need not worry about being left to sit out the evening.

Paula was not easily given to crying; the Eisenberth

children had all learned early to master their emotions. *Contenance,* Papa called it. But now, remembering the happiness of the convent festivities, all the suppressed homesickness of the last weeks broke out. She laid her arms on the letter she had started, put down her head, and wept. But in this house you couldn't even cry in peace. There was someone knocking at the door. It was Adolf, followed by the inevitable Aquarius, who straightaway laid a paw sympathetically on her knee.

"What's the matter, Paula? You mustn't bawl just because we make a bit of a row. We didn't mean to annoy you, and if Mama grumbles at you tomorrow morning, we'll all say it was our fault."

Paula stood up and wiped away her tears. "I know you don't do it on purpose," she said. She sat down on the edge of her bed, drew Adolf down beside her, and spread the thick feather-filled coverlet over his bare legs and across her own knees. Aquarius needed no invitation to jump up next to them, and the three of them sat huddled together, quite comfortable and warm.

"I know you don't do it on purpose, but it comes to the same thing anyway. I'm responsible whenever there's any mischief or anything goes wrong. If Karl comes to table with a dirty handkerchief because he has cleaned his shoes with it, if Ferdinand doesn't wash his neck or has forgotten half his homework again, who gets blamed? I do. The next thing will be that I'm reproached because he plays truant from school."

"He hardly ever plays truant in winter," said Adolf. "But just wait till the spring."

That was cold comfort. "You see, in the convent we were all children; we were told exactly what we had to do and what we didn't have to do, and after the first couple of weeks, everything went like clockwork. And now here I have to be grown-up all of a sudden and think of everything myself and do hundreds of things that I had no notion of two months ago. Baking bread! Yes, it's kind of nice when the loaves lie there finished, all round and brown and shiny, but my arms ache the whole day with kneading twenty pounds of flour, believe me. In Nancy the bread came white and fresh every morning from the baker, and we only learned to make fancy tarts."

"We haven't anything against fancy tarts. At Easter you'll bake us some, eh?"

"Oh, Easter's a long way off. First I've got to get through the ball on Sunday and either dance with complete strangers or sit out like a wallflower. I don't care a pin about being grown-up. I hate it. And the everlasting racket in the house! In the convent there were no loud voices, no banging doors, no din. There was no talking in the corridors and on the stairs, and from evening prayers till next morning after Mass, not a whisper was heard, for after prayers the *Great Silence* reigned."

"Terrible!" said Adolf in honest horror. "Did you hear that, Aqua? No whispering even!"

"Not terrible at all, stupid! When you lay in bed in the evening, it was as quiet as in church. You could only hear the rosary beads of the nun on duty rattling softly as she walked up and down between our white cubicles; that sent you off to sleep in no time. And during the day, you always found time to go to the chapel for a few minutes, *visiter le bon Dieu*, we called it. Here you're on the go the whole day, and everything revolves around ordinary things like mending pants, fetching eggs from the henhouse, and making beds, and Mama gets annoyed immediately when I forget anything."

"Oh, she doesn't mean it. You'll get used to us again soon, Paula," Adolf said to her. "You know Aqua was just like that! He was so funny at first, always uneasy, always looking as though he'd lost something. But now he's my dog, aren't you, Aqua? Now we belong together for life, and he's forgotten everything that happened before."

"I sometimes think . . . can you keep a secret, Adolf?"

"Like the grave."

"Truly? Give me your hand on it. Well, I've often thought in the last weeks that I should like to go back to the convent. For good, you understand. They wouldn't take me before I was eighteen, of course, and it isn't easy really to know whether you've got a vocation. In November, after my birthday, I'm going to speak to our parents about it."

"Oh, cut that out! You don't have to go back to the convent just because Mama's cross with you sometimes, and we make so much noise and get holes in our stockings and pants all the time. You know what? We'll make a real effort from now on, honestly."

"That cheeky Ferdinand called me a nun, as if we had been saints in the convent and did nothing except pray, but it wasn't like that at all. We were happy and light-hearted, full of fun and laughter. Sometimes when one of us had a package of food from home, we ate chocolate in bed at night and gossiped as soon as the sister on duty had gone to sleep. But we had to do it quietly, so as not to be discovered—because it was very wicked and we knew it!

Romper le silence, just think! Once our dormitory was forbidden to take part in the evening recreation for three days, but it was even worse that Mère Celeste didn't speak to us for the whole three days. We might as well not have been there, and we loved her so much. If I could only go back, I would gladly walk all the way barefoot!"

Adolf could scarcely understand all this. To be silent in the bedroom, where they often had great fun playing blindman's buff, having pillow fights, or being ghosts! But even if he didn't understand that you could be homesick for such a dreary place as a convent, he did understand that Paula was unhappy, and that made him sad, too. "You won't have to stay here forever," he said and put his arm around her shoulders. "Girls get married. Franziska got married at eighteen—only I was so little then that I didn't have much fun at the wedding. But I'm going to have fun at yours, see? And later I'll come and visit you every vacation, or perhaps you'll marry someone from here."

"Get that idea out of your head, Adolf. I'm not going to marry, and no one would want me anyway. Men want girls with a milk-and-roses complexion and with a *figure,* Aunt Rikchen's always telling me. And now, off to bed with you; otherwise, you'll oversleep in the morning. Perhaps I'll come to early Mass with you." She patted his hand briefly where it lay over her shoulder. "You're the best of the lot, Adolf."

He grinned, embarrassed. "*Toujours à votre service, mademoiselle.* Tomorrow you must come have a look at my falcon, won't you? His wing is already a little better. Janosch thinks it'll get all right again. But he's still just as wild as ever. Janosch says birds of prey can never be tamed. But I

know that you can tame falcons. I've always wanted a
hunting falcon, the same as the knights, you know, just as
much as I want Janosch to be my friend. But he doesn't
get any tamer either . . ."

The ball on Carnival Sunday every year was the last of
the season, and everyone of name and position in the town
assembled in the ballroom of the Casino. They all knew
one another, knew who and what everyone was; even those
from outside the town, who came over from Wetzlar or
Dietz or Bad Ems on such special occasions, were no
strangers. Bows and greetings went from table to table; the
ladies exchanged compliments on each other's daughters;
titles were tossed around liberally: Excellenz, Herr Hofrat,
Frau Professor, Frau Hofapotheker, for the women were
addressed by their husbands' titles and a minister's wife
was called "Your Excellency," just like her husband.

The first dance of the evening was always a quadrille,
in which everyone, both young and old, took part. After it,
the older members of the company withdrew to the white-
damasked tables that surrounded the dance floor on all
sides and talked or watched the young people dancing.
Later on in the evening, some of the tables would be
pushed together so that comments and gossip could be
exchanged more easily. The men would disappear for an
hour for hands of whist or tarots in the adjoining room or
to smoke a cigar and talk politics.

"She really does look sweet," said Aunt Stina as Paula
danced past them with a young man in an elegant yellow
tail coat. "What a pity the décolleté is not deep enough! It
wouldn't do at all at court."

"Look, that's young Overberg dancing with her for the second time," remarked Aunt Rikchen, who never missed anything. "I only hope he doesn't turn the poor child's head."

"There's no question of heads being turned," said Paula's mother matter-of-factly. "He's dancing with her because he's a friend of the family, like the sons of our other friends. No one would dream of leaving the Amtmann's daughter to be a wallflower at her first ball. Anyway, I must say she has learned to dance at the convent."

"It's all part of a young lady's education."

Aunt Rikchen was still busied mentally with young Overberg. It was the first time that he had been seen at a ball in the Casino since his affair with the daughter of Hofrat Brendel had ended. The *affair* hadn't been much more than that he had danced a great deal with pretty Natalie during one whole winter, and everyone had noticed it and drawn overhasty conclusions. The little town had buzzed with rumors, and then suddenly Konrad Overberg had disappeared on another journey abroad. It was obvious that he had been no more serious about Natalie than about any of the others he had courted before her. The mothers sighed, outwardly with indignation, inwardly with relief; he was still on the market. As for Natalie and her broken heart, things had not turned out too badly after all. After her parents had sent her off to spend a year with relatives in the country, she had gotten engaged to one of the Duke's young aides.

"That snowy white next to her pale face was perhaps a little daring." Aunt Rikchen was ruminating again. "It's a pity she didn't inherit your high coloring, Margarete."

"My high coloring, indeed! You've no idea how often I

WINTER IV   59

had to recourse to the flour barrel before a ball when I was young."

"I like her in white," said the Amtmann. "It accentuates her dark eyes and hair better than any color could. My compliments to the clever hands that made this lovely dress!"

"The design came from the very latest issue of the *Modenwelt*," Aunt Rikchen said proudly. "It would have cost you fifty gulden at least if it had been bought in one of the salons in Frankfurt."

"She is one of the most striking girls in the room," Uncle Emmo remarked. "Don't call her pale, Rikchen. That's an offense to her camellia complexion. She reminds me of a portrait in the Düsseldorf Art Gallery—with those big dark eyes that always look as if she were gazing at a Christmas tree. Moreover, our little girl is an enchanting dancer."

"My goodness, Emmo, you're getting quite romantic in your olden days!" Aunt Stina smiled, for she had just decided that the heroine in her next novel would look just like Paula, marry a count, and live happily ever after.

"It's easy to be romantic when it's no longer dangerous," Emmo replied. "What about a little game, Jacob? The doctor has signaled to us twice already, and I'm starved for a pipe."

At almost that very moment, Konrad Overberg was echoing Uncle Emmo's words to Paula. "*Enchanté mademoiselle!* You dance like a Parisienne."

"I learned it in Nancy from a Parisienne," she said, intoxicated with the music and the dancing and relieved not to be a wallflower. "Madame Hortense, our dancing mistress at the convent, would have been *dégoûtée* to see the mistakes the young men made in the quadrille. You are

the only one who can do the figures properly, Herr Overberg."

"My profound thanks. May I then ask for the pleasure
of the second quadrille? And for the next waltz?"

She nodded her assent immediately—without hesitation, without a trace of the coyness that had irritated him
so often in others. You could read her thoughts like an
open book. She liked dancing with him and did not
hesitate to show it. But he knew women well enough to
be aware that her pleasure had not much to do with him
personally. It was a tribute to his good dancing, which she
might have paid to anyone. Quite a new experience for him!

"Why were you so forbiddingly distant in the stage-
coach?" he could not help asking. "I should have liked to
talk to you. After all, we're old acquaintances."

"Are we? I can't remember! One doesn't talk to strange
men on journeys."

"Evidently not when one has come straight from a
convent school. Do you really not remember the day I was
riding past and found you having, I regret to say, a row
with three lads far bigger than you. There you stood, your
back to a wall, defending yourself like a wildcat. Your nose
was bleeding, your hair was a mess, and your dress was
torn. You hadn't a chance, not a chance in the world.
When I had chased the rascals away, you weren't even
grateful. It was obvious you thought it impertinent of a
stranger to interfere in your personal affairs. You just threw
me a furious glance from those dark eyes and ran away."

"*Mon Dieu*, that was you! You rode a dapple-gray horse,
right?"

"Yes. Immensely flattering that you should at least remember my horse!"

It had been an absolutely impossible situation. She must have been ten years old, and her instinct for taking the part of the underdog even in hopeless cases had led her yet again into doing something silly. The big boys had gotten hold of a much smaller one and were knocking him about. And she felt she had to stand up for the rights of the innocent, though it was pretty doubtful whether the case was one of snow-white innocence! "I must have been a real tomboy then," she said penitently. "If I were you, I wouldn't dance with someone like that."

She has a sense of humor, too, he thought delightedly. "I only do it because we dance so well together. Even the *minuet à la Reine* without a single mistake! In the meantime, they've turned the tomboy into a perfect young lady at the convent. Were you happy there?"

She made a graceful pirouette under his outstretched hand and then sank into the deep curtsy with which the dance ended.

He gave her his arm and led her back to her family's table.

"It was a wonderful time," she said. "I was very happy there." Later, when the orchestra started to play one of the new waltzes by Johann Strauss the younger, Overberg came to fetch her again, and now he talked French to her, as if he had guessed how much she liked this language. "What else have you seen in France besides Nancy?" he asked.

"The Strasbourg Münster," she said, "but that is not French. It was made by a German architect. We took a trip to Colmar, too. What a lovely, quaint, medieval city that is! Mère Monique, our teacher in art history, showed us Schöngauer's *Madonna im Rosenhag* and the wings of Grünewald's Isenheim altar. That's something you don't forget after you have seen it. And Matthias Grünewald was also a German, wasn't he?"

"The Alsace is borderland," Overberg said. "At the time the cathedral was built and when Master Matthias painted, it was German. Great art is universal, and it doesn't matter much where we find it. Strasbourg and Chartres, the founder's figures in the Naumburg cathedral, the Isenheim altar and the temples of the Acropolis— they all belong to each one of us because they are part of our Western culture."

"Have you seen them all?" she asked eagerly, and he told her about Greece and Rome and Florence, the French castles and cathedrals, and Sainte-Chapelle in Paris.

She listened, carried away by the vivid pictures he gave her, asking a question now and then and forgetting her shyness. And all the while she danced, following the gentle pressure of his hand, in complete harmony with the bewitching Viennese music and with her partner. She had never danced like that in her life, not even with her friends in the convent. And suddenly this beloved convent came back into her thoughts, and she felt a sting of remorse. Was it as easy as this to be distracted by the pleasures of the world?

"In March I must be off again," Overberg said. "To Russia this time. But in early fall I'll be back, and I'm going to ask you right now to keep the first quadrille and the first waltz at the first ball next season for me."

"If I'm still here then, I'll remember," Paula said.

"What do you mean? You don't intend to leave us and go back to the convent? Perhaps . . . perhaps for good?"

"How did you guess?" she asked in dismay.

"That wasn't difficult. You looked so radiant when you

told me that you had been happy there. And it's common enough to want to get back to a former period of our life when we haven't quite adjusted to the new one."

"But that's not the only reason." She stopped, surprised that she could talk to a stranger about her secret wishes. Yet somehow the fact that he *was* a stranger made it easier—and also that he would leave soon. By the time he came back, he would surely have forgotten.

"You are right," she continued. "It is not impossible that I may want to go back for good one day. But please promise that you won't tell anybody."

He pressed her hand. "You have my word, *mademoiselle*. And now will you promise me not to do anything in a hurry?"

She smiled. "That's easy. They won't even consider taking me before I am eighteen. I promise I'll do a lot of thinking and praying before I decide."

She looked up at him with her candid, serious eyes, and Konrad Overberg thought that this was the strangest ball conversation he had experienced in his life.

"How was the ball?" Adolf asked his sister the next day as he met her alone on the stairs. She had just helped August and Georg put on their costumes for the carnival procession through the town. Now she was dashing down to Babett's room, where the two little ones had to be dressed for the afternoon's entertainment.

"How did you think I looked?" Paula asked instead of replying.

"Fair. Nothing wrong at all. You weren't left sitting all the time?"

"No, everyone danced; there were more gentlemen than

ladies there. And Mama said that they couldn't ignore the Amtmann's daughter—it wouldn't be polite. Incidentally, I think Herr Overberg from Bad Ems didn't ask me just out of politeness but because we danced so well together."

"He's the one who has the finest horses for miles around here. I would have thought he was a bit old for dancing."

"Well—not *that* old. He dances better than all the younger men put together. Gavottes, minuets, and quadrilles, he can do them all, and he waltzes simply divinely. In March he's going to Russia."

"What for?"

"Oh, visiting the Crimea, you know. They're said to have good vineyards there. Aunt Stina said his Papa has wine vaults and vineyards on the Rhine. When his mother died, his father—the old gentleman—came to live at Bad Ems because the hot springs there are so good for his health. If I only knew why Aunt Rikchen warned me against him—I mean the younger one now. She said he was a Don Juan and had already made lots of girls unhappy. Do you know what she means by that?"

"It's from an opera by Mozart. They played the overture at one of those ghastly concerts our parents drag us to sometimes."

"That much I know myself. Papa said some people call him *Don Giovanni!* But how could he make me unhappy when he dances so well and tells such interesting things about foreign lands? Aunt Rikchen does have odd ideas at times. When are you going to the carnival?"

"Later," said Adolf. "First, I must feed my falcon, and then I'm going on the ice with Aqua, to give him some exercise. I don't want to take him into town today with all the noise and excitement."

"Call me if you need help with putting on your costume. Now I've got to help get the little ones ready in time."

The parade on Shrove Monday was the climax of the carnival time for the children. There was no mother so poor or so unskilled with her needle that she didn't manage to put together some brightly colored costumes out of old rags for her offspring so that they could join in the big parade. On Monday and Tuesday of this week, there was no school in the afternoon, and even the strictest teachers stretched a point and gave no homework for these days.

August and Georg were the first ones from the courthouse to make their way into the town. The previous week Paula had sewn gold braid onto two of her father's old tail coats. The boys wanted to go as officers of Frederick the Great. Just now she had put the finishing touches to her handiwork, bound pigtails of straw with a black ribbon, fixed a couple of cotton-wool curls on either side of their tall spiked helmets, and painted elegant mustaches on their upper lips. They looked quite realistic by the time she had finished, but it was reassuring to know that they would not encounter a living soul who had actually seen real live officers in old Fritz's army.

In Babett's room she found all the women of the house gathered around Ferdinand and Karl. Even the two maids were standing at the open kitchen door watching the transformation of the youngest members of the family. Karl had decided to go as Napoleon. He, too, had his gold braid, gold buttons, and medals sewn onto an old jacket. His mother had crocheted magnificent epaulettes of yellow wool, and Aunt Rikchen had stuck together a cocked hat out of shiny black paper. Babett, who was the only one in the house to have seen the great Corsican personally, subjected everything to a severe scrutiny.

"I tell you, boys, I saw him in the flesh when he came to visit his little brother Jerome, the king of Westphalia in Kassel," she told them, and they all listened respectfully, although they had heard the story many times before. When Babett spoke of Napoleon, she always meant Napoleon I, the Great. As for the Third, who now was on the throne of France, she hadn't recognized him yet.

"Don't forget Schinderhannes, Babett!" interrupted Ferdinand anxiously. He was going as the famous robber chief, who a century ago had kept the whole middle Rhine countryside in fear and trembling. "Did you know Schinderhannes, too?" asked Ferdinand.

"What are you thinking of, child? That would make me over a hundred years old, and to be sure my employers didn't mix with bands of robbers."

"But I want to look *exactly* like Schinderhannes."

"And so you will, so you will, my pet!" Aunt Stina comforted him. "I've had another close look at the picture in Uncle Emmerich's book."

The aunts rummaged in the big chest, full of oddments of material and old clothes that had been brought down from the attic. "There!" cried Babett as Aunt Rikchen pulled something out and held it up. "Just give that old tattered shirt and the ragged trousers to me. Try these on, Ferdinand. Why, you only need the legs a bit shorter, and they'll fit you fine."

Mother took up her needle and thread quickly.

"And we'll wind the red sash around your middle," said Aunt Stina. Meanwhile, Mama had found a damask ribbon that would do as a decoration for Napoleon.

"Look here!" shouted Paula, infected by the general enthusiasm. "We'll put this black raven's feather through one of the holes in Schinderhannes' hat."

"And now find a cork, Kettchen," Mama ordered. "Singe it over the candle, Paula; stand still now, M'sieu Schinderhannes."

She drew the blackened edge of the cork along the line of Ferdinand's already raven-black eyebrows and painted them twice as thick. On his upper lip, she drew in a martial-looking mustache, but then Napoleon started clamoring for one, too.

"Quiet now, child," said Babett firmly. "Napoleon was clean-shaven like your papa. But wait. Paint him in a few fringes on his forehead, Paula, like on the picture over there, so that our little Karl has a bit of black, too. And now have a look in the mirror on my desk. Well, how do you like yourselves?"

"It's odd what a bloodthirsty brood I've brought into the world," said Mama wonderingly. "I declare, you make me shiver. And where's Adolf, Paula?"

"In the stable. And then he wanted to take the dog on the ice."

"What? Isn't he going to join in the parade?"

"He has his last year's costume all ready, and he's going later," said Paula. She thought that he would probably have gone straight there if his bigger brothers had asked him to go with them. But it might not have occurred to them that an invitation was necessary.

Adolf took his falcon all that he was able to beg from the cook, the head or entrails of a chicken, some gristly bits of soup meat; often he would smuggle a piece of meat from his own plate, as well as anything he found in the traps in the larder or cellar, and an occasional rat that Aqua brought him.

"How is he?" was Adolf's first question whenever he came into the stable. Janosch would answer in a monosyllable, if at all. He had taken the splints off the broken wing now; the limb was still stiff, but it became visibly more flexible every day.

On this February afternoon, Janosch was leaning on his pitchfork at the open door of the stable and gazing out over the low wall that separated the farmyard from the garden. The sun had melted the snow in one or two places and left bare patches. For the first time in many weeks, there was the smell of damp earth in the air. Janosch sniffed like a hound that has found the scent. He always took his time over his work, as though he wanted to show that he was no menial whom anyone could order about. He gave his assistance here and there in cavalier fashion, as though bestowing a favor. His wound didn't seem to be giving him any further trouble; only when it was new moon, he would sometimes press his hand to the spot and give a momentary frown. The one thing he never neglected was to rub down the horse, keep its stall clean, and see that it had plenty to eat and drink. He looked after the goats and the pig, too, probably because he didn't want Holwein, whom he couldn't stand, to come to the stable. The two were like fire and water: they didn't mix—the independent vagabond and the docile employee, who in Janosch's eyes had sold his soul for the miserable guarantee of a secure existence.

Before, it had been Adolf who had cared for the animals,

for he had told his brothers, "Old Holwein hasn't the slightest idea how to treat animals." Adolf had always ridden the phlegmatic old white horse to the smithy and in summer to the watering place further up the river. The Amtmann had directed that the young gelding should be led by the halter until they had really found out whether it was good-tempered or not. But Janosch, who knew nothing of the order, had ridden Silver to the smithy over two weeks ago with Adolf and his dog running along behind them. The young gypsy sat careless on the horse's bare back, the reins loose in his hands, guiding him with the scarcely perceptible movements of his legs, while Silver pranced about under him like a circus horse. Terrific, thought Adolf; the horse had never looked so beautiful. He stood silent at the door of the smithy and watched how Janosch held the nervous young beast's head, covered its eyes with his hands when the blacksmith's fire flared up, and talked to it softly in strange, incomprehensible words, like a mother soothing her fearful child. When the horse was shod and Janosch had approved the old smith's work with a gracious nod, he lifted Adolf up and, without a word, placed him on the horse and walked alongside, while Adolf, dizzy with pride and happiness, rode the gelding home. On the way Janosch threw him a few words of instruction about his seat or the position of his legs, but otherwise he let him have his head.

That evening Adolf had said to his father, "I rode Silver today. Janosch was with me. Silver is awfully good, and Holwein is . . ."

"Holwein is an old man, and you will not say anything disrespectful about him," his father said firmly. "As far as I

am concerned, you can ride the horse when Janosch is
there. He worked for some time with a team of circus
riders and knows a good deal about horses."

Since then, Janosch had given Adolf a riding lesson
nearly every day, if you could count his short rough-and-
ready directions as instructions.

This Shrove Monday morning the Amtmann had been
to see that everything was all right in the stable, and later
he said to his wife, "He has a way with animals."

"With animals, certainly," she had to admit, "and ap-
parently with Adolf, too. He disappears there every spare
minute he's got. And when the gypsy plays his violin in
the evening, my maids go wild. Do you know that he's
playing at The Ox for the dancing this evening?"

"He told me he was going to," said the Amtmann
calmly. "I see no reason to forbid it."

What hurt his wife's feelings was the fact that after all
the good food given him at the courthouse, the gypsy was
still as thin as a stray cat. He and Paula, she thought
crossly, they do my cooking no credit at all.

While the costumes were being given their big rehearsal
in Babett's room, Adolf and Aquarius sat snuggled up to
one another in the straw in front of the cage, their eyes
fixed on the falcon. Adolf still hoped that he might gradually get to know the bird better and perhaps finally gain an
insight into the strange being that so stubbornly refused
his friendship. After a while, Janosch left his manure cart
and took up his stand silently behind the two of them.
The falcon hopped up onto the top pole, opened his beak,
thrust his head forward, and stared with his eyes of yellow
amber. It seemed to Adolf as though the two, the gypsy
and the bird, were looking at one another; from the very

beginning he had had the feeling that in some mysterious way they had something in common. Adolf had said not a word about it to anyone, he who had so often been the object of Georg's mockery because he talked naïvely about everything that interested him. In the last few weeks, he had learned not to give himself away.

"If you ever want to go on the ice," he said now, "I'll lend you my skates." He had tried again and again to think of something that would give the gypsy pleasure. But Janosch only asked, "What for?" When he wanted, he could be successful in anything he did. The maids brought him all sorts of kitchen and household utensils to mend: a cooking pot with a hole in it, a handle that had come loose from the broom, a blunt knife. The knives had never gotten blunt so quickly as they did this winter, thought the mistress of the house. Into the house itself, Janosch never went. He left the pails that he filled at the pump by the side entrance. Anyone who wanted him for something had to come to the stable. Every week he was given a small sum in payment for his work; the rest the Amtmann saved for him. At first, he had had to pay for the rabbit he had stolen from the farmer. Wittich had found the bloody pelt, a few bones, and a little pile of ashes from a fire, which had been carefully extinguished with snow, near the hay-loft in which Janosch had fallen asleep.

"Why didn't you make him go and work where he had stolen the rabbit?" asked Frau Margarete.

"That would have led to trouble," replied the Amt-mann. "The farmer is a rough, hot-tempered man."

Janosch would not sleep in the well-kept room reserved for stablelads, in which there was a bed, a table and chair, and a small stove, but preferred the stall with the birdcage.

There he lay on a truss of straw, wrapped in an old horse blanket. If only I could sleep near the falcon, too, thought Adolf.

"Do you need a knife?" he asked suddenly on an impulse. He had a pocketknife that had belonged to both Georg and August before him. There was always a lot of swapping of possessions among the brothers; each had a cardboard-box under his bed in which he kept his treasures, as if there were no cupboard in the house where such precious things would be safe. The previous fall, the knife had come into Adolf's possession after many complicated transactions, and although from looking at it you could tell its long and turbulent history in the hands of three boys, it was nonetheless one of Adolf's most prized possessions. Georg, the lucky dog, had recently acquired a brand-new knife, though where from he refused to say.

Adolf stretched out his hand with the knife quickly, before he could repent his offer. "There! It's a present."

Janosch took the knife, looked at it closely—without mockery or contempt but with the respect worthy of such a gift—and gave it back to Adolf. Then he said in a warmer tone than he had ever used to Adolf before, "Own knife. See!" And from the leg of his boot, he drew a blade of such splendor that Adolf held his breath, and all the famous swords of the great heroes began to spin around and around in his head like a blazing wheel: Excalibur, Balmung, Joyeuse . . .

"Oh!" he said.

"Beautiful?" asked Janosch with a smile that hid his pride, and he put back the long, slender lethal thing into its sheath, which was still hidden in his shoe.

"Terribly beautiful." Adolf sighed and felt as though he

had been given a present when he'd really intended to give one. He reached into his pocket again and pulled out his afternoon snack. "Do you want a Krebbel, Janosch?"

Janosch had already been given several presents of these Shrovetide cakes. Their mother had sent a plateful to the stable with Holwein, for Krebbel were an essential part of Shrovetide and everyone in the house had to have a share. Kettchen had hidden a few in a kettle that had a loose handle. Gretel had brought over two big ones filled with plum jam when she came to feed the hens in the early morning. In spite of this, Janosch did not say no, and he didn't seem to mind the fact that Adolf's cakes had shared a pocket with pieces of string, nails, an old cork, and a not very clean handkerchief. Contentedly, the three of them consumed the rich cinnamon-scented cakes. Aquarius licked his chops with evident enjoyment when he had finished and then cleaned the last few crumbs off Adolf's jacket with his tongue. He was now such good friends with Janosch that he visited him in the stable every morning when Adolf was in school.

"They bake two big laundry basketfuls every year," Adolf explained. "On Shrove Tuesday evening, there isn't a single one left. Then Lent begins, and on Ash Wednesday we all go to church early in the morning and have the ashes put on our forehead. You're not supposed to wash it off the whole day. Do your people do that, too?"

"We do it, too," said Janosch. He went to Mass every Sunday, which proved that the gypsies weren't heathens as Holwein said.

"And keep the fast days, also?"

"Roma fast whole year whether want or not." Romanies or Roma were what he called his people, and their father had told the boys that the word meant "men." Everyone else he called giorgios, barbarians. "Giorgios stuff themselves eleven moons and then fast one moon, bah!"

After their snack, Adolf stood up and went over to the bird again. The falcon flapped his wings and gave a hoarse, angry cry. "What if I open the cage door for him now?"

The gypsy shook his head. "Fly out, shwoosh . . . but not strong enough. Die."

"Hear that, you!" Adolf said to the bird. "And you, Janosch? Your leg is quite well again now, and you don't cough any more."

"Leg well, yes." He reflected for a moment. "Amtmann ordered, you no go to prison; stay here until I say. Amtmann word good; Janosch word good, too."

With that, he strode back to his cart and threw a forkful of manure onto it casually, like a gentleman taking a little exercise for the sake of his health. Then he seized the handle of the cart and pushed it over to the garden.

A second later, Adolf was at the gate in the wall, where he strapped on his skates, sprang onto the ice, and was away. Aquarius circled around him, barking his delight. If he knew there was water under the ice, wild horses wouldn't drag him here, thought Adolf. He himself was so happy that he felt like turning somersaults. He went as fast as he knew how, steering with his arms and singing at the top of his voice to his own tune: "Excalibur and Balmung, Balmung and Joyeuse," repeating it endlessly. "He showed it to me, his knife," he said to the dog. "He talked to me properly, really *talked* to me. He doesn't say 'Go away!' to us any more as he sometimes did those first weeks."

"Yap, yap!" barked Aquarius and joined in his master's pleasure. They were quite alone on the ice; all the others had long ago gone off to the carnival parade in town. There were just the two of them, he and his dog; they belonged together, and nothing could part them.

Bursting with sheer joy at being alive, Adolf even tried out a few figures. Today he was capable of anything, even figure skating, although in the ordinary way August and Georg were miles better at figure skating than he was.

But soon he had to turn back if he wanted to see anything of the parade. "Come on, Aqua. That's enough for today!" For Aqua, it was never enough, but where his master went, he went, too. Back at home, Adolf hung his skates up on his hook (the middle one of the five) in the hall on the ground floor and knocked at Uncle Emmo's door. He was sitting by the fireside, his pipe in the left corner of his mouth, pencil behind his ear, a notebook beside him, and an open Virgil in his hand. "Well then, I thought you'd all gone off?"

"Had to take Aqua out for a run first. Can he stay with you now?"

"All right," said his uncle, "if he doesn't whine or scratch at the door."

Adolf almost took offense at this. "You know him better than that. He has the manners of a prince. Stay, Aqua. There's a good dog!"

The dog lay down on the carpet in front of the fire and crossed his front paws, resigned to his fate. When Adolf said stay, there was nothing for it but to stay. On one of the bookshelves in a gap between Plutarch and Euripides sat Nicki, washing his haunches with studied indifference toward the latest arrival; but suddenly he stood up, arched himself, and the next minute landed on Aqua's back. He drew in his claws, put his paws around the dog's neck, and started to pummel him gently with the kneading movement that was his way of showing affection. Then he lay down between Aqua's paws, shut his eyes, and purred.

"Good-by, one and all," said Adolf and was off.

Earlier in the day he had gotten ready his old costume from last year's parade. It was his own notion of a minnesinger's attire: a short doublet of blue velvet, which his mother had embroidered in red along the hem with a diamond pattern, a cap of red brocade, a wooden sword at his belt, and a cardboard lute. Last year, he had spent days rummaging amongst the trunks of old clothes in the attic till he found something suitable for a courtly minstrel.

When he reached the town, everything was buzzing with the noise and gaiety of the carnival. Through the streets streamed children with or without masks but dressed up in some way, even if it was only a few rosettes sewn onto their everyday clothes and a harlequin cap. The boys were all armed with cardboard clubs with which they beat one another roughly and made the girls squeal with fright. Everywhere there were shrieks of laughter. People sang and shouted and danced in long chains through the streets. From the bay windows of some of the houses, the grown-ups who had not joined in the parade watched the young people enjoying themselves.

Now, the proper parade was coming along, and everyone joined it. The first float rolled along the main street to the accompaniment of admiring ohs and ahs from the onlookers. Every year there was yet another surprise. This time it was the ancient pagan god Neptune on a swaying cart pulled by four white oxen, decked out with strands of green-colored raffia, for where would you find seaweed in a place so far from the sea? He held a brand-new silvery pitchfork as a trident in his hand, and around him were stationed all sorts of ocean and river creatures in picturesque poses and costumes. Tritons with long fishtails blew on shell horns. On the second car stood Prince Carnival in person, in a cloak of royal purple trimmed with rabbitermine, a crown on his fair hair, a scepter in his right hand, and his left arm around his bashfully smiling Princess. There were no more floats. When all was said and done, this wasn't Cologne or Mainz, where the Shrove Monday parade lasted for hours. The citizens of Limburg thought their parade magnificent, and those who followed it on foot were many and gaily clad.

Adolf recognized almost all of them, even those in masks. There was Napoleon calling and waving to him in a condescending fashion; Schinderhannes flourished his tattered hat with the raven's feather; they seemed to be enjoying themselves enormously. Finally, there came Frederick the Great's two officers, haughty and elegant, accompanied by an eighteenth-century lady and a Spanish girl. Whistles were blown, tin trumpets sounded, dogs barked, and horses whinnied in the midst of the children's joyful shouts and the admiring cheers of the spectators at the windows.

From every house came the odor of deep-fried pastries, of roast pork and sausages. In the inns, the musicians were already tuning up their instruments. Today, Shrove Monday, even the maids from the courthouse were given time off to go dancing, taking with them the good advice of the *Hausfrau,* the aunts, and, above all, Babett. Kettchen had a sweetheart of honorable intentions in the Nassau militia. Gretel's betrothed would come in from the village. Both young men would eat supper in the courthouse kitchen with their girls, though the girls themselves were much too excited to swallow a mouthful. And afterwards they would go to The Ox, where Janosch was playing the first fiddle.

Adolf ran along with the parade for a bit until he met some friends and was caught up in a mock battle. Then he strolled along on the fringe of the parade, since that way he could see more than right in the middle of it. On the corner of Grabenstrasse, he almost bumped into Father Knodt. "Good evening, Father. Terrific, isn't it?"

"Magnificent, Adolf. It's seven years since I was in one myself, and do you know what I went as last time?"

"As a monk?" Adolf guessed. "As Saint George or the dragon perhaps?"

The curate laughed. "As a devil with a long tail, a red mask, and little black horns." It was so funny that they laughed like a couple of happy boys. The young priest's pupils said they had never had such a nice teacher before. Most teachers were strict and superior beings, demigods almost, dispensing knowledge as dry as dust. Father Knodt was different. With him even catechism, so dreaded before, was far from dull, and Latin declensions lost their terrors.

"Till tomorrow then, Adolf. I must be getting on," said the curate.

"And I must be off home. Here come August and Georg."

"There you are, Adolf," shouted August. "We've been looking all over for you. Have you seen Karl and Ferdinand?"

"They've just gone around the corner of Grabenstrasse with Philipp Derf and Anton Mehlhaus."

The three brothers doubled back and picked up Karl and Ferdinand in Grabenstrasse. They looked as though they had further plans but were rounded up and taken in tow.

"March, one, two! Home!" ordered August. "If we're late for supper, we'll be sent to bed with empty stomachs."

Once home, they rushed upstairs like a tornado. In their room costumes were peeled off like so many brightly colored snakes' skins. They washed their painted faces and hands, brushed their hair, and made a fresh parting, something Adolf, to his great annoyance, could never achieve. Whatever he did, two unruly tufts of hair stood up in the air on either side of his forehead like the horns of a faun.

It was striking seven from the cathedral when they came down the stairs. They were in luck. Uncle Emmo was just coming up from below with the two aunts, followed by Nicki and Aquarius, who greeted his master joyously.

On the supper table were two enormous plates of bread and butter spread with pink slices of home-cured ham, rounds of smoked sausage, liver sausage, and black pudding, all from their own pigs, and sliced hard-boiled eggs. Sausage was never bought outside from one year's end to another. "Who knows what those cunning butchers put in them," Mama would say.

Since it was a feastday, the boys were allowed to eat the rich food. Normally they were given only soft-boiled eggs, bread and butter, and milk for supper. "A heavy meal gives children bad dreams," was the saying.

"Was it good, boys? Tell us all about it."

They gave their report, interrupting one another in their eagerness. Ferdinand and Karl silently hoped that, while listening to their vivid descriptions, Mama would forget the cod-liver oil for once. There was still a big dish of Krebbel over on the sideboard—it would be a crying shame to spoil them with the taste of cod-liver oil. But they were much mistaken. It was Mama's firm conviction that the thick brown oil was absolutely necessary for the health of her brood. They were lucky that at least they had to have it only in winter.

"Paula!"

"Yes, Mama?"

"The cod-liver oil!"

Paula disappeared into the pantry, came back with the bottle and spoon and the box of peppermint drops, and gave each of her brothers the daily ration. She had to have her share, too, and by common consent she needed it even more than the others.

The three older boys had learned from long years of experience to swallow the hateful stuff with stoic resignation, but Ferdinand and Karl still protested.

"I shan't make my children have cod-liver oil," muttered Karl. "I'd rather they were ill."

"Or died young," said Ferdinand. "Then at least they wouldn't need to go to school."

Spring I

THE MARCH wind whistled down the valley and set the sap moving in the winter-blackened trees by the river. The avenue of poplars on the far bank still looked like a row of brooms that some giant's maids had left standing there. Only in the drooping branches of the willow was there a first shy glint of gold, and the silver birches had hung lilac-colored veils between their branches. At night you could sometimes hear the wild geese calling as they made their way north.

"Then he flaps his wings in the cage," said Janosch. "Flaps, screeches, wakes me up. Soon you can let him fly away."

"Fly away?" said Adolf. "I'm going to tame him, Janosch. You know I am."

"You won't—no! Have told you," said Janosch angrily. "You stupid? No taming grown peregrines. Must take them from nest when small."

Janosch turned away. He would not speak to Adolf for the rest of the day.

The winter stars sank slowly below the horizon. The cheerless season of Lent hung over the town like a gray mantle. Normally, it was a gay little town, being near the

Rhineland, which is so full of laughter and singing and where the wine gladdens the heart. Now there was no dance music in the inns of an evening. Christenings and weddings were postponed till after Easter; and at burials, which could not very well be put off, there were none of the usual sumptuous funeral meals. Instead, the churches resounded with the admonishing voices of the clergy preaching penance. In the houses, the lamps were put out earlier than usual; if you can only eat one full meal a day, you need to make up the food you miss in extra sleep.

The aunts, Babett, and Uncle Emmerich were excused from fasting because of their age, but it was inevitable that for them, too, the fare became leaner in these weeks.

"Fasting is healthy," said Mama heroically, for she cherished the pleasures of a good table. "But going hungry's not enough by itself. After all, my herbal tea, which purifies the blood, is as much an essential as the clapper is for the bell."

The efficacy of this medicinal purgative tea no one doubted; but the family kept a tactful silence on the subject of its taste. Every year from spring to autumn, its ingredients were gathered, dried, and hung up in linen bags in the storeroom. The first tender dandelion leaves, young nettles, sloe and linden blossoms, fennel seeds, rhubarb—all went into this tea, which was made from an original recipe of Great-Grandmother Thour. Now every evening the spicy bitter odor of the herbs penetrated the house. Uncle Emmo and the Amtmann exchanged wry glances when they drank their mugs of tea after supper instead of a nightcap of fragrant rum punch. They consoled themselves and the children with the thought that the hot, unsweetened infusion was a real purgatory for body and soul and that it cleared the blood and swept away any cobwebs from the mind.

Two of the brothers had special need of a clear head this year. It was more than doubtful whether they could maintain the class standard and be able to pass. Both, in the opinion of their teachers, had behaved like the foolish virgins in the Bible and not given any thought to oil for their lamps until the bridegroom was at the door. For the ever-cheerful Ferdinand, the thought of staying behind seemed to be anything but depressing. Wouldn't it be splendid if he and Karl ended up in the same class! But naturally he assured them all that he would make colossal efforts for his family's sake. Babett had promised to pray for him every day, which couldn't fail to help. And Uncle Emmerich had tortured him with questions and sums ever since Christmas, till he often felt quite faint with so much learning. So no one need worry about him.

"You certainly don't do any worrying yourself," said Mama. "But you've already had to stay behind once out of sheer laziness, and if it happens again, you'll have to go to the Jesuit fathers' boarding school in Feldkirch. So just remember that!"

"I know. But it would be awfully heartless of you to send a poor untalented child out into the world."

For Georg, it was a different matter. His vanity would never have borne the blow of having to stay behind; nor had he the slightest desire to prolong his dull time at school unnecessarily by a further year. So he had done what he did every year: right after the Christmas holidays he put his nose into his books and really worked. Since he had a fabulous memory, he quickly filled in his worst gaps and then relied on his ability to turn teacher's questions by every trick of oratory to a topic he did know something about. His friend, Carlo Trombetta, maintained that if Georg were asked about Charlemagne, he would manage to throw sand in the teacher's eyes and turn it into a brilliant discourse on Louis XIV, about whom he had happened to read something a few days before. "A pure juggler, that's what he is," said Trombetta.

"You could just as well say confidence-trickster," replied the thorough and reliable August. And Adolf, who had honestly worked his best and hardest the whole year (even if he occasionally got black marks for daydreaming in class), couldn't help feeling it was unfair that anyone as lazy as Georg should slip through in the end.

Staying behind was, therefore, Georg's least worry. One evening, however, after the little ones were asleep, the three older boys had an earnest consultation.

"How on earth did you get into such a mess?" asked August. "Borrowing money! If Papa ever hears about it, you'll get it! You know how annoyed he was last time, and it was only a few coppers for licorice at Maldaner the baker's. What in the world did you want money so badly for?"

"Don't ask silly questions," said Georg. "You know very well that Papa keeps us terribly short. And Trombetta always has his pockets full. I absolutely had to have a replacement for my knife that Adolf swiped from me last autumn."

"Swiped from you?" cried Adolf. "I gave you my best catapult for it."

"Anyway, I needed a knife. How can a fellow get on without a knife? And there was a beauty in Pinner's window." He pulled it out of his pocket and looked at it

lovingly. It was a fine specimen of a knife with a mother-
of-pearl handle, two sharp blades, an awl, and a corkscrew.
When the grownups were around, he had to keep it out of
sight; otherwise, there would have been awkward questions.
"That's no reason for borrowing money. Least of all
from Trombetta, when Papa meets his father so often."

"Aw—shut up, August! Carlo offered it to me on his
own when we were standing in front of the shop and I was
just looking in the window. 'How much d'you want me to
lend you?' he asked and clinked the money in his pocket.
'Of course, you must give me your word of honor that I
get it back before Easter. I need it then to buy a ring for a
certain someone in Wiesbaden.' That was in January, and
now it's only a fortnight to Easter, and I've simply got to
have three guilders."

"Three guilders, ouch!" Adolf could only groan at the
mere thought of such a vast sum. Three guilders was a lot
of money. Whenever he got that much from his godfather,
Papa had put it aside and saved it for him. "And where are
you going to get that from?"

"That's where you come in, Adolf."

"Your debts have nothing to do with me."

"Let him at least say what he's got in mind."

"It's quite simple. Papa said yesterday that Uncle Waterloo was in Dietz staying with Uncle Jean Baptist and
Aunt Helene, didn't he? What a pleasure it would be for
him if his dear godson Adolf paid him a surprise visit!
Perhaps Adolf wouldn't even have to say that he needed
money . . ."

"Why should I need money?"

"Obvious. You've got to help your brother out of a
scrape. Tomorrow's Wednesday, so there's no school in the

afternoon. Straight after dinner, you buckle on your skates, speed over to Dietz, drop in on Uncle Baptist, and tell him you want to say hello to your godfather. And if Uncle Waterloo doesn't have a brain wave all by himself and give you a present, I'll be surprised. I only wish I had such a generous one! So, if he doesn't hit on the idea of his own accord, you'll have to go about it a bit diplomatically and bring the conversation around to it—say, for example, that sometimes a fellow needs money for a noble but secret purpose and just doesn't know where to turn to get it. And if this isn't a noble purpose, then I've never heard of one. Go on, Adolf, don't make a fuss—do it for me. If you leave me in the lurch, I'll have to run away or put an end to it all. I can't bring shame on our parents."

"Stop talking rot," said August. "As if the shame would be less if you ran away. Have you asked Trombetta if he can wait a bit longer?"

"He says he can't wait. And if he doesn't get the money by Easter, he'll have to ask his father for an advance, and of course his father will ask why, and the cat will be out of the bag."

"If it's really like that, there's nothing for it but to go to Papa and make a clean breast of it. A gentleman owns up to what he has done." August's voice sounded so worried that it cut Adolf to the quick.

"Why didn't you think of all that about bringing shame on our parents beforehand?" he said angrily. "Nobody can afford to buy everything he wants. Put the idea of Dietz out of your head. You know we're not allowed on the ice when it's thawing anyway, and water has been dripping off all the roofs since the day before yesterday."

"Look at him! Who always thought it was most fun on

the ice when it was a little risky? And since when have you been such a good boy that you won't do something just because you're not supposed to? No, admit it, you're ducking. It's no good relying on you. If Papa finds out, then I'll run away, I tell you, as true as I stand here, and *then* you'll all have a happy Easter."

Georg wasn't standing at all—he was lying flat in bed —but it didn't occur to either of his brothers to correct him. "Perhaps you could do it by road, Adolf?" August suggested.

"You know how the road looks this time of year— knee-deep in mud. No, thank you! It would take three times as long as across the ice. I wouldn't get home before dark, and if Mama asks where I've been so long, then there'll be a nice row."

"Tcha, then there's nothing left for me but America," said Georg in a sepulchral voice. "I ask myself what's the use of having a brother who's the fastest ice skater in the whole school, and who has such a liberal godfather in the bargain, if when he could do you a little favor, he's afraid."

"Afraid!" cried Adolf and sat up in bed, his fists clenched, while Aquarius growled angrily. "Just say that again, that I'm afraid."

"Quiet or you'll waken the little ones, and then you might as well have the whole story shouted from the rooftops," warned August. "Perhaps Paula could help us," he suggested.

"No, no one here will," said Georg emphatically. "They'll all say that I shouldn't hide it from Papa, and they won't do anything behind his back."

The other brothers had to admit that this was only too likely.

"Adolf!" Georg tried once again. But this time there was no reply from the bed along the other wall. "I really think the heartless wretch has gone to sleep! There, August, you see that there's no relying on him."

"Shut up," Adolf heard his eldest brother say, for he wasn't asleep at all. "It's really a bit much to ask of Adolf."

A lot to ask indeed, thought Adolf. But could he really keep out of it? Uncle Waterloo would pull a couple of guilders from his pocket for certain—he always did. And how much trouble their parents would be spared! After all, Georg was his brother, even if he did often get mad at him. August had taught them all since they were little that none of them was ever to leave another in the lurch. And all that about the ice was, to be honest, just an excuse. Georg was right; he'd been on it often enough when it looked far more dangerous. A little bit of thaw was a challenge, and he'd never yet tried to avoid a challenge. Moreover, Georg had for the first time admitted he was the fastest skater in the school.

Adolf's head was almost bursting with all this deliberation. "Wait and see what the weather's like in the morning," he muttered into the darkness.

The next morning was fresh and clear. All the puddles had frozen over again when Adolf went to the cathedral. The rule on school-free afternoons was that the boys did their homework right after their midday meal and then were free until supper to do exactly as they wanted. If only it didn't come into someone's head to say something about the thaw in the last two days!

After Mass, Adolf and Father Knodt always had a little chat together. The young priest had heard all about Janosch and the falcon; he had even been to the stable with Adolf when he had come to the house to see Uncle Emmerich's old missal. He hadn't said a word to Janosch, just greeted him kindly, and that was all. This put him even higher in Adolf's esteem. Once they had gone around the cathedral together; the curate had shown Adolf the beautiful Romanesque baptismal font and the Knodt arms over the second choir stall on the right of the high altar. Canon Knodt, now long dead, had once sat here.

Today Adolf came out with a question: "If you had a brother, Father, and the brother was rather a louse generally and you didn't get on with him all that well either . . ."

"Get to the point, Adolf," answered the curate. "The one you don't get on with is Georg, right? And now perhaps you'll explain what you've got in store for him."

"Oh, I haven't anything in store for him. I mean, I wish he hadn't anything in store for me. But now all of a sudden he wants me to do him a favor. And what would you do, Father, if your brother, who does nothing but needle you the whole year through, suddenly asks you to do something for him?"

"Now, Adolf, you know the answer yourself. You can remember that much from your religious instruction: we must forgive our brother not only seven times but seventy times seven. If you can do Georg a favor, it's a good opportunity for showing him that you'd like to be friends with him, and then he'll do his best to be nice to you, too. Quite apart from that, I shouldn't be surprised if you irritated him just as often as he irritates you."

"You really think so?" asked Adolf. Yes, the curate really did. He knew all about boys, as one could see in school. He had grown up as the second youngest of seven brothers. "Now, be off with you," he said, "and do your brother the favor. And if you find it difficult, then do it *ad majorem Dei gloriam.*"

So it was that when he had finished his homework that afternoon, Adolf made his way down to the river with the best conscience in the world. No one had mentioned the thaw, since today glittering icicles hung once again from every gutter. Nor did anyone ask what he intended to do. Their mother was always in favor of their spending the few hours of daylight that remained in the open air. Paula was only supposed to know what the plans of the two youngest ones were.

Once again, Adolf had to leave Aquarius with Uncle Emmo, as his aunt in Dietz was a little pernickety and couldn't bear to have dog hairs on her furniture or dirty paw marks on her shining parquet floors. The ice felt firm and safe when he took the first long strides over it. He was always as happy and carefree as a bird when he was on skates. Swiftly he shot under the arch of the bridge and was well away. That he didn't see a single one of his friends on the ice didn't strike him as odd. Few were as keen on skating as the Amtmann's boys. Most of them had had enough of it by March, except for the fun to be had jumping the ice floes from one side of the river to the other, but the time hadn't come for that yet. They couldn't wait now to change over to spring games again. Two of them had already brought their bags of marbles to school. That was as sure a sign of spring as the first snowdrops.

Between Limburg and Dietz, there are several picturesque bends in the River Lahn, for it has a hard time winding its way through the narrow valley. But you can travel quickly on the river itself, in summer by boat and in winter on skates. To visit their relatives in Dietz was one

of the boys' favorite outings at any time of the year. Adolf
had already done nearly half the journey. Soon he would
see the gloomy outline of Dietz castle, still hidden by the
next hill.

When he noticed that there was a darker patch like a
shadow straight before him, it was already too late. The ice
shattered under his feet, he was pulled under, his legs sank,
and for a moment the coldness of the water and the shock
made him lose consciousness. Then immediately he was
wide awake again. I mustn't get carried away, he thought.
He felt how the stream was sucking and pulling him,
made swimming movements, and struggled with all his
might against the current. It was difficult in his clothes,
with shoes and skates on his feet. Luckily he had learned
from swimming and diving in the summer to stay underwater with his eyes open. So now he saw the faint light
coming through the hole where he had fallen in, made for
it, and when he got there, tried to pull himself up on the
ice with his arms. It kept breaking under him, and only at
his fourth attempt did he find a stronger place. I mustn't
stand up, he said to himself, mustn't trust my whole weight
on this brittle ice. He lay flat, his body spread-eagled
across the ice, and paused to get his breath back for a
moment. He felt desperately sick, spluttered out some
water, and then crawled a little further toward the nearby
bank. Soon he was able to get hold of the overhanging
branches of a willow and pull himself up. Now he lay
panting and spewing out water on the riverbank, until his
stomach had stopped turning over and over; then he lay
motionless. Not until now had he been conscious of his icy
clothes clinging to him, and although he would have given
anything to go on lying there, he suddenly realized that he

would freeze to death if he didn't start moving immediately. He sat up. He felt dizzy, and once again a nauseating stream of water came flooding up out of his mouth and nose. He choked and swallowed, groaning and cursing, but at last he summoned up the energy to undo his skates and pull off his shoes. He looked around him and saw where and why he had been caught. It was the spot where a narrow meadow lay between river and hillside. Every year in the spring, the boys found the first scilla and anemones here, because it got the benefit of all the noon sun. What a fool I am, he thought; if only I'd kept to the other bank in the shadow of the mountain, where it's still frozen hard, nothing would have happened to me. In the little meadow, there were only a few patches of gray-white snow left. The rays of the sun played among the golden-bronze of last year's grass—and nothing was more welcome to him at that moment than a little sun.

No human being, no house was to be seen. He took off his stockings next, rubbed his cold feet, and stretched them in the sun. Then he pulled off his thick suit and his underclothes. He wrung them out as best he could with his numb fingers, hung the clothes on the willow, and started to sprint around the small meadow. At first, he couldn't stop his teeth chattering, but soon the fast movement and the welcome rays of the sun, although it wasn't strong, warmed him up. Thirty yards up, thirty back. He ran up and down, flapping his arms, thinking what to do next. Dietz was now out of the question, even though it was within striking distance. His clothes had gradually stopped dripping. They couldn't get any drier in such a short time, but there was no help for it—he had to put them on again. As long as they hadn't missed him at home, there was still some hope that he would be able to slip back to his room unnoticed and get changed. He knew only too well that that was a temporary measure. He couldn't hope to keep the whole escapade to himself in the long run, but it would be something if he could avoid appearing dripping wet in front of Mama.

Paula! He suddenly remembered his sister, and it was as though a warming fire had been lit inside his cold frame. He must try to catch Paula before anyone caught him. She would help him; perhaps she could even dry off his clothes later in the evening in the washhouse. It was maddening that it was so difficult to get her alone. About this time she took tea to the old people in the side wing of the house, and if she wasn't with the aunts, she would be in with Uncle Emmo or Babett. It would be best if she were with Uncle Emmo, but it wasn't a matter in which he had any choice.

Well, into his clothes again. Ugh, they were dreadfully cold and damp! Stockings and shoes on again. He ran a little way up the river and strapped on his skates when the ice looked thick enough to inspire confidence. It had taken his weight before; it would take it again if he were careful not to get onto bad patches. Then he was off again; the faster he moved, the less he felt the freezing cold.

Paula sat with the old ladies for quite a while after she had served first Uncle Emmo, then Babett, with their afternoon tea. Babett always kept her for a while. The older she got, the more she lived in the past, and one had to listen to her when she poured out her reminiscences. Paula would dearly have loved to hear more about her father's first wife, whose picture hung in Babett's room among so many others. But at the time when the revels of the royal court at Kassel had been at their zenith, which was the time Babett most loved to talk about, the little Françoise had not even been born, and Paula did not like to ask a direct question.

The aunts' room had an old tapestry in white and brown on which a romantic landscape repeated itself endlessly: a ruin in the moonlight, tall trees, a spring with two lovers. It might have been an illustration for one of Aunt Stina's *novelle*. Here, too, there were pictures on the wall, an album of the past. The aunts' beds stood in the alcove behind white curtains. On Aunt Stina's writing desk lay closely written sheets of paper arranged in meticulous order, but at this time of day she wasn't writing; she was waiting for her tea. The aunts sat in their high-backed armchairs in one of the deep bay windows. At the second window, Aunt Ulrike's piano had its place. They looked up with pleasure when Paula entered with the tea tray.

"You always lay it out so prettily for us, my dear child," said Aunt Stina, as the embroidered cloth was spread on the little table that stood between the aunts. Paula poured out the tea; the thin bread and butter was arranged on a flowered plate. There were no little sugary milk rolls or currant buns in Lent! None were baked during these weeks, and anyway, the aunts would have considered such delicacies unsuitable in Lent.

"Come, sit and talk to us for a moment," said Aunt Rikchen. "Do you know when Frau Gerstenberg visited us earlier today she said that young Overberg had set off for Russia a few days ago."

The news didn't seem to make much impression. "He

spoke about it at the Carnival ball," said Paula. "Isn't he lucky to be able to travel around the world like that?"

"Eventually he'll have to settle down, in my opinion." Aunt Rikchen laid down the law. "When you get to thirty, you're no chicken any longer. The mothers in Nassau have had a grudge against him for long enough because he can't make up his mind to get married."

"Why should he marry if he doesn't want to?" asked Paula equably. "Perhaps he hasn't found the girl he's looking for yet. Or he may not have been able to get the one he wanted."

Aunt Rikchen flared up at this. "He could have any girl between the Rhine, the Main, and the Lahn, and you'd never believe, my dear Paula, how many have already tried to hook him. But he won't bite, not Monsieur Overberg. He courts a different girl every winter, and in spring off he goes into the far world, leaving tears and disappointments behind him. Be on your guard against him, child. I've told you once, and I'll tell you again! Anyone who falls in love with such a fly-by-night can expect nothing but sorrow."

"Dearest Rike," said Aunt Stina reprovingly, "in Lent we really oughtn't to gossip about our dear neighbor."

"You're right, Stina. But what's true is true."

Meanwhile, Paula had begun to dust the valuables on the commode, which were not to be trusted to Gretel's rough hands. A little clock under glass; painted straw boxes with ribbons and lace; an Iron Cross of 1813 mounted on red velvet; two groups of Meissen figurines. Paula lifted up each item carefully, wiped over it with her cloth and feather duster, and put it back in place . . . the flotsam and jetsam of a lifetime.

"You need not worry, Aunt Rikchen," she said. "I have no intention of falling in love. When I think of all the frightful complications in Aunt Stina's novels . . ."

"But it always comes out all right in the end, *chérie*," said Aunt Stina with a smile. It hadn't come out right in the end for her, though. She still wore in a medallion over her heart a lock of hair from the man who had been killed at Leipzig in 1813.

But now there was a knock on the door, and Adolf came into the room, blue with cold, his teeth chattering.

"Jesus, Mary, and Joseph!" cried the aunts. "Where have you been? You surely weren't on the ice after we've had three days' thaw?"

Just like women, he thought bitterly. Asking silly questions instead of doing something. But Paula, his big sister, was already moving. She thrust him quickly behind the screen around the big white stove, just the place where he belonged in his pitiful state of wetness and cold. "Off with those dripping things," she said. How willingly he obeyed! "I'll run and get you some dry ones."

When Paula came back with a bundle of clothes over her arm, he was standing stark naked behind the screen, rubbing his cold skin in the welcome warmth of the stove. She handed him his dry clothes over the top of the screen in exchange for the wet ones, which she carried straight off to the washhouse, where at this time of year there were always some of the boys' wet clothes drying. When she came back, she brought a fresh brew of hot tea. She had met no one, she said in answer to Adolf's anxious question. Mama had gone to the Stations-of-the-Cross devotions with the maids, Papa was still in the middle of a case in the courtroom, and Uncle Emmerich deep in his translation. "You just stay beside the stove," she said. "You can tell us from there what you've been up to."

"If only he hasn't caught his death!" he heard Aunt Stina say with a sigh.

"The ice was perfectly solid," he said. "It wasn't until I came to the bend halfway to Dietz, where the afternoon sun was shining straight down on it, that it suddenly gave way and I was under in a flash."

"Adolf! Halfway to Dietz? What on earth did you want to go to Dietz for?"

"Because Uncle Waterloo's there. Can't a fellow visit his godfather when he hasn't seen him for a long time?"

"You poor child," said Aunt Stina, deeply touched by so much devotion to the family. "Hadn't you heard that he's coming to see us on his way back to Montabaur? And you almost got yourself drowned out of sheer love for your godfather! Give me the smelling salts from the commode, Paula. I feel quite faint."

"There's something more than sheer love behind it," said Paula, who knew too much about brothers after the weeks she had been at home to believe in such tender feelings.

"Well, I did have something else to do, too," said Adolf. "For Georg, not for me. Georg had something he wanted me to do, and Father Knodt said it was to the glory of God to do your brother a favor."

"What has Georg got to do with it all?"

Adolf took a deep breath. Since the whole business of going to Dietz and getting something out of his godfather had gone wrong, there was nothing for it but to get the aunts to lend Georg the three guilders. "If you promise not to give anyone away, I'll tell you," he finally pronounced after lengthy consideration.

"Do you take us for gossips, child!" said Aunt Stina.

Adolf finished off his cup of tea quickly in order to win a little more time and because the hot drink was so comforting inside his cold stomach. "Well, Georg has absolutely got to have three guilders," he finally began. "There's something he had to buy, and he had no money, so he borrowed some from Trombetta. And if he doesn't give it back before Easter, then there's going to be the biggest row in the whole history of the world."

"Borrowed money!" said Aunt Rikchen. "Fallen into debt!" The aunts looked at one another, shocked and dismayed. They had suffered much distress years ago because of one of their brothers: among eight hard-working, honorable children, there had been one spendthrift and adventurer, a charmer whom no woman could resist. He had gone to his ruin and death somewhere in South America.

"Why didn't he come to us then, the silly lad? Of course we must help him. Papa mustn't get to know about it."

"But Aunt Stina!" said Paula and stroked the old lady's trembling hand. "We can't keep it a secret from Papa. That would be the same as deceiving him."

"But what else can we do, child? What else?"

"Georg must go to Papa and confess," said Paula. "There is no other solution."

"But what am I to do then?" put in Adolf, although he realized that Paula was right. August had said the same right away. "After all, I promised him I'd go to Dietz."

"I've got to lay the table for supper," said Paula. "Come up with me, Adolf, if you're a bit warmed up now. Have a word with Georg before supper, so that he knows what he has to do. When he sees that his carelessness almost cost you your life, it'll be a lesson to him perhaps."

"Oh, hum! He'll probably say I'm a silly idiot that you can't trust to do anything. And my life wasn't really in danger since I can see and swim underwater."

"Adolf!" said Paula, putting her arm around him as they went across the hall together. "I can't bear to think of how awful it would have been if they had pulled you out of the river dead. Even the best swimmer can drown if he's pulled under the ice."

"Funny," said Adolf, "it didn't occur to me that I might *really* drown."

But now Aquarius heard his voice from Uncle Emmo's room. He let out a howl, and jumped up at the door till he nearly brought it off its hinges. His paw caught the latch, the door flew open, and he was in the hall, almost bowling Adolf and Paula over with his joy at their reunion. From inside the room, they could hear a chair being pulled up and Uncle Emmo's voice grumbling, "Would you be kind enough to teach your dog, Adolf, to shut the door again after he's gone out?"

"Shall be done, Uncle Emmo," Adolf called back.

"This evening in bed I'll say a rosary in thanksgiving for your safety," said Paula.

"Thank you, Paulinchen," said Adolf and ran upstairs, two steps at a time, to tell his brothers the unfortunate outcome of the expedition. As he felt far from comfortable about it, he wanted to get it over and done with as soon as possible. Georg would reproach him or even pour ridicule and contempt on him. But that was not the worst. August wouldn't say anything, but what would he think of him?

When he slipped into bed that evening, he found a hot brick at his feet. What a jewel Paula was! And the incomparable Aquarius snuggled even closer up to his back tonight. Adolf was so tired by this time that the day's events swam before him in a soft mist; the adventure on the ice, the talk with his brothers—which had gone very much as he had expected—Paula's sisterly care, Georg's final decision to go and see Father in his office early in the morning before school. He felt only the blissful warmth and a deep thankful joy at still being alive. Already half asleep, he suddenly heard the dog growl softly and noticed the edge of his bed giving under a weight.

"Adolf!"

"Yes, August." He was wide awake immediately, and his heart almost jumped into his mouth.

"Georg and I," whispered August, "I mean . . . I just want to let you know that we think you're a decent sort, old man. Good night, Adolf."

"Good night, August."

Spring II

EASTER WAS EARLY that year. Already the equinoctial moon was rising a little later and growing a little fuller every day. Sometimes she made her silver way across a clear sky, like a heavenly shepherdess with her flocks of stars; sometimes she would play hide-and-seek among the racing clouds; and often she vanished from sight altogether, while the March rains poured down in an endless torrent. The roads became impassable. One day at table, there was talk about how the Duke's coach had gotten stuck in the mud somewhere in the Amtmann's district. Horses and men had to be sent for from a neighboring village to extricate a rather ill-tempered Serene Highness from the mud. Ferdinand and Karl tittered, but their irreverent mirth was quickly checked by a glance from their father. Under the roof of a ducal official, one does not laugh at ducal misfortunes—or at least not with all the family present, if perhaps *à deux*. However, even the Amtmann himself was not always in agreement with His Grace, and Uncle Emmerich and many of his fellow citizens were even less so. There was the hotly disputed question of the freedom of the press; there were the hunting laws, which people hated; and other things besides.

The constitution that the Duke had had to agree to after the troubles of 1848 he now interpreted rather arbitrarily, acting as a small scale Louis XIV: *L'état c'est moi!* I am the state!

The aunts, who were as conservative and loyal to the Duke as they thought nice people should be, nodded their heads sympathetically: how very embarrassing for Serenissimo! Uncle Emmo flicked a speck of dust from his lapel and remarked that a duke was mortal like everyone else, and it was wise of the Lord to remind him of the fact from time to time.

Mama was anxious lest a lively discussion should begin. In her opinion, discussions at meals were bad for the children and disastrous for the digestion. "*Pas devant les enfants, s'il vous plaît!*" she entreated.

Even Ferdinand and Karl already knew enough French to understand that. In middle-class homes, as well as at court, French was the second language for every cultivated person; even the language of the ordinary people was full of words taken over from French. The Rhineland was a border area. Many a marriage was made between one side and the other, and everyone had relatives or friends hither and thither.

The Amtmann was annoyed that the Duke's accident on the road should have happened in the district for which he was responsible. There were plenty of people at court who were irritated that the Duke should give a mere Amtmann such a free hand in the administering of justice. What an idea, not putting criminals in chains, they would say and would certainly use this opportunity to slander him at court. But that did not worry him. He had always gone his own way without bowing and scraping, and the

Duke was shrewd enough to know his worth. No, the Amtmann was irritated by the fact that he had still not quite succeeded in hammering into the village mayors' thick peasant skulls who it was that was responsible for keeping the roads in good order. "They are as stubborn as mules," he said. "Ah well, I shall have to do a good deal of traveling in the next few weeks anyway. That'll give me a chance to have a go at them again. Reports are coming in from all over about the danger of flooding."

"Janosch says that Silver is always upset when Holwein has driven him," put in Adolf. "He pulls on his mouth and uses the whip, and Silver can't stand that."

"I'll be driving him myself," said the Amtmann. He went on: "Do you think you could be trusted to drive him for a whole day on these soft roads if it were vacation time?"

"You bet!" said Adolf with absolute conviction, sorry that there wasn't a vacation right now to prove his point. To journey across the country with their father had always been a special treat for the boys.

It really looked as though there might be another flood. The rivulet called the Elb-Bach, which came down from the High Westerwald, the mountains that always had more snow than anywhere else in Germany, and joined the River Lahn just above Limburg, was swollen to a torrent. Big yellow waves were moving swiftly down the river past the town and the bottom of the courthouse garden. The water level was rising daily. This year there had been no chance to play the breath-taking game of jumping from ice floe to ice floe, so quickly had the thaw set in. In any case, the boys would probably not have joined in this year. After Adolf's adventure, and especially after Georg's carelessness, which had been the cause of it, they knew they could not risk getting into trouble with their parents again. Georg was pretty low-spirited after his interview with Papa, which made him much more bearable in Adolf's eyes. Until further notice, he had been confined to the house, or at least to the house and the yard, and this meant that for the time being there would be no more strolling up and down the main street between five and six o'clock when the older boys and girls promenaded. Instead, Georg had to give up his free time to bringing in wood for the stove and water from the pump and helping Holwein dig over the garden beds. Moreover, like Ferdinand, his future was still clouded by the possibility of a bad school report at Easter. But the brothers, however much they quarreled, stuck together whenever one of them was in trouble. Every day Adolf helped Ferdinand with his homework. August, instead of going out strolling alone, faithfully gave up time in the late afternoon to stay near Georg as he was digging in the garden and review history dates with him. Paula helped with his French, and even little Karl practiced arithmetic tables with Ferdinand as they walked to school. Uncle Emmerich did his share, too, in warding off the threatening crisis.

"Papa needn't have been so harsh," Georg complained as the brothers talked together in their bedroom one evening. "Cutting off my measly allowance just for those lousy three guilders!"

"It's not the three guilders; it's because you had debts," Adolf replied, and August explained that it wasn't long since people were put in *prison* for being in debt.

"Do you think I'm not in prison, then?" asked Georg.

"The real criminals Papa lets go free, and he locks up his own son."

"He doesn't let them go free," objected Adolf. "He just gives them a punishment that makes sense."

"I'm going to pass! I'm going to pass!" sang out Ferdinand happily from the bed he shared with Karl.

August looked up in astonishment and asked, "Since when have you been so pleased about passing? I thought you wanted to get into the same class as Karl?"

But Ferdinand had discovered a snag in being too near Karl at school. "They'd always be holding him up as an example to me. And if I ever had any plans for going on a little walk, he'd nag at me to be good and go to school with him instead of cutting."

"Of course I would," said Karl. "Do you think I'd want a brother in my class who was always being put in the corner with a dunce's cap and was thrashed after school in front of all the others? And how are you ever going to learn anything if you keep cutting school?"

"Oh, you and your learning, you old schoolmaster!" Ferdinand called upon his other brothers to witness that Karl was a solemn old schoolmaster and a grind in the bargain. Karl only grinned, showing the two gaps in his teeth that were his pride and joy. Even if they called him a schoolmaster, at least no one could call him "that pretty little boy" any longer.

Adolf's thoughts had gone back to the stable again. He thought of the two goats, who had had kids just in time for Easter; of Silver, who was becoming more and more obedient and friendly every day; of Janosch, who was gradually losing his mistrust toward the "son of the house."

There was only one point of real disagreement between them: the falcon. Adolf dreamed about the bird day and night. In his imagination, he kept seeing himself riding Silver through the forest, with the falcon on his wrist, like the Emperor Frederick seven hundred years ago, who had been one of the most famous falconers of the Middle Ages. In the rag box, he had found an odd glove, which he put on his left hand every time he fed the bird. Once or twice the bird had actually climbed onto the hand he held out to it in order to grab the mouse that swayed temptingly to and fro in front of it. Adolf would stand and hold his breath. He could feel the sharpness of the bird's claws through the leather glove, and a shiver of wild excitement would run through him from head to foot. "Look, Janosch, look!" he called out in triumph. "He's getting more tame. Now I must get Babett to sew a leather cap for him, a beautiful one with glass beads on it. I know just what you have to do with falcons. They're not unhappy either, Janosch, I assure you!"

He always hoped to be able to convince the gypsy. But Janosch only spat. "How do you know?"

"It's all in the book. I wish I could show you the pictures. Marvelous, with gold and red and blue, Janosch . . ."

"Bah, a book!" said Janosch with icy disdain. No, he had failed again. He might just as well have tried to persuade Janosch to settle down for good among the giorgios. And yet they were friends. Sometimes he was allowed to stay in the stable while the gypsy played his fiddle. For the first time, he felt a real desire to practice his piano playing more. Sometimes Janosch would even be persuaded to tell him something about gypsy life. The endless wanderings, the poverty and hardships, but, along with that, a wonderful life of freedom that dull, ordinary people could never know. Adolf dared not ask him why he had left his tribe and submitted to a life of exile for so many months. It was a mystery to which his father might have the key. But for him, it was not right to ask questions about it.

One day when he came across to the stable with a mouse he had just found in a trap, there was a woman there; she was old, with a dark brown, heavily wrinkled face and graying tufts of hair. She had rings in her ears, and under her black shawl she wore a bright scarlet blouse. There she sat on a bundle of hay, talking earnestly to Janosch with quick, strange-sounding words. The youth was standing with head bowed, leaning with his elbow on the gelding's withers. Adolf was about to withdraw when she beckoned him over, seized his hand, turned it over, and scrutinized it with her fiery black eyes. Janosch silently took the mouse and gave it to the falcon.

"Good hand," said the woman and nodded. "Long life, you hear, son? Much sorrow, much happiness." With her hard black-rimmed fingernails, she felt the little bumps at the bottom of his fingers, closed her eyes, and put her head on one side as though she were listening for something. Then she looked up again, straight into his face. "Good, yes. Easy, no. This here good house. Good to Janosch. Janosch go now with Dali."

"Not yet, Dali," said Janosch in a different tone from any Adolf had ever heard him use before: gentle, humble, caressing. "First speak with Amtmann, yes?"

She seemed to reflect. "Soon!" she said at last. It was a command. Somewhere behind them, the lambs were bleating. The hens were scratching about in the straw; they found it dull inside and too wet outside. The woman stretched out a brown hand for one of the hens, which squawked once and then gave in. Her fingers closed around its neck. She laughed soundlessly. Then she let it go again. As she did so, she watched Adolf, who was staring at the gnarled old hand, so like a talon, as though he were mesmerized. There was a question, a challenge in her look, perhaps a little sadness as well; but as she looked into his frank face, she saw no trace of suspicion there. Not for a moment had he believed she would steal one of the hens. Not here. She was a dirty and ragged beggarwoman with a fat bundle that might have contained goodness knows what, but she would not steal so much as a pin from the house that had given shelter to her son. She gave a nod of understanding and contentment. Then she stood up, threw back her head, and went without another word. She had the bearing of an empress.

Janosch followed her with his eyes. "I speak with Amtmann. I go soon," he said, more to himself than to Adolf. Then he lifted his hands, fingers spread wide apart. "Enemy dead. Dali magic, he dead." He shrugged. "If not, one day I dead."

Yes, thought Adolf, he could have guessed: a sorceress, with the power of those African tribal witch doctors explorers wrote about. "Where will you go?" he asked with sadness in his heart. "Won't you ever come back?"

"Cannot tell," said Janosch, still speaking in his new, strange tone. "Go here, there, everywhere. Each Christmas big feast; many many Romanies meet in south France. Much drink, much dancing, much singing, fights, too, yes!" Now he threw his head back, like his mother, and laughed. "Last year fellow take Janosch girl. Janosch knife, he knife."

"Did you . . . did you kill him?" whispered Adolf.

"He not dead. Janosch not dead either." He put his hand on his hip. "He soon fine, but belly full of wrath. Dali says: 'Go!' I go. Then this February moon, he hot, hot! Lies there, coughs, ill. Finished."

When Adolf came back into the house, still full of everything he had seen and heard, he met Paula in the lower corridor. "You've come just at the right moment," she said. "Everyone's needed to give a hand bringing up the provisions from the cellar. The water level's still rising."

Despite all the women's prayers and the candles they had offered, the water was rising. He ran down the stone steps with his sister, down into the vast cellar where once the monks and lay brothers from Eberbach had stored the goods that were their tithes from the farmers—here and in the attic and in the barns. The Amtmann and Uncle Emmo were already there, taking bottles from the lath-wood racks in the wine cellar and carrying them up to a higher room. The two maids were helping Mama bring the many glasses of jams and preserves to safety, and the stone pots with plum purée and salted green beans; there were cabbages, beets, and potatoes, too. Holwein was having difficulty with the big barrel of sauerkraut, and August and Georg had to give him a hand. Dirty trickles of water were seeping through the tiny barred windows high up in the solid walls. The stone floors were already covered with water, and you could see how the level was gradually rising. All the boys were down there, barefoot, their pants rolled up, helping with shouts and cries and merriment.

They knew what had to be done. Living so close to the river meant they must be always on the alert. For this river, most of the time a gentle friend, a playmate, could suddenly turn into a fierce adversary.

When there was nothing more to be cleared away, they went upstairs, wet and tired. The women let down their skirts, everyone put shoes and stockings on again, and hot tea was made to warm them up. In the cozy living room, the boys spread out their textbooks and paper on the big table and got down to their homework. But Adolf had something he wanted to tell Paula about first—he had to talk to *someone* about the events of the afternoon. Paula had withdrawn to the far end of the table with her mending basket, which never seemed to grow any emptier. Adolf bent over her and whispered, "She looked at my hands. She said I'd live long. 'Good, yes—easy, no,' she said. And she flashed those strange eyes at me till I began to feel quite queer."

"But Adolf!" Paula said. "That's all superstition; it's sinful. Only God can know what the future will bring."

"Well, I believe it, anyway. And guess what, she put a spell on Janosch's enemy and he died—the one who danced with Janosch's girl and stabbed him in the fight, so that he had to go away from his folk. 'Go, go,' Dali said, or else he'd have killed him, or Janosch would've killed the other man, or something or other, and then the whole tribe would have been in a fight. And last February, she said incantations, and the bad fellow got a fever and died in his bed, and no one can say that she or Janosch is to blame. *Dali* is gypsy for mother, you know."

"Killing someone with a spell! Surely you're not going

to believe nonsense like that," said Paula. "And it would be murder, in any case."

"Well, just you wait and see whether I live long. We'll talk about it again in forty years' time." Then he thought of something else. "You had a letter from Nancy today, didn't you, Paula? What did Mère Celeste say? Does she think you ought to go into the convent?"

"You get on with your homework now and keep an eye on Ferdinand to make sure he does his properly. Come to my room tonight, and then I'll tell you all about it."

Later that evening, when the boys were in bed, Adolf stayed awake until he heard his sister come up and saw the light of her candle pass the door. "Come on, Aqua," he said, and they slipped across to Paula's room. As usual, they all sat together on the edge of the bed, with the eiderdown over them. The candle flickered, Aquarius grunted contentedly, and they were blissfully warm and comfortable. While they talked, Adolf scratched the dog's head, and Paula stroked its back.

"You mustn't think it's easy to make a decision like this," Paula said. "There are hundreds of things to consider, and it's hard to tell if you have a vocation."

She had the nun's letter in her hand and read it, in French, to Adolf, translating parts of it now and again. Mère Celeste reiterated what she had said in an earlier letter, that Paula had never given her the impression, while she was at Nancy, of being one of the girls who would eventually return to the convent. Even then she had found obedience difficult, hadn't she? And now it appeared that she could not always obey even her own mother without inner rebellion. In the convent, as she well knew, vows of obedience meant not asking the whys and wherefores but doing blindly and without question what your superiors told you.

Paula sighed deeply, and Adolf sighed in sympathy. The Eisenberth children, as they well knew, were an obstinate brood, and more than once they had knocked their hard heads against an even harder stone wall. Among Uncle Emmo's treasures was an old book of names from the thirteenth century, which included the name Eisenberth. It came from two words meaning "iron" and "shining," and Uncle Emmo maintained this proved that the first person to bear the name had been a free man who would not let himself be ruled or pushed around by anybody. Was it any wonder, therefore, that his descendants found it difficult to submit themselves to others?

"I wrote to Mère Celeste to tell her I would like to pass my exams as a teacher and then go and teach in the convent," Paula went on. "And now she says in her letter what it would really be like. The superiors decide where you are to go, and even if I had passed my exams and qualified as a teacher, they might easily send me off to the kitchen or hospital to work if they thought it best for my spiritual good. Anyway, she advises me to try to practice obedience every day here at home first and says I'm to regard Mama as my superior. I'm really trying terribly hard. Mère Celeste also said I ought to get to know myself and the world a little better first before I make any decision to renounce the world forever."

With this, Adolf wholeheartedly agreed. "Get to know the world. Boy, that's what I'd like to do! Travel around like Herr Overberg, or, even better, go to Africa like Livingstone, or make voyages in the South Seas like Captain

Cook, or travel across Asia like Marco Polo. Just imagine that! You must get Uncle Emmo to give you that green leather book about Marco Polo's journey. But you'll have to read it in his room; he won't lend it."

"I often sit in his room and read for a bit when I bring him his tea. He always takes down something beautiful for me, and I think it's wonderful to read about things of which I know nothing. But that wasn't what Mère Celeste meant. She meant I ought to get to know the *pleasures* of the world, parties and balls and concerts and theaters and all the things my parents will take me to. You see, Adolf, it's important to know what it is you're giving up when you take your vows; otherwise, you might be sorry afterwards. She even said I might well meet a few men before deciding never to marry. A Christian marriage, so she says, is a vocation pleasing to God."

"A sensible person, this Mère Celeste," was Adolf's opinion. "I've always told you you ought to get married."

"I wouldn't know to whom," said Paula.

The next day there were three feet of water in the cellar, and outside, it looked as though it would go on raining forever.

"I bet that witch of a gypsy woman put a spell on us so we'd be flooded," said Babett.

"She *wasn't* a witch," Adolf contradicted her. He had been reading to Babett from the newspaper, not a favorite task for the boys, since they found the paper deadly dull. "At least, she wouldn't put a bad spell on *us*. There was a hen she could have pinched easily, but she didn't. She said the courthouse was a good house. The floods come from the snow melting and all the rain—any child could tell you that, Babett. And you couldn't do anything about it with your candles and your litanies. Remember last year— it was even worse then, without a gypsy woman around."

"Be off with you!" grumbled Babett. "I'll not have a boy in my room who doesn't believe in litanies and holy candles. Wait! Show me your hands."

Without presentiment, Adolf put out his hands, and then he noticed for the first time that the back of his left hand was covered with tiny warts. He stared at them in horror. They had not been there yesterday. Or was it just that he hadn't noticed them? Anyway, he was sure that Janosch's mother wasn't responsible. Indeed, he rather had the feeling that the warts must just have grown right now under Babett's gaze.

"There you are! You see!" said Babett, satisfied to see her suspicions confirmed. "That's what happens when you have dealings with gypsy folk. But don't worry; I'll help you. Wait till the moon is on the wane and then get one of those fat black slugs—you know, those snails with no houses—and let it crawl over your hand. Then stick the slug on a thornbush, and when it has dried up, your warts will be cured."

"Poor slug," said Adolf. "Oh no, I couldn't do that."

Despite this unpleasant discovery, nothing could dampen his adventurous spirit. Next day on the way to school, he pointed out to his brothers that the opportunities for navigation in the cellar ought not to be wasted and suggested a proper sea battle down there in the afternoon. Water had an irresistible fascination for him—the only point of disagreement between him and Aqua, who otherwise followed him through thick and thin. The dog, even though he had been named after the water carrier among the signs of the zodiac, still had a deep-seated horror of water. Now that the floods had covered the path by the riverbank and water was even trickling through the gate into the garden, it was difficult to get him to go beyond the yard. Adolf had to take him on walks uphill as far away from the river as possible, so that he could not hear the noise of the rushing water. Aquarius—that much was certain—would never take part in an escapade that had anything to do with water.

"What d'you think, August?"

But August said he had no time. Georg was in difficulties with his math, and Uncle Emmo had declared himself powerless to help. A sea battle without August? Adolf made a face. August had always organized the games when they had had floods before, for he knew better than any of the others what had happened in all the big maritime encounters in history.

"At least you might tell me a good sea battle we could play," Adolf begged him, although he could see that, with things as they were at present, August was more inclined to advise against any kind of adventures connected with water.

They were on their way home from school in the noon hour, and when the smaller boys met them, they joined in with Adolf at once, imploring their big brother: "Come on, August! Tell us about a nice juicy battle. You know all about them."

"Well, for heaven's sake play the battle of Lepanto, then," August said finally. He didn't want to be a spoilsport; he could well remember the fun they had had in the cellar on other occasions when there had been floods. There was no real danger in sea battles, except for their clothes, and if they took care not to get those too obviously wet, Mama need never know anything about it. "Lepanto, 1571," said August, "Don Juan of Austria, commanding the fleet of the League, beats the Turks. But watch out that none of you tips over."

"You and your history dates—you'll drive me crazy!" said Georg.

Adolf invited two dependable friends for that afternoon, and both the little boys were allowed to bring a friend along, also. All their pals knew the side entrance to the courthouse cellar. Everyone had to bring his own ammunition—cabbage heads, potatoes, and turnips—and if possible, one of the huge ladles that were used for stirring when the plum purée was made. They would serve as oars.

Unfortunately, Emil Müller, Adolf's old enemy, had caught wind of their plans and pushed his way in uninvited. And then, instead of being content with a modest role, he insisted on being Don Juan himself, but this was hotly disputed. Ferdinand, Karl, and the other boys supported Adolf's legitimate claims to the part, and Emil had to be satisfied with playing Ali, the Turkish sultan. Nobody else wanted to be a Turk, and lots had to be drawn to ensure an equal division of forces.

There were two washtubs for each side, and the combatants rowed their way skillfully about the cellar. All the boys in the town had learned to swim and row at an early age. First of all, declarations of war were made by both sides; then they proceeded to mutual insults. Finally, the bombardment began. After violent exchanges, the Turks were the first to run out of ammunition, but Emil Ali, defying historical fact, refused to admit defeat. In the end, his own crew mutinied against him, and Don Juan decided to ram the sultan's galley with his flagship. As a result of this maneuver, all the ships of the League and of the Turks were sunk, and the crews were left standing waist-deep in the water. They battled on bravely for a time with their ladles, but the din of war was so intense that finally Kettchen appeared on the steps leading down to the cellar, clasped her hands in horror, and disappeared again. It was easy to guess that she would call Mama. But before she had time to come down, all traces of the battle had been removed, except for the capsized washtubs, floating sadly in the yellow water.

So ended the battle of Lepanto. Adolf, Ferdinand, and Karl felt its consequences for several days every time they sat down. But then, as August pointed out, even Don Juan had had little joy from his great victory over the Turks. That was the way things sometimes happened in history.

Spring III

IN THE GARDEN of the courthouse, the first crocuses were making purple, yellow, and blue fringes around the rich brown of the freshly dug beds, holding up their little goblets for the pale March sunshine to fill with gold. In the forest, the scent of daphne filled the air with its bittersweet spice. Along the brooks, the pussy willows had brought out, just in time, their catkins from the protective hoods in which they had slept all winter. Every year on the Saturday before Palm Sunday, the children went out in droves to bring back the catkins that the priest would bless at High Mass the next day.

The boys had the afternoon free, and Georg was released from his house arrest for the first time, even though he and August were supposed to have their piano lesson from Aunt Rikchen on Saturdays. Their parents were disappointed that none of their sons made much progress with piano playing; but that was certainly no fault of Aunt Rikchen's. The boys always found excuses to cut their lessons and spend their free afternoons as they pleased elsewhere. "It's no use," they said. "We're just not musical, that's all." Despite this, they all liked singing and could sing well. They often sang either on their own or together.

Only August no longer joined in now; his voice had just begun to break. Paula was the only one who regularly turned up for her half-hour piano lesson. She had had lessons in the convent, and now that she was at home, it meant a welcome break for her from the daily round of domestic duties.

"Are you coming out with us?" asked Karl. "We're all going up into the forest, a whole crowd of boys, and Father Knodt is going, too."

"All boys?" said Paula. "What would they say if they suddenly found a girl among them?" It was an age-old tradition that the boys and girls went out separately to fetch the catkins, as she remembered, and she was surprised that Karl should have asked her. The boys had even been uncertain when Father Knodt had asked if *he* could go with them. A priest and a teacher on the first outing of the year? First, they had been embarrassed and rather doubtful. But they knew the curate well enough to be sure that he was not a spoilsport. Their last misgivings were dispelled when he told them he remembered from his own schooldays a pond deep in the forest where you could be sure to find frog spawn at this time of year. If any of them were interested, they could bring a jar with them and fish out some spawn; then at home they could watch the eggs turning into tadpoles and then later on growing into little frogs. The association of frog spawn and catkins for Palm Sunday was something new and exciting.

"Maybe your long skirts would be a nuisance dashing around the forest," Karl said, having thought about the advisability of taking a sister.

Paula admitted that long skirts were a nuisance for doing *anything* that was fun. She had found that out as a child and had always rebelled against the idea that life should be so much easier for boys in every way. "Yes, these wretched long skirts," she said to Karl. "Just be thankful that you don't have to wear them. Anyway, one of us must go for a music lesson today, though it's not really my turn. Aunt Rikchen is always so disappointed when you boys invent silly excuses every week. By the way, she's going to start painting the Easter eggs tomorrow, and she asked me to find out if there's anything you specially want."

The boys were all ready to set off, and they had no time for artistic questions. "Let her paint anything she likes," said Adolf for all of them. "I think we'd all like it to come as a surprise."

Only Karl had a special request. "I'd like a tree frog on mine," he said. "Bright green, and he must be sitting in the water." Paula promised to deliver his message.

The house smelled of soft soap and floor polish, which always made Paula homesick for the convent. The smell of extravagant cleanliness, mixed with incense, had been a special feature of the school. In the courthouse, as in all the other houses in town, there was a big housecleaning from the deepest cellar to the uppermost attic every spring and every autumn. It was a colossal upheaval, and the men of the house would take refuge, according to their personal inclination, either in the inn or in the fresh air. The Amtmann and Uncle Emmo were for fresh air. On these uncomfortable days, the two liked to go out for a long walk, or Jacob would take his brother with him on one of his trips into the country, which would become more frequent again now that spring was here. They also liked to sit together in Uncle Emmo's study, an island of peace in a chaotic world. He had made an arrangement with the

lady of the house that his two rooms were never to be
invaded by scrubbing brushes, pails of water, and carpetbeaters unless he was away, and even then there was a
strict ban on actually *touching* any of the books. On three
sides of the room, there were shelves full of books right up
to the ceiling, and even in the little bedroom next door, no
flat surface was to be found without heaps of books,
pamphlets, or loose sheets of paper. It was a real trial for
Frau Margarete, who regarded dust and cobwebs as her
archenemies.

In this room, with its homely smell of old leather-
bound volumes, paper, and tobacco, safe from the women
and their obsession with cleanliness, the two men often sat
together, smoking pipes, rummaging about with enjoyment
among books and catalogues, and having long conversations that were not always about literature. The Prussians
and their expansionist plans were an inexhaustible topic of
discussion at this time. Emmo was a liberal and used to
quote Freiherr von Stein's dictum: "I only know one fa-
therland: Germany." Jacob liked the rich variety of the
little principalities, although he did not always see eye to
eye with their rulers. He also had grounds for thinking
that the Prussian kind of strict bureaucracy would have no
place for his individual notions on the administering of
justice. Besides, he was too profoundly convinced of the
fallibility of human judgment to agree with the Prussian
use of capital punishment.

Today he was away in his coach, and Emmerich was
sitting alone in his room, with Nicki on his lap. He found
the monotonous purring of the big cat a stimulating accompaniment to his work of translating Virgil. Not that
he had any thoughts of publishing his work; he did it

purely for pleasure and as an insurance against his mind
running to seed.

When Paula had finished with her etudes and sonatas
on this Saturday afternoon, she came into her uncle's room
with her cloth and feather duster. He had agreed to let her
dust his books, an honor he would not readily have ac-
corded to anyone else. Today there was only one shelf left
to finish off; most of them she had already dusted in the
course of the week. As she went to and from the window
with piles of books, brushing the dust off them, shaking
them out, and carrying them back to their places, he
entertained her with comments on the various works. He
felt it was his place to initiate her into the secrets of great
literature, and she was so eager to learn. Her curious, naïve
questions reminded her uncle of a foal sniffing at every
blade of grass when it is let out into the fields for the first
time. In the convent, the literary diet of the schoolgirls
was even more carefully supervised than it would have
been in a secular boarding school: they had been given
well-stored hay, but nothing fresh and green. Now the old
bookworm felt the slowly burgeoning delight of his young
niece as under his guidance she made her first excursions
into the world of great books. She had read neither Kleist
nor Lessing, and of Goethe and Schiller they had studied
only the textbook selections. Of the great works of foreign
literature, she knew even less. He felt his fingers itching to
lead her further into the realm of letters but reminded
himself of the need for caution and patience.

"There we are," said Paula cheerfully as she replaced
the last book. "Tell me, Uncle Emmo, what are these
sweet little books here?" She spelled out the words in
faded gold lettering on the spines of the last books she had

put back in the Italian section. "Who was Giovanni Boccaccio, please?"

"A Florentine of the Trecento, child, a friend of Petrarch. Better leave them where they are; you have to be careful with these . . . old leather volumes. Anyway, it's in Italian, which you wouldn't understand."

"Does he count as good literature?"

"Hm. Opinions are divided on that point. And now it would be nice if you could bring some tea for us. I think we have both earned a little refreshment."

Paula went off with her cleaning things. Outside the door, she took off the red kerchief she had tied around her hair to keep the dust off. She came back with tea and bread and butter, found an empty corner of the table to put them down on, and sank back into one of the deep armchairs with a sigh of relief. "It's so cozy in here, Uncle Emmo," she said.

They spent a happy quarter of an hour together; Paula could not stay longer because the housecleaning still demanded her services. "I only wish there were more hours in every day," she said. "Do you think a person could ever manage to read *all* the books that ought to be read in one lifetime?"

"I should hardly think so," replied Uncle Emmo. "There's no such thing as books that *ought to be read.* Every person has to make his own selection. First of all, he has to find out the books he wants to *live* with, and then every few years he must reread those he likes best or that mean most to him."

"Why? Surely that just wastes more time?"

"That doesn't matter. The really great books are always new and different. They grow with you. It's the same with great music: the more you listen to it, the more you get out of it. Just wait; next winter I'll take you with me to Wiesbaden, and we'll spend a couple of days there together. There's always an excuse for me to go there. We'll stay with friends, and in the evenings we'll go to the opera or to a play. You've never yet seen a Shakespeare play, child!"

Paula looked at him with such a radiant smile that his old heart skipped in a quite unaccustomed way. "Oh, Uncle Emmo!" was all she could say. Then she suddenly remembered that she did not know for certain whether she would still be here next winter, but she kept her lips tightly closed. She was not going to blurt out her secret again, as she had done to Konrad Overberg. Surely Mère Celeste was right to tell her that she must get to know something of the world before renouncing it. Just at the moment, she felt like nothing less than renunciation and had a burning desire to acquaint herself with all the splendors that still remained to be seen and experienced.

She stood up and collected the tea things. A penny for your thoughts, thought Uncle Emmo.

"I must go now," she said. "You're so good to me!" She smiled and gave him a quick kiss on the forehead. "I can hardly wait for our trip to Wiesbaden. In the meantime, I'll dream of it day and night!"

The old gentleman smiled and followed her to the door with his eyes. She walked, as she danced, with the easy grace of a yearling fawn. "Heavens, to think I was once as young as that!" he said to himself.

Outside, the boys were just coming back with their booty of catkins and frog spawn; there was the usual confusion and laughing and teasing. "We had a wonderful time, Paula! We found more catkins this year than we ever did before. And frog spawn! Just wait; one day soon there'll be sweet little frogs hopping about all over the house."

"We shall be beside ourselves with happiness when *that* happens!" Paula laughed. "Don't forget to make a little spray of catkins for everyone in the house for Mass tomorrow morning."

Adolf took the tray from her and went into the kitchen with it. "Honestly, Paula, we've never had such a great time getting catkins before. The cuckoo's already calling up in the forest. We heard him, but we didn't see him. Father Knodt said you hardly ever see him—he's the shiest of all the birds."

"What about your falcon? Isn't he shy, too?"

"Oh, he'll grow tame one day. I know for certain he will. You must come and watch him sometime, the way he hops onto my hand when I bring him something good. Aqua brings me a big rat for him almost every day—there are hundreds of rats with all the flooding."

"Horrible! Aqua can't catch enough. The other day there was one in the larder. We fetched Nicki, and he was terribly afraid of him."

"Should've got Aqua! I say, the curate said today that the next time I ask him for advice when I want to do one of my brothers a favor, he's going to be sure and ask me *what* the favor is. How did he hear about my falling in?"

"I don't know, but he was visiting Uncle Emmo not long ago, looking at his books, and Papa was there, too."

On the Tuesday before Easter, school ended, and there were reports. Once again, Ferdinand and Georg had managed to scrape through. The whole house breathed a sigh of relief. Now they could spend a happy Easter all together without any worries.

On Wednesday, the women had started work on dyeing the Easter eggs. The stone jars were brought up from the cellar in which the eggs had been preserved in lime since the previous summer, for the hens were not yet laying sufficiently to provide all the eggs that were necessary at Easter. Five pans of boiling water were standing on the stove. In one, young nettle leaves had been cooked to make green coloring; in the second, onion peel for yellow. Madder for the red eggs had been fetched from the chemist's and indigo for the blue ones from the indigo mill further up the river. Mama was directing operations, Paula and the maids were running to and fro, Holwein was busy fetching fresh water from the pump, and Babett shouted advice through the open door of her room. At last, there were about a hundred eggs laid out on clean straw to dry. "Now watch them carefully, girls, to see they don't go blotchy! Keep turning them around. And as soon as they are quite dry, rub them with bacon rind. Have you the old rinds ready, Kettchen?'"

On Thursday morning after Mass, the five boys went off together to visit their old friend Michel Anderwand in his tower. He told them the story they had heard many times before, that on Maundy Thursday the bells fly off to Rome to be consecrated anew by the Pope. There was no bell-ringing to be done in the last days of Passion Week. A spell of silence and sadness hung over the country. It was as if the world held its breath. No sound came from the bells in the tower; no organ was played at the solemn services.

"On the first of April, I'm getting a new apprentice,"

said Michel. "But if you want, you can go on ringing the Angelus in the mornings for a bit. The young lad won't be able to learn everything at once." For forty years his bells had rung out the joy of high festivals and the events of everyday life. They gave warning if storms were approaching. They cried out Fire! Fire! if a blaze was sighted in the night somewhere. "You must feel it in the tips of your fingers," Michel said. "It can't be learned in a day."

Karl put a spray of catkins on the table, nicely tied together with box leaves, which had been blessed on Sunday along with their own. Michel fastened the spray over his bowl of holy water by the door. When there were storms, he would dip the catkins in the holy water and sprinkle tower and cathedral and town with them out of his four windows, once on each side, so that no lightning would strike.

"Of course we'll go on with the ringing," said August on behalf of the three older boys. "Good-by now, Michel, and happy Easter."

On Thursday, there was spinach and fried eggs for dinner in every house in town. Therefore, it was named Green Thursday. For Karl, it was Black Thursday. He had looked at the calendar and worked out that, with Easter coming so early, there couldn't possibly be any spinach to be had. But what had the market gardeners and his own mother gone and done? Brought on the spinach cunningly in forcing frames! And despite Karl's good school report, he was obliged to finish his plateful. He had had plenty of practice in the art of pouching green vegetables, especially spinach, in his cheeks and spitting them out somewhere when the meal was over. He sat there, looking a picture of innocence, replying in monosyllables to any questions that were put to him. Moreover, he had succeeded in smearing the remains of his spinach so carefully across his plate, that it looked almost empty. But Mama had long been up to his tricks. She scooped up a fair-sized pile from what was left on his plate and held his nose, so that he was obliged to swallow.

"I feel sick," said Karl, choking violently. "It'll serve you right if I'm ill on Easter Day."

"I'll risk that," said his mother, unmoved, and passed Karl's plate to Paula. "Up to the dovecote with him and his spinach."

In the loft, on the top floor of the house, lived the doves. They were sitting on their nests, brooding and cooing sleepily. Through their little door was a wide view across country. Down there were boys, who didn't have such cruel mothers, walking about freely, while Karl was a prisoner. He watched the young doves that had hatched in two of the nests and were being fed by their parents. He watched for as long as he reckoned it would have taken him to finish his plate of spinach; then he carefully scraped all the spinach off, stuffed it behind the nests and knocked on the chimney—the agreed sign that someone was to come up and release him.

Good Friday with its solemn mourning passed. Late on Saturday afternoon, there was the great celebration of the Resurrection in the cathedral. In a long procession, the consecrated host, the body of the Risen Christ, was brought up from the crypt; and at the same moment as the bishop replaced the host in the tabernacle on the high altar, the Easter music of the bells rang out, the organ came to life again, the altar boys shook their little bells, and down from the gallery came the jubilant angelic song of the choir of boys' voices: "Death, where is thy sting? Grave, where is thy victory?"

Before the service in the cathedral, the Amtmann had called Janosch to his office to give him the wages he had been keeping for him. "I'm proud of you, Janosch," he said as he handed him the money—more than the gypsy had ever possessed in a lump sum. "And I'm grateful to you for the sake of my horse and one of my boys: both of them have learned a lot from you." He held out his hand, and a deep red colored the gypsy's brown face. He wiped his right hand on his pants before he grasped that of the Amtmann. "I also proud of Your Honor," he said, and the Amtmann knew what he was trying to say.

After the service, Adolf went into the stable to take leave of his friend; the gypsy was going away first thing on Easter Day. Mama had knitted him a thick pair of woolen socks, Aunt Rikchen had painted an egg for him as well as for everyone else in the house, and the maids had almost certainly given him some present or other in thanks for so many mended pots and countless sharpened knives. Adolf had puzzled and puzzled over what he could give him. Finally, he had decided on a small book with the tunes and words of folk songs and folk dances in it. Perhaps Janosch would play the tunes on his fiddle and be reminded of him.

The gypsy was standing in the stall beside the gelding as Adolf came in. He turned around quickly when he heard footsteps and pretended he had only been putting down fresh hay for the horse. On the straw lay his battered old violin case and a bundle with a few tools in it and whatever else he might possess. He traveled light. He was ready to go now.

Adolf produced the book of tunes and held it out to him. "That's for you," he said. "Because you can play the fiddle so well."

Janosch shook his head. "Not read music," he said. "All here." He tapped his finger on his forehead.

They went together across to the falcon's cage. Adolf had brought the entrails and heads of the doves that they were going to have with bread stuffing for dinner on Easter Day. After a moment's hesitation, the falcon hopped onto his finger and took the delicacies back with him into the cage, where he tore them to pieces with his beak and his claws. Janosch and Adolf watched in silence. Beyond the open stable door, the evening sky was pale green. The bells still rang out their mighty resurrection song over town and countryside. When the falcon had finished eating, he flew up onto the topmost pole of his cage, moved his wings restlessly, and stretched his neck.

"Music, no, Adolf," Janosch said softly. "*Him.*"

The shock was all the greater for being quite unexpected. Give up the falcon when he was just beginning to tame him, the falcon he was one day going to take through the forest on his wrist, like the knights in the Middle Ages, while he thought of songs almost as beautiful as those of Tannhäuser? Day and night he had dreamed of nothing else.

"Janosch?" he said with a stifled voice.

The gypsy put his hand into the cage, and the bird hopped on to it at once. That was how it was, thought Adolf sadly. These two knew one another; there was some bond between them; they belonged together.

"Come," said Janosch. He stepped out of the stable into the pale green spring evening, the falcon on his hand. Adolf followed him. They walked across the yard and down to the garden. Behind them, the gelding whinnied; they could hear its hoofs beating against the wall of its box. "Look after him," said Janosch and nodded toward the stable.

"Yes, Janosch."

Of the horse he thinks. Of the falcon he thinks, Adolf thought. He does not think of me.

The western sky was now the color of gold in medieval illuminations behind the black filigree of the trees and the cathedral on its high cliff. The bells were silent now. A finch was singing in the garden. The falcon sat motionless on Janosch's hand; the yellow eyes stared into the distance as proud and as alien as on the very first day. The hand that held him moved gently up and down. Suddenly, the bird began to shift from foot to foot. Adolf held his breath. There was a tightening in his throat. He saw the air lifting the bird's wings every time the hand moved up and down; the wings began to stir gently. Heavens, how beautiful they were, those slate blue wings with their yellowish markings! Now they began to spread, and Adolf saw for the first time the amazing breadth of them. The white breast shone; the red of his stockings was as vivid as blood. Janosch's hand made a quick movement, as though he were throwing the bird up into the air. The falcon gave a hoarse cry—and flew up. They watched him as he landed on the acacia tree farther down the garden, fluffed out his feathers, and smoothed them down with his beak. Then he gave one more cry and climbed like an arrow into the golden evening.

Janosch looked at Adolf, and the boy nodded, blinded by the tears that he could keep back only with an effort. They walked back together across the yard and stood for a few moments at the open door of the stable. When Adolf could trust himself to speak, he said, "Good-bye, Janosch. All the best."

"You, too," said Janosch, and Adolf felt the hand that had held the falcon brush gently over his head.

Early on Easter morning, a morning bright as crystal and shining with dew, Paula walked through the garden. This is what it must have been like, she thought, when Mary Magdalene went to the grave, with sadness in her heart, thinking only of death—and there He stood, alive, saying: *noli me tangere.*

She had been to communion at the earliest Mass and had come back by the graveyard and through the top gate in the wall. As she walked among the graves, where crocuses and snowdrops were already in flower, she felt more strongly than ever that death did not exist. And now the garden, where life was forcefully breaking through once more, as though the whole earth was pulsating with it, reaffirmed her feeling.

"Happy Easter, child," said a voice behind her.

"Happy Easter, Mama," she replied radiantly. Her mother kissed her on both cheeks and said, "Come on, let's hide the eggs now. Why are you laughing?"

"Because you have to turn even Easter happiness into useful activity."

"That's what a mother and housewife is there for."

She's so secure, so sure of her place in the world,

thought Paula enviously. Perhaps one day I, too, shall have that certainty of what I am here for.

When they had taken the dyed eggs out of the big basket and hidden them all over the garden, they walked back past the stable. The door was open, and they could see that the animals had been fed and that fresh straw had been put out everywhere. Janosch had gone.

A little later the whole family came out, dressed in their Sunday clothes for church. The boys collected the eggs in little baskets to take to Mass with them, so that they, too, might receive the Easter blessing. Immediately after the service, the children had their traditional Easter-egg battle in front of the main door of the cathedral. It was an old custom. Two children would knock their eggs together, and the egg that broke first had to be given to the opponent. The two bigger boys no longer took part in this childish amusement, and this year, for the first time, Adolf did not join in either. He hurried back home to let Aquarius out of the stable in which he had been confined. They went for a long walk together, and by the time they came back, it was dinnertime.

In the living room, the big table was richly decked for the occasion, with crocuses and the first fresh birch leaves on the white damask and the egg tree as a centerpiece. Aunt Rikchen had sat up late the past few nights painting the shells that Kettchen always saved for her after the eggs had been blown out and used for the many egg dishes made during the long Lenten fast. The bare twigs of the egg tree blossomed with many gay colors. Some of the eggs for the tree were painted in traditional peasant designs of which Aunt Rikchen was especially fond. But every year each member of the family had an egg painted, with a special meaning just for him. Karl had one, as ordered, with a bright green frog on it. "I'm taking that upstairs with me!" he shouted. "I'm going to put it next to my jar with the tadpoles in so they know what they're supposed to grow into."

Now began the procession of Easter dishes, a real feast for eyes, nose, and tongue after the long time of fasting. First, there was clear meat soup with dumplings in it the color of buttercups; then the boiled beef with pickled beetroot, topaz-colored sweet gherkins, purple plums soaked in rum, and black nuts. After that came the Easter lamb, garnished with a circle of stuffed pigeons, noodles with brown buttered breadcrumbs, and the first fresh lettuce of the year from the cold frames. Finally, there was vanilla pudding sprinkled with chopped almonds, with raspberry juice poured over it. It was a festive meal, a real Easter banquet, a joy for the eyes and the palate.

Father and Uncle Emmo had fetched up from the cellar two dusty, cobwebby bottles of Schloss Johannisberger. Even the children had a little today in their silver christening mugs; and for the first time, August was allowed his without water in it. "It's time we began educating your palate with some good wine," said Father as he poured out his glass. "You will soon be sixteen, August Wolfgang." On ceremonious occasions like this, the Amtmann addressed his children by the full names they had received in baptism. "Always drink in moderation lest you spoil the true enjoyment of one of God's best gifts to man."

With a little bow to his wife and then to the aunts, he lifted his glass but did not yet put it to his lips. He set it gently in motion, passed it under his nose, savoring the fragrance of the grapes, the bloom of the wine. In silence, they all did the same; Father and Uncle Emmo exchanged a glance of deep mutual understanding, and then they took the first sip, rolling the wine slowly over the tongue and shutting their eyes while the precious liquid poured down their throats.

"Your good health, my dear ones!" said the Amtmann. "May we never see worse times."

Summer I

APRIL BROUGHT days of warm sunshine and soft winds but also another bout of slushy snow and frost at night. But nothing could stop Frau Margarete from starting work in the garden. All the domestic help and all the children were pressed into service. In other families, this might be done peacefully and quietly; but in the garden of the courthouse, the work went ahead with noise and excitement. There were shouts, commands, and occasional scoldings from Mama, for whom no one worked fast enough; there was laughter, teasing, and fooling among the boys, running back and forth among the maids, and grumblings from old Holwein, who loathed any sort of hurry from the very depths of his being. What a family, thought Paula, who was once more nearly dizzy with this swarming activity, the noise and speed, the overwhelming exuberance of her vivacious family.

With Georg's help, Holwein had spaded up all the garden beds, which Janosch had covered with manure from the stable in time for the last frost to break up the earth and let the melting snow soak it. Mama looked lovingly at the soft, rich brown earth, which was kin to her, as one woman to another. At this time of year, she was in her element. Under an old straw hat, her round face glowed as red as any of the first tulips that were just beginning to venture forth.

Plants that had been raised under glass were now planted out in the beds; radishes, carrots, and lettuce were sown, peas planted (they didn't mind a little cold, said Mama), and all the dead shoots removed from the perennial kitchen herbs so that there would be room for new growth. In the spinach bed, little furrows were made with the help of dibbers and string, and new seed was sown. Ferdinand and Karl discussed in whispers whether there was any means of preventing the hateful vegetable from growing. But they could think of nothing except urgent prayers to the ice saints, Mamertus, Pankratius, and Servatius, so that the Three Harsh Rulers would have pity on them and freeze the sprouts before they had a chance to grow.

Even Paula was drawn into the merry activity. The sun was warm and gentle; in the acacia tree a blackbird was singing; everywhere life was breaking out of the ground that had been frozen solid such a short while before. Who could have resisted the urge to bed young plants in this fertile soil, to sow seeds and cover them up like little children who still have to sleep for a while before the time comes for them to get up?

If I go back to the convent, Paula thought happily, I'll be the garden sister. She had forgotten once again that you could not choose your work as a nun.

The first violets were already pushing out their blue tips through the low leaves. The long tail-like catkins of the birches, the poplars, and the elder trees danced merrily in the wind. On the dark boughs of the plum trees lay white blossoms, like a last sprinkling of snow.

One night when Mama woke to hear a soft rain falling, she didn't hesitate to wake Paula and the maids at four o'clock in the morning to go out with her and plant young lettuces before the sun had dried the ground again. There was nothing like newly softened earth for bringing them on, she said.

On the Eve of St. Walpurga's day, when Adolf had taken something in to Babett, she said to him, "You must get up very early tomorrow and go out before the first cock crows. No one must see you; no one must know. Put your hand with the warts into the first May dew on the grass and say this prayer: 'Walpurga, holy flower, ward off the witch's power, all evil magic kill, and free me from my ill.' "

"She wasn't a witch," said Adolf stubbornly, for he didn't want to blame Janosch's mother for his warts. But unfortunately for him, the warts had grown bigger and bigger. The boys in his class were beginning to tease him about them: "Look at Adolf's hand; the devil's growing peas on it!" And there was nothing to be done but beat them up or be beaten up himself, one way or the other. Oh yes, he would have done anything to be rid of the wretched things. Perhaps the May dew would help them, even if they had nothing to do with witches and magic. He could try, at any rate. So on the first of May, he slipped out of bed and out of the house before dawn, followed by Aqua, who didn't count because he wasn't a human person. On the lawn he knelt down in the wet grass, bathed his hand in the dew, and said the words Babett had told him. But before he could get up again, he heard the cock crowing in the henhouse. So it was all no use, anyway.

When the day of the Three Harsh Rulers had passed

without any damage from frost this year, early summer came in with pomp and splendor. A delicate sickle moon rose in the evening sky; and there is nothing better for growing things than the pale light of a waxing moon. Now it was time to plant out the beans, which were too sensitive to frost to be put in before the middle of May. "Not too much earth on top, Paula," Mama reminded her. "Beans like to hear the bells ringing."

The garden was now blue with violets, whose scent flooded into the house through the open windows. Paula filled bowls and vases with them for every room. The picture of the young officer over Aunt Stina's little bedside table and the picture of old Goethe in Uncle Emmo's room were each given a bunch. When Paula went into her father's room to leave the most beautiful of the bowls of violets for him, she found a vase already there, blue and fragrant. It was standing beneath the picture of his dead wife, and for the first time it occurred to Paula that the winter sprays she had seen there, the twigs of fir and ilex, the first snowdrops or the catkins, had perhaps not been meant for her father only, but for this young woman also who had paid for her short happiness with her life. But who could it be that put them there? She suddenly felt a pang in her heart, a feeling of oneness with her mother. What must it be like for her to find that someone had brought flowers for the dead woman? Wasn't it painful enough that this picture was hanging there at all, always before the eyes of the man whose life she had shared now for twenty years, to whom she had borne six children! Was poor Françoise still moving among them like a sad little ghost, drawing sustenance from the life blood of the living? Had she, too, been taken along like the aunts and

Babett every time the Amtmann had moved house because she still lived on in his heart?

Before long, there were weeping hearts and gentle forget-
me-nots in front of the picture. Later on, it was the bright
glory of tulips and the first sprays of lilac, purple like the
bishop's biretta. Soon there would be roses. . . . But it was
still May, the month of Mary, in which all the lady altars
stood in shining candlelight and the sweet fragrance of
flowers. Every evening the women from the courthouse
went up to the cathedral to attend devotions to the May
Queen. It was a short interval of peace and happiness
amidst the work and the bustle of the day.

The days grew longer and the world wider. Once again,
as they did every year, the family went off on fine Sundays
for long walks in the countryside, through valleys and
meadows, over the hills, through deep forests, where they
met no one but an occasional forester out with his dog or
a journeyman on his travels. Often friends joined them,
families with children of the same ages as the boys or with
grownup sons and daughters. There were Paula's former
schoolmates, Caroline and Charlotte, and the older girls,
Ottilie and Melanie. There were the three Trombetta sons
and the Amtmann's young assistant judges, all sons of
Nassau families. In late afternoon, they would turn in at
one of the hostelries, sit in a garden in the shade of
gnarled lime trees under the ruins of some ancient castle,
and look out far over the beautiful countryside. The first
hay was already standing in stacks in the fields, and the
scent wafted up to them. They would sit down at scrubbed
wooden tables to eat the Sunday cakes they had brought
with them; the innkeeper's wife would bring coffee for the
grownups with brown-sugar lumps and rich cream, and

milk, warm and frothing from the cows, tasting of sweet meadow herbs, for the children. Then they would play round games or the boys would go for a dip under an ice-cold waterfall. Stories and legends were told, old tales that had their origins in these places; there was singing, or the young people would dance until the evening was late, for there was always someone there with a guitar or a fiddle. The moon hung in the branches, the scent of lime blossom filled the air, a cuckoo called, and from somewhere in the valley below came the melody of a nightingale's song. Paula danced, full of the sweet joy of life, enjoying the dance, the beautiful day, but her happiness had nothing to do with any of the young men who put their arms around her and sometimes drew her a little more closely to them than was necessary.

Whenever the aunts wanted to join in these expeditions, Adolf would drive them out in the chaise. Uncle Emmo at seventy-two was still a stout walker and declared he had no intention of being shaken about the country in the carriage "as though he were an old man."

Sometimes they spent their Sundays visiting some of the parish priests in the district. There were old churches to be seen, beautiful altarpieces to be admired. The priest would tell them the history of his parish, his housekeeper would bring in dark rich country bread with butter and cottage cheese, and a bottle of wine would be fetched from the cellar.

If any member of the family had a birthday, and there was scarcely a month in the year when there was no such celebration, or even two, then they made a special excursion the following Sunday. Sometimes they went by railway down the Rhine, changed at Koblenz on to a steamer, and puffed their way downstream past castles and woods and vineyards. The children would talk for months to come about experiences like these.

Corpus Christi came, and for the first time Adolf was allowed to take part as a ministrant in the big procession through the town. There were flags waving everywhere; statues of saints were carried in the procession. All the houses were decorated with young birch trees; every street was filled with the spicy smell of birch twigs, the heavy clouds of incense, and the delicate scent of fading rose petals on the dusty pavements.

This summer seemed the same to the boys as all the former ones in the courthouse, but as yet unnoticed by them, there were hints of coming changes in the air. The boys spent most of their free time down by the river, as they had done every summer. After May first, they had begun to go swimming, even though the water was still bitterly cold. They had worked together on caulking their boat, and then they would float downstream and row back again against the current. They landed on the leper island and repaired the damage that snow and winter storms had done to their old hut there. Fish were cooked on a fire between big stones, and the birds' nests in the tall trees had to be inspected to see if the young birds had hatched. They climbed up again to their cave in the cathedral rocks that they had fitted up and where they stored food every summer, collected more or less legally from attic and larder. Their rusty frying pan was still there, a chair with three legs, and the remains of a fire between rocks that served as a fireplace. But what had become of the glorious campaigns and adventures that had started from this cave? Where were the heroes of Hannibal's crossing of the Alps,

Caesar's victorious legionnaries, the questing knights of King Arthur? This year, August, who for as long as they could remember had been the unquestioned leader of all the boys of the neighborhood, only joined in their games on rare occasions. Most of the time he sat in Uncle Emmo's study and undertook a serious course in German history.

"You're crazy," said Georg angrily. "Don't you have enough swotting to do for school?"

"I want to find out," said August with a determined stubbornness that they had never noticed in him before. "I want to see if there is any sort of logic in all this jumble of events they call world history."

"Oh, come on; don't talk rot!" said Georg. "You can sit and read books when you're an old dodderer. The girls are always gaping at me now when I go for a stroll in the evening without you."

"Oh well, I expect you and Trombetta manage to console them," said August. Georg shrugged, picked a rose or carnation for his buttonhole, and went off for a stroll in the Schied, the main street that ran all the way around the town center. There the young people of the town promenaded every evening at dusk, like a stream, and who could tell where it would lead them?

Adolf still went swimming every day with his brothers, dived and rowed with them, but he was now no longer able to lead the completely amphibious existence of former years. The previous summer he had still hoped that after a while Aqua would forget his terrible experience in the floods and would get used to watching his new master spending hours on or in the water, or perhaps even come in swimming with him. But it seemed that Aqua's distaste for water was growing greater, not less. Adolf could scarcely bear to see him lying there on the bank, thoroughly miserable, and not howling only because he had been reprimanded so often for doing so. He suffered cruelly in the conflict between his urge to save his master and his horror of the water. As soon as Adolf was back on dry land again, the dog's agonies turned to wild delight; Adolf would lie down beside him in the warm grass, stroke him, comfort him, and assure him that he had finished with water for the day.

It was just as well then that the boy had taken on fresh duties this year that fitted in better with Aquarius's preference for terra firma. After Janosch had gone, Adolf had asked his father if he might take over the care of Silver entirely. The Amtmann had asked him if he realized that this was to be all or nothing. "You'll be solely responsible for the horse then, and that means you'll have to feed him regularly and look after him, see his box is kept clean, and so on. On days when I'm not driving out, you'll have to see he gets some exercise—you may ride him yourself or take the aunts out for a drive. You must see that he goes to the smithy when it's necessary, and now that it's summer, you'll have to take him out to the watering place from time to time. Think over whether you'll have time for all that with your schoolwork and your other activities."

Adolf could think of nothing more wonderful. "I'll get up an hour earlier in the mornings; that's all. It's light by four now, and the holidays will be here soon."

"Yes, but vacations don't last forever, nor does the summer. And in winter when it's cold and dark, you're going to find it hard if you have to do stable chores in the mornings as well as ringing the bells and serving Mass. I want you to think it all over; once you've taken the job, you'll have to carry on with it."

"I've thought about all that, Papa," said Adolf.

"And don't try to be too daring when you're riding him. I know you learned early to sit on a horse, but it was different with our old white one. This gelding is young and temperamental, and that's quite a different thing."

"But Janosch learned me how to ride properly."

"*Taught* you!"

"Taught me," Adolf repeated. "You told us yourself he was once a circus rider."

"Well, I don't expect you to perform any circus tricks. And don't get the idea that you can learn to ride properly in such a short time as that. If you manage to stay on and don't spoil the horse in any way, that's good enough for a start."

Since then, Adolf had fed and groomed the gelding every morning, and on days when he did not have to go up to the cathedral early, he usually went out for an hour's ride before school. Aquarius joined in these rides enthusiastically, and Adolf made the discovery that the forest is never so beautiful as it is in the early morning, with the slanting rays of the sun coming down in great shafts of light between the gray trunks of the beech trees and the reddish pines, changing them into pillars of a cathedral with the treetops forming a vaulted roof overhead. It would be wonderful to be a forester and live here all the time, thought Adolf. A hare leaped across the path. The bright red of a fox flashed among the brambles. What a mercy that Aqua was not a hunting dog! A whistle or a call was enough to bring him back to heel, though he enjoyed taking up a scent or barking at an impudent squirrel that hurled insults at him from the safe refuge of a tree.

He must have been trained as a puppy by someone who loved and understood dogs. Did whoever it was remember Aqua? Did he miss him? It would be impossible to forget a dog like Aqua. But why had he not come forward when they had put that notice in the local newspaper? And Aqua himself—did he remember that he had once belonged to someone else? Better not to think about that . . .

The forest was magnificent! Here and there the anemones were so thick that they made a white carpet, spotted with blue liverwort and scilla. Adolf would have been completely happy on these morning rides with his dog and his horse had there not been one thing missing: the tame falcon on his wrist, which had become a wild falcon again. And Janosch, too, had gone away, never to return. It was depressing to think that a man you had become fond of, a bird you had saved from certain death, could simply disappear, like shooting stars in the night sky, which shone out for a moment and then were extinguished and lost to sight forever. "Stay with me, Aqua!" said Adolf, and the dog looked up at him with complete devotion.

When he took the horse out to water it, Aqua had to be left at home. But Adolf's two younger brothers were always willing to come with him. They climbed up onto the horse behind Adolf, dressed only in their bathing trunks, which they put on every day the moment school was over. Behind the mill, where the river shelved gradually away from the bank, was the watering place. Silver gave a loud whinny, tossed his mane, and then stepped slowly down into the water. As soon as he felt the ground disappearing from under him, he swam out into the river, which flowed gently at this point. Sometimes one of the riders would slip off into the water, but that was all part of the fun. "Be careful you swim right away from the horse if you fall in," Adolf warned them. "Otherwise you might get a kick."

"I wish you'd come with us sometime," he said to Paula one day when he came back and found her in the garden. They sat together on the low wall, warm from the sun. "Not into the water—just on a comfortable little trot along the river. Remember the high wall and the old garden behind it that we used to peep into through the little iron gate? From the horse you can see right over the wall as far as the deserted house at the other end of the garden. Nothing but little turrets and balconies and bay windows and green ivy thick all over it."

Yes, Paula remembered the high wall farther up the river very well. Years ago she had imagined all sorts of stories about the deserted house and the green wilderness of the garden. The house belonged to a Frau von Savigny, who came to the Amtmann sometimes for legal advice. Since the death of her husband ten years before, she had not been in either house or garden.

"How I'd love to come with you!" said Paula. "But I've nothing suitable to wear for riding, and what do you suppose Mama and the aunts would say?"

"Oh, they need never know anything about it," Adolf said, and after some more urging, Paula had to agree that her wide skirts wouldn't look improper on a horse. So a few days later, at the crack of dawn, when everyone in the house was still asleep, they rode away together, Paula in front of her brother on the horse. Mist lay over the river, everything sparkled with dew, the veiled sky was like mother-of-pearl, and the world was fresh and new and all theirs. No one else was about.

"It's heaven!" Paula said, breathing deeply, her dark eyes shining. They looked over the wall, and everything was just as they had imagined it.

"See the frog prince?" Adolf whispered, slipping back into the fairy-tale world of childhood—and there he was, sitting on the moss-covered stone rim of a little pond, green and wet and sad-eyed. "Waiting for the princess and thinking she has forgotten him."

"But I haven't." Paula joined in the game and waved her hand at the green fellow. "Soon, soon, I'll come, my prince, and kiss you on your cold snout and rescue you!"

"Ugh!" Adolf giggled, but Paula was suddenly serious, touched by the melancholic beauty of the abandoned place.

"Not yet, my prince," she said softly. "Not yet," for the overgrown paths beyond the gray wall led nowhere. The box hedges were unkempt. The chestnut trees had put out a thousand candles for a feast to which no guests would come. Behind its green shroud loomed the white house, almost suffocated by ivy, a phantom . . .

"Let's go back," Paula said after a while, and Adolf turned Silver's head. When he put his sister down at the little gate leading into the courthouse garden, he said, "There we are. Nobody's caught us."

"I'll go straight in and pick some peas," said Paula. "Mama will be surprised to find me working in the garden so early."

She gathered courage from this morning ride with Adolf, and they repeated it more than once.

Her delight in the garden and in the life of all the growing things there had completely absorbed her. She never grew tired of it and would have been happy to spend the whole day working among the beds. "Don't forget to put a hat on," the aunts were always saying. Paula's face was already turning a deeper color. Under her dark hair, it looked like a carving of old ivory.

Ferdinand and Karl were happy that their big sister was generally to be found in the garden, for it often happened that they needed her help. More than in previous years, they were left to themselves and to friends of their own age this summer. This meant even more cut knees, bleeding noses, and other indications of a rough but glorious life, and Paula had the job of washing them off with cold water or patching them up with sticking plaster, which she always kept handy in her gardening basket so that Mama would at least not notice immediately that they had been on the warpath.

"Make sure you always have at least an idea of what those two young monkeys are up to," said Mama to Paula. "They're safest in the water or near it somewhere. You can't drown water rats." She had forgotten that it all depended how you *got* into the water in the first place. This was yet another one of Mama's funny notions, Paula thought. To keep an eye on Ferdinand and Karl, you would need a lookout tower and a telescope, and even these wouldn't always have been helpful, as neither Paula nor any other of the grownups knew that there was a piece of rock jutting out from the cliff and not visible from the house. For each of the boys, who knew these cliffs as well as his own pocket, there was an irresistible challenge to use the rock as a diving board. For years, the older boys had used it for this purpose. It took a bit of skill and a bit of daring—that was all.

Two years ago, Ferdinand and two of his classmates

had been initiated into what the older boys called the Death-Dive, something you had to do to prove yourself before you were fully recognized. Now it was Karl's turn. He had been nine on May seventh and could hardly wait to be accepted as one of *the gang* at last. That he and the two other novices his age did not jump too short and land on the path instead of in the river, breaking every bone in their bodies, was just one of the everyday miracles boys rely on.

"If there were no miracles," the Amtmann had once said to his wife, "then there wouldn't be any grown people. They would all have perished as children."

It was just as well for the boys that this summer the adults had other problems to occupy their minds. Otherwise, the jumping lessons for Karl, the apple of his mother's eye, might have been discovered.

Another thing that Paula could not see and that had its dangers was the younger boys' tree climbing on the leper island. One day Karl had ventured high up in the big elm, which he and Ferdinand had climbed in the spring to look at the pretty greenish-blue eggs in a thrush's nest. Karl merely wanted to have a look and see how the young ones were getting on, but this time the parent birds objected. They fluttered so anxiously around the boy's head that he had to put up his hand to guard his eyes and let go of the branch he was clutching. He lost his balance and tumbled down. The thick foliage broke his fall, but the sharp point of a broken branch tore a deep cut in his thigh through his thin cotton swimming trunks. Ferdinand had to drag him to the boat straight away and row him over to the courthouse. When they reached the garden, a green and sobbing

Karl fell into Paula's arms. "Run! Run and get the doctor, Ferdinand!" she said, terrified, and carried Karl into the house in her arms.

The doctor, the only physician in town, was a long, lean man with gray sideburns, spectacles, and a small black tube always sticking out of his pocket with which he used to listen to his patients' hearts and lungs and—in desperate cases—bellies. Every child knew him and saluted his one-horse, half-open carriage with the old chestnut mare and the old fat coachman. The doctor came at any time, day or night, when needed and also appeared without being summoned about once a month. He felt the pulse of the older people, looked at everybody's tongue, laid down the law, and then, over a glass of sherry, talked to the parents about the general state of health in the household, including the servants'. With the writing of bills, he couldn't be bothered. He expected his patients to make notes in their calendars whenever they consulted him. At New Year's, everybody would send him the money due him, often with a little present, the wealthier ones sometimes sending a choice bottle of wine. His fee was a guilder a visit. Poorer families weren't charged anything. And the doctor made quite a comfortable living that way.

On this occasion, Karl was given four stitches and a bitter white powder wrapped in rice paper, Ferdinand a sound box on the ears for not looking after his younger brother better. For him, the worst thing was that he had to stay in the next day during his free time and entertain Karl, who was confined to his bed. And on this, of all days, the news came that the Duke had ordered the mobilization of the Nassau militia. To have to stay indoors, whether in bed or tied to the bed of an ailing brother, was a bitter blow for two boys who liked to be in on everything that was going on.

Only when the older boys came up later that evening, did life become interesting again.

"Mark my words, men, the Duke has landed himself in the soup this time," August pronounced, and his brothers listened to him as though to an oracle. "Believe me, the whole thing'll be a flop. The people don't want war, and their representatives have for a long time favored a union with Prussia. The King promised our Duke he could keep his country if he stayed out of the war. And what does he go and do? Mobilizes his troops and allies himself with those Austrians. What do they want in the Rhineland, anyway? They ought to stay at home by the Danube. Bismarck'll soon teach them a lesson."

"If only he wasn't so anti-Catholic," Georg put in. "That's why the bishop and all the clergy are against Bismarck. They don't trust him."

"He's much too smart to molest the church, I'm sure. But on one point Bismarck is right. As long as every little tinpot prince can run his own political show, there'll never be a united Germany."

"And what would happen to Papa if Nassau became Prussian?" Adolf wanted to know.

"Oh, the Prussians would welcome him with open arms," said August with conviction.

The next day the town was full of soldiers. Ferdinand came home from school later than usual and went straight to Karl, who was out of bed but still under house arrest, to tell him what was going on in the town. "Eat as much as you can stuff in," he advised him. "Then you'll perhaps be allowed out again tomorrow. You've never seen so many soldiers all at once!"

Meanwhile, Paula had been given the task of getting the guest room on the ground floor ready for a major who had been billeted on the courthouse. She put the blankets and the featherbed out to air on the windowsill; later she came back and piled the freshly covered quilts and pillows on top of the bleached sweet-smelling sheet, so that the bed looked like a castle made of clouds. She dusted the shining surfaces of the little bedside cupboard and the chest of drawers, put a copper candlestick with a candle beside the bed, and relined all the drawers with fresh paper. Then she went into the kitchen to bake a cake for the guest's arrival. It looked perfect, and for once she hoped to have unadulterated praise from Mama. Instead she was asked, "Did you put some flowers in the major's room?" That was the one thing she had forgotten! "Now remember, a guest room isn't complete without flowers," said Mama. Paula never seemed to do anything exactly right!

When the boys came back from the town in the evening, the major was already sitting at table with the family. They were introduced to him in turn, each made his bow, said grace silently, and sat down.

The major was a small, friendly gentleman who did not look particularly warlike. But he could answer all Karl's and Ferdinand's questions about military matters to their satisfaction. Ferdinand had been particularly fascinated by the little drummer-boys whom he had seen marching behind some troops on his way home from school. Tomorrow, he promised, he would show them to Karl. These drummer-boys, usually the sons of noncommissioned officers, so the major told them, were about fourteen or

fifteen years old. As proud as young cocks that have just
learned to crow, they marched along, parade stepping bravely,
twirling their drumsticks, and trying to look as martial as
they could. With their gay uniforms, they were the envy of
every boy in town.

From now on, the boys only came home at mealtimes.
The bigger ones watched all the activity with a certain
reserve, but Ferdinand and Karl had to be everywhere
anything was happening. They watched the soldiers drilling, marched beside the band, and saluted the major whenever he rode past, to show that he was *their* major. Over
meals the talk was exclusively about uniforms, words of
command, and maneuvers. The grownups were quite content to listen to the boys' endless questions. It was better,
at any rate, than arguments about Nassau versus Prussia,
or His Serene Highness the Duke versus His Excellency
von Bismarck.

"When I'm fourteen, the major's going to give me a
letter of recommendation to the regiment," Ferdinand told
his brothers one evening as he marched up and down their
bedroom in his short shirt in the white moonlight, beating
an imaginary drum. "Ratatat, ratatat!" he chanted. "Then
I won't need to go to high school, ratatat! And I won't
need to take a final examination, ratatat, hurray!"

"You just wait and see whether there still is a Nassau
militia when you're fourteen," said August.

Georg went on: "You poor idiot! Even supposing you
became one of those drummer-boys, what'll you do later
on to earn a living when you're too old to go on drumming?"

"Then I'll become a lieutenant, and later a major, and
later a general. You'll join me, won't you, Karl?"

Karl was quite prepared to be a drummer-boy for a

while, but only in the school holidays. He had other plans for later on. "Mathematics!" he said importantly. "That's what I want to study, and I'll become a professor."

"The best of luck to you!" said Georg mockingly. "At least you two don't suffer from excessive modesty."

"Well, that's one who doesn't want to go to the university," said August. "Papa hasn't enough money to let us all study, anyway." His brothers pricked up their ears in the hope that they would hear something about his own plans for the future, but they were disappointed.

Georg stretched himself luxuriously on his bed. "Here's another one you can cross off your list, August. When I've done with boring old school, I'm going to enjoy life for a change and see a bit of the world. I'll go to Wiesbaden, where there are always lots of foreigners for the cure, and take a job as traveling companion to some rich English lord or a Russian count and travel everywhere with him. People like that need a good-looking and bright secretary who can take care of their affairs. And when I get to Nice or Monte Carlo, I'll try my luck at roulette and win a pile of money; then I'll pay for any of you to go to the university, if you really want to."

"Warmest thanks, my dear baron," said August. "I'll bet the lords and counts will be fighting over you. What about you, then, Adolf?"

"I expect Uncle Waterloo would lend me the money to go to the university, and of course I'd pay him back every penny later on. But I don't know if I want to go. Do you have to study to be a chief forester?"

"Of course, you nitwit. You'd have to go to the forestry academy. But the other day you said you wanted to be a priest, and before that it was an explorer."

"And a biologist!" shouted Karl from his bed.

But Adolf was in no mood for a discussion. His imagination always worked best at this time, in the dreamy state between sleep and waking. He had been thinking a lot lately about the white house in the overgrown garden, which he had already rented or even bought in his imagination. He would have to find out if there was a good enough stable there for Silver and a meadow where the horse could graze. Every winter he would invite Janosch and his tribe to visit him, and they would put up their gypsy tents in the big park. He saw himself sitting in front of an open fire, Aqua beside him on a soft rug, a little table with a big plate of biscuits and a glass of raspberry juice next to him. In his hand he held a book, or a notebook and pencil. It was a long time now since he had entertained his brothers and their friends by telling them exciting stories of travels and adventures he had made up on the spur of the moment. Later he had started to write his stories down, and in the summer vacation he was going to withdraw into the deserted cave and write like St. Jerome in his cave. Aqua could play the part of the saint's lion.

"You must go to the university, whatever happens, Adolf," he heard August say. "You've got the right sort of brain for it."

"Oh, I don't know. Perhaps I might become a writer," he said sleepily.

"Writer?" came the echo from all four brothers in varying degrees of surprise and horror. "What, like Aunt Stina, and never get anything published?" asked Ferdinand, who could scarcely comprehend how anyone could want to write of his own free will.

"Some writers do get things published," said Adolf. "Now leave me in peace."

When I'm living in the white house, he thought, I'll get August to come and visit me. Wonder if he'll be arch-bishop or professor of history or a Prussian minister by then. And Paula, if she doesn't go back into her convent or get married, she can come and run the house for me.

He felt Aqua's head nuzzling into his armpit. "And you, too, of course, Aqua," he murmured, already half asleep. "You'll always be where I am."

Summer II

GREAT PREPARATIONS were afoot at the courthouse. Everyone was busy washing, ironing, and sewing before the children went off on vacation. Paula was packing her traveling hamper and two rucksacks for Ferdinand and Karl. As usual, this year her half sister Franziska had invited the boys over for the vacation to give their poor parents a rest. This year the two youngest ones were to go over first, accompanied by Paula; for the second half of the holidays, the three bigger boys were going. For some years now, Franziska's husband had been in Schwalbach, a forest resort in the Taunus Mountains. The young boys were welcome guests, whose visits were eagerly looked forward to by the entire boy population of the little town every year. From the day they arrived, there was never a dull moment.

"They just can't wait for us to come," said Ferdinand. "We have a whole crowd of friends there." The grownups in the courthouse nourished suspicions that a few weeks later their relatives in Schwalbach would be scarcely able to wait for them to leave again.

Paula had seen her half sister only once since her return from the convent; in March, she had come over to Limburg for a few days for the Amtmann's birthday. They had had no time then for private talks together, and there were so many things Paula would have liked to ask her elder sister's advice about. In Limburg, she had found it difficult to take up the threads again with the girls she still knew from her schooldays at home. She had met them and their brothers occasionally at parties during the winter or now in summer saw them on Sunday excursions or at an occasional Kaffeeklatsch. But the two years she had been away in France were still a barrier between her and them. She was naturally reserved, and when the girls talked about their love affairs or about people and events she didn't know because of her long absence, she tended to withdraw into herself, without realizing that this only made her seem, as shy people often do, proud and distant.

She still corresponded regularly with the friends she had made in the convent. But they were a long way off, and often she felt as though they were also gradually slipping away from her. Françoise, with whom she had been most friendly, had gone back home the previous autumn, and to the surprise of everyone, there had come an announcement of her engagement at Christmas, even before Paula had left the convent. Her father was a wealthy silk merchant in Lyon; her fiancé, a young government official in Paris, secretary to a minister, with prospects of a successful career. The shrewd Françoise had been fully aware that the meeting had been carefully planned by their respective parents. "He worships me, and I like him quite a lot," said the letter. "Maman assures me that love will come after we are married; it was exactly the same way with her. Just think, we are going to live in Paris! You must all come to my wedding in April." Paula had not even

asked her parents whether she could go to the wedding;
the journey was too expensive even to be considered so
soon after her return from Nancy. But how she would have
liked to know more about this marriage! It was not un-
usual for marriages to be arranged by parents, but Paula
knew that she would have rebelled violently against any
such scheme. If she ever married . . . ah well, happily she
had quite different plans for her future.

The Irish girl Maura had gone back to her father's
sheep farm. She had been the most gifted of all the girls
in Paula's year. The nuns had hoped that she would go
into the training college run by the order and take her
exams as a teacher. But shortly after Paula left Nancy,
Maura's mother had died, and she was called home to look
after her father and her three brothers. Her letters sounded
contented, although she had been keen to become a teacher;
she accepted her duties as a matter of course, with no
thought of rebelling against them. "Perhaps later I may be
able to go to the training college in Dublin," she wrote, "if
one of my brothers marries and brings a young wife to the
farm."

The third, Monique, had gone off at Easter to become
an apprentice cook in her parents' hotel by the lake of
Geneva. In the evenings, she was taking a course in book-
keeping and English correspondence. She had no brothers
who could continue the century-old family hotel, and so it
was up to her to learn the hotel business from the very
bottom. What a pity, thought Paula. She had such a lovely
voice!

Paula was dismayed by the sudden changes that had
come over the lives of her closest friends. Monique had
always cherished the hope that she might be able to go on

with her singing. "I have no time at present to take lessons. Perhaps later I will be able to take them up again," she wrote. "Of course my parents hope that I will marry some expert in hotel management before very long, *ça va sans dire*. I'm only glad that as yet one hasn't turned up. The two young apprentices working here at present are both sons of hotelkeepers, so there's no question of my marrying them: they'll be needed in their parents' hotels! Isn't it a joke that I must be careful not to fall in love with an 'unsuitable person,' because that would make my parents so unhappy? I feel like a sort of heir to the throne who can't marry whom she pleases."

It all sounded so sober and sensible, and yet it was less than a year ago that the four of them had shared all kinds of romantic notions about what life would be like. All these things Paula wanted to discuss with Franziska. She knew about life; she had been married for nearly ten years. In the family it was said that hers was a happy marriage. "Even though they married for love," said Aunt Rikchen. "Generally marriages that are based on the sound and experienced judgment of older people have better prospects." Aunt Stina, on the other hand, was all for love matches; in her novels, at any rate, people married only for love. Paula would dearly have liked to know whether her parents had actually had a hand in Franziska's marriage or not.

She had written down in her notebook a whole list of questions she wanted to ask her. But suddenly all she had been looking forward to came to nothing. At the beginning of July, when the boys began their school vacations, the political situation had grown so uncertain that their parents decided to call off the visit. The friendly major disappeared with his regiment one day without warning, no one knew whither. The town buzzed with excited rumors. People who were hostile to the Prussians began to regard everyone else as a Prussian spy, and any harmless lamp might be taken as a signal to the enemy. Windows were broken. Old friends fell out because they belonged to different schools of thought. Gossip and mistrust flourished and bore evil fruit; it was enough to know that a person had different opinions from your own to doubt his sincerity and good character.

The Amtmann was busy day and night defending innocent victims of the spy scare. He had to use his full authority to prevent matters from taking a more serious turn; at the same time, he could not avoid his own actions being open to misinterpretation. His brother Emmerich supported him in everything he did; he counted himself a liberal, but there was much going on even among those of his party that could scarcely be called liberal.

Now that the major was no longer with them, conversation ranged more freely at table over current affairs, and differences of opinion between members of the family came to light. Without realizing it, the boys were getting a practical demonstration of tolerance that they were often to remember in later life. Everyone in the house was anxious not to allow these differences to develop into personal bitterness but rather to respect opposite views and keep a level head in spite of the confused situation.

The boys were bursting with eagerness to go out into the surrounding countryside and keep a watch for advancing Prussian troops. With this in mind, they paid another visit to Michel Anderwand in his tower, but even from up there, nothing was to be seen.

"One thing I do ask of you, you older ones," said Mama. "As we can't send Ferdinand and Karl to Schwalbach this year, I want you to keep a close eye on them. They might go marching off to meet the Prussians tomorrow out of sheer curiosity and desire for adventure. Stay close together, all five of you, as you did formerly. Please remember that in wartime people get shot. If you hear shooting anywhere, you are to come home at once."

Even Adolf's morning rides had been the subject of a parental ban; he must stay within a short distance of the town. This did not suit him at all, for he had recently become more and more enterprising in the things he did with his horse. He had discovered that Silver was a good jumper and enjoyed jumping, and after a few falls he learned how to stay in the saddle when he went over. There were plenty of ditches, streams, hedges, and low walls nearby for him to try out his new-found skill and test how well he understood the horse. Silver responded willingly and cleverly to all his directions. If only Janosch could see us now, he thought, I bet he'd be pleased with us. But all this could be done only at a good distance from the courthouse, and he now was forbidden to go so far. Instead, he sometimes took the two little ones with him and rode sedately and virtuously a little way up or down the river. All five of them now swam together almost every day, and except for Adolf, who had to think of Aqua, they often spent the whole day without drying off once. Aqua, whom the boys now sometimes called Terra, followed Adolf to the cave without any hesitation and was content to sit up there for hours beside him, playing lion to Adolf's St. Jerome. On hot summer days, it was wonderfully cool in the cave. Adolf was still near enough to the river to be fulfilling the order that they should stay close together, and yet he was sufficiently on his own to let his imagination roam freely. He sat there, chewing a pencil, scribbling sentences into an old exercise book, and then tearing the pages up again. He moaned and scratched his own head and the dog's alternately. What he wanted to write was a heroic epic about Richard the Lion-Hearted and his faithful squire Blondel, who freed him from prison. He soon realized that it was not so easy as writing an essay for school. In between, he looked out from his eyrie across the river to the fields on the other side, where wheat and barley were standing golden. He often thought he could glimpse a movement among the tall grain, but there were no helmets glinting, and he never heard a shot, however hard he listened.

Georg slipped away for a while every afternoon into town to learn the latest news and see his friends, who sorely missed him on their evening strolls. "I'll just see what's up," he would say to August. "You keep an eye on the young ones, meanwhile." When he came back, he brought the latest bulletins with him, for the news was always posted outside the printing office of the newspaper. One evening he rushed home breathless just as the family was sitting down to table and blurted out his tremendous news almost before he reached the door: the Duke had left Nassau and had gone to join his troops. The proclamation to the people was posted everywhere in the town, the town crier had announced it in the marketplace, and tomorrow everyone would be able to read about it in the newspaper.

Immediately afterwards, Father Knodt came in; he had been invited to supper with the family, and he was able to confirm Georg's report. As soon as the meal was over, the Amtmann, Uncle Emmo, and the young priest went out together. "To the bishop, I expect," said August to his brothers, and he was right.

No one could sleep much that night. Every hour one of the boys would get up, rush to the window, and look out to see if there were any enemy troops in sight. There was no Nassau soldiery in the town any more, and the duke had gone, but there was still no news of a declaration of war. Twice Paula came into the boys' room to ask if they could see anything and to have a look out of the window with them. But no, there was nothing to be discovered. The moonless night was dark and uncannily silent. Once there was a sound like distant thunder. In the garden, the crickets kept up their monotonous chirping, and down by the river a belated nightingale sang ceaselessly.

Their parents, too, had little sleep. The next morning the Amtmann went down to his office earlier than usual, fetched the files on a case he had to deal with that day, and began to read them. After a while, he heard steps and voices outside in the hall. Wittich burst in without knocking. The Amtmann looked up and raised his eyebrows. Whatever it was, there was no excuse for informality.

"Pardon me, Herr Amtmann . . . the Prussians!" stammered the beadle.

"Please ask the gentlemen to step this way," said the Amtmann.

A major and an adjutant entered; at the door they clicked their heels and saluted. They had come to the Amtmann, as the highest civil authority in the district, to inform him that the Prussian commander-in-chief had

declared a state of emergency throughout the whole of
Nassau. He, the Amtmann, would have to assume responsibility for peace and order and communicate the necessary procedures to the civilian population. The country
had been occupied without any resistance to speak of; the
general hoped to put an end to the state of martial law
very shortly.

"Now you'll be able to see what real soldiers look like,
fellows!" August said to his brothers. "These chaps have
not only occupied Nassau before you could wink, but
they've taken over Frankfurt, the thousand-year-old free
city. Think of it! The war's over before it's even started.
Here, at any rate."

The young people were disappointed that it had all
happened with so little to-do, but they had something to
make up for it. The victorious Prussians marched into the
town with flags waving and regimental music playing;
hussars rode up the main street; light artillery rattled past,
followed by such a vast crowd of schoolboys that the
drivers had to be careful not to run any of them over.
There was a general on horseback with a plume of white
feathers on his helmet, his adjutant beside him. People
said he was the commander-in-chief, General Vogel von
Falkenstein, but no one knew if this was true or not.
Others said that the bishop had been assured that Catholic Nassau would be occupied mostly by Catholic troops, a
noble gesture that did much to calm many people's fears.
In the courthouse, business was even more lively than
usual, people coming in from morning to night to get the
Amtmann's orders or advice in this exceptional situation.

As Paula was crossing the yard the next morning to
fetch the new-laid eggs from the henhouse for breakfast,

Adolf rushed out to her from the stable, full of excitement. "We've got soldiers billeted on us! There are two splendid horses in the stable and a hussar! Come and have a look. The trooper is a jolly fellow; he whistles like a canary and has settled into the stableboy's room already."

But Paula had no time to look at horses now. She quickly fetched her eggs, and as she had forgotten to bring her basket, she slipped them into her apron. When she was hurrying back into the house, she almost bumped straight into a blue and silver hussar officer. He stepped politely aside, clicked the heels of his high riding boots with a flourish that made the spurs jangle, put his hand to his cap, and said, "*Pardon, mademoiselle!* Lieutenant von Quitzow. Would you be so kind as to announce me to His Honor, Herr Amtmann."

Paula grasped the corners of her apron together with one hand and felt for the handle of the door with the other. It was embarrassing to have to face such an extremely elegant young man wearing her house dress! She realized that she was blushing, which made her embarrassment all the greater. One of the eggs tumbled out of her apron and smashed on the stone steps, and foolishly she bent to pick it up, although there is not much of a broken egg to pick up. The polite hussar could not do otherwise than bend down too, and this time they *really* did bump into one another—head on. "*Pardon, mademoiselle!*" he said for the second time this morning. Paula hurried into the house. He followed close behind her.

"Please wait here," she said, as distant and severe as possible. "The Herr Amtmann is not in his office as early as this. I'll go and tell him." She hoped this would make him realize that a visit at such an impossibly early hour

168

was far from being *comme il faut!* He looked like twenty at the most, a newly hatched lieutenant evidently, at least six feet tall, and from this height he looked down on little Paula, which she felt as an insult somehow, though one couldn't blame him for being so tall. The ridiculous little mustache on his upper lip didn't hide his attempts to suppress a smile. Without giving him a further glance, she ran upstairs. The family was already sitting down to breakfast—without eggs.

"Why are you bringing the uncooked eggs in here?" asked Mama in astonishment. "And what have you been doing with yourself?"

Paula realized for the first time that there was egg yolk dripping down her apron and onto her shoes. Apart from the one she had dropped, another one must have been smashed in her apron when she and the officer had bumped together. It never rains but it pours, she thought.

"I just wanted to tell Papa quickly that there is an officer waiting to see him downstairs," she said. "I think he must have been billeted on us."

The Amtmann finished his coffee without hurrying.

"Then you'd better get the guest room ready again straight away," said Mama. "But first, take off that dirty apron and have your breakfast. Did he really look so fearsome that it made you break the eggs?"

"What sort of soldier is he?" Karl broke in, saving Paula from having to answer her mother's question.

"A hussar," she said.

"With a bay and a brown and an orderly," Adolf rattled off. "Weren't you listening when I told all about it?"

Papa rose from the table. "You must see that Silver gets some exercise today, Adolf," he said as he left the room to go downstairs. "Please take this letter with you and hand it in at Frau von Savigny's house. You know the one, in the big garden behind the mill. You can tie the horse up at the gate while you go in. The house has been let for the holidays to an architect called Ippel from Wiesbaden. Our friend Winter recommended the family to me."

Adolf exchanged a glance with Paula. He had been waiting a long time for an opportunity to explore this mysterious garden. As soon as breakfast was over, he saddled Silver, whistled to his dog, and set off. When they reached the little gate in the wall, he dismounted and threw the reins over an ornamental curl in the ironwork of the gate. "Look! Lovely grass, Silver," he said. "You can help yourself; it'll have to be cut some time anyway. Sit, Aqua, be good! I'll be back in a moment."

He passed the fountain with the moss-covered rim that he had seen when he looked over the wall. From a rusty spout trickled a thin column of water. The frog prince was not at home today, but there was a big gold carp floating motionless among the duckweed. It was a hot July day, and it occurred to Adolf that the animals could do with a drink. Aqua came at once to his call and lapped thirstily at the water, which was clear and fresh under the thick covering of green. The carp disappeared under a water-lily leaf, all except its tail fin, which quivered indignantly—a grumpy old man's gesture of dismissal when his nap has been disturbed. Silver had a drink, too, after Adolf had cleared away some of the duckweed with his hand. Then he took the animals back to the little gate and left them there in the shade of the wall and the old chestnut tree. Aqua whimpered a little as the boy left him, and Silver rubbed his nose against his face. It was almost as though the two of them wanted to dissuade him from penetrating the enchanted green wilderness.

The main path, as far as it was recognizable between the thick bushes, turned a corner, and after a few more yards, Adolf realized that he was no longer walking toward the house. Instead, he found himself between tall box hedges, higher than himself; once upon a time they must have been trimmed into elegant shapes, but now they were all ragged and grown over. He turned right, in the direction he thought the house must lie, but found himself trapped between more hedges. It was the same thing wherever he turned—to right or to left, the same narrow paths, the same hedges. The air was curiously silent. There were no birds singing in the shady tangle of leaves and branches. Once he heard a whinny from Silver and a short bark from Aqua. They sounded surprisingly distant and as if they came from a completely different direction than he would have imagined. Being Adolf, he at once began to weave a story in his mind, turning into Theseus in the labyrinth of the Minotaur. His imagination made his situation even eerier than it was. About time for Ariadne to turn up and rescue me, he thought, and he began to whistle loudly to dispel the unpleasant feeling of being lost. Then he stopped and listened. From somewhere he thought he could hear voices and laughter.

"Hello!" he shouted and waited for a moment. "Hello!" he shouted again.

"Is someone there?" replied a girl's voice.

"You bet there is!" he called back. "I've lost my way in these bushes."

Again he heard voices and laughter somewhere behind the impenetrable walls. Was a consultation in progress as to how long they could go on teasing him like this? Finally he lost patience. "Aqua!" he shouted as loud as he could. "Aaaaquaaa!" At the same moment, he heard footsteps very close to him, though he could still see no one they might belong to. Then there came a nerve-shattering shrill barking, and from nowhere a tiny white dog appeared, jumping about at his feet, yapping for all he was worth as though Adolf had been a burglar. A second after, Aqua came bounding around the corner—it had been easy enough for him to follow his master's scent. The big dog pulled up with a jerk, evidently disgusted by the sight of this ludicrous little thing that leaped at him as though it were intending to eat him.

"Help!" cried a voice, which presumably belonged to the footsteps Adolf had heard, and Ariadne appeared. "Help! He's eating Powder Puff!"

A little girl emerged out of the tangle of hedges, bent down, picked up the yelping little dog, and held it high above her head, as though to defend it from the knightly Aquarius, who would never have dreamed of attacking a dog smaller than himself. "Call him off!" she begged. "What are you two doing here, anyway?"

"Come here, Aqua, down!" said Adolf. "You'd ruin your digestion if you swallowed so much cotton wool. I've a letter here for Herr Baumeister Ippel."

"Oh, I see!" said the girl. She must have been about eleven, a slender little thing with a mass of shining brown hair that flowed over her shoulders and down her back in a thick mane, held back from her forehead by a silken ribbon. Now that her dog was no longer in danger, she looked at Adolf with laughing eyes. Ariadne could not have appeared more charming to Theseus than this small

girl in her white dress, which was short enough to show
quite a stretch of white stocking, did to Adolf. She wore
black strap shoes and a red coral necklace around her neck.
Obviously she thought it a great joke that Adolf had lost
his way so completely.

"This is a la-by-rinth," she said importantly.

"I almost guessed it," he said, but the irony was lost on
her.

"Please keep tight hold of your monster and see he
doesn't bite my dog," she went on.

The little dog was still growling fiercely down at Aquarius, who did not so much as look at him. "What? Do you
suppose a real dog would attack a thing like that?" said
Adolf.

She cuddled the thing tenderly to her. "His name is
Powder Puff. Isn't he sweet? We call him Püffchen. What
about yours?"

"Aquarius."

"That's a funny name! Come on, I'll take you up to the
house. Look, you only had to take this turning here, and
then this one, and there we are."

"How was I to know that?"

They actually had merely turned two corners of the
maze when it opened up and they were standing on a lawn
in front of the house. (Big enough for a gypsy encamp-
ment, Adolf decided.) Steps led up to a veranda, where an
elderly lady was sitting in a garden chair. At the edge of
the lawn, a swing had been slung between two trees, and
there were two more girls sitting in it, also in white, one a
little bigger than Adolf's rescuer, the other a little smaller.

"Who's that with you, Toni?" asked the elder. "And
what's that terrifying dog doing?"

"The boy said he wouldn't do anything. He's called Aquarius. The dog, not the boy." She looked at him questioningly, and he said, "Adolf's my name."

The two sisters came over. "You remind me of that good-looking boy who was so nice to us and showed us all the sights of the town the other day. Doesn't he?" the youngest one asked, and all three girls stared at him.

A thought came into Adolf's mind. "Would you mind telling me this good-looking boy's name?" he asked.

"Georg," replied Toni. "And these are my two sisters, Lina and Emmi. Come on. You can give the letter to Aunt Käthchen. Her name is Fräulein Stritter. Papa only brought us here last week, and then he went back to Wiesbaden. And now we're stuck here with Aunt Käthchen and can't go back to Papa, and he can't come to us because that horrid general has forbidden all journeys."

"Well, that's only a temporary thing," said Adolf. "My brother August says they always do that in occupied territory at first."

Toni took his hand and led him up to the veranda where her aunt was sitting, knitting something red. Gosh, she's a hunchback, thought Adolf. But her face was so friendly and serene that he forgot the hunchback. He noticed that the house had many more bay windows and turrets and little decorations than he had been able to see from over the wall. It looked jolly but a little odd.

"He lost his way in the maze," Toni explained, and the aunt joined in the girls' gay laughter. On a table beside the garden chair stood a big jug of lemonade and a plate with thin bread and butter. Adolf had never seen anything so thin. "You must be thirsty," said Fräulein Stritter. Lina ran into the house to fetch another glass, and Toni poured out

lemonade for everybody. Adolf sipped his cool drink and
ate some bread and butter, or rather inhaled it—there was
nothing there to chew. Then he had to tell them the story
of how Aquarius received his funny name, and they all
listened attentively. Afterwards, the conversation came back
to the "good-looking boy" who had taken the aunt and her
nieces around the town. Or rather, dragged them around,
thought Adolf. They had been to the bishop's palace and
the bishop's chapel and to the fish market, where he had
told them that a man with a trumpet always had to walk
in front of the mail coach and any other heavy carts to
warn the butchers and the bakers to move their wares back
from the street. Here in Limburg was the narrowest point
on all the main cross-country road from Cologne to Frankfurt, and there was an ordinance about the exact width the
loads on the carts could be—if they were any wider, they
could not get past. Then he had taken them up to the
cathedral and shown them the beautiful Romanesque font
and his family's arms above one of the choir stalls. Adolf
could well imagine how he had made himself seem important and shown off all his knowledge in front of them. "He
knew *everything*," said Toni. "Don't you think Adolf looks
rather like him, Aunt Käthchen?"

Adolf put one foot on the other with embarrassment.
His left hand he kept tightly stuffed into his pants pocket,
so that at least they couldn't see his warts. What a rotten
fellow and show-off he was, that Georg! And he had
dragged this poor old lady, hunchback and all, up the hill
to the cathedral. It was a miracle she hadn't dropped dead
with the effort in the boiling heat they'd had last week!
"That's my brother," he said gloomily. "If I'd taken you
around, I'd have taken you in the carriage."

"Have you any more brothers?" asked Lina. "Yes, you must have; you mentioned another one just now."

Adolf had to run through the whole family for them. "Next time you need a guide, you just ask me. I'll take you out in the carriage," he said. "And now I'm afraid I've got to go." He would have liked to stay longer. It was fun to hear the old lady and the three girls laughing, each at a different pitch; it sounded like a glockenspiel. He didn't care much for girls generally, but these three didn't look at all bad in their white dresses with the coral necklaces and the silk ribbons in their hair.

"If you really have to go, I'll see you as far as the gate," said Toni. She was easily the prettiest of the three sisters, with her brown eyes with little gold specks, like larks' eggs. "I don't want you to lose your way again," she said and laughed. When the light fell on her hair, it looked like a ripe chestnut fresh peeled from its shell, new and shining.

"Do you really think I look like Georg?" he asked her as they walked down the avenue of trees together. She stopped and looked at him carefully with a little frown. "Yes. No. Perhaps a bit, but not so much as I thought at first."

"I bet. You said he was good-looking. It's true. His hair is always smooth, with an absolutely straight parting, and mine's just a mass of cowlicks."

"Is it?" she said, as though she had not noticed, and ran the tip of her finger quickly over one of the little tufts above his forehead. "Never mind. Cowlicks are fun."

They had reached the gate. He found himself wishing they had gone back through the maze again, and then it would have taken longer.

"Heavens, a horse!" cried Toni as she caught sight of

Silver, who was standing in the shadow of the trees looking as shining as his name. He threw back his head and whinnied when he saw Adolf and Aquarius.

"You can stroke him if you like," said Adolf. "And if you want to ride him a little way, I'll lift you up."

"Ooh, I don't know," she said, wrinkling her nose. "I've never been on a horse. It's so terribly high up there. Can you ride properly, trotting and all that?"

Adolf nodded, climbed up on a stone, swung himself into the saddle, and tried to look as elegant as one of the English gentlemen in the engraving in Uncle Emmo's room. Toni caught her breath at his skill. Georg can go and boil his head, thought Adolf. The girl made no move to go back to the house. "You've got two aunts," she said. "We've got only one. What do you have aunts for when you've a mother?"

"Well, you see, Papa was married before, and then his wife died and they came to look after him. It's an awfully long time ago now, and they've been with us ever since."

She nodded seriously. "Just the same with us. Aunt Käthchen came to look after Mama when she was so ill. She's her sister, you see. And then when she died, she stayed with us. We were very small then. It's a good thing there are aunts, eh?"

Adolf agreed with her. Luckily, in every family there was an aunt or two who could come to the rescue when needed.

Toni walked out onto the path by the river behind the horse. She looked so tiny beside the big horse, but at last she summoned up courage and stroked Silver's smooth neck, as delicately as she had touched Adolf's tangled hair before, just with her fingertips. "Like silk," she said. "Can you gallop as well?"

"You don't think I always just walk or trot, do you?" He laughed down to her with pride. Admiration had gone to his head a little. "Sometimes when I want, I jump, too, over ditches or hedges. It's easy when you know how. In the beginning, I fell off head first, just once or twice, but now I know how to stay on."

"Ooh!" she said again and put her hands to her eyes, horrified at such daring.

"Of course, Georg can't do it," he threw in casually. "Good-by for now, Toni. You must come and see us soon. Mama told me to ask you, and it's in the letter, too."

"Yes, we'll come soon," she said. "Good-by, Adolf!"

He trotted elegantly away, and she watched him go. When he turned around, she waved at him, the charming little Ariadne with her speckled eyes the color of larks' eggs.

Summer III

IN SUMMERS to come, whenever Paula passed an orchard and smelled the scent of ripe fruit, she could remember the summer of 1866 as if it were yesterday.

Under the chestnut tree by the steps leading from the side wing into the garden sat the aunts, each swathed in a large white apron, stripping red currants off their stems with forks into a large bowl. In the kitchen, the jelly was being made. The deep red juice simmered in the copper cauldron; bees hummed in through the open window, attracted by the sweet smell. When bubbles rose to the surface in the cauldron, it was time to throw in the pieces of sugar loaf, which had been broken up by one of the boys. This was done in a yellow chopping box with a knife that came down like an ax again and again until the pieces were small enough. In the storeroom, there still stood a long row of pointed sugar loaves wrapped in blue paper, each weighing ten pounds; by the end of the summer, there would be none left.

Once the sugar had dissolved, the froth could be taken off, and a little later a few drops had to be tested to see if the juice would set. The glass jars, covered with a clean cloth, stood ready to receive the boiling-hot juice. Once it had cooled, a little round of pergament paper soaked in rum was placed on top. Finally, the jars were covered over with squares of old linen and tied firmly.

The abundance seemed never-ending. Everything was ripe at once. Green gooseberries for fruit tarts had been put into empty wine bottles, covered with water, and sealed at the beginning of June. The blue stone jar, which was the rumpot, was already a quarter full of fruit, and whatever ripened in the garden was added to it with a spoonful of sugar, crushed fine in the mortar, sprinkled on top, then Jamaica rum poured on until everything was covered. In winter, when the fruit was thoroughly saturated with rum, it tasted wonderful with the boiled beef that was served as an *hors d'oeuvre* on Sundays.

Apart from syrups, jellies, and jams, Frau Margarete also made red-currant, black-currant, and gooseberry wines. She had an old family recipe that she would not entrust even to her dearest friends. The sweet heavy wine that resulted enjoyed great prestige among their circle, even among the canons of the cathedral chapter.

Tant de bruit pour une omelette! thought Paula, as all this fuss over preserving and wine making went on around her, but at least by now her sense of humor had asserted itself and she could smile at Mama's industriousness instead of shedding tears over it, as she had done at the beginning.

Her thoughts these days were occupied almost all the time with whatever book she was reading, and luckily, there was plenty of time for thinking while she stirred the thick syrups or picked berries in the garden. Sometimes she would hear the happy shouts of the boys from the river as she worked, the splash of the water when one of them was thrown in, or see the blue and silver of the hussar's uniform over the garden wall when the young officer rode past on the beautiful Krimhilt, the boys' delight. But all this was on the fringe of her consciousness. With Uncle Emmo's help, she had come to realize how little she knew of the immense treasure of poetry there was in the world. Now she felt like swallowing it all at once. If Uncle Emmo had not been such a wise and prudent guide, she would probably have ruined her stomach for good on the unaccustomed richness of the diet.

On her father's bedside table, there was always a volume of Goethe; every morning as she dusted, she would hold one of these volumes in her hand, leaf through it for a while, and then lay it aside again with a sigh. What did she know of the greatest poet in the German language? *Dichtung und Wahrheit* in the school edition; *Hermann und Dorothea;* a few ballads; of the plays only *Torquato Tasso, Egmont,* and little else. In Nancy she had read mainly French and some English literature, and this also had been carefully selected. At the moment, Papa was reading Goethe's play *Iphigenie auf Tauris* aloud, while the ladies kept on with the unending task of stripping the berries from the stems every evening. Paula was so entranced that she could think of nothing else all day long. Recently, too, she had discovered the love poems of the young Goethe. She had learned them by heart and recited them as she worked, whenever she was on her own:

> *"Wie herrlich leuchtet*
> *Mir die Natur!*
> *Wie glänzt die Sonne!*
> *Wie lacht die Flur!"*

Her heart beat faster at this stormy and yet tender outpouring of love's exaltation in which the whole of nature joined. If it could happen to another young heart, then it might happen to her, too. In the evening, she would often sit for a long time at the window of her room. The moon was mirrored in the river, the heavy scent of the meadows wafted over to her, and the crickets chirped their monotonous song. Then she would repeat to herself softly the words of Goethe's poem, "An den Mond." A sadness swept over her, a longing for she knew not what, a premonition of how much there might be waiting for her at each corner of life. Every line of these poems throbbed with the power of life itself: the joy and the tears, the happiness and the despair, the anticipation and the renunciation. Was she ready to experience it all and pay the price? She did not want Mère Celeste to think that she was one of those feeble souls who sought an escape from life in entering a convent. If she took the step, she would take it with open eyes. But more and more she became aware of the danger, her very personal danger: self-deception, vague doubts. She felt that the time had come to speak to her confessor about it as Mère Celeste had long ago advised.

The wise old parish priest Father Meinert had looked after the spiritual welfare of the grown-up members of the family ever since they had come to Limburg. After Paula had broached the subject, he remained silent, surprised at how carefully the child had kept her struggles and her plans hidden from him up till now. Paula was beginning to think that he had not understood when at last he answered her.

"You are still very young, my daughter," he said. "Wait a while. You do not know yourself yet. If the Lord has chosen you, He will call you. For the moment, your appointed task is to be a good daughter and sister and a comfort to the old people in your parents' house—for, believe me, old age has need of consolation." He lapsed once more into silence behind the curtain of the confessional and in this silence recollected all he had learned of his penitent in the last few months: her impatience, her rebellious feelings toward her energetic mother; the common failings of a young and spirited temperament that like new wine was still fermenting; a passionate heart that had not as yet found its lodestar. "I wish you to practice charity," continued the old priest, "constantly to practice charity, my child. Charity toward your nearest and toward those far off, to the poor whom your good mother sends you to visit and whom you may sometimes find repulsive. Poverty is not beautiful to look upon. It doesn't smell nice; it tastes bitter even to those who only see it from the outside; it offends our aesthetic feelings. I give you nothing else for your penance today than the practice of charity. Test yourself daily in the here and now; you can safely leave the future in God's hands. Enjoy the beautiful things in the world around you. Joy is an important food for the soul, particularly when we share it with others; and piety without joy is a sad sort of piety."

Here was further food for reflection. She knew that one of her faults was to take offense easily. Mama's justified reproofs hurt her out of all proportion, and then her thoughts were far from charitable. The boys' noise was still a constant source of irritation. The dear aunts got on her nerves when they continually admonished her about her health and her complexion, things about which she felt little concern. And what became of charity when old Babett held her back with her never-ending tales, when her only thought was of finishing a book or doing some job in the garden so she could let her mind wander. Now that she began to think about it, she was shocked to find a lot of omissions at the end of each day. The thought of confessing her failings to a severe novice master each evening when she became a nun made her shudder. Her fellow novices, in front of whom she would confess, might be far ahead of her on the stony path to a saintly life.

At table, the young hussar now occupied the place where the major had formerly sat, on Mama's left. He was a guest, albeit an uninvited one. Mama took care that he had everything he needed; everyone at the table did his best to see that he was included in the conversation. Once again it was the boys who saw to it that the talk did not lag. They had hundreds of questions to ask the lieutenant, and this time it wasn't only the little ones but the older brothers, too, surprisingly enough, August most of all. Herr von Quitzow seemed to have a special liking for him.

It suddenly occurred to Paula that she had not put any flowers in the guest's room, and Mama had not reminded her to do so this time. Was this not failing in charity, too? She had told herself that flowers were going beyond what was due to the representative of a foreign power with which they had not even yet signed a peace treaty. At the same time, she harbored a faint suspicion that personal feelings of resentment had something to do with it. The business with the broken eggs had been such a ridiculous beginning to their acquaintance that she felt justified in some slight resentment. It was true that the boys had gone over to the enemy with all flags flying—all except perhaps Adolf. But the magnetism of the elegant, courtly officer and his splendid horsemanship seemed to be gradually having an effect on him, too.

At table, Paula now took pains to look after the two youngest boys with increased zeal. Mama never needed to remind her now to fill up their mugs with milk any longer, to indicate with a glance that Ferdinand's elbows had to be inconspicuously removed from the table, or to tell her to watch that Karl really ate his vegetables and did not merely pouch them in his cheeks and get rid of them later in the wide open spaces. In between these duties, she kept her gaze fixed on her own plate, since whenever she looked up, she met the eyes of the young officer gazing at her in a disconcerting way, sometimes seriously, sometimes with a little smile. It was the smile that irritated her. Was he remembering their first encounter? Or was something wrong with her—a lock of hair come loose, her collar crumpled, or a speck from the kitchen range on her nose? She turned her head quickly toward Ferdinand on the right or Karl on the left or looked straight down at her own plate.

In the stable, the two Prussian thoroughbreds got on well with Silver, who after all was no more than a simple country horse. The boys got on equally well with the officer's orderly. Adolf was able to learn a lot from him when they were both rubbing down the horses in front of the stable door. But the other boys, too, were now to be found in the stable more frequently than before. The lieutenant's orderly was called Orje Priske. They learned that Orje was Berlin dialect for Georg. He was the first Berliner they had ever come across, and everything he said or did was new and funny to them. When he rubbed down a horse with his cap stuck on the back of his head, whistling a march or a soldiers' song as he worked; when he saluted the lieutenant smartly and made some report or other in his twangy voice; when he rode out ready for duty on Vulcan in full uniform, lance and all, he could be sure that admiring glances followed him. They found out that the lieutenant's mare Krimhilt came from the famous Trakehn stud and had a pedigree as long as any nobleman's family tree. When the lieutenant didn't need his horse for duty and had no time to go for rides on his own, Orje would sit the two small boys on Vulcan and lead him alongside by the bridle while he himself rode Krimhilt. This won their hearts completely! Their own language rapidly took on an equestrian, Prussian flavor. The drummer-boys of the Nassau army that they had envied so fervently not long ago were forgotten; as far as Ferdinand and Karl were concerned, the Prussian cavalry was everything.

When the lieutenant went for a ride off duty, he would often ask August to accompany him. They talked together about the noble equestrian art, about German history and the Prussian army. Quitzow spoke of the brilliant prospects that an officer's career offered a young man with the necessary qualities and implied that August had these qualities. Sometimes he would take Georg with him instead of August, but it was clear that he preferred the older boy. Adolf went on riding Silver by himself. Silver was *his* horse, even if he looked a little heavy next to the two elegant Prussian mounts. "We like Silver, don't we, Aqua?" he said to his dog, and Aqua gave the horse's muzzle a friendly lick, as though to assure him of his unaltered affection.

One day the lieutenant asked, "Why do you never come riding with your brother and me, Adolf? You're a promising young horseman, and your gray is a good mount.

Perhaps I could give you a few tips." Adolf secretly doubted that anyone, even a majestic Prussian hussar, could know more about riding than Janosch. But he soon found out how much he still had to learn, especially in jumping, which he had taught himself in a rough and ready fashion. A riding course with hurdles had been laid out for the hussars on a piece of fallow land, and when he had time, the lieutenant took the boys out with him either for a proper riding and jumping lesson or to watch while he drilled his squadron. "You can learn a lot from watching, too," Quitzow said. Best of all was the riding to music every Wednesday afternoon. Then all the schoolboys in town would gather at the riding course while the regimental band played gay marches or waltzes and the slim young officers rode with perfect skill. All the spectators were agreed that there had never before been such a glorious summer vacation. Often the boys who had friends among the hussars—or in whose home an officer was billeted— would be given a ride on a regimental horse. Then even Hannibal, Caesar, and Alexander, the boys' heroes of previous summers, paled in comparison with the hussars. "*Sic transit gloria mundi,*" said August, their former commander-in-chief, but he, too, voted this the best summer ever.

A few days after Adolf's first meeting with the architect's family, he fetched Fräulein Stritter and the nieces for afternoon coffee in the courthouse garden. The table was set on the terrace by the river in the shade of the acacia tree. It was easy to see that Fräulein Stritter was delighted to have some other middle-aged ladies to talk to at last. She clearly felt lonely out there in the enchanted garden, and on many days she was not well enough to go shopping in the town. Of course she would not consider letting her nieces go by themselves, and her young serving maid wasn't an experienced shopper, either. Only yesterday evening a letter had come from the architect, by the mail coach, which was now traveling regularly once again, with the news that he could not join them for a holiday in the country as had been planned. One of his houses, which he normally rented for the summer to guests who took baths in the hot springs, had been requisitioned by the Prussians as an officers' mess, and it was vital for him to stay in town to make sure everything was all right. Frau von Savigny's house had been rented for the holidays chiefly because of the aunt. She was asthmatic and could not stand the heat of the summer in Wiesbaden. Under the shady trees of the old park, it was never oppressively warm, and even on the hottest days a fresh breeze blew off the river morning and evening.

Frau Margarete and the aunts urged her not to cut short her stay in the country. "We'll gladly send you fresh fruit and vegetables from the garden every few days. Why else have we so many young people in the house? It will be a pleasure for the boys to bring you provisions from the baker or the butcher or grocer whenever you need anything." Mother threw her sons a glance that said clearer than any words: Now don't dare disgrace me! But miraculously they all declared themselves instantly available for the messenger service, although normally they were so busy that they had trouble finding time for their duties in the house and garden. The little ones were for rowing up in the boat, and Georg brazenly offered to ride over daily on Silver to inquire what was needed and how he might otherwise be of service to the ladies. This made Adolf speechless for a moment, especially as he already had his own plans. At the very next opportunity, he must make clear to Georg that it was he who groomed and fed Silver all by himself; so it was only fair that he was the one to decide who should ride him, and, anyway, Georg's equestrian skill was so limited that Adolf would not have trusted him alone with the horse.

When the coffee table had been cleared, Ferdinand and Karl took the three girls into the house to greet old Babett and to visit Uncle Emmo in his library. They weren't allowed to disturb Father in his office, but he had promised to come into the garden later on for half an hour.

"And now," said Paula, who had fetched three baskets from the kitchen, "let's go and pick some fruit."

Followed by the Ippel girls and all the boys, she climbed up to the top terrace where the fruit trees were and where the grape arbor leaned on the graveyard wall. In this garden, there was no maze, no pool with a frog prince or a fat goldfish, only a few toads hopping around among the vegetable beds. Everything here was plain, orderly, useful, and without mystery. The beds were marked out in rectangles with flowering shrubs around the edges, the paths straight as a die; the rose garden without a single withered leaf. Two big mirabelle-plum trees were golden with ripe fruit, and the three little town girls went on eating them until they almost had stomach-aches. Georg obligingly climbed up to the highest branches to bring down the sweetest and ripest plums for them, so full of juice that their skins were already bursting. At last, Adolf seized the opportunity of slipping away with Toni. He had promised to show her the stable that smelled wonderfully of hay and horses. Swallows flitted swiftly in and out of the tiny windows; the Prussian horses were chewing peacefully at their evening meal of hay. Orje was away on duty. Adolf fed Silver and took Toni with him into the stall to show her how gentle and good-tempered he was. She stroked him more confidently this time and gave him a piece of sugar that Adolf had remembered to bring away with him from the coffee table. "Your hand must be stretched out absolutely flat," he explained to her and Silver took the sugar lump carefully with his soft lips from the out-stretched hand. Krimhilt and Vulcan, too, had their share of sugar. Next the goats had to be visited and the pig, lying fat and lazy in his sty. They reached the henhouse just as a hen was announcing to the world with a loud cackle that she had laid an egg. Adolf felt under the hen, which was still sitting on her nest, took out the warm brown egg, and put it into Toni's hand. "If you don't take it away from her, she starts brooding," he explained, and the town child, who up till now had only seen eggs in the market women's baskets or in the kitchen, fingered the newly made product in amazement.

"I guess you know almost everything," she said, and her respect for Adolf's profound knowledge made his heart swell.

"About Silver," he said with feeling. "*I'm* the one that looks after him, and up till now Georg couldn't have cared less about him. I'll teach him a thing or two, the show-off."

"He said he would teach me to ride," said Toni.

"What? He can't even ride himself. I'll teach you, Toni. When I bring the fruit and vegetables, I'll take you up on the saddle in front of me to see what it's like. Nothing can happen to you then. And later on, you may try it by yourself. Don't go with Georg, whatever you do, or you'll fall off and break every bone in your body."

"All right, Adolf," she said docilely. "If I go on a horse at all, then I'll go only with you."

They climbed up into the hayloft from which they could see over the garden where the others were picking mirabelles. They talked about all sorts of things, and Adolf found out why these Nassau girls spoke such pure German without swallowing syllables and with only the slightest hint of local dialect. It was because they went to a private school in Wiesbaden where dialect was not allowed. A very exclusive school that must be!

"Later on," said Adolf, "I'll probably rent or buy the Savigny house. Will you marry me then, Toni?"

"I think I will," she said at once. She was a sensible girl.

"That's settled then!" said Adolf. "But we've got to keep it a secret." That was all right with her, too. But now they were being called from the garden. The baskets were full, and Aunt Käthchen wanted to go home on foot with her nieces. In the cool of the evening, she always enjoyed taking a walk. The boys went with them to take turns carrying the baskets of mirabelles, peas, and beans. Paula took the third basket and started off in the opposite direction toward the town.

"Don't forget to take a few flowers to Frau Mauser," Mama had reminded her. She never sent a gift to her little old women without a spray of flowers from the garden, or a fresh branch of spruce in winter, or a piece of cake, and Paula had come to understand that it was this little touch of luxury—not the necessities—that made the recipient happy.

The long shadows cast by the willow trees lay like black

beams across the yellow gravel of the river path; on the water, a few families of ducks were swimming, inconspicuous brown females with their brood, each accompanied by a magnificent drake. Water hens with their red beaks and a red tuft of feathers on their foreheads dived among the reeds for insects and other small water creatures. Their families, too, were out of the nest by now and took to the water just as confidently as the old ones. Paula stood there watching them for a few minutes before going on her way again. Her long skirt swung to and fro over her black-buttoned boots; the broad rim of her straw hat with its bright band of red poppies, blue cornflowers, and golden ears of corn shaded her face; and since she was going into the town, she wore gloves, white summer mittens crocheted by Aunt Stina.

Frau Mauser, to whom she was taking the basket, was one of a dozen or so of her mother's protégées who had to be regularly visited and cared for. She lived in one of the narrow-fronted houses in Fish Market, high up under the pointed gable. The staircase leading up to her room was so steep and narrow that the old woman only came down it on Sundays to go to Mass, when some of the other inmates of the house helped her. The landlady's children saw to it that there was always enough wood on her hearth and brought up her quarter-liter of milk in the morning and the two rolls that the baker's boy put into one of the white bags that were hung up for that purpose in the ground-floor hall.

"How are you today, Frau Mauser?" asked Paula as she came into the room in which the old woman spent her day from the moment she got up in the morning till she went to bed at night.

"Thanks, Fräulein Paula, quite well," she said. She was

one of those contented people who find something to give them pleasure in every one of their hard days. Her room was neat and clean, and it wasn't difficult to like her. Not all Mama's protégées were like this. "When I heard you on the stairs, I thought: Here comes the Frau Amtmann," she said, and Paula heard the politely suppressed disappointment in her voice. What was it that made them all so pleased to have Mama visit them? Certainly not just the material assistance that she brought. Yet she was no softer with her poor wards than with her own children. She let no one pull wool over her eyes; she asked awkward questions; any little trick to get something out of her was noticed immediately. Women who did not keep their houses clean or who let their children run wild knew she would have something to say about it. Once Paula had been with her when she had hauled a drunken father over the coals. The man was a carter and earned enough for the modest needs of his family. But he drank his money away and even took from his hard-working wife the little she earned by cleaning in various houses in the town. The big, heavy fellow, who could have crushed her with one of his hands, stood there like a schoolboy in disgrace in front of the little woman with the flashing blue eyes, promising that he would reform. He had even kept to it, these last few weeks at least. Probably even his thick skull had sensed the love behind the reproof, which was what Father Meinert had meant when he recommended the practice of charity to Paula as her penance.

"Mama sends her good wishes," she said, "and wants you to have what's in the basket. Only eat it up soon, while it's still fresh. There's more where that came from."

"Thank you indeed," said Frau Mauser, and, "Oh, the

beautiful flowers!" Her wrinkled face lit up. "I'm sure I don't know what I've done to deserve all this in my old age. Your good mother sends me food and flowers, and the Women's Guild pays my rent. And there's no better room in the whole town, either. Just you take a look out of that window, Fräulein Paula. I can even see a little piece of the river down there. And the Herr Ratsschreiber's canary next door here sings all day long for me. If I lean right out of the window, I can push a lettuce leaf in his cage sometimes. I'm mighty glad the mail is traveling again and the carters with their wagons, too. There's always a to-do when they have to squeeze their way through the narrow street. I never get tired of looking down."

Paula sat and listened, throwing in a question from time to time, but she wasn't as good at it as Mama. It was oppressively hot under the slate roof, even though it had grown much cooler outside. And Father Meinert was right: poverty didn't smell nice, even when it was clean poverty. But precisely because of that, she stayed a little longer than she had meant to and listened to Frau Mauser's accounts of her children and grandchildren, some of whom lived in Wiesbaden and some in Giessen and did not often find time to visit her.

When Paula finally set out for home, the shadows of the willow trees had lengthened, and there were red and yellow streaks across the blue-green of the western sky. On the top of the cathedral tower further up the river, a blackbird was singing in the peace of the evening. The water lapped drowsily around the roots of the willows. No one was to be seen, for it was suppertime all over the town. Since there was no chance of meeting anyone, Paula took off her hat and swung it by its ribbon as she went along.

It was good to feel the cool evening air on her forehead. But suddenly she heard footsteps behind her. A man's footsteps! Her first impulse was to put the hat on again quickly, but before it was properly back on her head, the man had overtaken her. Who should it be but Lieutenant von Quitzow!

"Good evening, mademoiselle," he greeted her. Perhaps he had thought she would give him her hand, but she couldn't do that because she was still fussing over her hat, and probably she wouldn't have thought of it anyway.

"Do leave it as it is," he said. "You look delightful. The shadow of the brim across your face is simply ravishing . . ."

"All right, make fun of me if you like," said Paula. "At table, you always look at me as though I had a hole in my stocking."

"But neither at table nor anywhere else can I see your stockings, oh gracious lady!"

She glanced up quickly at him with her big eyes, which were almost black in the shade of the hat, saw his young laughing face, and had to laugh herself. "No, of course you can't see my stockings, Herr von Quitzow. Can one see the ladies' stockings in Berlin?"

"That depends on the ladies," he said. One of the tower clocks struck three times. "A quarter to seven!" he exclaimed. "I know enough of the rules of your parents' house to realize that unpunctuality is one of the unforgivable sins. If we don't hurry, we'll be put in the corner together. However much I would welcome the rendezvous, it would go against my honor as an officer to get a young lady into trouble."

"*Enfin: allons!*"

"*Allons* or quick march, just as you command. Amazing how much French you still hear in the streets here in the Rhineland!"

"That's because of the nearness of the frontier," she said as they hurried along the river path between the willows on one side and the thick undergrowth on the other. For him with his long legs, it was no trouble at all, but Paula, who had been taught that a young lady should walk slowly and modestly in the street, had become unused to running. Suddenly, she stumbled, and though she caught herself immediately, he had already grasped her hand and held it firmly until they were near the courthouse. Breathless, with glowing face and disheveled hair, hat still awry, Paula hurried into the house. The lieutenant pressed her hand quickly, with a conspiratorial glance as if they had been stealing apples together, and went to his room to wash his hands. She intended to put her empty basket back in the kitchen but ran straight into Aunt Rikchen's arms on the way.

"Good evening, Tantchen," she said. "I'm . . . I've . . . I had to hurry terribly not to be late for supper."

"One can see that," said her aunt dryly. "Completely *échauffée!* You have still time to put your hair straight and run a cold sponge over your face. It's poison for your complexion to get so hot, simply poison!"

Late that evening in the boys' room, the inevitable fight between Adolf and Georg took place.

"You want to give Toni riding lessons when you scarcely know how to sit on a horse, you old show-off!" Adolf began the dispute.

"Show-off yourself. Do you think you have a monopoly

on the Ippels just because you took Papa's letter to them?
I knew them long before you."

"Disguised as a guide! It's enough to make a cat laugh."

"A cat perhaps, but not intelligent people. The ladies
were pleased that a person of culture could show them
around the town, I can tell you."

"Did you say *culture!* Well, culture or not, you're not
riding Silver. You never bothered yourself one bit about
him, and now suddenly you want to swank with him.
Keep your dirty hands off my horse and off the girls;
they're far too good for you."

Dirty hands was too much for Georg to swallow, con-
sidering he used so much soap on his well-shaped hands
that it was sheer extravagance. "You can talk about dirty
hands, you and your beastly warts."

This hit Adolf on a tender spot. He jumped out of bed,
took Aquarius by the collar, and led him over to Paula.
The dog had been growling the whole time, and if it came
to blows between Adolf and Georg, he would certainly not
remain neutral.

"Look after him for me a few minutes, will you?" he
said as he pushed the dog into Paula's room, and before
she could ask any questions, he had disappeared again.

Georg was already waiting for him. "Say dirty hands
just once more, old wart hog!"

"Dirty hands, three times!"

They went at one another like fighting cocks. "Just a
minute!" said August from his bed. "You can fight it out
between you; it's been coming for a long time. But keep it
fair and clean; and when I shout stop, there's an end to it."

They fought silently and savagely, and the other boys

watched in silence, too. If there was any noise, Paula would come over or, even worse, Mama would come up from downstairs.

First Georg was down, then Adolf. Blood was already dripping from Adolf's mouth, and Georg's left eye was starting to swell. Suddenly, Georg was sitting on Adolf's chest. "Who rides Silver now?" he gasped. "Say I can ride him and I'll let you go."

"Not you, even if you knock me out cold."

"Say it."

"I won't. I won't."

"Idiot!"

"Even . . ."

At this moment, Adolf managed to throw off the over-confident Georg. They were both up on their feet again, wrestling fiercely. Another two minutes passed, and then Adolf had Georg in a stranglehold. He was bent double, his head in a vice between Adolf's muscular legs, while Adolf seized his arms and twisted them up on his back in a double nelson. No one can stand that for long.

"One, two, three . . ." August counted slowly.

"Say you'll leave Silver in peace or I'll press tighter. The horse and the Ippels, too. Toni, anyway. What about it?"

"You miserable rotter," groaned Georg. "You can keep your wretched horse . . . and your Toni."

"Finish," said August. "He's turning blue." The two combatants went over to the washbowls, still gasping for breath, and washed off the blood and sweat with cold water. No further word was spoken.

The next day two battered and noticeably silent boys sat at the breakfast table; the story of the fight was written clearly on their faces. No questions were asked; their parents knew that the boys would sooner die than betray the cause of the quarrel, and they respected this silence.

Father glanced at Adolf's swollen lip and Georg's many-colored eye and the swollen noses of both boys. "You are to stay in the house and garden until you're fit to be seen in public again," he decided.

Two voices answered, "Yes, Papa."

The air was cleared as after a storm. One thing was obvious; the hostile brothers had made their peace for the time being. That the younger had won this time brought him honor and esteem, even from Georg, who from now on treated him with a certain respect.

Summer IV

EVERY MORNING right after breakfast Ferdinand and Karl disappeared to the stable with the lieutenant to inspect the horses. Together, they made sure the hay was fresh and the mangers clean. The lieutenant lifted up the horses's hoofs to see that no trace of straw or dung had gotten stuck to them; he ran his hand the wrong way over the smooth backs of Krimhilt and Vulcan—and the boys did the same with Silver—which showed quite infallibly whether any dust from yesterday's ride was still there. From one stall to the other, comments were exchanged on horses and horsemanship. During the inspection, Orje stood at ease, a self-satisfied grin on his face, in the corridor between the stalls. He kept his horses in first-class condition. "Nobody can tell me anything when it comes to horses," he had remarked to the boys. All three horses gleamed as though they had been lacquered, for Adolf had groomed Silver, too, before breakfast. When the ceremony was over, each horse was given a sugar lump, the goats a potato, and the pig a piece of stale bread.

"And now come and visit Babett with us," said Karl. "You've promised three times already. Everyone who belongs to the house has to go and see Babett."

The lieutenant gave them to understand that he had one or two other matters to attend to, but. . . . "You think I belong to the house, eh?" he asked. "Very flattering, comrades! Forward then, if we must."

"I'll run on and tell her to put her teeth in," exclaimed Ferdinand and rushed into the house.

The lieutenant had heard so much about Babett that he had gradually become curious. The boys were forever talking about her: Babett says this, Babett says that. Even Gretel, who brought a pan of boiling water for his shaving in the morning and served him tea in his room in the afternoon, sometimes passed on Babett's words of wisdom, which the lieutenant either because of the dialect or because of the obscure meaning often could not understand. Babett seemed to be a sort of family oracle, rather like Pythia of the ancient Greeks, and who could expect a mere mortal to comprehend the sayings of an oracle?

"In November she'll be ninety," Karl told him as they went into the house behind Ferdinand. "If the Prussians hadn't come, she would've gotten a letter and a present from the Duke."

Quitzow laughed. "I can't promise that she'll have any congratulations from H.M. The news will hardly spread as far as Berlin in the time, I fear."

"Who is H.M.?" Karl wanted to know.

"His Majesty the King of Prussia."

"Whew! Do you really know him?"

"Well, distantly," Quitzow said with a boyish grin while Karl knocked at Babett's door. Ferdinand put his head out and said they could come in. Good heavens, a mummy! the young man thought when he saw the figure sitting at the window. She was wearing a fresh white cap on her head, which was probably bald. Her hands with the knitting dropped into her lap as she looked up with red-rimmed eyes at the newcomer. They were the sharp amber eyes of an old owl, and the almost fleshless nose was like its beak. The yellowish dentures behind the thin lips reminded him of the keys of a piano. This showpiece was saved for social occasions only; for actual eating it was not suitable.

Ferdinand had taken up his position beside her chair. "Lieutenant von Quitzow." He made the introduction, and Karl with his liking for fancy expressions added, "He wishes to take the opportunity of paying his respects."

The only thing we need now is a master of ceremonies to rap on the floor with his stick, thought the lieutenant.

"Pleased to make your acquaintance at last, young man," said Babett. "How long is it you've been with us already? Two weeks? Three weeks? Well, sit down. Karlchen, draw the chair up a little. You were fortunate to be billeted in the courthouse, Herr Lieutenant."

"I realize that," he answered politely and looked around the room. Over there Napoleon's death mask was hanging on the wall, an ivy wreath around his white forehead. How young he looked! What peace, what nobility in the face of the man who had flooded a whole continent with blood and war! Was a vanquished conqueror so transfigured when death had spoken its final word? The Prussian lieutenant shook his head; he was still too young to understand with what suffering the purification had been achieved.

"A great general!" he said, and Babett inclined her head as though he had complimented her personally.

From the mask, his glance strayed to the portrait of a man next to it. There was the Bonaparte nose again, but this time in a gentler face and over a weaker mouth. On the yellowing paper, there was a dedication he could not read from his chair.

"Jerome, King of Westphalia," said Babett, who had followed his gaze. "The dedication below was for my own dear lady, Madame la Baronesse Dudon d'Enval. Over there she hangs, and close beside her is her husband, the Capitaine. Handsome but irresponsible. I hadn't the heart to throw him out even if he did leave her high and dry with her child."

"Leave her?" repeated the lieutenant and looked at the boys questioningly. They knew all about it. "He had to go with Jerome to help Napoleon when he came back from Russia," Karl declared.

"Quiet! You two don't understand these things!"

"Yes, we do," Karl insisted. "An officer's got to put his Emperor first, hasn't he, Lieutenant?"

Babett's stick rapped the floor in annoyance. "You'll hold your tongues now. The poor lady would've died of grief if she'd not had me. We brought the little one up together, and a lovely girl she was. Have a look over there, Lieutenant. That's my madame's daughter on her father's arm, that good-for-nothing Capitaine. When she was nineteen, she became the Amtmann's wife, and in a year she had died in childbed, and my madame soon after her." The mummy-like hand made a gesture that took in all the walls, covered end to end with pen-and-ink portraits, silhouettes, and daguerreotypes. "All dead," she said. "I have them nicely together, so I can talk to them. Sometimes at night they come to visit me."

The lieutenant was silent. What could he have replied

to that anyway? The boys nodded their heads in confirmation. Babett smiled, showing her yellow teeth. "You're a Prussian, young man," she said. "Well, you can't help that. The good Lord made the Prussians, too; he must have had his reasons. French, Russians, Prussians, Saxons, Hessians, Austrians, not to mention the folk here in Nassau—I've known them all. There were good and bad mixed up together everywhere. They come and go. History's like a seesaw, young man; it goes up and down. When you're as old as I am, you don't take it so seriously any longer."

"History, madame, yes indeed," said the lieutenant. "That's why we're here. It's time for a united Germany once again."

"History," repeated the old woman obstinately, "is as inconstant as the moon. Full today, half tomorrow, disappeared the next day; then it starts all over again. It's my opinion the Lord God hung this changing moon up there to make us understand that power grows and wanes. But everyone thinks he gets a personal call from the Lord to set the course of history straight. You Prussians have pocketed Schleswig-Holstein and Hanover and now Hesse and us, and even the ancient free city of Frankfurt. Perhaps you'll keep it fifty years, perhaps a hundred; then someone else'll come along and change it all over again. Before Him, as you'll perhaps have learned even in your Prussian schools, a hundred years are but a day. But you can tell your Bismarck one thing from me: he'd better leave the Church alone. She's nearly two thousand years old, and in history that's quite a nice piece of time. Others than Bismarck have broken their teeth on her before now."

"Your message will be delivered, madame," said the

lieutenant. "You need have no worries on that score, anyway. As long as the Roman Church makes no attempt to
claim secular power, she has nothing to fear from Bismarck."

"Glad to hear it," said Babett.

Holy thunder, thought the lieutenant! She sits there
like a sibyl talking about world history as if she had seen
it all personally. And what was he, a lieutenant of the King
of Prussia, doing in this room, which was itself just like a
piece of history, with pictures of the dead on all the walls,
nothing but the dead. He shivered suddenly, although the
sun shone warmly through the window. He stood up. His
sword clattered; the spurs on his high riding boots clicked
together.

"It was a pleasure, Lieutenant," said Babett graciously.
"Look in another time. And there's one thing more I have
to say to you—take good care that our boys don't fall off
when you're teaching them all your riding tricks."

"If we want to be officers, we've got to learn to ride,
Babett," said Ferdinand stoutly.

"So it's officers you want to be now, is it? A few weeks
ago, it was drummer-boys. But if you break your necks
first, it won't matter one way or the other."

"I'll see to it that they stay in one piece, madame. We've
need of such splendid lads."

"H.M.," said Karl importantly. "The King of Prussia
needs us."

"Kings and commanders always need cannon fodder.
Look at Napoleon. All he needs now is a fresh wreath; he's
grown more modest. Remember to get some ivy when
you're out in the garden, children."

The lieutenant bowed once again from the door. "It was a pleasure, madame. *Auf Wiedersehen.*"

"God willing and we're still alive," answered Babett; it was like a damper on his Prussian bravado.

What a land he'd been sent to, thought young Quitzow when Karl had closed the door behind them! What a house in which an old woman thought she could explain world history to him! In Berlin he knew no one whom the dead visited at night; nor did he know any children who would listen to all that stuff as if it were the most natural thing in the world. Well, Berlin was the future and all this was past; a bit of queer old-world country life on which they would soon shed the light of reason. But the boys had to be won for the future, and for Lieutenant von Quitzow the future meant Germany. They would make magnificent officers.

"We must go now to do some weeding in the garden," said Ferdinand, and they ran on ahead together. The lieutenant followed more slowly, so deep in thought that he almost bumped into Paula in the narrow corridor of the side wing as she was on her way to Babett's room. Were all their meetings going to start with a collision?

"*Pardon, mademoiselle!*" he said and stepped back against the wall to let her pass. His hand touched her fingers as she did so. They exchanged a quick smile, and then she had disappeared into the room of ghosts. Well, at least she was alive, and no one could prevent him from enjoying the fact.

"Here's some more wool, Babett," said Paula, a little breathlessly, and laid the ball in the old woman's lap. "Mama thought you needed more."

"Of course I do. The lads' feet get bigger and their legs

longer all the time, and the wool's never enough. And how are you looking, my sweet? A bit of color in your cheeks at last. But perhaps that's because of the young goldfinch who has just paid me a visit?"

"What sort of goldfinch?" asked Paula, really going red this time.

"Goldfinches are colorful birds and so is the hussar, eh? Blue and silver and easy on the eye. But don't look at him too much, my girl, d'you hear?"

"Dear Babett, I have other things to do than stare at Prussian soldiers," said Paula with dignity. "Shall I close the windows? It's going to be hot today."

"Yes, close the windows and open the door into the kitchen. Today we're having potato dumplings, and they'll be as hard as rocks if I don't keep my eye on them."

"What would we do without you, Babett?" said Paula and laid her smooth cheek against the old woman's wrinkled one.

"That's what I'd like to know," grunted Babett. She needed a little appreciation from time to time, as dried-up plants need watering.

Later when Paula was standing on the ladder in the garden picking the last apricots, she had time to shake her head over Babett's sharp old eyes, which never missed a thing. Farther down the garden, Ferdinand and Karl were weeding between the young Brussels sprouts.

"Isn't the hour over yet?" they shouted up to her. "We want to go down to the riding course to watch. The older ones have gone, and Philipp and Hannes have whistled for us twice already."

"Let them whistle. You've hardly even started."

"It's all right for you to talk. Picking apricots is far nicer than this beastly weeding."

"But if you did it, there wouldn't be any left over. Come on up. You can each have one since it's so hot."

They came bounding up the steps, stretched out their earthy hands, and then took a big bite out of the ripe apricots so that the juice ran down their chins and dripped onto their bare chests.

"Thanks, Paula," said Karl. "Two would refresh us even more, and then we really could get on with the work better."

"Here's one more for each of you. But I don't want to hear another word from you now until the hour's up."

They withdrew. Halfway back, Ferdinand stopped and shouted, "This afternoon the lieutenant's giving us lessons in vaulting on a trotting horse. All five of us. Are you coming to watch?"

"Get on with the work. Vaulting's just about all you need. Don't forget to wash your hands before you go."

She broke off each of the golden crimson-tinged fruits carefully and laid it in the basket, which she had hung from the top rung of the ladder. They mustn't be pressed or dropped or they would be bruised and no longer any use for preserving in jars. The overripe ones had to be used immediately. Luckily, there was no shortage of takers. Almost daily a basketful was given to Father Meinert, who had no garden of his own. Mama's protégées were provided for, too, and Adolf or Georg took Fräulein Stritter all she needed—Adolf on Silver or on foot, if Father had taken the horse; Georg in the boat. There was such an overwhelming abundance of fruit this year that all hands were busy gathering it in. Wherever you went, the gardens smelled of ripe fruit; out of every kitchen window wafted the steaming sweetness of fruit cooking; and on what was left too high on the trees to be picked, the sparrows, blackbirds, and wasps made their midsummer feast.

Vaulting! thought Paula as she filled her basket. Does he really have to teach them new ways of breaking their necks when we all give a sigh of relief every evening to see all five of them sitting more or less unharmed around the table! Karl and Ferdinand ran after him as though he were the Pied Piper of Hamelin. Through their friendship with Orje, their already varied vocabulary had become even more colorful. With their familiar Nassau dialect were now mixed all sorts of Berlin sounds, not always to the grownups' pleasure. The older boys were more inclined to take the young officers from the riding course as their models and try to imitate their bearing and expressions. Georg, in particular, could say, "Phenomenal!" "Colossal!" "Fantastic!" through his nose; he would click his heels and touch an imaginary cap in salute with two fingers, as he had seen the young lieutenants do. Yesterday as he and August were pouring watering-cans full of river water on the beds, Paula had heard them discussing a project of the Prussians to set up a cadet school in nearby Schloss Oranienstein.

When the cathedral bells chimed out at noon, Paula had filled two big baskets with apricots and one with mirabelles. In the afternoon, she intended to pick the first really ripe peaches from the trellis along the upper wall and put them on her father's desk. All the others had to have a plate of fruit taken to them, too. "All?" she asked herself and, "Of course, all of them," she answered. It would not be right or hospitable to make exceptions.

When she went up to the living room to lay the table, the aunts were already sitting in their usual armchairs at one of the bay windows, while the Amtmann with Uncle Emmo was standing at the other. Every day before the meal was served, they would have a brief midday chat together, and if Paula could manage it, she liked to stand there listening quietly. Just now they were discussing icons, and Paula had only a very hazy idea of what icons were. "Konrad Overberg is back from Russia," she heard her uncle say. "More than a month earlier than he intended. He was worried his father would have difficulties about billeting, which fortunately wasn't so. Quite unexpectedly, he sailed into my room this morning; sends his compliments to everyone. You must come and have a look at the icons he's brought me, Jacob."

"Thank you for the greetings, Emmo," said Aunt Rikchen. "You surely weren't in the garden without a hat, child? Your mother shouldn't let you work so much in the garden, anyway."

"But I do prefer garden work to housework, Tantchen," said Paula. "And under the fruit trees, there's so much shade that I don't need a hat."

"Enough sun filters through to spoil your complexion!" That was Aunt Stina, if anything even more worried than Aunt Rikchen. "Be a good girl and put a compress of distilled rain water on your face straight after the meal. The Empress Eugénie . . ."

But at this point, the lieutenant came in, surrounded by the boys, who gave an enthusiastic account of the cavalry practice they had been watching, and put an end to any disclosures about the Empress Eugénie. "With music!" exclaimed Karl. "One of them had a drum on the horse with him. Potdrum it's called."

His brothers burst out laughing. "Kettledrum, blockhead, not potdrum!" Georg corrected him. But August nudged him in the ribs and threw a warning glance to the two little ones. They didn't have to enthuse about the Prussian army within the family circle.

At table, the conversation turned back to icons once again, a good neutral subject. Paula listened with great attention, as she wanted to learn more about this art form of which so far she knew very little. She had the impression that the same was true of Herr von Quitzow as far as ignorance about icons was concerned. He put a polite question, and Uncle Emmo began to explain. The older boys, too, were eager to find out all about them, and so there was a far livelier conversation during the meal than usual.

After dinner, when the calm of the afternoon had descended on the household, Paula climbed up to the farthest terrace, a book under her arm. She had not made a compress of distilled rain water. What an idea to waste her precious rest hour with such nonsense! The aunts and Uncle Emmo withdrew to their rooms after dinner for their afternoon rest. The parents were sitting together over a cup of coffee in the living room before Papa went down to his office again. A greenish light came in at the wide-open windows, filtered through the thick foliage of the old trees; the scent of roses blew in from the garden, although the month of roses and the summer solstice were already past.

"My roses have never bloomed so long or so luxuriantly as this year," said Margarete to her husband, and each knew what the other was thinking: that it would probably be their last summer in this beloved house in which they and the children had been happier than in any other.

The grape arbor up by the cemetery wall was an ideal place for solitude at this time of day. It was so still that one would think some of the timeless peace of the graves had spread over the old damp graveyard wall. The vine dated back to the time of the monks. With the years, it had become as gnarled as an old farmer's hand, but every fall it bore a small harvest of sweet golden grapes. In its deep shadows were two old garden seats and a round table, the top of which had once been a millstone. Paula put her book on it and, before she opened it, listened for a few minutes to the silence. She heard the boys on the river and the clatter of plates from the kitchen, accompanied by the voices of the maids who were singing in a slow drawl and with great feeling the song of the three lilies:

> "O rider, O rider, let the white lilies be,
> In their beauty and bloom for my sweetheart to see."

Orje, a rider himself, sat in front of the stable and accompanied the tune on his mouth organ. It all sounded so muted and distant that it made the quiet seem even quieter.

The lieutenant sometimes went for a walk in this peaceful hour after the midday meal, and when he passed through the garden and over the cemetery, he looked into the arbor and exchanged a few words with Paula. Once she had given him a ripe apricot, and he had seemed as pleased as a boy with the sweet golden fruit. He had kissed her hand gallantly—or rather just the tips of her fingers.

How much easier life was in summer! The cold and early darkness of the winter months drew the family together in the few heated rooms. Now their world was larger. The arbor in which Paula spent the siesta hour was like a room of her own in which no one disturbed her as she read or wrote letters or simply sat thinking her own thoughts.

She felt freer, much more her own master now that she had learned to organize her duties, to do what had to be done without waiting for an order. She didn't forget so much since she had become accustomed to the well-established routine of the big household. Understanding its needs made it easier for her to satisfy her mother's requests, instead of feeling too much was being asked of her. Only lately had she realized that Mama made the heaviest demands on herself. One difficulty remained—that she and Mama were so different, in temperament, in disposition, in what each one considered important or trivial. But was this really so very important? Couldn't they be tolerant of one another like Papa and Uncle Emmo, who had different opinions on so many things and yet got on so well together?

Recently she had made yet another discovery that had given her food for thought. She got on better with men than with women. When she did copying for her father and sat talking to him for a while afterwards, or when she talked to Uncle Emmo while she dusted his bookcase, she felt relaxed and free from cares; the French word *à l'aise* best expressed her mood. When she had a chance to glean something of the conversations that her father and Uncle

Emmo had in the garden in the evenings with the canons,
the doctor, and other gentlemen of mature years, she was
far more interested than in the talk of the ladies around
Mama's coffee table. And with Father Knodt, who as a
relative of the family sometimes came to supper, she
talked more readily and animatedly than with girls her
own age. This realization put further doubts in her mind,
for if she really went into the convent, her life would be
spent exclusively in the company of women and, under the
strict rule of obedience, it was women she would have to
obey. The idea did not appeal to her. It was strange, too,
how the radiance of these summer days made her memo-
ries of Nancy fade. Was it possible to forget so quickly
something that only a short time ago had been her whole
life?

But now she opened her book. If she was not careful,
her precious free time would slip by without her having
read anything. Uncle Emmo had given her Heinrich von
Kleist to read. "He is the most Prussian of all German
writers," he had said, "and with things as they are, we have
every reason to learn to understand the Prussians. Here, in
Prinz Friedrich von Homburg you have everything: the
glory and the hubris, the strength and the danger of
absolute obedience. A splendid play that you should read."

Indeed, she found that such was the quality of the
dramatist's writing that, after a few pages, she had a clear
picture of the prince in her mind without realizing that it
seemed strangely familiar. This was no figure of paper and
printer's ink but a man of flesh and blood who demanded
one's sympathy and interest. She liked him; with every
page she liked him more, this cavalry general of the Great
Elector of Brandenburg, young, handsome, burning with

ambition, enthusiastic about the idea of a growing state that still had to struggle for its existence. And what a lover! When he kissed his betrothed, Paula caught her breath and trembled, as though it were she that had been kissed. By contrast, for the Elector, uncle of the girl the prince loves and his commander-in-chief, Paula conceived a definite dislike. After a bloody battle in which the prince fights valiantly and the Elector's forces are victorious, Paula felt certain the prince would be given the hand of his betrothed in marriage. Instead, because the brilliant young general had led his riders in the attack without waiting for the command, he is ordered by the Elector to give up his sword and is led off a prisoner. The tribunal will sentence him to death, and neither his friends nor his beloved Natalie will be able to save him.

At this point, Paula could read no more. Everything in her rebelled against this kind of justice. She felt the agonies of the prince facing death as though they were her own. She hated the Elector, despised this inhumanity that recognized no other law than that of blind obedience. It was too much for her defenseless heart; tears of anger and pity fell on the old stone table in the arbor.

Suddenly, she heard a voice close to her saying, "For heaven's sake, my dear demoiselle, whatever has happened?"

"There, read that," she said, without even feeling ashamed that he should see her so out of control of herself. "Read that—or do you know this terrible play?"

He sat down on the edge of the table and looked into the open book. "Oh, yes," he said, taking out his handkerchief— it smelled of saddle leather and horses and *eau de Cologne*—and dabbing her tears with it. "But take comfort, *ma belle;* you haven't read to the end yet."

"I can't read any more," she sobbed. "And I don't *want* to."

He put his arm around her and went on dabbing her eyes with his white cambric handkerchief. "But listen a moment. True, I don't know much about literature. As a professional soldier, I have to occupy myself with other kinds of books. But of course I read Kleist's *Prinz Friedrich von Homburg* when I was a cadet, and afterwards I saw it on the stage in Berlin. A fantastic play! If only you would read on to the end, I'm sure you would agree with me. You can imagine that Natalie goes and begs the Elector on his behalf, can't you? And the Elector is ready to pardon him. There is only one condition attached to his pardon: he must sign a document declaring that he finds his sentence unjust."

"Thank goodness for that!" Paula sighed with relief.

The lieutenant hesitated for a moment. He was reluctant to cause her further sorrow, if only for a moment. "Remember that he cannot sign it without lying."

"Lying?"

"Of course, for at bottom he knows that his sentence is just. Don't forget, he *had* attacked too early and against the Elector's strict command. He cannot buy back the favor of the Elector, or even his own life, with a lie; that would offend all his principles of honor and decency. You must understand, my dear, that if he is challenged on this point, he has to admit the justice of his sentence."

"What a mean trick for the Elector to play on him!" said Paula, quivering with indignation.

"You still don't understand. Prince Friedrich doesn't sign the document, he can no more sign it than I or any of my companions would. No, challenged to the core of his being, he now accepts his fate like a man; he can look death in the face as he has done a hundred times before on the battlefield. His eyes are bound, and he is taken away. On the way to execution, he pauses for a moment to rest in the garden of the castle. Suddenly, the officer of the guard takes the bandage from his eyes. He looks around, he is dazzled by torches, the whole court is gathered around him, and Natalie—Natalie presents him with the gold chain and the wreath of the victor, for he has now won a victory over himself and the Elector has pardoned him. Are you satisfied now, little Paula?"

She had to draw deep breath before she could speak again. "Satisfied?" she said. "To put someone through the agonies of death first and then make all that fuss with wreaths and torches and forgiveness! No, if this is masculine logic, I don't want any part of it. This Great Elector of yours was a despot and a cruel Prussian monster."

"Just a moment! The Great Elector you seem so angry with was not, as it happens, a Prussian. He was a Hohenzollern, and his family's ancestral castle is in the south, in Swabia. The first Hohenzollern came into the March of Brandenburg in about 1400, sent by King Siegesmund to create order there and teach the wild barons some manners. The Quitzows were the wildest of them all. Robber barons, highwaymen, I suppose you'd call them today. Great fellows! The Hohenzollern had to burn down their castles and hang half a dozen or more of them before the rest would acknowledge their new masters." He laughed. "The Brandenburg robber barons became first-class officer material under the Hohenzollern."

Paula was silent, for she remembered that her own

name had something to do with the proud independence of a bygone age. She was still thinking about the Prinz von Homburg, and even the happy ending of the play could not dispel her feelings of disgust at the Elector's behavior.

Good Lord, thought the lieutenant! Here's this child weeping for a man who's been dead two hundred years. He could think of no girl or woman in Berlin society—and he knew a fair number of them pretty well—who would have reacted with such passionate sympathy.

"Little Paula!" he said and took her face in his hands. Her eyes, still liquid with tears, looked reproachfully at him, although he really could not be blamed for what happened in the play. He saw now for the first time that those beautiful eyes were not black, as he had thought, nor brown like her brothers', but a soft, deep gray. There were two tears still glistening on her long lashes, and since he was one of those men who ride to the attack without waiting for an order, he did not bother to pick up his handkerchief, which lay white and fragrant on the table, but drew her slim shoulders closer and kissed the tears away, and since it was not far from her eyelashes to her mouth, he kissed that, too.

Paula did not resist. For a moment, time stood still. Then she gently released herself from his arms, stood up, and took the basket, which she had left there that morning. "Please go now, Herr von Quitzow," she said, breathless still but quite firm. "If I'm not mistaken, you've promised my brothers to teach them vaulting this afternoon. I can't say that I approve—but even robber barons, I think, ought to keep their promises."

"Unquestionably." He took her hand and kissed the tips

of her fingers as he had done when she had given him the apricot. *"Adieu, ma belle chérie,"* he said with great tenderness.

In her light summer dress, she went out into the bright afternoon sunshine, her basket on her arm, her book in her hand, very straight, only her head under its heavy tresses tilted slightly to one side. He watched her go. Then he was down the steps in a few bounds. In front of the stable, the boys were waiting for him, the three horses already saddled. As he felt for his handkerchief, he realized that he had left it lying on the stone table.

Autumn I

AT THREE o'clock that afternoon, Paula came into her father's room with the peaches she had just been picking. He looked up from his files. "The first ones? How thoughtful of you, Paulinchen!"

"I remember from before how much you like the ones from that tree," she said. How far away this "before" now seemed!

"Can you do some writing for me?"

"Yes, oh yes, I'd love to!" She would have to concentrate while she was writing, and there was nothing she needed more urgently than that just now.

At four o'clock, she took tea in to Babett and then to the aunts, with freshly baked apricot tarts, for overripe fruit had to be used up. Babett was complaining about her rheumatism and prophesied a storm, even though there was not a single cloud in the sky. "Put my brick in the oven to heat while there's still some warmth left in it; there's a good girl," she said. "I'll be needing it later on today—you just see if I won't."

The aunts were worried about a mouse that had disturbed them the previous night with its gnawing and scurrying about. They discussed all the possible means of getting rid of mice. Poison or traps were dismissed as being too cruel; here in their own room, at any rate, the aunts would not hear of using them. Uncle Emmo might well have loaned them Nicki for a night, but everyone in the house knew what a spoiled cat he was; he had no need to go out of his way to earn his daily mouse. Aquarius, who was a great hunter of rats, weasels, and martens, would have made more disturbance with his mouse hunt than the mouse itself.

"If you could find the hole and stop it up, Paula, I'm sure that would be the best solution," suggested Aunt Rikchen.

"Then at least we wouldn't need to reproach ourselves with having killed the poor little animal," said Aunt Stina. "I'm sure you'll be able to find the hole. It must be behind the cupboard. Or perhaps underneath it. Or I wonder if it's behind the chest of drawers?"

Paula crawled about on her hands and knees for some time before finally finding a hole. Whether or not it was *the* hole, they wouldn't know until the next night. She fetched some old rags, poured petroleum on them, and stuffed them into the hole. The aunts were relieved and most grateful. "Just think if the little beast should nibble at my manuscripts!" Aunt Stina said.

Paula sat down with them for a moment, poured out their tea, and laid a napkin on their knees. How old they are, Paula thought! Not so old as Babett, who was a relic of a bygone age, but still very old. How terribly sad it must be to be old, she felt with a sudden flash of insight. There they sat, the two of them, yet they had been young once and must perhaps have experienced the bittersweet felicity of love and been kissed by a man. Aunt Stina for sure, for there was that picture of the young officer on the wall, the one she had loved and who had been killed in battle half a century ago. And now she wrote novels that no one ever read, telling herself stories that she hadn't had a chance of experiencing. And when she read them to her sister, they were moved by the joys and sorrows of imaginary people. Their lives were over; they had nothing more to hope for, or so, at least, it seemed to Paula, and suddenly she felt a warm, sad sympathy for her aunts. How right Father Meinert had been when he said old people needed consolation! She embraced them and kissed their faded cheeks. "Now enjoy your tea and your tarts," she said, and the casual words sounded like a declaration of love.

Next she went to the kitchen to fetch Uncle Emmo's tea. When she went into his room with the tray, Konrad Overberg was sitting there, and she had to go back again for a second cup and plate. Konrad Overberg? But Uncle Emmo had said that he had been there that morning. It appeared that he had been kept in town all day on business and had just looked in for a moment before going back to Bad Ems. "I must have smelled that there were fresh apricot tarts in the courthouse today," he said.

"How was Russia?" Paula asked. Not that she was much interested in Russia right now, but when someone had been on such a long journey, it was only polite to ask.

Overberg readily told them about Russia, about the Crimea, Moscow, St. Petersburg, about a Russian Orthodox convent to which he had had a letter of recommendation. He was a good and vivid narrator, and Paula listened. She looked at him occasionally, and as she did so, he discovered what someone else had noticed before him— that her eyes were a lovely soft gray, a tender gray, thought young Overberg. Her face was tilted to one side as she listened; a loose strand of hair fell over her forehead, a result of her mouse hunt, and heightened the impression she gave of eager attention. He had no means of knowing that today her thoughts were far from Russia and far from the narrator, too.

"At long last a woman who can listen," said Overberg to Uncle Emmo after Paula had gone out again; she still had plenty to do before the evening meal. "Mademoiselle Paula has changed a great deal since last winter, by the way."

"Children grow up," said Uncle Emmo. "I've been devoting myself to the task of widening her somewhat one-sided education a little, at least as far as literature is concerned."

As much as Konrad Overberg admired literature, he doubted that the change he had noticed could be due to that.

Paula made up another basket of fruit and vegetables for Fräulein Stritter. There was now a lively traffic between the two houses; the ladies at the courthouse enjoyed Fräulein Stritter's company, and the three girls found it much nicer to pick fruit in the Eisenberths' garden or watch the boys doing their daredevil jumps into the river than to play by themselves in the gloomy garden of Frau von Savigny's house. How often Adolf went out to the house on his morning rides and how often there was a little white figure waiting for him by the gate there, nobody knew!

"Here's the basket for the Ippels," said Paula after she had run him to earth in the stable. "Would you mind riding over there and leaving it?" He certainly appreciated having a tactful sister.

"I'll walk," said Adolf. "I've already cleaned up Silver for my trip to Montabaur with Papa tomorrow." They were going off for a few days together, and, as always, Adolf was looking forward to it—if only it hadn't meant that he would miss Toni's last few vacation days.

"Are the little ones still in the water?" Paula asked. "It's a wonder they don't grow webs between their toes and fingers in summer!" When Adolf told her that he had left them in the river about an hour ago, she hurried down to fetch them.

"Out you come!" she said. They both had blue lips and crinkled fingertips, but no webs so far. She herded them up to the house, taking good care that they didn't slip away again. "And how was the vaulting?" she asked.

"Colossal!" Karl assured her, and Ferdinand bragged, "The lieutenant said we'd done really great for a first time. None of us broke even the littlest bone. If we practice enough, the lieutenant said we could either join a circus or go to the cadet school in Oranienstein."

"Yes, but they take only good students," said Karl. "Like me, for instance. I'm doubtful about Georg, and *you* would never do, Ferdinand." But Ferdinand, always an optimist, said he still had nearly a year left to become a good student, though he preferred the circus.

The lieutenant had been a cadet also, they told Paula. He was the youngest of five brothers, and they counted them up on their fingers. "There's the eldest who inherits the family property, see? The next two are at the university, but there wasn't enough money left for the two youngest to go and study. Well, they didn't mind; they wanted to become officers, anyway." The boys seemed to know all about the Quitzow family.

At supper, Quitzow's place was empty. He had sent his excuses by Orje. Sometimes he would eat in the evening with his friends at the Golden Goose.

At long last, after the exhausting day, came the moment when Paula was alone in her room. Babett had been right as usual: there was lightning over in the west, and now and again distant thunder rolled behind the hills, sounding like heavy carts making their way along a bumpy road. The window was wide open as the room was still heavy with the heat of the day, and it was good to feel the fresh breeze coming in. The still thick summer foliage of the trees rustled. The row of poplars on the far bank of the river swayed in a wild dance. A few lights were still shining. A dog barked.

"I must think!" Paula said to herself and pressed her hands on her throbbing temples. "Heavens, what has happened to me!" He had taken her off her guard, this descendant of robber barons, but she was too honest to blame him for it. She had not thought for a moment to reprove him as she should have done. No, not for one moment, for it had been sweet to be kissed by him—so overwhelmingly sweet that even now, in remembering it, her heart almost stopped beating under the storm of a passion she could never have anticipated.

But now she would have to collect her thoughts. Arms folded, she walked up and down her room, from the window to the door and back again. The rain had started, and for a while at the window she turned her hot face to its cool touch. Then she closed the window.

What was it Mère Celeste had said in her last letter? She lit the candle and took out the letter. Yes, there it was: "God has given you a clear head and the capacity for

self-criticism. I am surprised to see what little use you are
making of these gifts at present. Your all too vivid imagination is obviously preventing you from seeing your situation in focus. Here lies the danger for you, and you must
overcome it and face the facts in this crucial period of your
life."

What had become of this clear head that Mère Celeste
said she had? Just at the moment, when she needed it
most, it was not much in evidence.

How naïve she and her friends in the convent had been
to believe that the first man to kiss a girl would hurry
straight to her father and ask for her hand. That had been
what had happened in all the noble books they had been
allowed to read in the convent. But would she really have
wanted Quitzow to go and talk to Papa? Good heavens,
how little she knew about marriage and all that it implied!
Nobody had ever told them anything about it. It had been
so remote, so far away—and now it seemed completely
new and frightening. How could she decide about her
entire life in this utter confusion into which she had
fallen? She felt so young, so ignorant, and so vulnerable.

Suddenly, she remembered that Quitzow was a Protestant. The boys had seen him lead a small group of soldiers
of his regiment to the only Lutheran church in town. This
was a crucial point. Besides, didn't he come from a background completely strange to her? He was of Prussian
nobility, which was supposed to be much more exclusive
than that in the southern part of Germany. He belonged
to an army that only lately had come to Nassau as an alien
occupation force! What did she know about him but that
she loved him? And hadn't she had quite different plans
for her future? Or had they, too, been put in question now

after the first encounter with the tenderness of a man? So Mère Celeste, even without knowing about these recent events, was quite right when she said that Paula had let her imagination run away with her.

Outside, the storm had finally broken. Lightning flashed in quick succession over the night sky. Thunderclaps came nearer and nearer. She didn't pay any attention to the storm while her thoughts flared up and died away like the lightning in the dark sky among the racing clouds. If only she could be on her own for a few days, she thought, away from everything and everyone! She needed time to reflect. She knelt down in front of the Madonna on her little shrine. When reason lets you down, only prayer is left.

She had no idea how long she stayed there kneeling. Suddenly, a huge flash of lightning lit up her room with a bluish-white light. At the same moment, the solid house shook with an earsplitting crack of thunder.

From the maids' room came a scream, followed by the murmuring of prayers. Paula knocked on the wall. "It's all right, girls. Nothing happened!"

Then came a knock at her own door, and Adolf entered. "That was a real big one, wasn't it? Did you get a shock, Paulinchen?"

And now Mama's voice from below: "Is everything all right up there? Have you looked into the boys' room, Paula? Are the maids awake?"

"Yes, it's all right, Mama. Everybody is awake. Should I go down to the aunts and Babett? They'll be upset."

"Papa has taken them some Valerian drops. Just wait a minute or two, children, and then go back to bed. I think the worst is over."

Everything was soon quiet in the maids' room. Adolf

sat down on Paula's bed. The rain was falling in torrents now, but the thunder sounded farther away already. They went to the window and looked out, but there was no glow, no fire, to be seen. In that case, they would have heard the fire brigade racing through the streets with clattering hoofbeats and bells shrieking. Michel or his young assistant would have rung the fire bell, and Papa would have gone in to town to see if he could be of help somewhere.

"Go to sleep now, Adolf," Paula said. "How I wish I could go with you and Papa tomorrow!"

"Why not ask if he'll take you? Do! It would be such fun if you came along!"

"We'll see," she said, took off her fichu, folded it neatly, and put it on the chest of drawers. As she did so, something fell out of it, and Adolf bent to pick it up. "Leave it," Paula said, but he had already sniffed at it.

"Gosh, that smells like our lieutenant!" He giggled.

"What an idea!" she said, shoving him out of the door; then she unfolded the handkerchief and looked at it. In one corner of the fine cambric, there was a monogram and, above it, a tiny seven-pointed crown. The robber barons have gone elegant, she thought tenderly, and pressed the handkerchief to her cheek and mouth. Then she put it under her pillow.

At roughly the same time, Lieutenant von Quitzow was sitting with Rittmeister von Bassewitz, a friend and neighbor of his family, in the Golden Goose. Their fellow officers had been wise enough to return to their quarters before the storm broke. Bassewitz was a good deal older than Quitzow, happily married, the father of two sons. He had suspected that his young friend had something on his mind, and so he remained sitting after the others had gone, waiting in silence to see what the trouble was.

"Something has happened, Basso," said Quitzow when the Rittmeister had ordered another bottle of Rudesheimer.

The captain raised his eyebrows. "Debts?"

"Worse: love."

"Nothing new for you."

"This time it's serious."

"I've heard that before, too."

"Don't be so frivolous. I'm telling you, this is something quite different from ever before."

"Of course. You young cubs always think it's the end of the world. I suppose you are talking about the daughter of your involuntary host?"

"Yes! I kissed her."

"Are you crazy? Kissing the Amtmann's daughter, you lout! That could mean a fine scandal, my good fellow."

"Tomorrow I'll go and ask for her hand."

"And what do you propose to get married on if you'll excuse the question?"

"Stop that! I guess he would throw me out, anyway. Imagine his face: a penniless Protestant Prussian officer! A few days ago it was mentioned at the table, in some connection or other, that there had never been a mixed marriage in the family."

"You should have considered all that before, you irresponsible young whippersnapper. You might even have given your parents a thought: members of the nobility with a pedigree older than that of the Hohenzollern; Protestant to the very marrow! Do you think *they* would shout for joy at the thought of a bourgeois Catholic and presumably just as penniless daughter-in-law? You would have to put away your elegant blue tunic and think about some means of feeding a family. Twenty years old and you haven't learned a single practical thing, and now you talk of marrying! No! There's only one solution: clear out, straight away, before you lose your last little bit of horse sense and turn the poor child's head completely."

"What do you mean, clear out, you heartless, dried-up Philistine! I've got to see her again, explain everything to her, say good-by. Can't you understand *that* much?"

"Lieutenant von Quitzow!" This was his superior officer's voice. The lieutenant stood at attention. "*Jawohl, Herr Rittmeister!*"

"You will report tomorrow as early as possible at headquarters in Wiesbaden. It happens that I received an order today to transfer one of my officers to that post. Report to the staff there at six o'clock sharp. Understood?"

"*Jawohl, Herr Rittmeister!*" And after a pause, through his teeth: "You miserable, insensitive . . ."

"All right, boy, calm down. You'll thank me one day. And the young lady, too."

The young lady . . . oh Lord, she wasn't feeling in the least like a young lady, more like an abandoned child. She had never spent such a night in her life before. When she heard her brother August going downstairs first thing in the morning, she got up, bathed her swollen eyes with cold water, and dressed quickly. He had already gone out when she came downstairs, but she met Mama coming across the hall with a basket of freshly cut rosebuds. "The rain has spoiled all the ones that were already in bloom," she said, "but the buds have suffered no harm. Are you off to early Mass?" She lifted up the roses for Paula to smell. "If you wait a couple of minutes, I'll come with you. I just want to put these in your father's room."

"Oh?" said Paula as her mother disappeared. "Oh, I see." Now she knew who it was that put fresh flowers every day before the picture of her father's first wife.

A little while later, they walked up the alley to the cathedral. The morning was wonderfully fresh. As they passed the graveyard, they caught the strong, pure fragrance of wet herbs: lavender, rosemary, thyme. . . . The sky was the palest blue, washed clear by the night's rain. A hint of red shimmered in the east, veiled by the morning haze over the soaked meadows. Birds were singing. Paula saw and heard and smelled it all with an intensity of perception she had never known before.

"Were you going to ask me something just now?" her mother asked her.

"No . . . no. I don't think so," Paula replied.

Her mother took her arm. "All right," she said quietly. Paula gave a quick sidelong glance at the short, rather plump woman who looked so homely by comparison with the beautiful aristocratic girl whose picture hung in Papa's room. But would she, lovely Françoise Dudon d'Enval, still have been so slim and pretty after thirty years and as a mother of six children? She was dead, she could live on forever as a dream of loveliness. The other one, middle-aged now, was alive, and from the bounty of her happiness, she granted the dead girl a place in the memory of the beloved man. It was all very simple and so easy to understand. Only the day before yesterday young Paula would not have been able to understand.

She prayed fervently during Mass, and in doing so,

what she would have to do grew clearer. She must go away. If today and tomorrow and goodness knows how many more times she let herself be swept away by the sweetness of his embrace—and she well knew she would if she stayed—then it would be the end of all reason, and nothing but grief would come of it—for him and for her, for her parents and his parents. Yes, she must go for a few days at least. She needed time to regain her composure, her *contenance,* as Papa called it.

"I've just thought of something I do want to ask you, Mama," she said as she walked back after Mass with her and August.

"Yes, my dear?"

"If you could spare me for a day or two, I'd love to go with Papa and Adolf. I haven't seen all the aunts and uncles in Montabaur for such a long time."

"Good idea!" said August. "You look run down. You sure could do with a few days' vacation, little sister."

"Why not?" Mama said, and brother and sister exchanged a quick glance of surprise at this ready agreement. "I'm sure Papa would be glad to take you. Your good white dress is hanging in the cupboard freshly laundered and ironed. There is sure to be a big family gathering at Montabaur for which you must look your best."

Now they were on their way, and there was no turning back. Up to the last moment, Paula had feared that her resolve would weaken and that she would find some pretext for staying at home. Quitzow had not appeared at breakfast, and Adolf mentioned that the lieutenant and Orje had already gone when he went to the stable to feed Silver this morning. "The horses also. Some training or other," Adolf said. Perhaps it was better that way, thought Paula. And yet she would have liked to see him again, to explain at least with a quick look across the breakfast table that she was not angry with him and that he was not to be angry with her for going away. In a few days, when she came back, she would have mastered her emotions. He must not have the slightest suspicion of how desperately she longed to be kissed by him again. No—no meetings in the arbor, no secrets. She was firmly decided on that. And no one in the family must ever guess what she was feeling. What a help it was now that all the children had learned early to control their feelings! "Control yourself!" Mama would say when one of them cried because he had fallen down or was disappointed about something or had to have a tooth out. Their father need only tap on the table if anyone showed signs of temper or sulks, and say "*Contenance!*" He need not even raise his voice; that was enough.

Self-control was a fundamental principle in the house; with so many impulsive people under one roof, they could not have managed otherwise. And self-control was what she had to regain in these few days. Her abysmal grief was not the only thing she had to master and for which she must find a perspective. Behind it stood the fundamental question of what God was trying to tell her through this experience, for she never doubted for an instant that it had a meaning and that from all this sadness she must distill some wisdom.

"Are you unwell, Paula?" her father asked anxiously.

"A slight headache, Papa. From the storm, I expect. It will soon pass."

His calm, reliable presence was a great comfort. Up on

the box of the carriage sat Adolf, whistling cheerfully. He was happy that she had come, and that also consoled her. Silver trotted gaily on. They were already over the bridge, and the town lay behind them. Only a few more houses and farms, then open country, meadows, and forest, and above them the silvery trickle of the lark's song. Aquarius, who had been in a torment of anxiety up to the last that he might be left behind, sat beside Adolf in front, nudging his master's knee gently with his head.

"Just take a look back, children," said Papa. "The cathedral looks beautiful in the morning light, and you can see the courthouse down by the river. I think there's someone waving there." A white handkerchief fluttered from a window.

It was one of those clear days that often follow a storm; the cloudless sky was by now a deep blue over the pale orange of the sheaves of wheat in the harvested fields. "The colors of the House of Orange," said the Amtmann. "Orange and blue, those good, warm colors of the line that gave us the first dukes of Nassau. Every fall they will shine over the country, even when the black-and-white flags of Prussia fly from the towers."

He also knows about unhappy love, Paula suddenly saw with her new perception, for was not this little country his great love? He had been born and raised in it and had lived here all his life except for his student years in Bonn and Göttingen.

Soon the beech trees would be turning into an even deeper orange, she thought, feeling the first hint of autumn in the late summer day, a foreboding of parting. *Adieu,* orange and blue . . .

They made their first stop in one of the clean, pretty

little villages where Father had business with the mayor. He was an elderly farmer, a redhead, with deep, shrewd eyes behind heavy lids. He invited them to the midday meal in an old half-timbered house with texts from the Scriptures on the crossbeams. His wife brought in a huge bowl of rice, over which brown butter had been poured and which had been sprinkled liberally with sugar and cinnamon. The mayor and his wife, their two sons, an old manservant, and a young maid sat with them around the table of lime wood, silent and serious. The mayor muttered a prayer; then they each seized a tin spoon and started eating from the dish in the middle of the table. Not a word was spoken, for eating was important business. If you didn't pay proper attention, you had only yourself to blame if you didn't get enough. The Amtmann's children liked nothing better than to have a meal in a farmhouse when they were off on trips with their father. There was almost always rice on such occasions, the accepted dish for special visitors, and the boys loved it. Occasionally in the courthouse, there was rice pudding as a main dish on fast days, but it could not be compared with what the farm folk made. It was not swimming in a pool of butter, and served in individual portions on plates, it tasted different from rice taken out of a big communal dish. Not a grain was left over now, but there was a little more in the big pot in the kitchen, which the farmer's wife scraped out for Aquarius, who lapped it up as though he, too, had never tasted anything so good before.

After the Amtmann had finished his business, they drove on, and in the afternoon they arrived at Montabaur. They pulled up in the marketplace in front of yet another timbered house, this time a patrician one. It was the family home of the mayor of Montabaur, Peter Modest Waterloo, who was married to the Amtmann's sister Helene and whose son was Adolf's godfather. Whenever Jacob Eisenberth came to Montabaur, he stayed with the Waterloos, and he often took one or two of his sons along, for this was a place where they could meet the family *en masse*.

"What a lovely surprise!" Aunt Helene said when she took Paula into her arms—Paula, whom she had not seen for almost three years. "What do you say, Modest? A grown young lady!" It was really a surprise, for there had been no way to send a message ahead, but the Waterloos' guest rooms were always ready. While young Waterloo took his godson Adolf into his bachelor apartment in the same house, the Amtmann and Paula were led to their rooms by Uncle Modest and Aunt Helene. Again Paula felt the warmth of her aunt's welcome when she walked up the stairs, her arm around her young niece, almost enveloping Paula in the folds of her wide skirt, which made her stately figure even statelier. One of the guest rooms was under the gable. It was light and airy, the high bed covered with snowy linen, and this looked so inviting to Paula that she would have liked to climb right into it. She was still tired from her almost sleepless night.

"Now, freshen up, child, and have a little rest," said her aunt. "I'll send the maid around to summon the whole clan for supper. They'll hardly be able to wait another hour to see you!"

Sure enough, when Paula came down an hour later, the living room was already brimming over with a welcoming crowd, and she found herself surrounded by aunts in black and gray silk, uncles in tail coats, and handsome young cousins, male and female; one of the young families had even brought two small children to greet the visitors from Limburg.

It was difficult to sort out the generations. Paula's father had four sisters and five brothers, some much older, some younger than himself, so that some of their children were really in the age group of aunts and uncles, like Adolf's godfather, Adolf Waterloo. Then there were a few of the even older generation; it was a little confusing, and Paula exchanged an amused glance with her brother who was handed around by young Waterloo. They were embraced and patted. Paula kissed a variety of cheeks— smooth young ones, wrinkled and stubby old ones. She had to answer questions about the folks at home, she smiled about family jokes she dimly remembered from childhood, straightened out pillows or shoved footstools under the feet of the elder ladies, and allowed her white dress to be admired and fingered, the same one she had worn for the Carnival ball last winter and for all parties since. By the standards of the remote little hill town of Montabaur, it was in the most modern style, and Paula heard much praise for her skillful mother who had turned her out so prettily.

Over supper, the dignified Uncle Modest, with his handsome white sideburns, made a gracious little speech in honor of the guests, and the Amtmann replied with a toast. Supper was cold because of the short notice but as excellent as one would expect it to be from such a perfect housewife as Aunt Helene. And the wine—well, Montabaur was still near enough to the Rhine and Mosel to have well-equipped wine cellars. The cut glasses rang as they touched. The atmosphere grew even gayer, and once again,

as at her homecoming the previous December, Paula felt
overwhelmed by the exuberance and high spirits of her
family. There was only one short interval of quiet while
one of the cousins gave a horn solo and an aunt played the
Moonlight Sonata on the pianoforte.

A nursemaid in traditional country dress brought in the
two children to say good night: a three-year-old girl and a
tiny baby. "May I hold him?" asked Paula, and the young
mother, only a few years older than herself, put the warm
little bundle of life into her arms. She held it, sniffed the
clean, healthy baby smell, felt the flower-petal smoothness
of the soft skin, and thought: I want a baby! Oh, how I
would like to have such a little treasure of my own! Even
that fulfillment was now out of the question forever, alas!

Then there were more questions to be answered, about
things at home, about Mama and the aunts and Uncle
Emmo and Babett, her brothers and the Prussian occupation, of which they had heard but had seen nothing up
here in the Westerwald.

Paula began to feel sleepier and sleepier; she had to
make an effort to keep her eyes open. Gradually, the whole
room full of friendly relatives began to swim before them.

At last Aunt Helene noticed. "The poor child!" she
exclaimed. "In another moment, she'll fall over with ex-
haustion. Traveling all day and then the strong mountain
air to which she is not accustomed!" And after another
round of kisses and embraces, Paula was handed her bedroom candle in the hall and climbed slowly up to her
room. The window was wide open, and she could see out
across the quiet marketplace, which seemed—in its way—
like a continuation of the family gathering. Over there,

under the lantern, which was not lit tonight because of the bright moon, stood the Red Ox, the house her great-grandfather had built and in which widowed Uncle Adam now lived. On the corner beside the town hall was the house of Uncle Heinrich, the youngest brother. Because of that, this branch of the family was called the *Eisenberths of the Corner.* In the neighboring streets, she knew, were the homes of some of the relatives by marriage, the Waldorfs and the Wingens, the Knodts and the Corceliuses.

A fountain murmured drowsily. From an invisible church tower, eleven strokes fell into the peace of the late-summer night. Down below she heard the leavetaking of the guests.

Paula piled the eiderdowns and one of the heavy woolen blankets on the little curved sofa, slipped in between the cool sheets, and slept undisturbed into the bright morning, when the tempting aroma of coffee and fresh rolls wafted up through the house.

That day the Amtmann went for a drive with his brother-in-law to attend to some business matters. The previous evening he had avoided talking about his future plans, but now, alone with Modest, he spoke more freely. "We haven't decided yet," he said. "The Prussians have made me a fair enough offer of a government position in Koblenz. There is a good deal to be said in favor of it, and against it, too. True, it would mean greater financial security, and the boys must get an education. But I am no longer young enough to get used to this separation of legal and administrative duties. I'm not cut out for a desk official. I need contact with the people I am supposed to lead. I want to talk to them, to explain to them why I expect this or that of them, not to send them written ordinances that they'll hardly read anyway. You know that

the peasants up here need a lot of personal persuasion not
to grow so many potatoes to make schnapps but to think
of years when the potato crops are bad and what they'll
feed their livestock with during such a calamity. It's not
too long ago that you had a potato famine up here. What
a job it was to knock some sense into these blockheads!
Margarete and I think our two older boys have some plans
of their own. I don't want to talk about it all yet. If things
work out, we may be able to get along on my pension.
And what about you, Modest? I don't think the Prussians
will be in a hurry to change things up here."

"No," the mayor said. "I guess they'll let us go at the old
pace at least as long as I am in office. It's not easy to
imagine you as a Prussian official, Jacob."

"They'll give me until next spring to decide," the Amtmann said.

Paula and Adolf had been sent up to the graveyard with
a basket of flowers from the garden to pay their respects
to the family graves. The first stone they found in the cool,
shady cemetery around the old church was that of Johann
Emmerich Eisenberth and his wife Christine. He had
been called to his rest in 1712. The date of his birth and his
wife's maiden name had been worn away by the years.
"They must have seen the Thirty Years' War!" Adolf said.
"Think of it!" There they lay, or what was left of them,
surrounded by children and grandchildren and their offspring, a family gathering as impressive as that of the
evening before.

The children found the same names on the tombstones
as those on the front doors of the town houses. "So many
of them!" Paula said to her brother. "Such an awful lot of
them!" There was also the grave of their father's first wife.

A bunch of asters was lying on the gray stone; Papa must have been up here early in the morning. Young as they were, they felt the hint of death and transiency, the swift, relentless passage of time. Quickly they put their flowers on the well-cared-for graves under their stern crosses, said a prayer, and hurried out from the shade into the warm sunshine, where Aquarius was waiting for them impatiently.

Adolf went back to fetch his godfather, who had promised to take him fishing. He felt like an important grown-up guest in Adolf Waterloo's bachelor apartment, with its collection of long pipes, the colored caps of his student brotherhood, and the two crossed swords on the wall—altogether a wonderful masculine atmosphere. Paula walked on alone up the wooded slope behind the church to a spot from which she could see far over the austere beauty of the Westerwald landscape to the bare basalt summits in the east. She sat there for a long time among gorse and blooming heather, content to be alone.

After dinner, Aunt Helene took her out into the garden, where a hammock was slung between two gnarled apple trees. "Have a good rest now," she said. "Young girls need a lot of sleep. It'll be another late evening." A lot of sleep, indeed! Paula smiled. Aunt Helene should hear Mama! It was easy to see that this aunt had never raised a girl. But it was nice to be treated with so much tender consideration for once!

That evening the family met in the house *On the Corner* at the invitation of Uncle Heinrich and Aunt Gertrud. He was the head of the tannery and leather business his father had founded, was quite a wealthy man, and was considered a trifle fast by the ladies of the family and a spendthrift.

Well, he seemed to be able to afford his extravagances. His elder brother, the Amtmann, he called jokingly "our poor relation," since he drove out unpretentiously with only one horse. Heinrich always drove in double harness. "And believe me, he would drive a four-in-hand if he weren't scared of our wagging tongues!" old Aunt Maria Anna informed Paula. "Can you imagine—he has brought up his children with butter and jam on their bread every day of the week?" No, of course Paula could hardly conceive of such unheard-of extravagance. But later, when Uncle Heinrich made a speech in extempore verse in honor of the ladies, mentioning in particular his young niece, who had blossomed into such a charming young lady, she understood why he was considered the gay spark of the family.

One more night in the room under the gables, lit by the full moon, with the lullaby of the fountain from the marketplace, and then it was time to say good-by. It was Adolf who found the parting hardest after the short spell of bachelor life with his admired godfather. For the first time in his life, he had been invited to smoke a pipe with real tobacco, which didn't make him feel sick at all like the pipes filled with chestnut leaves that he and his friends smoked in secret on the island to prove their manliness. They had come back from their fishing trip with a big pike and three beautiful trout. The pike had gone to the main kitchen; the trout were prepared by young Waterloo's housekeeper and served with new potatoes sprinkled with parsley, fresh butter, and a green salad from the garden. As a farewell present and partly as a birthday present, since his thirteenth birthday had been just a couple of days ago on August 25, Adolf received five guilders from his godfather, a staggering sum. He thought he would venture to ask Papa to allow him to keep the money instead of saving it for him. He needed it for all kinds of things—first of all for a present for Toni, secondly for a new collar for Aqua, thirdly for a nice birthday present for Paula in November, and after all that, there had to be enough left over for Christmas presents. Now that he looked after the horse all by himself, his allowance had been raised to a guilder a month. When you came to think of it, he had become a kind of Croesus.

The road along which they drove dipped down into a valley at first, then climbed up to one of the higher ridges from which they had once more a splendid view of the highland country near and far, rolling away under a carpet of purple heather, gorsebrush, shaggy woods, and meager pastures. There were no signs of life, no villages, no people, except for a solitary shepherd with his flock on a distant slope. His blue linen smock caught the sunlight as he stood near his long shepherd's cart, which served him as bed and shelter from early spring until fall and which he pushed along from one pasture to the next. It looked like a coffin on wheels.

"It must be a peaceful life," Adolf said. "No one ever disturbs you when you're thinking your own thoughts, and you are always out of doors with your dog and your sheep."

They had stopped to eat the provisions Aunt Helene had packed for them. They filled their traveling mugs at one of the springs so abundant in these parts. Aqua drank his fill also, and so did Silver, whom Adolf had unharnessed to let him graze on the rough mountain grass.

"Come, let's be on our way, children," Papa said after they had sat for a long while, each occupied with his own thoughts. "I still have an hour or two's business to do in Hadamar."

The narrow road with its deep, grass-grown ruts ran downhill, frequently twisting and turning. Foxgloves grew at the roadside. Around the tree trunks stood little families of toadstools. The briar bushes were dotted with red hips, and the sloes full of black berries. As they came farther down, they saw a village here and there or a lonely farmstead. Once again they caught sight of a shepherd on a steep meadow, waving to them. When they saw he was hurrying down the slope, they stopped. The man had recognized the Amtmann's carriage, and he stood and talked for a little while, hungry for company, eagerly asking for news from "down below." As he stroked Silver's head, Aquarius came up and sniffed the man's shoes.

"If I didn't know that old Kasper's dog Bello had drowned in the flood in March '65, I could have sworn that was him," he said, knitting on a long woolen stocking. All the shepherds in the Westerwald knitted during the long, lonely summer months.

"Is that so?" said the Amtmann without looking at Adolf. "Where does the man live?"

"High up in the Elbbach Valley. He was a good dog, that Bello was. Let me see your hand, lad. It's covered with warts."

Adolf held out his hand, and the man ran his fingers over it. "I'll take care of them, lad. God bless you all."

"God bless you, shepherd," said the Amtmann, and Paula nodded a farewell to the man, who walked back to his dog and his flock. Adolf called Aqua to jump up beside him on the box. The dog had spent almost the whole journey running behind or in front or beside the carriage, sometimes bounding off to scrabble about among the trees or dig up molehills or sniff an alluring scent. Only now was Adolf aware that whenever they had seen a flock of sheep in the distance, Aqua had stood quite still for a few minutes, his head lifted, with quivering nostrils, and had whined softly. The boy remembered what the shepherd had said, and a cold fear crept into his heart.

They drove down to the village of Hadamar in silence. Paula thought of getting back. Would she see him today? Tomorrow she must tell him that everything between him and her had to be over.

An hour later, when the Amtmann had attended to his business with the Hadamar mayor, they made their way home along the Elbbach stream. "You silly little stream!" said Adolf crossly to the harmless brook that hurried down between meadows and wooded slopes. But it was not always harmless. It came from the Westerwald mountains, where there was for months every winter deep snow. There is a story told of these mountains in which a rider loses his way at nightfall one winter evening and, as he cannot find village or hamlet or house, ties his horse to a post, wraps himself in his cloak, and sleeps till dawn in the soft snow. The thaw came that night, and when he woke, he saw his poor horse hanging from the top of a church steeple.

When they arrived home, Ferdinand and Karl were in the yard, waiting impatiently to blurt out their great piece of news. "The lieutenant's gone! Our lieutenant and Orje and the horses! Transferred to Wiesbaden. He left a letter for you and Mama on your desk, Papa. It told all about it and thanked you for your hospitality."

"Good evening, gentlemen!" said their father, and the

boys remembered their manners and greeted the home-coming party properly.

When Adolf had unharnessed Silver and put the carriage in the coachhouse, he gave the horse his food and water. As he was doing so, he saw his father standing in the open stable door, black against the last evening light. "You drove well, Adolf, and looked after everything properly," he said. "Uncle Modest noticed, too, what good care you took of the horse. Thank you."

"Oh, not at all, Papa," murmured Adolf, his heart in his throat, waiting for what was coming. It came.

"Think about what that shepherd said. He may be mistaken, but on the other hand, he may be right. And now it's time to come in to supper."

The next day, when Paula went up to the arbor with a book in the noon hour—there was no longer any danger to her peace of mind—she saw something white stuck between the stones of the wall at the back. She pulled out the little note and read: "*Adieu, ma belle amie. Pardonnez-moi. Je ne vous oublierez jamais. F.Q.*"

Autumn II

THE NEW September moon, a delicate crescent, sailed above the stubble fields. Everywhere in barns, the flails were beating time, as though the great clock of the seasons were ticking out its message all over the land: autumn is here, autumn is here.

The first apples were just showing a pale yellow, still sour enough to turn the milk, as the grownups said, but nevertheless eaten by all the boys in town when they had a chance to pick them up under the trees. It was the same this year as every year. The hard, unripe apples gave them a stomach-ache, but for some mysterious reason, they preferred them to the fully ripe pears and damsons that plopped into the dew-wet grass, dripping with sweet juice.

These were the mild days of ripening after the summer's heat, the time when in the Rhineland and the neighboring valleys the grape harvest begins, made more brilliant by the first shadows of the oncoming farewell. In the courthouse, too, there was an underlying mood of farewell, though the word itself was still avoided.

When the October moon looks like the thin sickle up there now, Adolf thought, the autumn vacation will have

started. Much as he liked vacations, he would willingly
have given up this one, because then he would have to
walk up the Elbbach with his dog and look for the man
who might be Aquarius's rightful owner. But justice had to
be done; there was no need for words to be wasted on that
subject in the Amtmann's house. At Eastertime, the falcon
had flown away to freedom because Janosch said it was
wrong to keep a bird-of-prey in captivity. When his time
had come, Janosch himself had gone, and no one had kept
him back. Now it was Aquarius's turn, and that was harder
than anything else. The moon would wax and wane and
disappear, and when it appeared again, it would be time.
After that perhaps only Silver would be left.

In recent weeks, the Amtmann had been in Wiesbaden
a few times and had visited Frau von Savigny, who had
once again asked for his legal advice. As a civil servant, he
had not accepted either money or presents from the lady
for his friendly help. But now she suggested that he might
be willing to take over the administration of her affairs for
a fixed salary. She presumed that the Amtmann hesitated
to take office under the Prussians.

"That would mean our having to move to Wiesbaden,"
said Jacob Eisenberth to his wife when he came home that
evening.

"And getting a welcome addition to your pension, too,"
practical Margarete replied.

"Besides all kinds of other good things that only a large
town can offer. The theater will now enjoy royal patronage
instead of ducal. We'll at last be able to see plays and
operas and hear concerts with soloists from all over Europe.
There is an excellent reading room in the Kurhaus, also.
And as far as parties and balls are concerned, Paula will

have far more opportunities than we could offer her in rural Limburg."

"The hand of fate, Jacob. But how will the children settle down in a city apartment? They are used to almost unlimited freedom here—in the yard and garden, in and on and by the river, and in the forest."

"How many of them will still be with us then?" said the Amtmann pensively. "Paula, Adolf, Karlchen . . ."

The parents were well aware of the plans August and Georg had discussed with Lieutenant von Quitzow during his stay in the courthouse, though there had not been any actual discussion of them as yet. "I hope they realize what a hard life it will be in the cadet corps," the Amtmann said, but his wife thought that strict Prussian discipline might do Georg a lot of good.

"Especially as August will be able to keep an eye on him there," she said. "And they would get a thorough education and have a prospect of a fine career, too." She gave a little sigh; she had given up the idea of her eldest son becoming a priest, anyway. And to study law, his parents knew full well, was a long and costly business.

It had been decided that Ferdinand was to start next Easter at the Jesuit school in Feldkirch. His inclination toward a vagabond life had become even more evident after the long summer vacation. Whenever the weather was fine and the urge came over him, he managed to slip away from school unobserved during the first recess and wander off happily into the wide open spaces. To all the questions of his parents and teachers, he gave no reply, his small dark-skinned face looking more puzzled than defiant. What should he have answered to all those penetrating, probing questions when he didn't know himself what it was that was driving him? Only to Karl, as they lay in bed at night, would he sometimes confide what he had been doing: lying on his belly in a hedgerow, watching a late dragonfly that slowly peeled its transparent wings out of the hard chrysalis; fishing in a hidden pond; stealing a few apples that he could have had for the asking at home —only, "It's different," said Ferdinand. There were tales about giants and dragons also, his favorite dragon being Fafnir, who guarded the Nibelung treasures. Not that Ferdinand was particularly interested in those, though they would have come in handy. His main concern was to overcome Fafnir and have a bath in his blood, which would give him a horny skin, like Siegfried's in the legend, and would make him safe from spears and arrows and swords. "And just think how useful it would be to have such a tough skin on your backside, Karl! You'd have a big laugh at those silly hazel rods and carpetbeaters and wouldn't feel a thing!"

"Why can't you stop this stupid tramping around?" said Karl miserably, for he suffered almost as much as his brother when Ferdinand received a well-earned beating. "Anyway, your horny skin wouldn't protect you from weapons since they have invented powder and shot."

Now, whenever Mama looked around the big family table at mealtimes, happy about the abundance of life under her roof, she seemed to see it shrink and dwindle away before her eyes.

"And what about our old ones?" she asked her husband when they were alone.

"Perhaps Emmerich might start a bookshop in Wiesbaden," said the Amtmann. "He has several good customers there and in nearby Frankfurt, too. And as far as the aunts are concerned, you well know how lonesome Adam is feeling in the big Red Ox since his wife passed away. He would be only too pleased to have Aunt Stina and Aunt Rikchen go to live with him."

"But it's not good to transplant old trees."

"Don't forget that they grew up in Montabaur, and they were no longer young when they came to live with me. The big family will receive them again, as though they had never left."

"And Babett . . . ?"

"She has sometimes talked of going into the home, after all. And if not, we'll certainly find a place for her. At her age, it won't be for many more years."

Margarete suppressed a sigh. Those few years might easily become a decade with a person as tough as Babett. And an extra room would make the apartment more expensive.

Adolf visited Paula almost every evening now, and they would sit on her bed with Aqua crouching between them. The dog's head rested on Adolf's knee, where Aqua could feel the reassuring touch of the hand from which nothing but good had ever come to him. Paula knew what was on her brother's mind, and sometimes she would give his rough, long-fingered hand a little pat, since he would not have liked to be comforted by words. He spoke as little about his grief as she about hers. One day, touching his hand, she made a discovery. "Adolf, your warts have gone!"

He nodded. "I know," he said without interest, although before he had been disgusted with the ugly things, most of all while the Ippel girls had still been here. They had gone, as everything seemed to be doing this year. And now next Easter, August and Georg would leave for cadet school. They talked about nothing else every evening when the little ones had gone to sleep. It bored Adolf to death, it hurt him, and rather than stay and listen, he would creep out and go to Paula's room, where he and his dog were always welcome.

"Those old Prussians have to fill up their officers' corps now that they own half of Germany," he said to his sister. "You should have heard how tempting the lieutenant made everything sound when he talked about it. A boy as keen and smart as August would be pretty sure of being promoted to the Academy of War later, he said, and that was as good as a university, at least for a military career. August's sound knowledge of history would come in handy there. Only the pick of the crop got to this academy, and from there it was only one step to the great General Staff. . . ."

"I am sure August will be tops, whatever he does," Paula said.

"Yes. But Georg, the silly idiot, of course he has to go also, as he has always copied everything August does. And I can just as soon imagine him in a military school as a cow in the church choir."

"Don't you worry about Georg. The Spartan discipline may very well bring out the good qualities he certainly has. But, tell me honestly, Adolf, wouldn't *you* like to go there, too?"

"I? Not on your life!" he exclaimed with sudden violence. "With that Georg around, I've been odd man out all my life, and I'm fed up with it. Besides, it's no life for me anyway: drilling and standing at attention and talking fancy Prussian and doing what you are told every minute of the day just like a hundred other boys! *No!* I'd feel as though I were one of a flock of sheep. Old Georg, of course, he only thinks of how he'll be a lieutenant in three or four years, and then just wait and see how he'll fool around with the girls in his fine uniform! But why August is going in for a thing like that beats me."

"August knows what he's doing; you can bet on that. And he'll be just his own self, even among a hundred other boys."

"Maybe," said Adolf. "I only wish I were sure what *I* want to be."

One couldn't be a wandering minstrel in these stupid modern days—that he knew. In fact, all the knightly careers were out, and if August thought that being an officer was the next best thing to being a knight, he might be in for a disappointment. Except that August would be knightly no matter what he became, Adolf thought.

The eldest of her brothers, sixteen now, had seemed to Paula to be almost a grown young man when she came home last winter. Now he had really matured. Even his voice was deep and masculine; only very seldom did it slip back into the funny, croaking stage. While Paula was thinking about August's calm and composed ways, her eye was caught by Adolf's shadow on the wall, thrown by the flickering candlelight. Strange, how all the essential features stood out there, free from distracting detail! This wasn't any longer the round childish face that had welcomed her last December—Adolf, too, had changed in this year. The structure of his skull had become more defined; one could already guess how he would look as a man. He is no longer a child, she thought. He's a youth who has undergone all kinds of transformations in these last nine months. How many things he has thought he wanted to be and what will he finally end up with? She was deeply attached to this young brother of hers who was trying so hard to find himself.

And wasn't that what she was doing also? She felt as if she had aged in the last weeks by just as many years—and still she was on her way, still far from reaching her goal. What had become of the young thing who thought that to enter a convent would be an easy and pious solution to all her present and future problems? She had had to learn that one could not go back to an earlier stage of life just because one didn't like the present one. Mère Celeste and Father Meinert had warned her, but everyone must learn by his own experience. And since she had come to know herself a little better, she was not surprised that she was not destined to be a bride of Christ. But why, then, had God shown her the man she could love only to take him away from her again? Every morning when she woke, every night before she went to sleep, she would hold his white handkerchief against her face. "He is gone!" she would tell herself for the hundredth time, and every time it was like a fresh shock, received just at this moment. "He is gone, and I will never see him again!" If only she knew whether he had asked to be transferred because he didn't want to bring even more confusion to her and to himself. Or had he simply been ordered away with the blind casualness of military commands, which know nothing about human feelings and care less? It never occurred to her to doubt him. It was impossible to think of him as a Don Juan or as an *homme fatal*, which was what Ottilie and Melanie, Caroline, and Lotte called Overberg. She was sick and tired of hearing it.

Each year he had been "arousing hopes" in another

young girl, they maintained. It was one of their favorite phrases: "arousing hopes," turning a girl's head, leaving tears and broken hearts behind him.

"And people say he has even more exciting adventures on his travels!" Lottchen whispered.

Paula had never been able to stand hearing someone attacked who was not there to defend himself—her old weakness for taking the side of the underdog, though it was difficult to see Konrad Overberg as an underdog!

"His adventures in foreign countries take place mostly in libraries and museums, I suppose," she replied bravely, overcoming her shyness, "and in the mountains. Uncle Emmo says he is an accomplished mountaineer."

"Hear, hear!" said Melanie, but Paula was warming to her subject. "I think it's silly, just because he pays her some attention, for a girl to fall in love with him—a nice, middle-aged man, who is fond of dancing but has no intention of settling down. Surely everyone must have realized that by now. Then why do they go on making fools of themselves?"

"Why? Why?" said the girls in chorus and cast their eyes to heaven at such innocence. "Because no one can resist him if he pays her the slightest attention. That's why, you little lamb!" And Ottilie, the oldest of the circle, informed her, "He's what they call an *homme fatal!*"

But now Paula was thinking of Friedrich von Quitzow, not of Konrad Overberg. What a blessing it was that during the day she had so little time to think, to brood, to lose herself in the torturing fact: he is gone . . . he is gone! There was so much work to do in the house, the kitchen, the garden, and she was grateful for the strength she drew from this ordered and demanding routine that she had learned to accept.

Still nothing definite had been said to the children about the coming changes, but from an odd remark here and there, they could guess a lot. Babett, always inclined to making dark pronouncements, grunted, "An old body must go to a home, just like old hats have to go to the lumber room. I know, girl, I know! But I always figured to die with my Herr Amtmann holding my hand."

"Don't talk about dying, Babett," Paula said. "You're looking forward to your ninetieth birthday, aren't you?"

"God willing and I am still alive," said Babett and crossed herself, but she was evidently cheered at the thought of the great day. "Roast goose," she said. "You hear me? A real fat one—that's what I want for dinner at my jubilee, with chestnut stuffing and potato dumplings, and trust me to see to it that Kettchen makes them properly. The boys must give me a hand upstairs, so I can eat with all of you in the living room, and the Herr Amtmann will toast me. Perhaps the bishop'll come in person to congratulate me. And the mayor, of course. And you see to it that someone comes from the paper. I want to see all about my life in black and white."

Paula promised to tell the editor of the local paper in plenty of time about THE EVENT. Then it was time to take tea to her aunts and to set Uncle Emmo's tea tray. She always left him till last, for she liked to stay with him for a little while. Sometimes she found her father there, and it was good to listen to him and Uncle Emmo having a quiet conversation. She had grown used to taking three cups and plates, one for her uncle, one for her father or for any old book lover who might be visiting, and one for herself. Even if there were no visitors, her uncle enjoyed her company over a cup of tea. Recently, it had rarely been an old book lover that she found visiting Uncle Emmo. More frequently it was young Overberg. She had grown accustomed to calling him "young Overberg" as everyone else did, to distinguish him from his father. But for her, he remained the fatherly, solicitous older man who had put half his warm fur rug over her knees in the mail coach. If for other girls he was an *homme fatal*, they had only to blame themselves.

The conversations in Uncle Emmo's room were almost always about books. Once Uncle had read some of the *Odyssey* in Greek—evidently he and Papa had been discussing the Voss translation of Homer into German. It sounded like music, even though Paula could not understand a word, and she found herself regretting, as she had so often done, that the great classical education of the humanities was denied to girls. If Overberg was there, Uncle Emmo would not read aloud himself but would ask his young friend to do so. And Paula heard lines of Goethe, Schiller, and the Romantic poets, some of whom she had often read for herself but who took on a new, warm life when they were read aloud. Overberg had a deep voice—like a cello, Paula thought. One day he was in the middle of reading one of her favorite poems as she came in with the tea tray—Goethe's "An dem Mond." She stopped at the door and motioned Overberg to go on reading, not to jump up politely as he would otherwise have done. It was wrong to interrupt a poet, she thought, no matter who was coming into the room. With the tray in her hands, she stood motionless and let the verses flow over her:

> *Fliesse, fliesse, lieber Fluss!*
> *Nimmer werd ich froh,*
> *So verrauschte Scherz und Kuss*
> *Und die Treue so.*

The words had always moved her, but now they went straight to the marrow of her bones.

> *Ich besass es doch einmal,*
> *Was so köstlich ist,*
> *Dass Man doch zu seiner Qual*
> *Nimmer es vergisst.*

As she put down the tray, the cups rattled slightly, and she was glad that she had an excuse for looking down at the little table, her eyes hidden, for what she had seen and felt now was no longer the gentle light of the moon over river and valley—it was a cry of despair at the transiency of love.

Overberg stood up and bowed to her silently; after the emotional force of this poetry, words would have been meaningless. The three of them drank their tea in silence. Then the two gentlemen lit their pipes, and at length Uncle Emmo said, "Just fancy, child, the elder Herr Overberg wants to know if I would like to be his librarian. You have heard me say that his library is as exquisite as his wine cellar."

"My father has always been a passionate book collector, but not a very systematic one," said Konrad Overberg. "And as for me, I've only learned in the last few years from your uncle what a library should look like and how it should be arranged and complemented. Father and I have now decided that the time has come to establish a proper catalogue for our collection."

"I am most grateful for the trust you place in me," said Emmo Eisenberth. "And you can depend upon it, I will consider your offer seriously."

"And what about us?" asked Paula. "Here you are luring our uncle away, and who's going to tutor my two lazy brothers, Georg and Ferdinand, every year before Easter and attend to the gaps in my education?"

"But you would be welcome to visit your uncle in Bad Ems any time," said Overberg. "Oh, by the way, I have another invitation to deliver. A week from Saturday, we're going to celebrate the beginning of the wine harvest, down in our old house, Rheingold, in Assmannshausen, with a few friends. We'll take the train to Ehrenbreitstein, and from there a chartered steamer will take us up the Rhine. When we get to Assmannshausen, the older folk will probably want to sit quietly on the terrace for a while and drink coffee. The younger ones will prefer to go up to our vineyard with me for an hour or so, and after that there will be a tour of the cellars. Then, after dinner, we'll all go over to the Crown—there's dancing every evening at this time of year. Young Hufnagel, the Crown host—in the third generation—was at school with me and has promised to reserve the best tables for our party. There's room enough for everyone to stay the night at Rheingold if the young gentlemen don't mind being a bit cramped. The next morning after breakfast, we go back by steamer, and on the way we can hear Mass in the pilgrims' chapel at Bornhofen. What do you think of that for a program, Fräulein Paula?"

"It sounds wonderful. Don't you think so, Uncle Emmo?" said Paula. "But I wonder what my parents will say?"

"Their permission has already been granted. May I remind you that you still owe me a quadrille?"

"I haven't forgotten," she replied. "The first, Herr Overberg?"

He knew from last winter's Carnival ball that Paula liked dancing with him because he was a good dancer. And that's all, my dear Konrad, he said to himself with a touch of self-mockery. Besides, she had told him at the same dance that she intended to go into a convent. If that was still her plan, it was no wonder men made no impression on her.

"But now that I come to think of it, they won't play quadrilles at a wine-festival dance, any more than at our little summer parties," he told her. "At this time of year, they play folk dances on the Rhine—quick polkas, Rheinländers, a schottische, and of course waltzes. How many waltzes are you willing to trade me for a quadrille?"

"That I'll leave you to figure out, Herr Overberg. I'm sure we can reach agreement on it." So now she was giving him sums to do!

Paula began to gather up the tea things, and he stood up and offered to take the tray for her. "No, it's all right, thank you. It's not heavy. You just stay here with Uncle Emmo. I'll see you later, Uncle. *Au revoir, monsieur.*"

He held the door open for her and closed it again behind her. Then he knocked out his pipe, looked at the clock, and found that it was time for him to leave. "My father doesn't like to be kept waiting for his meals. And apart from that, Nikodema has brought us up to be strictly punctual during her long dictatorship, twenty years and more." The two men laughed; the strictness and at the same time the unswerving loyalty of the Overbergs' house-keeper was known all over the little principality. Konrad took his leave and set off toward the hotel, where he usually left his horse when he came to town. As he was crossing the yard, he saw Adolf unharnessing Silver; the Amtmann had just returned from a short trip. Overberg stopped and watched for a moment with approval the experienced way Adolf was handling the horse. He could never pass a horse anyway without tapping its crupper and giving it a few friendly words. "Hello there, Adolf. Hello, Silver."

"Hello, Herr Overberg," said Adolf, always ready for a little horse talk. "I've been meaning to ask you what kind of stallion you ride."

"An English hunter, Adolf. He's called Eastermoon. The hunters are bred from Norfolk mares, sired by thor-oughbreds. Do you like him? In November I'm expecting a foal by him, from my little Arab filly Suleika."

"How terrific!" Adolf beamed at him. "A foal from an Arab filly! That's the white horse with the little head and long tail, isn't it? And what about your carriage pair?"

"They are Hungarian coach horses. Your Uncle Emmo tells me you like to ride. And I can see for myself that you know how to look after a horse. If you come to our party, I'll show you our stables before we start from Bad Ems."

"What party?"

"The beginning of the wine harvest in Assmanns-hausen. You're invited, too, because you belong with the bigger ones now. The two old ladies have decided to stay home and look after your two youngest brothers."

"Thank you, Herr Overberg. But I can only come if I may bring Aqua."

Aqua heard his name and came out of the henhouse; someone must have left the door open. Adolf looked at him closely; either he was innocent this time or else he had licked his mouth so clean that no circumstantial evidence could be seen.

"Hello, Aquarius, you old Water Carrier who hates going in the water," said Overberg. "Do you mind going on a boat, old chap?"

"Oh, he'll go in a big boat all right," said Adolf, running his hand over Aqua's back. "He won't come out with us in our little boat, but he has nothing against a regular steamer, I'm sure, not if I'm there as well. Isn't that right, Aqua?" Aqua affirmed this with a few wags of his long tail. Then something else struck Adolf. "If you really think I'm good at looking after horses, Herr Overberg, can't you leave your stallion here with me in the future instead of at the hotel? I'll see he's all right, and it won't cost you a penny." But if he lets me have a ride on the stallion by way of reward, I'd have nothing against it, he thought to himself.

"That's a tempting proposition." Overberg laughed. "If the Herr Amtmann has no objections, I'll leave Eastermoon down here in the stable from now on."

Fräulein Nikodemus, called Nikodema for short, the Overbergs' housekeeper, had gone over to Assmannshausen two days before in the carriage to air the house and make all the necessary preparations for the big party, with the help of the coachman and two maids from the village.

"It smells like a tomb up here," said Frau Schickel, the wife of the steward, who lived with her husband on the ground floor behind the firm's offices, next door to the oak-paneled room where the wine tasting took place. She always kept a room ready for the young gentleman, who came over from Ems once every week to attend to business matters and to be the host at wine-tasting sessions. Down there, where coopers and cellarmen, customers and distributors were always coming and going, the house was alive; but in the upper part, where the family had once lived, there was the smell of death and times long past. "Just like a tomb," repeated Frau Schickel. "A shame for the lovely house."

But Nikodema had neither the time nor the inclination to talk to Frau Schickel about the reasons for this house not having been lived in by the Overbergs, father and son, for over twenty years. At that time, she had just joined the household, a young thing who had strayed from Hamburg into the Rhineland; and she was still with them, the strength and mainstay of her two gentlemen, whom she adored and ruled. This year for the first time in many years there was going to be a big party at Rheingold. The excuse for it was the wine harvest, but only Nikodema knew that it was really Konrad's thirtieth birthday they were celebrating. Even on this occasion, however, the old gentleman would stay at the Crown, as he invariably did when he came to Assmannshausen.

"How are you going to put all those people up?" asked Frau Schickel as the maids went around taking the dust sheets off the furniture.

"There's no need for you to worry your head about that," replied Nikodema. After all these years, she still

spoke with a Hamburg accent instead of the softer local
dialect. "There are only eighteen coming this time, and in
the old days we often had twenty weekend guests. Herr
Konrad's room is ready. Herr Emmerich Eisenberth will
be sleeping with the old gentleman at the Crown—I
gather they've all sorts of things to talk about. The Herr
Amtmann and his wife go in the south room; Fräulein
Paula next door, in the red boudoir that was Herr Konrad's
grandmother's room. One of the young ladies in the white
room, two in the green room, and another one we'll put in
the Chinese room—that makes five. Then there are two
more married couples, one in the east room and one in the
southeast room. The young gentlemen will be on the top
floor. It's just a question of organization, you see."

"Is there one of the five girls that our Herr Konrad
seems to be . . . I mean . . ."

"I know what you mean, but that's no business of mine,
Frau Schickel, and it's no business of yours, either. If it will
put your mind at rest, I can tell you that the five boxes of
chocolates from court-confectioner Schilling in Wiesbaden
that I had to put out, one for each of the young ladies, are
all exactly alike. Now come on, down to work, girls. I want
the eiderdowns out on the lawn. The covers must come off
the chandeliers in the dining room and the salon, and the
silver must all be polished. The flowers I'll arrange myself
later on. Now I'll go down to the kitchen. When you're
finished up here, you can come and help me with the
baking. And you, Johann, please see that there's a good fire
burning in the range and enough wood's cut."

When on Saturday afternoon the steamer moored by
the bridge in the village, Nikodema was there to welcome
the guests in her black dress and white collar, looking as

dignified as a châtelaine from one of the old castles along
the river. She led them into the house and to their rooms
where they could freshen up. After that, the young ones
set off to the vineyard, led by Konrad Overberg. The older
people met in the shade of the ancient plane trees on the
terrace overlooking the Rhine for coffee and cakes.

In the vineyard, which was reached by a narrow path
through the park and then by climbing up the steep, slaty
slope, there was great activity. The girls in their white
blouses and gaily colored headscarves and the lads in their
green smocks had been working since the morning, and in
the middle of the day the sun had been hot. But they were
still joking and laughing and singing. The girls' baskets
were quickly filled with bunches of grapes, and the men
tipped them as quickly into zinc tubs and carried them
down the slope on their backs. On the road oxcarts were
waiting to take the grapes in large containers to the wine
press.

The guests helped with the harvesting for a while, but
more grapes went into their mouths than into the baskets.
Konrad Overberg had a hundred questions from the ignorant city folks to answer, to the unconcealed delight of the
harvesters. August climbed farther up the slope with his
sister, to the edge of the woods, and they enjoyed a wide
view of the proud river. Here and there old castles rose
above the river bank, gray with age, watched over by
ivy-grown towers, relics of a bygone era. Peaceful little
villages slept in the valley, surrounded by the autumnal
yellow of the meadows, the brown of plowed fields, the
gold of the orchards. On the opposite bank, rows of cherry
trees bordered the road that Napoleon had built for his
armies.

Adolf had not gone up to the vineyards with the rest of the party. He had set off along the river with Aqua toward the ruins of Castle Nollich, a few kilometers downstream. As he walked, he dreamed his old dream: he was a wandering minstrel, on the way to a castle where beautiful ladies and great lords would listen to his songs, and it was no surprise to him that the ladies who waved to him from a window of their bower were three sisters whose faces seemed familiar to him.

Meanwhile, young Overberg had taken his guests into the park again and was showing them the cellars, which had been cut into the rock of the slope and which ran far back into the mountain like an underground town, with streets bordered by oaken barrels and shelves with thousands of bottles—catacombs of wine. It would have been easy to lose one's way in these vaults had there not been a Caliban of a cellar-master, dressed in a big leather apron, walking in front of them with a miner's lantern, and had not Overberg himself taken care that none of his little flock wandered off in a side turning. Right at the back, there was a kind of grotto, with water dripping from the mouth of a big fish into a stone basin; above it, the arms of the house of Overberg were cut into the stone—a grapevine with three grapes underneath the cross and the date of the founding of the firm: 1752. Caliban shed light on it all with his lantern: cross and fish and vine, age-old symbols of the faith, woven together as in an ancient hymn.

They came out into daylight again and went to look at the wine press with its grooved wooden rollers, which very gently pressed the wine out of the grapes without pulping the stems or the pips. "For the best kinds of Spätlese, the grapes are taken off the stems by hand," said Konrad. "The juice that drips from these hand-picked grapes, without any pressure, gives the noblest wines. But now, ladies and gentlemen, it is time we were dressing for dinner."

In Paula's room, there was a glass vase with twelve beautiful yellow roses on a little table, which stood beside the voluptuously curved bed under a canopy of red brocade. Used to the simple charm of the homely Biedermeier furniture in her parents' house, she found herself surrounded now by the extravagant elegance of the rococo period. The red walls set off the white and gold of the two graceful armchairs; the chest of drawers, too, was lacquered in white and gold, the doors painted with scenes in delicate pastel colors. The engravings on the walls, of ladies in swings wearing crinolines and powdered wigs, dated from the century that was already darkened by the growing shadow of the guillotine. On the ceiling, there floated cherubs with garlands of fruit and flowers, and on the big screen in the corner was a pastoral scene such as Watteau or Lancret might have painted; Paula had seen similar ones in Uncle Emmerich's illustrated books. When she peeped behind the screen, she found a tin bath filled with hot water, beside it a ewer of cold water, and in a little flowered china dish a piece of scented French soap. She remembered that it was Saturday evening, when every clean person took a bath. The little curved tub looked funny and inviting. How different from the rough wooden tubs at home or in the convent! She undressed quickly and climbed into the bath. In the convent, there had always been long white calico shifts put out beside the tubs. When she took a bath there for the first time, she had not used the shift and had been reprimanded later by the

bathroom sister. Surely mademoiselle hadn't taken a bath
. . . *naked?* Yes, she had. But in the future, to spare the
feelings of the lay sister, she took care to soak the chaste
shift in the bathwater and hang it up to dry on the
clotheshorse provided for the purpose. She found it too
difficult to wash properly in such long drapery.

After the bath, she put on her clean cambric chemise
with its embroidered edging and, over it, the bone stays—
the aunts insisted that a young lady's waist should be slim
enough to be encircled with two hands—the long under-
drawers with the crocheted frills, and the under petticoat
of piqué, called *the modesty petticoat.* So attired, she stood
in front of the mirror to do her hair. Beside her face in the
polished glass was reflected the picture of a beautiful
woman that hung on the opposite wall, and on a sudden
impulse she tried to do her hair the same way as the
woman's in the picture. Part of her thick dark hair she put
up on top of her head in a braided crown, the rest she let
fall on her neck in a deep chignon. Last of all, she put on
the crinoline petticoat stiffened with horsehair and, over it,
the skirt of her new green dress. She had chosen the
material herself this time when Isidor came to the courthouse with his wares from the Frankfurt Fair and unrolled
a length of delicate green silk before the ladies of the
house. It was to have been put aside as a birthday present
for Paula, and her birthday was not till November. But
when the invitation to Assmannshausen came, Mama had
decided to sew next winter's ball dress now.

"Green!" the aunts had protested with one voice. "Impossible."

"Green with my daughter's pale complexion? What are
you thinking of, Isidor?" Mama had said.

But, "Green! Yes, this green, please!" Paula had pleaded. Even Babett, who was always ready to take Paula's side, insisted that in this color she would look "like a cheese."

But Isidor stood firm. "Apple-green" was the very latest color, and he quickly put beside the beautifully soft silk for the skirt a piece of a deeper jade for the bodice. "Not like a cheese, if the gracious ladies will permit a humble old man to say so," he had assured them. "Like a princess, that's how demoiselle Paula will look in it."

"Please! Please, Mama, nothing else!" Against the unanimous opposition of the four women, Paula had had her way. And now the full apple-green skirt swayed over its crinoline. The darker bodice was close-fitting, with tiny puff sleeves, but fortunately with a much more modest décolleté than that of the beautiful lady in the picture. Wondering whether it was Konrad's mother, the woman whom old Herr Overberg had mourned for the last twenty years, she felt a surge of gratitude for her own father, who after a long period of mourning had again given life a new chance. Otherwise, none of us would be here, she thought.

Next door, in her parents' room, she heard the murmur of their voices as they dressed. She knocked at the communicating door, opened it a crack, and handed Mama the big box of chocolates she had found beside the roses. "Let's keep them for the aunts and Babett and the two little ones, since they had to stay at home," she said. As she shut the door into her parents' room, there was a knock at her own door. Nikodema entered to ask if she could help the young lady get dressed, and when Paula said she was ready now and was not used to any help, the housekeeper said, "Just a moment, demoiselle!" took two of the yellow roses from the vase, cut the long stems, and fastened one in Paula's hair, the other on the neckline. "From the Wiesbaden florist," she said. "There! And now have another look at yourself in the mirror."

Strange, what a difference two roses made, Paula had to agree, as she contemplated herself in the mirror. They seemed designed by one of the great Paris *couturiers* just for this soft-green dress. "Can you tell me who she is, Fräulein Nikodemus?" Paula asked.

"The Empress Elizabeth of Austria, by a famous painter," replied Nikodema. After twenty years in such a house, she knew a little bit about the art treasures.

There was giggling and whispering outside in the corridor, and as Paula came out of her room, she met the other four girls in their ball dresses. "Those boxes of chocolates!" Lotte said. "From Schilling's in Wiesbaden! Have you ever seen anything like it? And the flowers—a different color for each one of us! Doesn't Ottilie look a dream, Paula? Her dress is from the Odenheimer Salon in Frankfurt, an original!" It was pink tulle over white silk, a border of wild roses around the skirt. It suited Ottilie's rosy complexion perfectly, and the darker pink carnations on her décolleté emphasized the pastel tints of the outfit.

"We must look upon it as an investment," Ottilie's mother had said when they had purchased the expensive dress. Ottilie was twenty-one and still not engaged.

When Paula went down the stairs in her green dress with the yellow roses, Pedro, the eldest of the Trombetta boys, her partner for the dinner, was waiting for her in the hall. "My word!" he exclaimed. "Look what's become of our skinny schoolgirl! A creature with bewitching eyes and a complexion like a pearl."

"Since when do pearls have complexions?" Paula teased

him. They had known each other for years, but since
Paula's return from Nancy, they had met only a few times
when Pedro was home on vacation from the university.
Once upon a time, he used to pull her pigtails and pinch
her skinny arms. In revenge, she had scratched his noble
Roman nose, and it had ended with his buying her a bag
of sticky candy to make up. In the meantime, in Bonn, he
had acquired the impeccable manners of a member of one
of the most exclusive fraternities at the university. He
bowed deeply, offered her his arm, and, both laughing at
the formality of it all, they entered the dining room. It was
decorated in Empire style, the first Napoleon's period. At
table, Paula found Konrad Overberg on her left. Ottilie
was his partner. She smiled radiantly and waved to her
equally radiant mother at the other end of the table. What
else but marriage could a girl of good family hope for? She
might become companion to some temperamental old
lady, or governess to other people's children, or one of
those maiden aunts who helped the family whenever and
wherever they were needed.

Once the two older boys have gone to the cadet school,
I'll ask Papa to let me attend the teacher's training course
at the Ursuline college in Wiesbaden or Geisenheim, Paula
thought. I won't sit around and wait for a marriage. If I
can't have the man I love, I'll have a career.

Konrad interrupted her train of thought. "How many
waltzes, my gracious lady?" he asked and raised his wine
glass. She touched it with her own.

"Oh, I thought *you* were going to work that out."

"All of them," he said, looking at her over the rim of his
glass. Paula noticed Melanie and Lottchen exchanging a
glance and felt the blood rush to her cheeks. She bowed

her head on its slender, a little too long neck, and Konrad
saw the faint red rise into her ivory-pale face and disappear again.

"The first one you must dance with your dinner partner," she admonished him softly. "And I with Pedro."

"Of course," he whispered reassuringly. "And after that,
I'm only staking a very modest claim to the waltzes; all the
polkas and mazurkas and Rheinländers are entirely yours
to dispose of as you will."

In the Crown, the dancing was well under way when
the Overberg party arrived. On the terrace overlooking
the river, tables with white cloths surrounded the dance
floor. Red, blue, and yellow lanterns were strung in the
overhanging branches of old plane trees. A steamer passed
on the river; music and singing drifted across the water. In
the garden of the Crown, the small band, which was
known as one of the best dance bands between Cologne
and Frankfurt, struck up a waltz by the younger Strauss,
whose melodies were bewitching all Europe. Paula danced
with Pedro, and she had to admit that he had learned to
dance in his student organization, not to be compared to
Overberg, but fair enough. Even the older ladies and
gentlemen joined in dancing this first waltz, although
usually they only took part in quadrilles. Paula saw her
mother's black silk dress, which she had worn on all such
occasions for as long as she could remember, going past
with the brown frock coat of Herr Overberg Senior, and it
was clear that they were both enjoying themselves, even if
they went back to their table again after a few turns
around the floor. August had booked the next dance with
Paula, and Georg cut in for the second half. Adolf was still

off with his dog somewhere; as yet he had no interest in dancing. Then came a polka with the doctor's son and a mazurka with the second Trombetta boy, Georg's friend, and after that Overberg's waltz, *Spring Voices*. The young people were so carried away by the enchanting melody that the band had to play the waltz twice again. Even after that, the dancers clamored for more, but the band leader, who played the first violin, insisted on a rest for his musicians.

"And now you should cool off, Paula," Overberg said. "Let's walk along the river."

"Quite clever, our convent girl, hm?" whispered Melanie to Caroline, Lottchen, and pretty Ottilie, in her Odenheim original, who had grown more and more quiet as the evening went on. "That green dress with her pearl complexion—that's what Pedro called it just now when he danced with me—and the yellow rose in her dark hair! And how she's done her hair today! Very clever!"

Paula had nothing against a little walk. She put her hand on the sleeve of Konrad's lavender-blue dress coat, and they disappeared into the shadow of the plane trees, as other couples were doing. They walked along the river, away from the noisy gaiety of the dance floor, which had swallowed up all the more delicate sounds of the night— the gentle murmuring of the river, the lapping of the little waves against the quay, the rustling of the leaves. Soon even the village with its few drowsily winking lights lay behind them.

"It's been a long time since I saw my father so cheerful," Konrad said. "He even danced with Madame your mother."

"Yes, and he really looked as though he were enjoying

it. Tell me, there is such a beautiful picture in my room. I thought it might be a portrait of your late mother, but Fräulein Nikodema said it was the Empress Elizabeth of Austria."

"Yes. A copy of the Winterhalter portrait in the Hofburg." He stopped walking and turned his face to the river. "There is no picture of her in our house," he said. "She is not dead, Paula."

"Not dead?"

"No." In the silence that followed Paula regretted that she had asked about the picture.

Not dead. . . . But what else?

"Gone." he said at last. "Father and she were on Lake Garda together at the time. There she met another man and went away with him. When Father came home, he said she had been drowned when swimming in the lake. Only your father, who was a friend even in those days, learned the truth and was a great comfort to him. I was nine, when it happened. On my twentieth birthday my father told me, and he never talked of it since."

"Ach!" Paula said, utterly shocked. How was it possible to leave a husband, and young child! Could something so unthinkable happen even when one believed in the security of a marriage? Was there never an escape from the terrible uncertainty of human existence?

So that was what had happened. . . . And Konrad had been told about it, a young man, unsuspecting and unwarned. The long-healed scar of his mother's death had been torn open by the bitter realization of her unfaithfulness.

If only there were a word to tell him about my sympathy and my gratitude for his confidence, she thought miserably.

"Perhaps it's easier for you to understand now why I have given people reasons for criticizing me," said the man at her side. "I don't want to make excuses. It's the talk of the town and it's true what they say. I courted this and that and the next girl and allowed them to fall in love with me. But every time, when the moment came for me to declare myself, I lost my nerve. Yes, I'll admit it, I was cowardly, afraid that I might be as fatally hurt as my father."

"And so you went off on your journeys."

"Yes, I went off. But luckily each of the girls forgot about it sooner or later."

"What makes you think women forget so quickly?"

"What makes you think that men forget quickly? Look at my father. He has never forgotten. As a Catholic, he could not have married again, but even without that, he would have stayed alone. Enough of this."

He turned his face back to her, and they continued walking. "And you, Paula?" he said. "Are you still thinking of going into a convent?"

"No," she replied. "I've realized that it would only have been an escape. I'm not cut out to be a nun. Let's go back now, please. I don't really mind much what people say, but I wouldn't like it to look as though I might be the reason for your next big trip."

"Can't you trust me a little, Paula?" he asked, and—aware of the unfairness of all this gossip—she considered seriously.

"I could," she said at last, "provided everything between us is quite clear. I haven't forgotten how kind you were to me in the mail coach, and I certainly wasn't anyone to be courted then, a shivering, skinny schoolgirl with a red nose."

"Objection! It wasn't red!"

"Was it blue? Horrible! Honestly, I like finding you in Uncle Emmo's room when I take his tea tray in. I could sit there by the hour drinking in your discussions like a dry sponge. I enjoy dancing with you more than with anybody else. I like you, Konrad, and you know it, don't you?" She looked up at him with unaffected sincerity. "But if we are to be friends, you must promise me something."

"Whatever you ask, Paula."

"You must never think that one day you might have to pack your bags because of me. As far as I'm concerned, you are completely safe because my heart isn't free any longer, and it won't be for ever and ever, even if there's not a bit of hope."

Now it was Konrad Overberg's turn to say, "Ach!" and after that he said not another word until they were near the garden of the Crown again. There he stopped and gently took the yellow rose from her hair. "It's faded. May I keep it—because it's my birthday today? But please don't tell on me. Thirty years old! Old enough to have learned patience."

"My very best wishes, Konrad. I do hope you'll soon find the woman with whom you can feel secure."

"Thanks," he said, put the rose into his breast pocket, and kissed her hand.

On the terrace of the Crown, the young people were still dancing as eagerly as before. It had grown quite cool. Herr Overberg Senior was taking his older guests back to the house. Mama looked over at Paula, wondering perhaps where she had been so long. Adolf had returned and was going off with his parents and Aqua. Both he and his dog were tired from a long day.

The band struck up the *Blue Danube*. "Our waltz," said Overberg and led Paula onto the floor.

From the village street came the clatter of horses' hoofs. A mail coach and four pulled up in front of the Crown, full of young Prussian officers from Mainz or Wiesbaden. They had been spending the evening in nearby Rudesheim, and although it was late, they had decided on the spur of the moment to drive on to Assmannshausen when they heard that the famous dance band was playing in the Crown. They came just in time to take the now empty table of the Overberg party, and a waiter hurried over with the wine list. Paula was aware of August and Georg greeting someone joyously. For a moment, she turned her face away and looked over Overberg's shoulder, up to the moon that sailed against the velvet of the night sky, so reassuringly unconcerned. Then her eyes were drawn back irresistibly by the familiar voice, to the shimmer of blue and silver.

"I'm tired," she said and stopped dancing. With Overberg's arm still around her, she stood as though turned to stone, her eyes dark, her lips slightly parted but with no trace of a smile. Overberg had only to follow her gaze to understand everything.

There he was, coming toward her through the dancing couples like a swimmer breasting a choppy sea. "Allow me, Herr Overberg!" His spurs jangled. Overberg returned his bow and yielded to what nothing and nobody in the world could have prevented.

They danced. His arm held her tightly, his mouth was close to her ear. "*Ma belle chérie*," he whispered, as he had done in the arbor. They had never before danced together—and where dancing with Overberg had been pure pleasure in music and rhythm and the perfect coordination of movement, now it was ecstasy, a helpless captivity in the net of the bewitching melody, a merging into one another without resistance or reserve. "*Ma belle chérie,*" he said once again with sad tenderness. "That this should have been granted us!" And then, "The division is being replaced. We leave for Berlin tomorrow."

"*Adieu,*" she said. "*Adieu, mon ami.*"

They danced around the circle, silently now, once, twice, and a third time. It was an instant. It was an eternity.

"Enough," she said at last, completely exhausted, as if she had reached the summit of a mountain with her very last strength.

Quitzow led her to the place where Overberg had been standing all the time, waiting, and put her gently beside him as if entrusting something fragile to him. The two gentlemen bowed. The hussar's spurs jangled. Paula bent her head without looking at him again. She did not even notice that her friends were watching her.

"We must continue dancing," said Overberg.

"Yes," she said. From far away she seemed to hear her father's voice: "*Contenance,* child!" And still the waves of the *Blue Danube* were coaxing, alluring.

When the music came to an end at last, Overberg said, "I'll take you back to the house now, Paula."

"Yes," she said again and let him lead her along the river, in the other direction this time, back toward the house. The stars wandered across the sky, still faithfully watched by the moon, the celestial shepherdess. The river murmured softly. The silence of the night received the secret of Paula's tears, which ran down her face. Overberg felt the soundless weeping but did not disturb her with a word or even a pressure of his arm. She had to overcome this alone. He was there; from now on he would always be there when she needed him—that he knew, overwhelmed by the depth of his tenderness for her.

They walked on in silence a little longer, past the house until he thought she might now be tired enough, and then back to the house.

"Sleep now," he said at the door of her room. "Sleep, my dear."

He did not even kiss her hand.

In a very small, very controlled voice she said, "Thank you, Konrad."

Autumn III

IN THE FIELDS, the potato fires were burning, and the schoolchildren had what was called the potato vacation. This meant hard work for the farm children, since everyone except tiny babies and the old and infirm had to help with the potato digging. In rainy weather, they stood in the ankle-deep mud of the fields, an empty sack tied about their shoulders; in fine weather, the burning sun beat down on the backs of young and old alike. The pungent smell of burning potato tops drifted over the fields and meadows to the very town. It was the smell of fall, the odor of death that nourishes future life.

For Adolf, the time had come to go and search for Aqua's rightful master.

"Tell me when you're going. I'll come with you," said August—August who was now making an effort to speak good German, *Hochdeutsch,* and not swallow syllables or the endings of words any more, August who would be going away with Georg next Easter and leaving Adolf behind. His offer was a present, a farewell present, the meaning of which Adolf understood but could not accept, however hard it was to refuse. This was something he had to perform alone, just as the Knights of the Round Table had to go out on their quest for the Grail alone. They hoped to find something, but he, Adolf, had to give something away; that was the difference. One as well as the other was a solitary business.

"Thanks, August," he said. "No . . . thanks."

And his elder brother slapped him on the shoulder. "I know what you mean, old man."

On the third of October, the whole family went to Gretel's wedding at Dietkirchen on the other side of the Lahn. The wedding took place on the feast of St. Lubentius in the great cathedral that stands on the steep white cliffs high above the Lahn and daily sends its greetings to its sister cathedral of the same age across the river in Limburg.

Country wedding festivities went on for three days, and the feast of the patron saint, with its fair, was celebrated for three days, too. The family from the courthouse came only on Sunday, the actual wedding day. They walked in the long procession that led the bridal pair to the cathedral, where the marriage took place after the High Mass; then back to the farm belonging to the bride's parents. Here there was a wedding feast that the old Flemish painter Breughel might have painted. Long tables were set under the two linden trees in front of the house; the gaily dressed company in traditional country Sunday costume sat down on the benches, and the parade of plates and dishes began. First came a tureen of steaming soup and dumplings; then an enormous cut of boiled beef with horse-radish and gherkins and beetroot; next followed a platter of river fish swimming in golden butter and surrounded by new potatoes. Then came roast ducks and pigeons with salad and vegetables, and at the end, for dessert, the inevitable dish of rice, this time stiffened with whipped cream in honor of the great occasion. All this was washed down with quantities of fresh grape juice, wine, and beer; otherwise, even the stoutest trencherman could not have managed it. After the meal, the men lit up their pipes, the parish priest took his leave because he had to go on to another wedding, and an hour later coffee and damson cakes big as cartwheels were served. The young people withdrew to the threshing floor, swept clean for the occasion, to dance. The girls stood against the wall on one side and the lads on the other until the Amtmann had danced the ceremonial round of honor with the bride. Then the village musicians struck up a livelier tune, and the lads seized their girls and stamped away till the dust rose from the earthen floor and the sweat ran down their red faces. Paula, too, danced a few rounds; held in an iron grip by the country lads, she was whirled around and around, until her mother came to remind her that it was time to go, as dusk was falling. Adolf harnessed Silver, the family said good-by to the young married couple, their parents and the other guests, and the carriage, now driven by August, started down the steep village street homeward bound, accompanied for a long way by the fiddles and pipes from the wedding celebration and the gay noises from the fair. The smell of incense from the morning's procession, mixed with the earthy odors of fresh grape juice and damson cakes, still lingered in the narrow streets.

Adolf did not drive back to Limburg with the family. Since he was now on the right side of the Lahn and not far from where the Elbbach joined it, he wanted to set out on his hike early the next morning. Gretel's mother had packed his rucksack full of good things from the wedding feast, and he spent the night in a farmer's barn, some little way from the noisy fun of the fair. In the sweet-smelling hay he fell asleep quickly, his dog beside him—but his sleep was not so deep and peaceful as usual, whether because of the heavy food he had eaten or the heavy task that lay ahead of him. At dawn, he shook the straws out of his hair and clothes, washed the sleep from his eyes at the well, and said good-by to the farmer's wife, who was just coming out of the barn with her milk pails. She held one of the pails out to him, and he took a drink and then wiped the foam off his mouth with the back of his hand.

"Thank you, and God bless you," he said. "Come on, Aqua." And they set out on the road.

A few days previously, after early Mass, Father Knodt had asked him if he had any plans for the holiday. "A trip up the Elbbach," said Adolf. "The shepherd who used to own Aqua is supposed to live up there. Why on earth didn't he claim his dog when we put the advertisement in the paper, Father?"

"People in the country only read the paper if someone brings it back from a trip to town, and then they only look at the cattle and potato prices."

"But why did God send me Aqua in the first place when *He* knew the whole time where he belonged and that He would take him away from me one day? A gift's a gift, after all!" said Adolf, disappointed in the heavenly Ruler who evidently had no regard for the rules of fair play valid among schoolboys. Adolf had no idea that he was asking the same question as his big sister—Job's question, the ancient and forever unanswered question of all mankind.

"If we begin to ask why, we don't get very far, Adolf," said the curate, who had himself encountered this Why when he went into the seminary to become a servant of God and had to leave behind the beloved tabby cat with which he had grown up. He had never forgotten and so could understand that, for the boy standing before him, blinking resolutely to keep back the tears, his world was going to pieces. He knew as well that he would patch the pieces together again, this time and many more times in his life.

As Adolf set off into the slowly brightening autumn morning, he thought to himself that perhaps God might have let the man die in the meantime and only wanted to put him to the test. Or it was also possible that the shepherd had found himself another dog and no longer needed Aqua. Or that Aqua would refuse to stay with him. There was still a dim ray of hope.

The world glistened with dew. Hips hung like drops of blood among the brownish twigs of the briar. High above, in the thin blue air, two birds of prey were circling. Adolf thought of his falcon—that was a scar that had almost healed, but it still hurt each time it was touched. He had come to understand that a falcon had to be free and have a mate, like the one up there, but a dog belonged to his master.

From Dietkirchen and Limburg came the sound of the morning bells, and the bells from the village of Elz joined in the glad song. It was easy going in the clear autumn air, which had no trace of heaviness in it. The forest was brown and red and gold, punctuated by the dark autumnal green of the conifers. Aqua enjoyed the walk wholeheartedly and, without any suspicion of what was in store, ran on ahead, barked at the crows on the poplars, came back and went off again following a trail. Whenever he saw a flock of sheep grazing on the fallow fields, he would stop for a few minutes and sniff the scent, which was carried on the wind. Once Adolf had a word with one of the shepherds. "Do you know this dog?"

"Couldn't say. Sheep dogs all look alike. See, my Molli could be his brother."

Yes, of course, all the sheep dogs in the district resembled one another. They weren't bred according to a stud book or for their beauty but for their ability as sheep dogs. The shepherds would often make a trip of several hours on foot to secure a young dog from the litter of a reliable and intelligent female if they knew she had been mated with a similar sire. There were sheep dogs whose intelligence, faithfulness, and courage were known from the Westerwald to the Taunus, and it was true they all had a kind of family likeness. Perhaps, thought Adolf, the shepherd that day had been mistaken after all.

The higher he and Aqua went up the course of the stream, the fewer the farms became. They had climbed up the footpath into the forest behind Hadamar, whence you could get a wonderful view of the valley. It was peaceful up here; the forest covered the hills like the thick fleece on a sheep's back. At midday, they stopped for a rest, and Adolf unpacked bread and bacon and wedding cake from his rucksack; they ate and quenched their thirst at one of the springs that rose everywhere here. Then they had to press on.

The valley grew narrower and the slopes steeper. Sometimes the winding path would climb higher up into the wood, then drop down into the valley again if there was a farmstead or hamlet. At each of the lonely farms, Adolf asked whether they knew anything about the dog. Once Aqua ran on ahead and stood sniffing by the fence of a farmhouse; in the garden, a few bright asters nodded beside red and green cabbages. An old woman was sitting in front of the door stoning plums into a big tub. In the courthouse, too, they would begin to stone the plums for the plum purée soon. Throughout Nassau, the time had come to cook the "Hoink," the plum purée, which was made without any sugar, with only a few sweet pears, and simmered and stirred for twenty-four hours in the enormous copper kettle otherwise used for boiling the linen. The women would sit on benches along the wall of the washhouse, knitting and telling stories and taking turns at stirring the pulp day and night, until the purée started to grow stiff and could be poured into the gray stone jars.

Adolf called a greeting to the old woman. A basket with a sleeping child in it stood beside her; everyone else from the valley was probably still in Dietkirchen. Only the old people had been left at home to look after the cattle and the tiny children. "Do you know whose dog this is?" asked the boy. The old woman, evidently stone deaf, held her hand to her ear and shook her head, but she stood up and passed him a handful of the little wrinkled plums, as sweet as honey, over the fence. He thanked her and went on his way.

A little later, they saw a lame man driving a calf back into a shed; from inside the shed came the doleful mooing of a cow. " '*Tag*. Has anyone around here lost a dog?"

"Run away?"

"No, pulled him out of the Lahn in March last year in the floods."

"So-o, a lot drowned then; dogs and cats, calves and lambs, scores of them. Never got none back. Kasper, the shepherd, lost a dog at that time, too."

"And where'll I find him?"

"Way up over yonder, an hour or two. There's two farms over the other side. If he's not there, he won't be far away."

"Thanks," said Adolf.

"So long, lad."

"So long."

The path climbed up into the forest again. They walked on and on. Even Aqua started to get tired and trotted along close to Adolf's side. Occasionally, he lifted his head and looked at the boy; what further plans did he have for today? Home lay in the other direction; he knew that much. At last, the track began to descend again, across a steep meadow and down to two small homesteads on the other side of the stream. A flock of sheep was grazing along the bank and up the slope. An old man stood nearby, his hat pulled down low on his forehead against the slanting rays of the sun. A dog lay near him but stood up watchfully when he saw the two coming down the opposite bank. There was no plank across the water, which at this point foamed over small boulders. Adolf stopped and held his dog tight by the collar. Aqua did not move, but a shiver ran through his body and from it through Adolf's hand and arm right down to his toes.

"Turn back with your dog, lad," the shepherd shouted over to him. "Or else they'll be fighting and biting."

When Aqua heard the voice, there was no holding him any more; he was down the slope, through the water, and up to the shepherd in a flash. Adolf, who followed more slowly, saw how the other dog lowered his head for the attack, but before he could leap, Aqua had seized him by the neck and given him a shake, like a mature man admonishing a cheeky boy. The shepherd sent him over to the flock with a wave of his stick. "Bello?" he said, and now Aqua jumped up at him barking loudly, almost knocking him over with the force of the impact, licked his face and hands and circled around him with wild bounds.

"Bello!" said the man again, still half incredulous, and he looked at the boy, who had meanwhile crossed the stream, too, jumping from one stone to another, but was now on the point of turning for home again. Aqua had *gone through water;* there was nothing more to be asked or said. He had recognized his old master . . .

"Wait, lad!" shouted the man, and now Aqua ran back to Adolf, seized his sleeve, put a paw on his shoulder, ran his rough tongue over the boy's face, torn in confusion this way and that, between one love and the other.

"The flood in '65, eh?" questioned the man.

"Yes."

"That day," the old man told him, "as the stream was rising, I tied Bello to his kennel because he was always so crazy about water. If he saw anything floating in water, even if it was a dead cat, he had to get it out and bring it to me. We'd already brought the sheep back across the mountain into the old barn in the afternoon. If only I'd known the water would rise so quick! Next morning the stream was up to the door, and the kennel and Bello gone. Did you fish him out, lad?"

"Yes."

"Where'd that be?"

"In Limburg."

"Jesus, Mary, and Joseph!" He crossed himself. "Might have drowned yourself. Is he still so silly about water?"

"No. Won't go near it."

"And how did you know he belonged to me?"

"Shepherd in the Westerwald thought he might. Well, God bless you, shepherd," said Adolf. He couldn't bear any more questions. It was enough. It was all over. He jumped over the stones in the stream with big strides, Aqua whimpering behind him, then running back to the shepherd, barking, complaining loudly of the stupidity of human beings. Couldn't they stay together?

"Want to go with the lad?" asked the shepherd, more used to talking to his dog than to people. "Wait, lad!" he shouted again. "Wait. You pulled him out of the water . . ."

Adolf ran up the far slope as fast as he could. Aqua looked at the shepherd. When the shepherd turned his head away, he followed Adolf. The water splashed his belly, but he didn't even shake himself; he leaped up the bank and lay down right across the path in front of the boy, who stopped, his hands thrust deep in his pockets to keep himself from fondling the thick coat just once more. "Go," he said hoarsely. "Go to your master, Aqua. *Allez!*" With one stride he stepped over the dog and scrambled farther up the slope, stumbling over stones, blinded by the tears gathering in his eyes.

Down below stood the old shepherd; up there on the opposite slope was the boy. Neither called the dog; neither tried to entice him. Aqua stood looking after Adolf and then back to the shepherd. . . . Suddenly his body tensed; head and tail stiffened. He had seen a lamb straying onto a rock that fell steeply to the stream on one side. The younger dog was barking at the animal, confusing the poor lamb. The experienced Aqua, calm and prudent, jumped right into the deeper water and, under the side of the rock approaching from the stream, drove the lamb gently back to the flock.

From the edge of the wood, Adolf had watched the proceedings. Aqua was now standing beside the shepherd, who was stroking him for the first time. The dog was still hanging his head, but his tail was waving gently to and fro. Already he was Aqua no more. He was Bello. Not a happy dog, but back where he belonged and where he would one day be happy again.

Adolf returned the same way he had come. Dusk was falling. More and more stars came out. The Milky Way stretched out across the sky; like a pale mist with its millions of stars, it looked down on the dwarf planet called the earth by its inhabitants. He could have asked in any village or farm for a night's lodging, but he wanted to be alone. Since no one could see or hear him, he cried himself to sleep and then slept deeply on a bed of leaves, covered by shadows, alone beneath the wandering stars.

When he awoke early the next morning, it was raining softly, and he felt cold. Swathes of mist hung between the trees. Still half asleep, his hand reached out for the warm pelt of his dog. He drew it back empty, stood up, stretched himself, ate a piece of bread and bacon from his rucksack, and looked for and found a spring to drink from and to wash the sleep from his eyes. Then he set off at a brisk pace down the narrow path to keep warm.

It was afternoon when he arrived back at the court-house. First of all, he went to the stable to see Silver. He stood for a while in the stall beside the gelding, leaning his forehead on the smooth neck. The horse pawed the ground and looked over the wooden half gate as if he were searching for the dog who was usually inseparable from Adolf. Then he rubbed his nose against Adolf's cheek and held out his forehead to be scratched. "We two'll stay together, eh?" said Adolf and went into the house. He knew that no one had been worried about him. The boys were often out on expeditions for a few days, either by themselves or together in the holidays. It was a safe district. For years now, no one had been attacked by robbers. Old Isidor traveled about untroubled and unmolested, even up into the High Westerwald once a year.

In the kitchen, the smell of freshly baked bread greeted Adolf. Kettchen had just put the brown loaves on a wire tray to cool and was showing Anna, Gretel's younger sister, who had now come to be housemaid in the courthouse, how to wipe out the oven so that it didn't rust.

"Good day, Kettchen, good day, Anna," Adolf said.

"Good day, Adolf. Sit down and I'll spread you a slice of new bread. We made the butter today. Want some buttermilk?"

"No, something hot, please. Was it fun at the wedding after we left?"

"Ah, yes! Eh, Annchen? The mistress let us stay there till this morning. Sunday night we danced till we were fit to drop and ate till we were near bursting."

The hot milk did Adolf good. He was still feeling a little chilly from his night in the open, and his throat was sore. If only he didn't catch a cold! Mama had a nasty way of waging war on colds if ever one of the boys started one. Wet compresses, quarts of hot, bitter herb tea, warm salt water that had to be sniffed up one nostril until it came down the other. . . . Adolf hadn't even had a cold after he'd fallen in under the ice last winter. He certainly wouldn't yield to one after a single night in the open air and a bit of rain.

"Where are the other boys?" he asked.

"Yesterday someone brought a letter from Madame Franziska. You were all to go for a week to Schwalbach, the weather being so good. So they set off straight away."

"Has Paula gone with them?"

"No, Fräulein Paula stayed. She's in with Babett. She's poorly, Babett is. The doctor was here, and then Father Knodt had to come to hear her confession."

Only now did it strike Adolf that today the door between the kitchen and Babett's room, which normally stood open, was shut. He stood up, turned the door handle softly, and peeped through the crack. She was lying in bed quite peacefully. Paula was sitting next to her, holding her hand, and when his sister became aware of Adolf, she signaled to him not to come in. He went upstairs and took off his damp suit. It was his best Sunday suit that he had worn to the wedding; luckily, all the boys' clothes were of good, strong material that could stand any amount of wear and tear.

At suppertime, the long table looked empty without the other boys. "Good evening, everyone," said Adolf and found that today his napkin ring was at the place next to his father. It was a rare honor, reserved for birthdays or when you brought home a particularly good school report.

Mama nodded to him. "It's good to have you home again, Adolf dear."

And once Papa leaned over toward him and asked softly, "Everything all right?"

"Yes, Papa," he said, and then as he glanced quickly around the table, he asked, "Where's Aunt Rikchen?"

"She took over from Paula and is sitting with Babett," said Mama. "It's lucky the little ones are out of the house. We have to be quiet. Babett has had a heart attack."

A heart attack! Adolf knew that was something serious. A schoolfriend's father had died from a heart attack last year. He hoped Babett would not die. She had been looking forward to her ninetieth birthday for a long time, and the boys had thought out all sorts of surprises for her, beginning in the morning with a serenade of songs and music on their recorders. Everyone in the house had planned something to make the day happy for her. Adolf himself had written a poem to celebrate the momentous occasion. Paula, to whom he had read it, had pronounced it a beauty, very moving and here and there a little funny, too, for that was an essential part of a birthday poem. He didn't of course consider for a moment reciting it himself: he would have died of embarrassment. Georg and Ferdinand were the actors in the family, and Adolf had offered it to Georg first as the elder, since he thought it an honor to read his poem. But Georg had not accepted; he said he had enough to learn by heart for school. Just like old Georg! Ferdinand, on the other hand, was all for it. There wouldn't be a dry eye in the house when he recited the seven verses; whatever else you might say about him, Ferdinand certainly had *feeling*, and moreover he was always willing to do anyone a favor if it didn't actually run counter to his own plans.

"Yesterday evening, when I said good night to her, Babett was quite cheerful," said the Amtmann. "She said she didn't want to go into the almshouse after all; she had lived all her life with the family, and she wanted to die with us when the time came. The curate described the old people's home in glowing terms to her, but *all those old women*, that wasn't her cup of tea at all, she said. If we were moving to Wiesbaden, then she would move with us."

"To Wiesbaden?" asked Adolf.

"Yes. Of course, you weren't there when we talked about it with Paula and the boys yesterday evening. August and Georg told Mama and me that they would like to enter the cadet corps next Easter, if we have nothing against it. They discussed it all with Lieutenant von Quitzow once again when they met at the Crown in Assmannshausen, and he's going to put in a good word for them with his uncle, who's going to be the commandant at Oranienstein. Well, we won't stand in their way—and we told them and the little ones that next year, as soon as the roads are clear of snow, we'll be moving to Wiesbaden."

"But what about Silver? Where shall we keep him in Wiesbaden?"

"I shan't need a horse in town. There won't be any more official trips around the countryside for me," said Papa. "If I have to make a journey on business for Frau von Savigny, she will provide a carriage and horses for me, and besides I can always make use of the mail coach or the railway."

Oh, Silver! Silver! Adolf could think of nothing else.

"I'll relieve Aunt Rikchen now with Babett," he heard Mama saying. "If you want, you can go to the Rosary this evening, Paula. Take Adolf with you if he's not too tired."

"I've something more to see to in the office; then I'll join you, Margarete," said Papa. "We can sit with Babett together and wait for the doctor to come—he's promised to look in once again before nightfall. Adolf, we are all proud of you today. Now don't look like a dying duck in a thunderstorm just because we're going to Wiesbaden. It's a beautiful and interesting town. Just think of all there is, theaters and opera and lectures. The Taunus Mountains will be on our doorstep, and we'll be able to go for splendid hikes and rambles. And Franziska will be so near us that you can easily visit her on a Sunday. Mama and I are looking forward to seeing more of her and her family. And besides that, we intend to see Mozart's *Don Juan* and *The Magic Flute* at least once every winter."

If I have to give up Silver, too, thought Adolf, I don't care about all that! But then, as though his own grief had made him perceptive, he suddenly had a flash of insight. Perhaps the truth was that Papa had to comfort himself and Mama with *The Magic Flute* and all the other things they could enjoy in the town. Wasn't he just as fond of his career as Adolf was of Aqua and Silver? Weren't he and Mama just as sad at heart when they thought of having to part with their sons and with all their friends in Limburg? And what would Mama do without her big garden?

"Yes, Papa," he answered. "I guess it's quite possible to live in Wiesbaden, too, if we must."

Later as he walked up to the cathedral with Paula, she put her arm through his. "Was it very bad?" she asked.

"Oh, all right," said Adolf. "Just think, Aquarius went through *water* when he heard the man's voice. . . . Then I really knew that the time had come."

"Yes. But now it's a good thing that Aquarius is with his old master after all, isn't it? He'd never have managed to become a town dog—he's been used to the freedom of the country all his life."

"I know, I know," said Adolf.

"You'll like it in Wiesbaden once you get used to it. And won't it be nice to see a lot of the Ippel girls, whom we all liked so much when they were here in the summer."

Adolf's face cheered up a little at this. "We're engaged to be married," he said. "Don't tell anybody."

"Engaged?"

"Yes. Toni and I."

"Congratulations," said Paula. "I couldn't wish for a nicer sister-in-law."

"I gave her a little garnet heart for her birthday. Isidor bought it for me at the Frankfurt Fair, then he delivered it to her for me, and I'm sure he'll bring me a letter from her when he comes before Christmas. He got me something for your birthday, too, Paula, but I won't tell you what it is."

"I can hardly wait to see," she said, and he nodded happily.

In the cathedral, the Lady altar was radiant with candles, and the statue of the Mother of God stood above a cloud of autumn flowers: asters, dahlias, and sunflowers, and bouquets of bright fall foliage with red and blue berries, silver thistles, and delicate wild grasses.

"October has always been one of my favorite months," Paula whispered to Adolf as they went up the side aisle together. "It's such a lovely thought that the Queen of the Rosary is honored everywhere. So you mustn't be so sad if we leave here. In Wiesbaden we can go to October Rosary devotions and on Holy Saturday to the Easter Vigil and at Christmas to Midnight Mass, just as we can here in Limburg or anywhere in the world."

The voice of the priest leading the recitation of the

Rosary resounded in the vaulted roof, and the response of the small congregation was like the murmur of an underground river. After the Rosary, the organist played one of the beautiful hymns to Mary, the *Ave Maristella*. Adolf heard his sister's voice next to him as clear as a blackbird's song, and he joined in the singing even though his throat was still raw with grief and soreness. Then the mysterious invocations of the Litany to the Blessed Virgin rolled out, which always conjured up strange pictures in his mind's eye: "Tower of David! Tower of ivory! House of gold! Morning Star! Comforter of the afflicted!" "Pray for us!" answered the congregation and "Pray for us!" Adolf begged, too. His grief was still overwhelmingly big and dark. Aquarius! he thought; Silver! August! Nothing, nothing would ever be the same again, nothing as it used to be. Aqua had left him for an older loyalty. He was a clever dog; he must have known that he would never again have such a good life as he had with Adolf. No nice soft bed that he shared with his master on cold winter nights, but instead hard service and short rations and constant bother with the silly lambs that were always getting lost. But he had chosen what he had to choose. And he, Adolf, had done what he had to do without anyone's forcing him to it.

Strange, he thought, that with so much sorrow, one still remained the same person as before; it didn't make one rot inside; one didn't get disfigured by sorrow as by a wound. It almost seemed as though something had been added to his own essence and not taken away, as though he had found something and not just lost on his agonizing journey. Not the Holy Grail, like Parsifal, to be sure . . . then what? Himself perhaps? The self that would later grow into a man? He couldn't have expressed it in words. It was only a dim foreshadowing of what he might perhaps be able to understand much later—just as he could only guess at what his sister meant when she said that always and everywhere, even in the strangest places, there was an unchangeable constancy ever ready to comfort you if only you were willing to let yourself be comforted.

"But you, Paula," he said on their way home. "You will stay with us, won't you? You're not going to the convent to be a nun?"

She shook her head. "Don't worry, Adolf. I'm going to stay with you. If Papa'll let me go to the Ursuline college in Wiesbaden and become a teacher, I'll always be able to live with Mama and Papa and look after them later on when they're quite old."

That night Adolf slept for the first time alone in the boys' room, without any of the others and without Aqua. He woke once or twice and felt involuntarily for the dog or listened for his brothers' breathing. There was a lot of stirring in the house of which he was aware even in his sleep. Suddenly Paula was standing by his bed, and at once he was wide awake, even before she shook him, although he usually slept heavily. "Wake up, Adolf. Babett's worse. The doctor has been, and Holwein's gone off to fetch Father Knodt. We must all be with her."

He dressed quickly and went downstairs with his sister. Babett, he thought. Babett who had been with them as long as he could think! It wasn't possible that Babett would die?

The entire household had gathered in Babett's room. She had already received Holy Communion; now she lay there, her face a waxlike yellow against the white pillows, but her bright bird's eyes still watched everything that was going on. She even acknowledged Paula's and Adolf's presence with a quick glance. Then she turned her attention to the hands of the young priest as he anointed her with the oil of Extreme Unction, the last sacrament. She watched him with an alert attentiveness, for now it was important that everything was done properly to prepare her for her last hard journey.

On the little table beside her bed, covered with a white cloth, two candles were burning. The Amtmann himself put the crucifix into the hands of his old friend, and as she took it, she kept hold of his hand also.

When the curate said the prayers for the dying, they all knelt and made the responses.

The breathing of the dying woman was now so heavy that it filled the room. The sunken chest rose and fell, as though every little breath of air demanded a painful effort from her tired heart. Adolf could not take his eyes off this struggle: he watched with burning curiosity. He had never seen anyone die; death was as yet not the reality for him that is at the end of every life. He was frightened. He felt his own skin going cold, his young healthy limbs getting stiff, his breathing becoming heavy. Sweat was breaking out on his forehead, and when he suddenly felt Paula's hand clasping his fingers, it seemed to him that this hand was the only thing that still linked him to life.

Babett's face strained with the effort of a last urgent contemplation. Her whole life she had been a faithful steward of all the things entrusted to her. Now she trusted that her credit of intercessions would be rewarded. Prayers had to be repaid by prayers; that was only fair. She sought the eyes of the Amtmann, who had been the very personification of justice for her on this earth, and as though he had followed her train of thought, he nodded his assurance. Between his hands he was now holding hers, and that also was in order and as she had always wanted it to be at the end. Her gaze wandered once more over his face, then to the pictures of the dead on the walls, and finally to the young priest, who had done everything there was to be done. Then her features relaxed and smoothed out. The tough old heart stopped fighting; it yielded and consented. A last quivering sigh came from her tortured breast, and the bluish eyelids closed of their own accord.

The curate said the final prayers, made the sign of the cross over the dead woman, shook hands with everyone in the room, and went out.

Uncle Emmo escorted the quietly weeping aunts to their room. The Amtmann put his arm around his wife, who looked near to collapse with tiredness. "Go to bed now, dearest," he said. "And you, too, children, off to bed. I will stay."

Kettchen and little Anna were wailing loudly, for loud lament was proper at a death. So in primitive times women had wailed over their dead. Kettchen opened the window to allow the soul free passage and veiled the little mirror with a cloth. The Amtmann did not interfere. Age-old customs must be fulfilled; the simple folks' sense of propriety insisted on it. As soon as he was alone, he would close the window again.

Two o'clock was chiming from the church tower as Paula and Adolf made their way upstairs again. Paula held her brother's hand as she had often done when he was a small boy and would not admit to being frightened in the dark.

"I'll sleep in your room tonight, in August's bed," she said. "Then you won't feel lonesome."

Winter

O N ALL SOULS' Day Paula's half sister, Franziska, came over from Schwalbach and drove out alone with her father to Montabaur to visit her mother's grave as they did every year.

November, the last month of the Church year, belongs to the dead. In the twilight of the short winter days, candles burned in little blue glasses on the graves after the lovingly tended flowers of summer had faded and been cleared away. On All Souls' Day, even on the oldest graves, where the writing could no longer be deciphered under the heavy coat of ivy, there would be twigs of evergreen and a candle burning, lit by someone for the dead whom no living person mourned any longer, a symbol of the love that forgets no one.

This year Franziska had taken leave of her family for a whole week, since after the visit to Montabaur, she wanted to have a Mass said for Babett on the fourth, which was her birthday, and put a wreath on her grave.

For Paula's eighteenth birthday on the seventh, a small party had been planned but now that Babett had died, six weeks of mourning had to be observed for the household's oldest member. Paula was quite content to cancel the party, for with all the preparations that would have been necessary, she would have had far too little time left to spend with her sister. Naturally her parents and the aunts wanted to enjoy the visitor, too, and the boys demanded their rights when they came home from school in the afternoon.

Paula left it to her sister to keep the aunts company at tea every day while she was there; they had brought her up from the very first when she was a tiny baby and loved her like a daughter, although according to their age, she could have been their granddaughter. This meant that Paula had more time for taking tea with Uncle Emmo and with Konrad Overberg, who was there almost every day now. It had been decided that shortly after the New Year Uncle Emmo would move to Bad Ems and take up his position as librarian of the Overberg collection. From time to time, he drove over to make the necessary arrangements. It had been agreed that there, as in the courthouse, two rooms would be at his disposal for his own books, and his clients could visit him as they had done in Limburg. When his trips to Ems fell on a Saturday, Adolf was invited, too, and in good weather would enjoy a ride with Konrad Overberg or would sit in the stable with Suleika as long as he wanted, gazing his fill on the newborn foal.

Franziska had been installed in the upstairs guest room. The chimney of the kitchen stove ran up behind one wall of the room, so that it was always comfortably warm, however violently the autumn storms blew across the valley. The two sisters sat there every evening far into the night and talked about all sorts of things that were not suitable for discussion in the wider circle of the family.

"So you thought of the convent, did you, little sister,"

said Franziska when Paula had told her of the difficulties
of her first months at home. "It was a bit different in my
case, but it comes to the same thing. I still thank the Lord
even now that my dear Karl appeared on the scene before
I had a chance to marry someone just in order to escape
Mama's severe discipline. She's a magnificent woman, even
if not an easy task mistress. It wasn't until much later that
I realized how much reason I have to be grateful to her for
teaching me the essentials of housekeeping, even if it did
cost me many tears."

"So you, too, shed tears occasionally under Mama's
stern rule?"

"Of course! Do you suppose she would have been more
lenient with me than with her own daughter? But just you
wait and see, one day you, too, will remember her with
gratitude when you have to cope with your own house and
children."

"That will never happen, dear Franziska, since I don't
intend to get married."

"Really? Well, now that you've put the idea of the
convent out of your head, which seems fortunate both for
you and the convent, nothing stands in the way of a
sensible marriage."

"A sensible marriage! Aunt Rikchen has told me several
times already that they're often the happiest. They may be
for someone who has never experienced love. If you have,
it's enough for a lifetime, Franziska, even if you pay dearly
for it. For me, it was hopeless right from the beginning.
Just think how shocked Mama and Papa would have been
if a Protestant and a Prussian officer to boot had asked for
my hand."

Franziska didn't seem to be as astonished at this sudden

confession as Paula would have expected. From Aunt Rikchen's letters during the summer, she had learned of a
certain anxiety in the family. "This Prussian lieutenant,"
her aunt had written, "is making me worried. Fair as the
young Alcibiades, Emmo calls him (whoever that might
be). Anyway, he's attractive—on that point even two old
women like Stina and myself are agreed. We thank God
that he disappeared before anything serious could develop.
A Protestant! We've never yet had a mixed marriage in our
family."

"It is hardly a good basis for a happy family life if the
mother and children go to one church on a Sunday and
the father to another," said Franziska in her sensible way.
"On such fundamental matters as religion, there should be
conformity in a marriage. Don't make the mistake of
thinking that such a passionate first love is enough to last
you a lifetime, as you said a minute ago. A lifetime is long,
child, and it would be a poor thing if it was all over after
the very first love. You may not believe me now, but there
can easily be more than one love in your life, even if it isn't
necessarily the same kind of love."

Paula sighed. Those were the views of a mature older
woman, who was comfortably settled in a happy marriage.
She found it difficult to believe that she herself would ever
be so reasonable. "Do you think that the parents noticed
anything?" she asked.

"They're not precisely blind, you know. But in our
family, emotional things aren't talked about more than
they have to be. What isn't discussed isn't given any more
importance than it deserves."

So that was the reason, Paula thought, Mama agreed so

quickly when she had asked her if she could go to Montabaur with Papa. "I've already told our parents that I'd like to go to the Ursulines' training college in Wiesbaden and prepare for my teachers' exam," she said, "so that I can earn my own living. I like children and get on well with them. Besides, I find it humiliating just to sit and wait till a man comes along and has the goodness to marry you."

Look at the little sister now, thought Franziska. There she sat, working out her own solutions. Out of the immature convent girl she had seen in March, a young adult person had developed, taking her life into her own hands. For the time being, at any rate, her plan sounded sensible enough. "Up till now, there hasn't ever been an unmarried daughter in our family who had to 'earn her living,' as you put it," Franziska said. "That's one of these modern ideas, but there may be something to be said for it. You'll be reasonably occupied for the next year, and by the end of it, perhaps you'll think differently about marrying."

"What else should I do all day long in Wiesbaden?" Paula said. "A little town apartment, no garden, three of the boys away from home—how will Mama find enough to use up her own vast energy? She hasn't even said a single thing against my suggestion."

Franziska would have liked to ask a few more questions, but she let the matter rest there. About this young Herr Overberg, for example, of whom two elderly ladies had been whispering in the mail coach. He had been paying court to the Amtmann's daughter lately, they had said, but with him you could never tell. . . . She wouldn't be the first he had left in the lurch after he had turned her head.

And then on the morning of Paula's birthday, there

came a box from the big flower shop in Wiesbaden; the postillion had put it down at the posting station, and the stableboy had brought it to the courthouse. By the afternoon, the whole of Limburg would know that the Amtmann's daughter had received a box from the flower shop in the former ducal residence.

The box was opened and revealed twelve yellow roses, still almost buds, each wrapped individually in a soft sheath of tissue paper; roses of such perfection that Mama, the aunts, and Franziska, who were all standing around when Paula opened the package, breathed an enraptured Ah! "They must have cost a small fortune!" said Aunt Rikchen, who was the first to come down to earth again.

"How nice of Herr Overberg!" said Paula. "We really must invite him to have coffee with the family this afternoon. He is almost always with Uncle Emmerich about that time, anyway."

By now Aunt Rikchen could keep her anxieties to herself no longer. "Nice of him, certainly, providing you don't run away with the wrong idea because of it, dear heart. Probably he only wants to show he's grateful for the tea he has so often with Uncle Emmo. After all, you're the one who has the extra work to prepare it."

The four women held their breaths in anticipation of Paula's reply to this. Perhaps it was a good thing that Aunt Rikchen had seized the opportunity to take the bull by the horns, after all.

"You can set your minds quite at rest as far as I'm concerned," Paula said and gazed with delight at the exquisite roses. "I'm well aware of what's said about him, and he himself knows better than anyone. We've spoken about it quite frankly. He's told me that he probably won't ever marry, and I told him that he'd never need to set out on another journey because of me."

"You told him that . . ." said Aunt Stina, flabbergasted. Well, these young people nowadays! It seemed she still had a lot to learn as far as her writing was concerned.

"Of course," answered Paula without a trace of embarrassment. "If you see as much of one another and dance together as much as we do, you have to have everything clear, don't you?" And she went off to find a suitable vase for her roses.

"Well, I declare!" said Aunt Rikchen, and Mama expressed the opinion that it was a good thing the family was moving, so that *all that* would come to an end of its own accord.

But, "Who can tell?" Aunt Stina, the old romantic, murmured hopefully. "They look so perfectly matched when they dance together."

Once on her own and no longer under the inquisitive eyes of her relatives, Paula picked up the roses one by one and held them in her hand for a moment before arranging them with care in a pale green vase—those yellow roses that brought back to her so vividly the farewell in Assmannshausen. How would she ever have survived that day except for Konrad's understanding, for the masculine calm and strength that had emanated from him and that had given her strength, too. He had been silent then, and he had never since spoken so much as a word about it. And now he sent her the roses that said gently, "I remember." Hidden among the leaves was a white card with only his name—"Konrad."

November was passing, wet, cold, and dark; the month of fogs lived up to its reputation. The flames of autumn had been extinguished. The whole world was gray.

The sun seemed to have deserted the world; it shone dully for only a few short hours each day over the veiled mountains and left the little town with its narrow streets to the gloomy atmosphere of late autumn. The narrow, high-gabled houses in the old quarter of the town seemed to have huddled up closer together, freezing in the darkness and cold.

And to add to the general gloom, the cod-liver oil bottle in the courthouse had been filled to the top again at the chemist's.

In Uncle Emmerich's room, it was always cozy and warm, even though here, too, they had to economize on light during the hours when dusk was falling. The flames on the hearth danced and crackled, and the candles on the table were sufficient for her uncle and Konrad to talk by. Since the weak light was not enough to read by, they would now sometimes recite poems they knew by heart or share the parts of a play. So it happened that Paula, when she brought in the tea tray, would hear the first act of *Faust*, and it needed no great feat of the imagination to change the room with its bookshelves up to the ceiling and the open fire glimmering red on the hearth into the study of a medieval scholar.

Uncle Emmo spoke the first of Dr. Faust's monologues, Overberg the voice of the Erdgeist, then Wagner, and at last the second Faust monologue when the doctor prepares to drink the poison. Paula, who heard all this for the first time, was completely carried away. She felt as if she could never be the same person again after this encounter with overwhelmingly powerful poetry. The two men, also, forgot about the tea getting cold, and when they finally shook themselves free of the enchantment, Paula had to go back to the kitchen and make some fresh tea.

With December came the beginning of Advent, and how many times in later years the children from the courthouse would tell their own children of the magic of these days leading up to Christmas and how they had been spent in the old house, which had been their home in their happiest childhood days.

Electricity had not yet replaced the more intimate warm light of candles and oil lamps, and even the street lamps still ran on oil, although in the big towns they had had gas lamps in the streets for several years now. In Limburg, the lamplighter still went through the streets every evening to make sure the people of the town didn't have to take their own lanterns with them when they went out after dark. Like little friendly islands of light, the lamps shone out every evening through the mist that billowed up from the river, though their circle of light did not reach very far into the darkness. In the window of Mergel's, the baker, there stood an almost life-size Father Christmas made of gingerbread, which the children of the town looked forward to seeing every year as the first sign of the Christmas season. It was always the same splendid figure, never for sale, with a rod of gorse twigs bound around with three ribbons of shiny colored paper, with his beard and hair made of thick icing, with prunes for his eyes, and with shelled almonds for his buttons, as elegant as genuine ivory. His coat was sprinkled with stars of raisins, sultanas, and candied orange peel. The children squashed their

noses against the cold pane, which was covered with delicate tendrils and flowers of icy crystals whenever there was
an early frost. The clockmaker Mehlhaus in Grabenstrasse
had put rows of candles behind his window, as they did in
the big towns, to prevent its freezing up and hiding all the
fine things laid out there: little bracelets and pocketknives,
tiny ladies' watches and big fob-watches, each with its
appropriate chain, a few rings with sparkling stones. "If
only I had some money!" groaned Georg, who would have
liked to give princely presents all around at Christmas, and
not only to his own family either. But his brothers were
now always in a hurry to get home, for there, in the living
room, was the Advent wreath hanging over the table, fresh
and green and smelling of the forest. The boys had made
it themselves and fixed the four candles to it. Every Sunday a new one was lit, until in the last week before
Christmas all four were burning. Until suppertime, the
only light in the living room was from the candles, for the
oil lamps burned only for three or at the most four hours
at a time, and it would have been dangerous to try to refill
them during the evening.

"The range in the kitchen is glowing all day long now,"
Aunt Rikchen wrote to her relatives in Montabaur. "The
house smells of cinnamon and cardamom, lemon and rum,
'all the spices of Arabia' says our Ferdinand when he
comes home from school and starts sniffing around to see
if he can't snatch up a gingerbread man or an almond star,
'because they taste so much better before Christmas,' the
little monkey says. Paula is being initiated into the secrets
of the Christmas baking this year, and even her mother
has admitted that she is doing it quite well. Stina and I are

still vainly doing all we can to teach the dear child the fundamentals of skin care, but she insists that cold water is quite good enough for her. It is true she has a perfect complexion, if only she weren't so pale—even the cod-liver oil doesn't seem to make any difference.

"At dusk all work stops, even in this busy house. Then we sit around the big table in the living room and knit—the Advent candles give enough light for that. Margarete is always urged to tell stories—she has such a talent for storytelling. Even the big boys want to hear the same old fairy tales over again—about the fellow who went off to learn fear, about Jorinde and Joringel and Tom Thumb. I think their favorites are still the Christmas legends—about the wintry forest that burst into blossom on Christmas Eve, or about the animals in the stable talking about their good or bad masters while an angel sits up in the rafters and writes it all down. Often I sit down at the piano and we sing Advent carols together, and when Jacob hears us from his office, he comes up and joins in.

"Ah, my dears, Stina and I often grieve to think that this will be the last time we spend these happy weeks of the year in the big family circle that has been our own for so many years now. But Wiesbaden would not be the right place for us, and it is a comforting thought that He who has each one of us in mind should lead us back at the end of our long lives to the place where we came from. We know that it will be lovely with you all and just like home again for the short time that still remains to us.

"As soon as the lamp is lit and supper is over, we all take out our sewing. The five boys are each having a new suit for Christmas, the same as every year. Margarete has had one of these newfangled sewing machines for the past two years, and for Stina and me it is still a miracle that you need only to turn a wheel by hand and the needle will make beautiful, regular stitches of its own accord along the thick woolen material that Isidor brought back for us again this year from the autumn fair in Frankfurt. One day, what with all these new inventions, I can see that a woman's work in the house will be made so easy that she won't know what to do with all her spare time.

"Stina sends her fondest greetings to you all. She is writing another novella at the moment. With her great talent, I just can't understand why none of the magazines will ever publish any of her wonderful stories."

The last Christmas Eve in the courthouse! Candles were burning in the big Christmas tree that Papa picked out every year at the Christkindel market. The boys had painted nuts with gold, polished red apples till they shone, and made chains of colored paper as decorations for the tree. Laid out on the white-decked tables were the presents, with sprigs of fir and ilex scattered between them. This year Emmerich's waistcoat had been embroidered with rosebuds in petit-point. "Because I grow younger every year," he said and kissed the aunts; and the two old ladies dabbed away a few tears, for there was an unspoken agreement between them not to let the sadness of leave-taking spoil their last Christmas in the courthouse.

When the maids and Holwein had gone downstairs with their presents to eat a piece of Christmas stollen and drink a glass of punch at the kitchen table, and when the boys had been sent off to bed to get an hour's sleep before the family would set off for Midnight Mass, the others watched in silence, each with his own thoughts, as the candles on the tree burned down one after the other.

Paula read for a while in the old leather-bound volume of Goethe's poems that was Uncle Emmerich's present to her; then she closed it and thought back over the year that had changed the course of her life, no matter what might happen to her from now on. She thought of the letter from Mère Celeste that had arrived the day before, a friendly, motherly letter, in complete agreement with her plan of going back to school again next year. Her friends had written to her, too, and each had disclosed a little piece of her life; how much they had told her and how much they had kept to themselves, it was hard to tell. Paula herself had not felt able to tell her friends, who had once been such intimate confidantes, of all her experiences of the past year, of joys and sorrows, of renunciation and self-knowledge gained. The neatly folded handkerchief with the little crown still lay under her pillow, and from time to time she would press it to her face, but the smell of horse and leather and eau de Cologne was all but gone.

She had a purpose in life now, and that counted for a good deal—a temporary goal, which left the distant future open. She did not want to ask yet what might be waiting for her around the next corner.

The time between Christmas and Twelfth Night came, a time of ghosts and magic dating back to pagan days. In the kitchen, on an earthenware plate, smoked an incense candle, for these were the nights when one had to ward off the Wild Hunter who came storming over the roofs with his army. The more dreadful the neighing of the ghostly horses, the louder the croaking of old Woden's two ravens, the more fruitful the next year would be, but it was frightening to behold.

Even for those who did not believe in ghosts and witches, time seemed to stand still in these twelve days, the days *between the years* as they were called. Following the rule of tradition, there was no washing done, no scrubbing or sweeping, no new work begun. It was a time for visiting and being visited by neighbors; there were evening gatherings and coffee parties, and in the courthouse, preparations had already started for the New Year's party, which this year was going to be a farewell party as well, for soon afterwards packing would have to begin, even though there was still much time before the move was due to take place.

As on every New Year's Eve, the family had an early supper, so that the maids could get away for the dancing in the Golden Goose. Around nine o'clock, the guests arrived. To fill the time before the traditional Silvester salad would be served, there were big bowls of cinnamon stars and Nürnberger Lebkuchen, gingerbread and macaroons, and dainty little hearts and fruits of marzipan. The boys, who had been allowed to stay up until the beginning of the New Year, helped eagerly to finish the rest of the Christmas goodies. The big salon had been opened up, the white tile stove heated, and the parquet floor waxed and polished. Two prelates and the worldly dignitaries with their wives joined for a while in the party games and charades, for which young Kaplan Knodt served as master-of-ceremonies. Later, the older people retired to the living room for a quiet talk or a game of whist, along with a glass of rum punch. In the meantime, the younger set moved tables and chairs in the salon to the wall to get space for dancing. Aunt Rikchen sat down at the piano, which had been moved into the salon beforehand, and accompanied the young peoples' dancing untiringly, playing waltzes and polkas or whatever they asked for. Even a quadrille was organized, with Overberg calling the figures as he danced with Paula. Aunt Rikchen, caught up in the enthusiasm of the youngsters, smiled reminiscently as she played, moving her gray head with the dainty lace cap in the rhythm of the melodies, her old fingers dancing over the keys. When she looked up, she saw shining eyes, a hand pressed, a tender smile, overheard a whispered word. Young folks, she thought; some things at least haven't changed much in half a century. *We* were the actors of the eternal play then, and it seems only yesterday.

Toward half-past eleven, Mama beckoned Paula into the living room and reminded her that she had to go down to the kitchen and stir the salad once more, ladle it into the cut-glass dish, and then decorate it with the big star, which like the herring salad itself was a traditional part of New Year's Eve. "The red beetroot, the green gherkins, the egg yolk and egg white have all been chopped up fine by Kettchen and put in the larder. And don't forget to put the cheese straws in the oven. They have to be golden, please remember, not brown."

"Yes, Mama," said Paula, far from happy at being called away from the dancing. It was the first time in her life that she had been given the honor of decorating the salad with the traditional star, its eight sections in the four alternating colors. If only it doesn't go crooked, she thought anxiously, throwing a quick glance back into the salon. Overberg was dancing with Charlotte, and Paula thought with approval how well he had behaved this evening, treating all the girls equally, singling out none of them, neglecting none. Konrad did not always conduct himself as diplomatically as today. Usually he made no attempt to disguise the fact that Paula was his favorite partner, and even the most anxious mothers had to admit that they danced well together. However, they shook their heads and sighed with pity for the poor young thing who was in for such a shock. What else could be expected with such an unstable partner? There was even a rumor that it might not be the first time the Amtmann's daughter had had a disappointment. That elegant Prussian lieutenant at the Overberg party in Assmannshausen—well, nobody knew for sure. And as long as young Overberg had not declared himself, there was still hope for other people's daughters.

Now Paula stood in the kitchen with a white apron over her green party dress. She had already put the cheese straws in the oven, ladled the salad into the crystal bowl, and smoothed the surface. Now she was figuring with a worried frown how she could best divide the star into eight equal parts. Adolf had followed her; he stood beside her at the kitchen table and watched attentively while she began to fill in the eight sections; he knew something was being done that would have to pass Mama's strict scrutiny.

"You've got a problem there!" said a voice behind him, and a hand was laid on his shoulder. "Will you go to the stable for me—there's a good lad. I quite forgot to tell you that I brought an extra sack of oats with me. The horses shouldn't be left out of things on New Year's Eve—give Silver some, too, with my compliments."

Adolf, who would have unhesitatingly climbed Kilimanjaro for his friend Overberg, only paused to ask after Suleika and her little son and then went straight off to the stable.

"And now let me take over the construction of the star, Paula, for it seems to me that it's gone a bit awry."

"Oh, I'll manage," said Paula. "Men needn't think they can lord it over us in the kitchen, too!"

"Nothing is farther from my mind," he said, but nonetheless, he took the two forks she had been using without much success so far. "This is less a matter of cooking than of geometry and so falls more into the field of masculine endeavor, if you will permit the comment."

But to Paula's mischievous delight, he discovered that the slippery salad put up strong opposition to superior male geometry, too. Nonetheless, the end product was recognizable as a star.

"The first person to take some will ruin my glorious performance, anyway," said Overberg. "And now let's forget about stars. We don't need to go up again before it strikes twelve, and I want to talk to you, Paula."

"My cheese straws!" she exclaimed and hastily pulled the beautifully golden straws out of the oven and put them on a warm plate on the side of the range. But then he gently pushed her onto the bench behind the kitchen table and sat down next to her. "I've got to go off on another trip," he said. "To St. Gallen in Switzerland. There's a famous library in the monastery there with over two thousand illuminated manuscripts, incunabula, and other treasures. . . . My father is anxious that I should examine them thoroughly."

"Incunabula," she said. "What on earth's that?" But she wasn't thinking of the St. Gallen library as she spoke, for his words had given her a shock, and she was yet more shocked to find that there had been a shock in the first place. Would she no longer find him in Uncle Emmo's room when she brought in the tea, nor hear that deep voice reading or reciting any more? And when he came back, whenever that might be, she would no longer be in Limburg but in distant Wiesbaden, and Uncle Emmerich would also have gone—Uncle Emmerich, who had been Konrad's excuse to come almost every day.

"But you are not going because of me, Konrad?" she asked anxiously. "For that would be against our arrangement."

"Because of you, yes, Paula." He laid his large hands over hers where they rested on the table. "Although I'll admit St. Gallen is an attractive excuse. I am going because I want to give you time to think. . . . I believe you know what I mean."

She looked at him wide-eyed for a moment. Then she dropped her eyes and shook her head, not over what he had said but over herself. If it had been anyone but Konrad Overberg, perhaps she would have understood earlier. Hadn't he said that he did not want to marry? That had made her feel completely secure with him, so she had let him become part of her life, had enjoyed his friendship and taken it for granted. And all the time she had been so preoccupied with her own grief that she had not given a thought to what he might feel.

"Oh, Konrad!" she said, alarmed. "What an awful, selfish, blind egotist I have been!"

"No, don't feel badly, little Paula, please don't! How could you possibly know that someone like me would suddenly be serious? Look, we all must overcome our own troubles first before we can understand other people. I don't want you to give me an answer now. That's why I'm going away. It took a long while for me to realize it, but now I know that it all started a year ago when I laid half my fur rug over the knees of a frozen little schoolgirl and she blushed so enchantingly."

"Oh, Konrad, that was simply an act of Christian charity!"

"I doubt it! I think it would be wise for you to go on with the plan you were talking about in Uncle Emmo's room the other day. That will help you to gain perspective. A year isn't long when you're thinking of a whole lifetime."

"But you won't be away a whole year?"

"I couldn't leave my father alone that long. I'll be at home again when you're in Wiesbaden. That's a little further away from Bad Ems than Limburg, but what have we got the railway for? It's still near enough for us to see each other as often as you'll permit me to come."

"I'll miss you, Konrad."

"That's more than I dared to hope and certainly more than I deserve." He lifted her hands and pressed them to the sides of his face. "I love you, I love you," he said scarcely audibly but with such sincerity that she felt it in the very depths of her heart.

"Be patient with me," she said.

From the cathedral came the first stroke of midnight, and one clock tower after the other followed with its chimes.

"Paula!" Mama's voice was calling from above. "Where have you got to?"

She took the tray with the cheese straws; he carried the heavy crystal bowl, and while they climbed the stairs, the clocks of the town ended their twelve strokes. For a moment, there was silence; then all the bells began their triumphant song to welcome the New Year.

About the Author

BORN IN 1889 in Saarbrucken, Germany, Margot Benary-Isbert lost her beloved mother at seven years of age. The stepmother she acquired soon after, insisted that the children should be sent away. At the convent little Margot retreated into a fantasy world, making up stories and telling them as if they were true. She was punished for being a liar, but a sympathetic nun took her aside and said, "If you write these tales down they will be called fiction and nobody will call you a liar any more." That was the birth of Margot Isbert the author.

Having published her first short story at age 19, Margot enrolled at the University of Frankfort. While working at the Museum of Ethnology and Anthropology, she met her husband-to-be, Wilhelm Benary. The young couple eventually moved with their daughter to the Benary farm in Erfurt, located in what would later be East Germany. For many years Margot lived here, writing and—among other things—raising Great Danes, but finding no publisher for her full-length manuscripts, since she refused to write for the Nazi regime.

A new day arrived in 1945. The war had just ended. A publisher suggested she should write for teenagers. By that time she had fled Erfurt before the Russian army's advance. After a time on a friend's farm, she and her husband and daughter found space in two rooms of a house in a city near Gottingen and Kassel. Electricity, like other necessities, was strictly rationed, so she often wrote by candlelight. In this way she completed *The Ark*, her first post-war story. *The Ark*, a book written for young people, is about a family of refugees from the East of Germany who slowly grow new roots in a West German town. This experience paralleled Margot Isbert's own. Her second book, a sequel called *Rowan Farm*, also had much success. During the next few years she wrote many more books for youth, including *Under a Changing Moon*, a book whose inspiration came from her father's childhood near the Rhine in the middle of the 19th century.

In 1952 Margot and her husband immigrated to the United States, to Chicago, where their daughter had been living for several years. Margot's books were soon published in English. Margot would write her books in German first and then have them translated. She carefully checked the translations for faithfulness to her original style and intentions, and eventually did her own translations. Awards and honors came her way.

In the spring of 1955 the Benarys moved to Santa Barbara, California, where Wilhelm had dreamed of living for a long time. He died three months after the move. Again Margot returned to her fantasy world and let the stories flow from her imagination onto paper. She turned to writing for older adults, starting with the book, *The Grandmother and Her First Grandchild*. This story humorously relates Margot's visit to her daughter and 8-month-old baby in Chicago. Three more books followed, all from the viewpoint of growing old and relating to the younger generation.

In the last five years of her life Margot's mind deteriorated. She was taken care of in a retirement home in Valle Verde where her daughter visited her often and she was treated with loving kindness. She died in 1979, almost 90 years of age.

Adapted from a biographical sketch by Margot Benary-Isbert's daughter, Eva Hearst